He cupped her face in his hands. "Spoil what?" he asked with strained patience. "Your maiden's dream of chastity inviolate? I don't intend to spoil what is between us. I want to make a woman of you." He felt her tense in his arms. "A kiss, only a kiss, Deirdre," he soothed.

She was burning, she was freezing; she wanted to resist him, she wanted to yield to him; she hoped he would stop, she willed him to go on; she hated him, she loved him. The fervor of his kisses threatened her sanity. Rathbourne sensed her weakening and pressed his advantage.

The ache to claim her fully went beyond carnal need. He wanted nothing less than her unequivocal acceptance of his title to who and what she was. Let her try to disavow him, and he would soon teach her the error of her logic. By God, he would compel her to accept that she was destined for his full possession sooner or later.

"A kiss, only a kiss, you promised," she hissed at him.

"If a kiss is the limit of your generosity, girl, you had better make it memorable, or I swear I'll take what I want from you, and to hell with your blushes."

She held nothing back. He would not have allowed it. And when he had finished with her, she would have allowed him anything . . .

THE PASSIONATE PRUDE

ELIZABETH THORNTON

ZEBRA BOOKS
KENSINGTON PUBLISHING CORP.

ZEBRA BOOKS

are published by

Kensington Publishing Corp.
475 Park Avenue South
New York, NY 10016

First printing: October, 1988

Printed in the United States of America

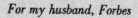

For my husband, Forbes

Chapter One

My Lord Rathbourne's indolent gaze flickered indifferently over the crush of noisy diners in the White Swan's public parlor and came to rest on his silent companion.

"I beg pardon, Wendon, I wasn't listening."

Viscount Wendon, of an age with his friend although of a more pleasantly boyish aspect, was at that moment leaning hard back in his dining chair, which was balanced precariously on only two legs. He brought it slowly down to rest squarely on the carpeted floor and leaned his elbows on the white damask of the covered table.

"I merely remarked, Gareth, that out of regimentals, to all intents and purposes, we veterans become indistinguishable from the rank and file. I have been attempting this age to attract the notice of our estimable landlord, to no avail. I own that the poor fellow may have good reason to be so hard pressed with every man and his dog taking refuge from the elements, but dash it all, don't he recognize Quality when he sees it? Here we are, a couple of peers of the realm, not to mention heroes of the Peninsular Campaign, and we are passed over as if we were a pair of negligible country bumpkins."

This good-natured complaint brought a ghost of a smile to the Earl of Rathbourne's pensive countenance. "Speak for yourself," he said in an amused baritone. He turned slightly in his chair, bent a riveting glance from glittering amber eyes upon the harried landlord, and raised one hand imperceptibly. In a matter of moments, the landlord was at his side with mumbled apologies, and Lords Rathbourne and Wendon had given their order for the best nuncheon the inn had to offer.

"Boiled brisket! I ask you!" said Viscount Wendon in disgust when the landlord was out of earshot. "I swear we did better under Wellington. Well," he amended on noting Rathbourne's incredulous expression, "there were occasions."

"Yes, but very few and far between," averred Rathbourne as he leaned across the table to fill his friend's glass from the opened bottle of Burgundy which stood at his elbow.

Wendon lifted the half-filled glass to his nostrils and savored the bouquet. "The real thing! I wonder . . . do you think that they ever went without anything or gave us a thought whilst we squandered the best years of our lives on those squalid treks across the Peninsula hunting down Boney's elusive armies?"

"Not *always* elusive," responded Rathbourne, his face taking on a grimmer aspect. "We are lucky. We came back in one piece. Thousands didn't."

"Do you miss it at all?"

"Do I miss what?" There was a shade of disbelief in the Earl's voice. "The near starvation? The utter exhaustion? The executions? The needless savagery? The loss of friends I've known since school days? What do you think?"

"Then why didn't you resign your commission?" Wendon persisted.

Rathbourne took a moment or two before replying. He relaxed the imperceptible tension across his shoulders and settled back in his chair. "Who knows? Youthful idealism? Loyalty to one's comrades? Duty to King and Country? It seems such a long time ago now, I hardly remember. It becomes a habit. Sometimes I have to remind myself that the war is over, that I'm not the autocratic officer whose every command must be instantly obeyed. I suppose it will take time

8

to adopt more civilized ways, to resume my former existence. I have little practice in the role of chivalrous gentleman."

Viscount Wendon gave a shout of laughter, and heads turned to look disapprovingly in his direction. He lowered his voice. "Gareth, you scoundrel. You . . . chivalrous? Never! I've known you most of your thirty years, since we were both in short coats. Being autocratic comes naturally to you! You didn't learn it in the army! Good God man, when we were at school, at Harrow, who commandeered the best bunk in the lower school dormitory, drawing the cork of no less a pugilist that George Gordon, the present Lord Byron? And that was only the beginning of your scandalous career! And after that, when we were newly up at Oxford, who cut out all the other hopefuls with the fair Griselda, the wife of our illustrious dean—yes, and fought a duel with the poor old codger who was only trying to protect his own?"

Rathbourne suppressed a shudder. "Some episodes in one's life are best forgotten and that is one of them. Can you imagine? He didn't know one end of a pistol from the other! He might have killed himself, poor devil! If I cut you out with the lady, I am sorry for it, but I did you a favor, albeit unconsciously."

"Think nothing of it," said Wendon magnanimously. "I couldn't afford her. My father, the old skinflint, kept me on a very tight leash. I hadn't a feather to fly with from one term to another. You, on the other hand, were never short of the ready." He fell silent as he belatedly recalled that Rathbourne, as an undergraduate, was wont to laugh away his affluence by intimating that his widowed mother bribed him to stay away from the ancestral home. The joke had been too close to the truth for comfort, as he remembered—something to do with a falling-out between mother and son after his younger brother had lost his life in a climbing accident.

A bold-eyed serving maid brought an ornate platter with their dinner, and the two gentlemen fell silent as she set it on the table before them. Her roving eyes darted from one to the other in open appraisal, eliciting an inviting smile from the friendlier of the two gentlemen, but her glances were for the handsomer although austere Rathbourne, who gazed steadfastly out the window until his companion addressed him.

"Nice," said Wendon appreciatively.

"I didn't think you cared for boiled brisket." There was a twinkle in the Earl's eye.

"Never mind." Wendon shook his head. "You were telling me about your sister—the reason for this trip to town, as I recollect. Or could it have anything to do with the darling of Drury Lane, Mrs. Dewinters, who, as I hear, has taken up residence in Chelsea—in one house among many of which you are the acknowledged landlord?"

"Absent landlord," said Rathbourne emphatically as he carved a generous portion of beef. He offered the platter to his friend. "How very well informed you are, Wendon. We could have used you in Intelligence, if only we had known of your penchant for listening to gossip."

"Not I," retorted Wendon with some vehemence. "Your methods are not compatible with my gentle turn of nature. I suppose somebody had to do the dirty work, but . . ." He fell silent, realizing the implied insult in his words.

It was only the merest chance that he had ever discovered that his companion was not all that he seemed to be when they served together in Spain with Wellington (or Wellesley as he then was). Wendon had been on a reconnoitering mission with a detachment of cavalry when he had been captured by the French and taken to their headquarters for questioning. The Earl had walked in on that interview, but posing as a French officer. If he was surprised to see the Viscount, he covered it well, much better in fact than Wendon did, who almost gave the game away.

It was the Earl who saved Wendon's hide when things turned ugly and it appeared that he would be summarily shot. Rathbourne had spirited the Viscount away before anyone was the wiser. In so doing, he had almost blown his cover. Wendon supposed that he owed his life to the fact that his acquaintance with the Earl went back to the playing fields of Harrow. He wondered whether Rathbourne would have risked so much for a perfect stranger. He very much doubted it. Once safely back behind British lines, he had been sworn to secrecy and had in fact been close mouthed about the Earl's clandestine activities during the war since then. Until recently, he recalled, with an uncomfortable flash of memory. Still, the war was now over. Rathbourne was safe from a French assassin's hand, and his confidante was someone who could be counted on not to betray his confidence and who posed no threat to the Earl. Nevertheless, he wished he had kept his mouth shut.

He threw a quick glance at his companion and was relieved to note the amused quirk of one dark eyebrow. "Woolgathering?" asked Rathbourne quizzically. Avery recovered himself quickly and rushed into speech. "Forget the war! Old Boney is Emperor of only a pile of rocks on Elba. England is safe from attack, and we are military men no longer. Tell me about your sister."

Rathbourne shrugged his shoulders. "There is nothing to tell. Now that Caro is eighteen, my mother wishes her to make her come-out. My presence will simply add a little countenance to all the parties and balls which she is bound to attend. What the devil is this?" he asked distastefully as he removed the lid from the vegetable tureen. He brought up a ladleful of soggy, dark green leaves.

"Boiled cabbage. What did you expect at an English tavern? Here, put it on my plate. It is the perfect accompaniment to boiled brisket. Yes, and I'll have some of those boiled potatoes too, if you would be so kind."

The Viscount's appetite, apparently, was not impaired by the quality of the food. The Earl, of a more fastidious palate, confined himself to the Burgundy and the Stilton.

"Do you happen to know anything of an Armand St. Jean?"

11

he asked casually after an interval. "You are in town more often than I. I thought perhaps your paths might have crossed."

"I haven't been in town this age, but yes, I know of him," Wendon replied, looking speculatively at his friend's carefully impassive countenance.

"And?"

"He's a young hothead—no more than twenty, I should say. His propensity for gaming is legion, as are his women, and he hardly out of leading strings. Shocking, ain't it? He's half French, of course. There's an older sister in the wings somewhere who exercises not the slightest restraint upon him. He's a charming devil though. Come to think of it, he's a bit like you were in your salad days. But your cousin, Tony Cavanaugh, can tell you more than I. He's taken him under his wing, so to speak, and has tried to restrain some of St. Jean's wilder impulses—to no avail, I'm sorry to say."

A smile flickered briefly on Rathbourne's lips. "Now I know we should have seconded you to Intelligence, Wendon. The war would have been over in half the time if we'd set you loose behind French lines. You have a veritable talent for gathering information."

Wendon laughed self-consciously. "Well, I do go about a bit. I can't settle into running my estates as you seem to have done. The war has made me restless, I suppose. Perhaps I should find myself a wife and secure the succession as my fond mama keeps telling me."

A thought suddenly struck the Viscount. "Good Lord! St. Jean isn't angling after Caro, is he? He's got nerve, I'll give him that!"

Rathbourne demurred but Wendon continued as if he had not heard the denial. "Be careful, Gareth! He's a dangerous cub with a demon temper! It don't matter to him whether he dispatches you with foil or pistol. He's blessed with cool nerves and natural talent, you see, a deadly combination."

12

The Earl spoke in a soft undertone, humor lacing every word. "The prospect terrifies me! A callow youth, you say? I'm thankful I never met the hellion on the battlefield. I'd have been tempted to put him across my knee and paddle him."

"You'd be a fool to underrate him," Wendon went on pleasantly. He cut himself a thick slice of brisket which he proceeded to attack with relish. "I've done my duty. If you don't wish to take him seriously, that's your lookout. Don't say I didn't warn you."

The door to the parlor opened and the chill draft of that cold, wintry morning ruffled the covers of their lordships' window table. Rathbourne looked to the door, his brows knit together.

Two women stood on the threshold. The elder was smaller in stature and hung back as if unsure of the propriety of entering the inn's public dining room. The Earl's eyes became riveted to the younger woman, and his fingers tightened on the stem of his wineglass. She stood with head held high, one hand securing a green mantle which hung in loose folds from her shoulders, her clear eyes coolly assessing.

He would have known her anywhere! Five years seemed to slip away as he absorbed every lovely feature, every soft contour, every endearing detail which had been a constant memory since their last encounter. Yet she was different—no longer the fledgling, but a woman with the bloom of promise fulfilled. He felt the constriction in his chest—a reminder that the sight of her classic beauty had always set his pulse to an erratic tempo.

His hand went absently to finger a small faded scar on his left cheekbone. He had hoped for a different setting in which to make himself known to her. No matter. He was not one to cavil at Providence. Better sooner than later.

She removed her high poke bonnet to reveal the thick burnished braids at her nape. He could almost feel their silken smoothness between his fingers. His hands itched to unpin the heavy skein of spun gold and wrap themselves in the curtain of hair that he knew would fall to well below her shoulders. He smiled as she pushed back a stray tendril from her smooth, high forehead in a familiar gesture of impatience. She flashed an encouraging look over her shoulder at her companion then took a halting step into the room, a small smile of anticipation curving her generous mouth, as if she was enjoying every minute of the novelty of finding herself in the White Swan's public dining room.

Her eyes traveled around the interior, lighting with undisguised interest on the various occupants, and Rathbourne had the sudden urge to rob her of that fragile composure, to drive down those thick, dark lashes in confusion and bring the blush to her creamy complexion. He had the overpowering desire to make her as disturbed by his presence as he was by hers.

Her eyes alighted on Wendon momentarily, and he saw the smile on her lips deepen. Then her eyes met his and Rathbourne held them, inexorably, unwaveringly. He was conscious of the startled lift of her dark eyebrows, the defiant tilt of her head, the sudden shock of recognition in the depths of green eyes widened in alarm at the unexpected sight of him, and still he held her.

He knew she was breathing rapidly, fighting him off with every breath, as if they were locked in mortal combat; he knew that she was remembering in vivid detail, as he was, that other time so long ago when she fought him with every ounce of strength which she possessed, and he was determined that, in this contest, he would not be the loser. His smoldering gaze captured her, compelling her to yield to him. The blush on her cheeks deepened, and a slow smile touched Rathbourne's lips. He would have continued the contest, but someone moved between them, and when he sought her eyes again, they were carefully averted.

"Who is she?" Wendon asked softly as she allowed the landlord to seat her at a table, her back turned resolutely against Rathbourne.

"Someone I once knew, a long time ago," said Rathbourne noncommittally.

"Don't think I ever met the lady." Wendon could hardly contain his curiosity. "Don't seem as if she cares to renew the acquaintance."

He looked at his friend expectantly, but Rathbourne's only comment was, "Shall we have coffee and brandy?"

The Earl tried to catch the landlord's eye but he was unsuccessful, for the girl in the green mantle had at that moment crooked her index finger and he was hastening to her side. Rathbourne saw the flash of an emerald ring and he smiled enigmatically.

"If that don't beat all!" exclaimed the Viscount with mingled astonishment and chagrin. "How shall we ever live this down, Rathbourne? To be outranked by a slip of a girl with only a pretty face to recommend her! Look at our host positively drooling over her!"

"Yes, it is a bit of facer, isn't it? But console yourself with the thought that if she were a man and could be persuaded to accept a commission in His Majesty's service, she would quickly rise to the higher ranks."

"Oh?" Wendon intoned encouragingly.

Rathbourne's thoughtful gaze took in her straight spine and squared shoulders. "Defensive strategy would be her forte, I should say." After a moment or two's reflection, he added, "But this is one occasion when she shall not out maneuver me."

He felt in the breast of his dark frock coat and withdrew a scrap of lace from an inside pocket. "Mrs. Dewinters's," he explained with a hint of apology. The stale perfume of carnations was in the air, and Wendon grimaced.

"What do you mean to do?"

"What else? Merely renew an acquaintance of long standing."

The Earl pushed back his chair and rose to his feet in a leisurely manner. There was something in his expression which provoked the Viscount to exclaim, "Good God, Gareth, she's only a slip of a girl! Have a care, man! What on earth was her offense that you look so blasted . . . punishing?"

Rathbourne evinced surprise. "Punishing? You are mistaken, Wendon. Say rather 'determined.' If you will excuse me?"

Deirdre sensed his approach rather than saw it, and her shoulders tensed, but her conversation continued unabated, and the smile on her lips became fixed. She saw her aunt's surprised glance become focused on a point above her head, and she carefully half turned in her chair to look dispassionately into the familiar face which had persistently tormented her waking and sleeping hours since he had flung away from her on their last, never to be forgotten encounter.

He loomed over her, a menacing masculine presence, and Deirdre had to force herself not to shrink from him. His eyes, coolly polite, met hers briefly then he ignored her as if she did not exist.

"Rathbourne at your service, ma'am," she heard his deep baritone say gravely to her aunt. She had forgotten how husky and liquid his voice could be—soft, soothing, or seductive, as he chose to make it. "I believe this article of feminine apparel belongs to you? You dropped it as you entered, I collect."

Deirdre's aunt, Lady Fenton, examined the friendly gentleman who stood towering over her. His presence compelled attention. His dark hair shot with auburn was cut long on the collar; broad shoulders encased in restrained black superfine; the flash of white teeth in a deeply tanned face; but it was his eyes which arrested her—amber eyes, flecked with gold—tiger eyes, but gentle as he waited patiently for her response.

"Thank you kindly, sir, but it does not look familiar." She turned it over in her hand to examine it more carefully. "Perhaps some other lady . . . Deirdre, is it yours?"

Deirdre's nostrils detected the stench of stale scent on the lace handkerchief and her eyes flickered in annoyance. "I

16

think you should try some other lady," she said coldly and pointedly.

Her aunt glanced sharply at her niece with questioning eyes, but Deirdre looked steadfastly at the shining, silver cruets on the table.

"Then I apologize for the intrusion, Miss . . . ?" He waited expectantly.

Deirdre preserved a stony silence, but her aunt, now startled by her niece's lapse of good manners, hastened into speech.

"Permit me to introduce my niece, Miss Deirdre Fenton. I am Lady Fenton."

"Charmed," responded the Earl, raising Lady Fenton's fingers to his lips. "Miss Fenton? I recall that name. Yes . . . come to think of it, I believe I had the pleasure of making your acquaintance prior to my embarking for Spain. That would be about five years ago. Your mother, as I recall, was undertaking your come-out at the time." He captured Deirdre's hand and brought it to his lips. "And who could ever forget the dazzling emerald? You still wear it, I see."

Lady Fenton was conscious of the charged atmosphere. Deirdre, who had been sitting throughout as if frozen in her place, her pale cheeks as white as the linen covers of the table, brought her head up and looked at the Earl with a flash of temper.

"I regard it as my good luck piece," she said, snatching her hand away.

"Indeed?" The Earl deliberately fingered the scar on his cheek and Deirdre's defiance seemed to crumble. Her gaze reverted to the cruets. "Superstitious, Miss Fenton?"

"Hardly that, sir. I wear it because it was my late father's. That is all."

"Touching, I'm sure. But I have already taken up too much of your time. Lady Fenton, I hope I may call on you in town? Miss Fenton, your servant, ma'am."

It was the longest hour that Deirdre could ever remember. Hardly aware of what she ate, or the pleasantries she

17

exchanged with her aunt, she concentrated on keeping her back turned rigidly against him, checking her unwilling eyes from roving from table to table. She knew when he took his leave, for her aunt's smiling eyes followed him out and she nodded her head in silent salute. Deirdre breathed more easily again, relieved to be rid of his threatening presence.

Chapter Two

As Deirdre walked the short distance across the White Swan's pebbled courtyard to the waiting carriage, she glanced stealthily over her shoulder, half expecting him to be lying in ambush, ready to pounce on her and—and what? she asked herself breathlessly, unwilling to finish the thought. Even *he* would not dare assault her in broad daylight with her aunt at her elbow and ostlers and grooms standing by. But she could not shake herself of the conviction that Gareth Cavanaugh, Earl of Rathbourne, was capable of anything.

Five years had made a remarkable difference. His face was leaner, more weathered, no longer so boyishly handsome— tempered, she supposed, by his years of active service. The familiar fire was still present, close to the surface, but less unpredictable, held in check by a strength of will which, if anything, made him appear more formidable.

But the eyes were unmistakable—those unusual amber eyes which could quickly flame to gold and intimidate her with a look, or convey a message too transparent to be misunderstood. He always had the power to compel her to a self-conscious awareness of all that was feminine in her nature, and it irritated her beyond bearing.

She knew that he had returned to England. She had, in fact, covertly kept herself informed of his whereabouts, slightly bemused at her own perversity. Really, he meant nothing to her! And she had supposed that should their paths ever cross again, he would not acknowledge the acquaintance, perhaps not even remember her. That he had remembered her was very evident, and Deirdre could not suppress the thought that she was glad of it.

Of course, she had given him something to remember her by—the scar which he had deliberately fingered, evoking memories she wished to forget. Deirdre shivered as the carriage swayed into motion and her aunt solicitously patted her knee.

"Are you chilled, my dear? Would you like the rug? Are the bricks at your feet still warm?"

Deirdre forced a wan smile to her lips. "Everything is fine, thank you, Aunt Rosemary. Just a draft from the window. There, now I've shut it properly. You are a dear to fuss over me so."

A smile warmed Lady Fenton's eyes. "Nonsense," she said emphatically. "You deserve a little coddling. Your uncle agrees with me. My dear, I hope we can make you change your mind and stay on with us. It's not every girl who is given the opportunity to travel on the continent. Think of it, Deirdre—Vienna, Paris, perhaps even Brussels. Sir Thomas is uncertain as yet where his diplomatic mission will take him, but it's the chance in a lifetime for you. Won't you reconsider, my dear? Of course, I know I'm being selfish. But you would be such a help to me. You know how I dread mixing with strangers."

"As though you could ever be accused of selfishness," Deirdre chided gently. "I wish with all my heart that I might accept your offer, Aunt Rosemary. But don't you see, I cannot consider my own wishes only. I promised myself that I would try to persuade Armand to return home with me. If things were different, you know that there is nothing I should rather do than accompany you. But at present, it is impossible."

Lady Fenton's eyes assumed a guarded expression. She gazed unseeingly at the darkening landscape of the Thames valley for a moment or two as if trying to frame the words which would be most acceptable to the thoughtful girl sitting opposite. Finally, she seemed to come to a decision.

"Deirdre, how much longer are you going to act as wet nurse to your brother? You have a life of your own to live. You are neither Armand's mother nor his guardian."

The criticism in her aunt's words stung Deirdre. "Aunt Rosemary! That's not fair! Armand never had a guardian—not in the true sense of the word! My stepfather's brother has no notion of how to guide a young man! He has never exerted himself in the least on Armand's behalf, but cuts himself off like some old recluse dreaming of all that might have been if things had been different for France. Other émigrés have made something of their opportunities in England. But the St. Jeans never had any ambitions to speak of." She clamped her lips together as if she had said more than she ought, then went on more reasonably. "Armand reaches his majority in less than a year. It is natural for me to worry about him. You know our circumstances. My income is adequate but scarcely extravagant. What is to become of him?" Her voice took on a desperate edge. "He must look to the future and settle in some respectable position which will at least put bread on the table. I cannot turn my back on him. I have to try to make him change his ways."

"Armand? Respectable?" The incredulous note in her aunt's voice brought a rosy glow to Deirdre's complexion. "I'm sorry to be so blunt, my dear, but be realistic. He is a notorious womanizer; he frequents the worst sorts of gaming hells; he fights duels at the slightest provocation and he is only twenty years old! If your uncle had been appointed Armand's guardian, as he was yours, he would have purchased a commission for him and persuaded one of his military friends to take him under his wing. It would have been the making or breaking of him. But you could never be persuaded to such a course of action. If Armand is ever going to mend his ways, it is going to take something catastrophic to bring him to his senses.

21

Happy as I am to have you spend a month in town with me, my dear, I cannot see that your intervention will make the slightest dent in Armand's mode of living. There, there, I've said too much," she said consolingly as she observed the stricken look in Deirdre's face. "I'm an interfering old busybody. I know Armand is not related to the Fenton branch of the family, but in spite of everything, I cannot help liking the exasperating boy, and whatever touches you, touches me. Please forgive an old woman for speaking out of turn."

Deirdre reached across the coach to clasp the older woman's hand. "Aunt Rosemary," she began earnestly, "what you say of Armand may be true, but as long as I have breath in my body, I will try to protect him. He isn't bad. Don't you see? I grant that he is wild, unthinking, unmanageable even, but he *isn't* bad! Mama, before she died, was an invalid so much of the time as we grew up. He never had a strong hand to guide him. I have tried to be a mother to him, but I suppose I indulged him more than I ought."

"You were four years old when he was born, as I recall," retorted Lady Fenton dryly.

Deirdre continued, heedless of her aunt's interruption. "Perhaps Mama and I did spoil him, but with Mama widowed twice by the time she was only four and thirty, surely what she did is understandable. We were everything to each other. I think I can make him listen to reason. At any rate, I must make the attempt! I must!"

Lady Fenton examined her niece with shrewd eyes. "There's some particular reason for your coming to town at the present, isn't there? It's not just Armand being Armand. Has he fallen into a more serious scrape than usual? What are you up to, Deirdre?"

Deirdre's thoughts flew to the letter she had received from an old school friend, Serena Bateman, now Mrs. Reginald Kinnaird, and the tidbit of gossip she had imparted, namely that her darling Armand had stolen the affections, if not the virtue, such as it was, of a Drury Lane actress, the toast of the demimonde, a certain Mrs. Dewinters. Her protector, a noble peer of the realm and, by all accounts, more than a match for the hotheaded Armand, was still in ignorance of the unchivalrous conduct of the foolhardy boy. The betting books in all the gentlemen's clubs in town, from which source Mr. Kinnaird had gleaned the information, were odds on favorites for Armand to be soundly trounced in the expected duel, if not permanently eliminated. It was this alarming piece of news which had induced Deirdre to accept her aunt's open-ended invitation to take up residence for a month in Portman Square. Since Lady Fenton, at the time of the letter's arrival, had been on the point of returning to London after spending a few days at Henley with her favorite niece (Sir Thomas fortuitously being with the British delegation in Vienna), Deirdre concluded her arrangements to make for London and her brother without delay. But she thought it prudent to conceal Armand's latest folly from her aunt since that dear lady would without a doubt forbid her to consort with her delinquent brother.

Deirdre hesitated, then embarked on a subject which she was sure would be pleasing to her aunt. "I am thinking of getting married."

It wasn't true, of course. She had made up her mind long since, that marriage, that men, could be no part of her life. Still, she had of late been flirting with the idea. Somewhere, there must be some man who would treat her with respect, with reverence, with loyalty. And there was Armand to consider.

"Married?" Her aunt was startled. "To whom, may I ask?"

Deirdre burst out laughing. "Oh dear, I'm afraid I've led you astray. What I should have said, dear Auntie, was that it has occurred to me that it is time I was wed and I am hopeful of finding a suitable parti in town."

Her aunt was interested. "Indeed? And what, may I ask, has brought about this change of heart? As I recall, you have rejected past suitors, many of them most eligible, with the excuse that you wanted to devote your energies to the care of your brother."

Lady Fenton had a shrewd idea of what was at the bottom of Deirdre's aversion to the estate of matrimony and it was not merely devotion to Armand St. Jean. It went deeper than that. Deirdre was a confirmed cynic. As a young girl growing up, she had watched her mother endure the humiliation of marriage to an attractive but improvident philanderer who wasted his wife's small inheritance on a succession of loose women. Lettie St. Jean's bitterness had instilled a deep distrust of men in her daughter, and now Armand looked to be in a fair way to following in his father's footsteps.

"Marriage? Are you serious, Deirdre?"

Deirdre looked thoughtful. She sighed. "I don't know. I am almost resigned to the thought of marriage. And if I found the right sort of man, undemanding but with character of course, strong yet . . . persuadable, I think it would work out for the best. Oh Auntie," she said on impulse, "if only I could find someone who would be a moderating influence on Armand. Don't you see, he's never had a father's guidance? The right man might work a salutary change in him."

"Armand! Armand! That's all you ever think of. Child! This is idolatry. Don't you see it? One doesn't choose one's life partner for such a frivolous reason. Armand is a man. *You* will never change him. Why, if anything, Armand would make mincemeat of such a one as you describe—yes, and you would too—'undemanding and persuadable.' You would never respect such a specimen, Deirdre, and you know it!"

"You misunderstand! Of course I shouldn't wish for a husband who can't stand up to me!"

"Oh don't you? I am glad to hear it, for I shudder to think of the fate of any poor, gormless creature who thinks himself qualified to manage a filly like you. You would make his life miserable!"

24

Deirdre laughed self-consciously. "Auntie, you don't really believe that of me, do you? That I could be so . . . well . . . unfeminine?"

"Of course you're not unfeminine! Did I say so? I am not finding fault with you, Deirdre, merely stating the obvious. You are a headstrong girl, and it is the law of nature for the strong to master the weak. I am merely suggesting that if you are serious in your intention to wed, you cast around for someone with a little gumption, a man of some substance who comes up to your weight."

After an uncomfortable interval, Lady Fenton spoke in more moderate tones. "Deirdre, what think you of the gentleman we met at the inn? Rathbourne? That would be the Earl, as I recall. Sir Thomas has spoken of him on occasion. He is a seasoned soldier, and most eligible in every respect. I would not even think of him in normal circumstances—too exalted by half for a mere gentleman's daughter—but I thought he showed some . . . interest."

"I disliked him on sight, and further acquaintance has merely confirmed my opinion," asserted Deirdre flatly.

Lady Fenton's eyebrows elevated a fraction at the heat of Deirdre's words, but she wisely forebore comment and soon turned the conversation into more convivial channels, and the two ladies became happily occupied in discussing the various outings and parties which a month in London might reasonably offer a provincial miss on the hunt for a husband.

The following morning, Deirdre set off with abigail in tow for the lodgings of her brother, which he had but newly acquired. In company of many young bucks aspiring to fashion, Armand St. Jean had rooms above one of the innumerable shop fronts lining the elegant district of Bond Street. Since Portman Square was north of Mayfair and Armand's rooms were close to Piccadilly, the southern boundary of the most exclusive residential area of London, Deirdre had a good half-hour's walk ahead of her, but since most of that time would take her on a slow stroll through the most prestigious shopping district of England, if not Europe, Deirdre was nothing daunted.

She knew from Armand's infrequent letters that he lived hard by "Gentleman" John Jackson's "Academy," that gathering place for more than a third—so it was rumored—of the pugilistically inclined male members of the aristocracy who self-styled themselves "Corinthians." Such gentlemen vigorously embraced the manly sports and virtues, eschewing the indolent life and effete manners of the despised fop. Nevertheless, Deirdre harbored the hope that Armand St. Jean, Corinthian or no, could be reasonably expected to be still abed after a late night of dissipation.

As she entered Old Bond Street, her eyes began to scan the numbers above the shop doors. She heard her name called in a soft baritone at her back, and her pulse began to race. She paused, taking a moment to compose herself. He said her name again and she turned slowly and looked steadily into his eyes, meeting his gaze squarely.

He seemed relaxed, almost gracious, his eyes regarding her warmly, as if the sight of her gave him pleasure, and Deirdre wondered at the change in him.

"I would recognize that back anywhere," said Rathbourne without the least trace of malice. "You have a way of carrying yourself and of walking. I remember, you see." He took her arm to lead her a little apart from her abigail so they might be private.

Deirdre hardly knew what to say. If he noticed her surprise, he gave no sign of it. "Ah—I see that my flowers arrived safely."

Her hand flew to the pink rosebud which she had pinned that morning to her dark blue, velvet redingote. She had done it on impulse, never thinking that he would ever see it. The bouquet

26

of roses had been waiting for them at Portman Square. When she had first set eyes on them and read the simple inscription, "Rathbourne," she had taken for granted that the gift was for her. But on turning the card over, she had immediately seen her mistake, for the card was addressed to her aunt. Deirdre had been amused, but she had sobered in the next instant. She told herself severely that she had no wish to become the object of his interest yet again. In the five years since their last disastrous clash, she had tried to forget him, but without success. She did not trouble to deny that he had left an indelible impression on her mind. But the primitive masculinity, barely held in check by the fine garments he wore, both fascinated and frightened her.

"You received my flowers?" he prodded gently.

Deirdre came to herself with a start. "The flowers were quite lovely, my lord, and the gesture most thoughtful. My aunt was touched by your gallantry."

She came under that hard scrutiny again, and Deirdre maintained her passive exterior with no little difficulty.

"Deirdre." His tone was gentle. "You must know how deeply I regret what happened between us on the eve of my departure for Spain. It would please me to think that that unhappy memory had altogether faded from your mind. May I assume that it has? For my part, I should like nothing better than for us to cry truce. We could be friends, I think, if you would meet me halfway." He hesitated only fractionally. "My friendship is not something to be cast away lightly."

Deirdre said nothing.

His voice grew impatient. "Friend or foe, Deirdre, which is it to be?"

There was something in his eyes which disturbed her. He was too confident, too watchful, too much the hunter who had cornered the hare. When she spoke, she managed a normal, neutral tone.

"I have no wish to be your enemy, sir. To be frank, such a

prospect terrifies me. But this discussion is pointless, surely? Friendship is born of trust, of common interests, of shared ideas and reflections." She could not meet the intensity of that steady regard and allowed her eyes to flit to her abigail, whose attention was caught by a display of fine gauzes in the window of a draper's shop. She might not wish to further his acquaintance, but she could scarcely avoid him, not if it was his intention to enjoy the Season. They were bound to be thrown together at various functions. She spoke carefully. "To speak of 'friend' or 'foe' in our case is unnecessary. There is neutral ground, I think, on which we might meet if we must. Yes, let us be neutral, polite acquaintances, from a distance."

"Neither hot nor cold, in fact, but lukewarm?" She heard the smile in his voice.

"If it pleases you to put it like that, by all means."

"Ah, but it does not please me, Deirdre."

There was bright mockery in his eyes when she looked up at him. It burned her to think that he was laughing at her. "It has never been my object to please you, Lord Rathbourne. I trust you will not be too distressed if I choose not to indulge this whim which seems to have taken your fancy?"

His tone of polite sarcasm exactly matched hers. "But it does distress me—deeply. I am afraid I cannot allow it."

"You think you can wrest my friendship from me?"

"If I must."

His gall was insupportable. She spoke with slow emphasis as if she were addressing a backward child. "Friendship is not something that can be coerced."

"No? I beg leave to differ. Yesterday the French were my enemies, today we are bosom bows. In Paris, at this very moment, many of my comrades are finding a welcome from the French mesdemoiselles that yesterday was unthinkable. Do you wonder, Deirdre, that I consider my case to be far from hopeless?"

The innuendo, his boldness, left her speechless.

"Dee! Dee! Where have you sprung from?"

Armand St. Jean, at that moment catching sight of his sister as he made his exit from Jackson's Academy, came striding swiftly along the walk. Rathbourne ignored the interruption, his eyes fixed on Deirdre. She had half turned on hearing her name and the aloof reserve was gone from her face. Her whole expression softened and she laughed—a gay, clear melody of unrestrained joy. Her green eyes, which could freeze to ice with cold contempt, were soft and luminous, glowing with an animation Rathbourne had rarely seen. He drew a deep breath and his hand reached out to her, but she was swept into the arms of a tall, broad-shouldered young man with flashing white teeth and velvet black eyes. Rathbourne's hand dropped to his side and his expression darkened.

"Armand! Put me down!" she exclaimed, pushing feebly against her brother's shoulders, her head thrown back, her dancing eyes giving the lie to the reproving tone in her voice.

Armand became aware of the tall, disapproving figure at his sister's elbow, and he flashed his teeth in an amused grin. He released Deirdre without haste, and spoke rapidly in a soft undertone in her ear. The words were French, and uttered too softly for Rathbourne to hear, but he noted Deirdre's dull flush of color and the slight shake of her head as she glanced uncertainly up at him.

"Lord Rathbourne, permit me to present my brother, Armand St. Jean," she said with a hint of reluctance.

There was a moment of electrified silence, then he threw back his head and laughed.

"So! St. Jean is your brother?" he asked, the amusement lingering in his voice. "I don't recollect . . . ah yes, he would have been at school when I first made your acquaintance." He turned to the young man with the frozen expression and said affably, "How do you do! So you are the young rakehell who has set the ton on its ear? I have been in hopes of making your acquaintance. I don't suppose that surprises you?"

Armand St. Jean's look of astonishment quickly gave way to a furious scowl. His lip curled in a sneer and he spoke stiffly. "I too have been impatient for the honor of an introduction, my lord. My sister has performed a service for both of us, I assure you!"

His eyes swept the Earl with studied insolence, measuring the perfection of his tailoring, the diamond pin in the fold of the white neckcloth, the muscled legs displayed to advantage in tight pantaloons and hessians polished to a military shine.

Rathbourne remained unmoved by this show of unprovoked spite, but Deirdre was deeply alarmed and she took a small step forward as if to shield her brother from the Earl's wrath. Rathbourne observed the gesture and raised one haughty black eyebrow.

"I see," he said half to himself, his eyes growing thoughtful as they absorbed Deirdre's protective posture. "Your brother takes precedence, naturally. But do you think it wise to shield a troublesome boy from the consequences of his folly?"

Before Deirdre had time to frame a reply to the Earl's question, Armand broke in hotly. "I am man enough to meet with you, any time or place of your choosing."

Deirdre blanched at the challenge in Armand's words, but the Earl merely held up a restraining hand. "Spare me the rhetoric, St. Jean," he said with deadly calm. "And you may save the scorching glances for those who are likely to be frightened by them. Troublesome children need to be taught a lesson, in my opinion, and I intend to deal with you at a more propitious moment. At least, have a care for your sister!"

Deirdre felt her brother coil as if ready to spring and her hand fastened firmly on his arm. "My lord," she began, her eyes seeking Rathbourne's in urgent appeal, "thank you for seeing me safely to my brother's lodgings. It was most kind of you, and should we never meet again, please believe that I wish you every happiness."

"Do you so?" asked the Earl gravely, his eyes searching Deirdre's. His features relaxed as he smiled down at her.

"Then I take leave to tell you, Miss Fenton, that we shall most assuredly meet again."

He ignored the erect and unbending figure of St. Jean, and drew Deirdre's fingers to his lips, his glowing amber eyes mesmerizing her with the intensity of their expression. As he bent over her hand, she observed the tawny cast of his dark head, and then he turned on his heel and walked quickly away.

Chapter Three

Deirdre was scarcely aware of the jumbled disorder amid the elegant furnishings of her brother's second-floor lodgings. In other circumstances, she would have been highly amused to note that bachelor living had little improved Armand's incorrigible habit of slovenliness, but at that moment her energies were directed to presenting a mask of indifference to Armand's keen eye while inwardly her brain seethed with speculation about the scene she had just witnessed between the two men. Only the rapid clenching and unclenching of the gloved hands in her lap gave any indication that her unwavering composure was as fragile as the crystal prisms which hung like teardrops from the glittering chandelier on the ceiling.

Her veiled glance flickered briefly over the angry young man whose frantic strides carried him to the two long sash windows at the far end of the saloon, and she watched him covertly as he turned in his pacing, his tread muffled by the thick pile of the rug on the sanded floor. She listened with only half an ear to the string of obscenities he uttered which she made not the slightest effort by word or gesture to curb. A thought was growing in her mind which she was impatient to verify, and she waited only for him to give her an opening. At length, he came to a halt in front of her, the worst of his fury spent.

"It's Mrs. Dewinters, isn't it?" she asked, her voice betraying her emotion in spite of her resolve. "Rathbourne is her protector, isn't he?" she persisted. "That's why you lost your temper when I introduced you!"

At the sound of his rival's name, Armand's black eyes flashed with anger. "That arrogant cur! Who does he think he is? To call me a 'troublesome boy'! I'll deal with him soon enough and make him regret that he ever took it into his head to insult a St. Jean."

"Cut line!" Deirdre said wearily. "To him you *are* a mere boy. He can give you ten years, Armand, most of them spent otherwise than acquiring a little town bronze."

"How do you know him?" Armand asked, a hint of suspicion creeping into his voice. He brushed his coat tails aside and took the chair flanking the striped satin sofa which Deirdre occupied, and looked at her closely. "How do you know him?" he repeated when Deirdre did not immediately reply to his question.

"How does one usually meet gentlemen?" asked Deirdre, her green eyes lifting innocently to meet his. "It was five years ago at some party or other. I can't remember the details exactly," she prevaricated. "Why? Does it make a difference?" She steadied herself to give him back look for look.

Armand was not completely satisfied with her answer. "I trust the man means nothing to you, Dee," he said at last, a slight frown furrowing his brow.

"No! Why should he? I scarcely know him." She managed to inflect a hint of surprise in her voice.

"Don't you? I had the distinct impression that Rathbourne was more than a little taken with you. You looked to be on terms of familiarity."

Even to her own ears, her laugh sounded convincing. "You are imagining things, Armand. And even if he were taken with me, as you say, what is that to you?"

Armand's frown deepened. "He is completely ineligible, Dee. I mean it! I won't have my sister encouraging a man who

34

is lost to all sense of decency. Rathbourne may be an earl, but that doesn't make him a gentleman." His voice softened to an appeal. "Don't let your head be turned by rank and fortune, Dee. This man doesn't play by the rules. You'll only end up the loser."

"Take care, Armand!" Her smile was bright and her voice teasing. "You make the man sound positively irresistible! Why on earth should I avoid him? As I understand, Rathbourne has been in England for only a matter of months—scarcely time to become the blackguard you paint him. What has he done to deserve this character assassination?" She flashed him an artless smile. "Are you warning me off because he is your rival for the affections of Mrs. Dewinters, or is there more to tell?"

"I've heard enough to know that I have no wish to see him dangling after my sister," he snapped. "The man is a barbarian!"

This was unexpected. She knew Rathbourne to be a dilettante, but it had never been suggested, as far as she could remember, that he had been unprincipled or unfeeling except in his treatment of women, and that minor transgression, in a man, was easily forgiven by his peers.

"What are you suggesting?"

"You must know the man's nickname!"

"Le Sauvage? A nom de guerre that the French gave him, as I understand, because he made a formidable enemy. What of it?"

"A barbarian, in fact, and an epithet that his own men were not slow to take up. I've heard stories about his inhuman treatment of the men under his command as well as the enemy that would make your blood run cold. He hates the French, be they friend or foe."

"What stories?" Deirdre demanded.

"They're not pleasant, Dee. Are you sure you wish to hear?"

"I'm not a child." She was past masking the impatience in her voice. "Tell me!"

Armand's tone was damning. "Men flogged to a pulp for

35

minor infractions of regulations; the wounded left to die where they fell and their comrades forbidden on pain of execution to go to their aid; and for the enemy, for the French"—here his jaw tightened—"no quarter given! He hanged two of my countrymen, like myself, the sons of émigrés, who deserted to the French lines. He caught up with them, of course. So you see, my dear," he went on with a bitter twist to his mouth, "my antagonism to the man is based on more than rivalry for a woman's affections."

Deirdre let his words sink in. Something deep inside of her would not admit the truth of what Armand was saying. She had her own reasons for disliking the Earl; she knew from past experience that he set little store by conventional morality, that he gave no quarter to any woman who had the misfortune to fall into his hands. But this was something else. She knew him to be single-minded of purpose, ruthless even. But cruelty had not been in his character. Of course, the war had changed many men. She brought her mind back with difficulty to concentrate on what her brother was saying.

"I suppose he thinks to find a suitable wife to continue his line. But make no mistake about it, I would not, could not tolerate Rathbourne as a brother-in-law."

"A brother-in-law?" Her incredulity was genuine. "Gareth Cavanaugh? He is not the marrying kind! Nor have I any wish to bracket myself with a man who has the morals of an alley cat. But don't try to turn the subject, Armand! I know perfectly well that the primary cause of your quarrel with Rathbourne has nothing to do with me or his war exploits. It's Mrs. Dewinters, isn't it? She's the real bone of contention between the two of you, isn't she?"

Armand did not try to deny the truth of her words. His face relaxed into a sheepish grin. "Wait till you see her, Dee," he said warmly. "I'll take you to Drury Lane sometime soon, then you can judge for yourself. She is everything a man could want in a woman."

Deirdre clamped her lips firmly together. There was much

that she wished to say, but she forebore comment knowing from past experience that overt hostility would have the opposite effect to the one desired. She managed a suitable rejoinder, but her mind was furiously engaged in devising a way to save her impetuous brother from quarreling with a man who would, by all accounts, deal with an adversary in the most ruthless manner. Inwardly, she railed at Armand's stupidity, but she forced herself to silence and calmly began to strip the kid gloves from her fingers. She removed her plumed bonnet and set it on a small, ivory inlaid table at her elbow and cast an inquisitive eye around the spacious interior. After a moment of quiet assessment, she rose gracefully and strolled around the room, surveying the delicately carved furniture and fine objects with a desultory eye. She picked up a bronze figurine of some Greek deity and examined it closely, then replaced it on its ivory stand.

"How can you possibly afford to keep yourself in this style?" she asked with an all-encompassing wave of her hand. "Not from your meager allowance, I'll be bound."

Armand's eyes sparkled with amusement. "I came by it honestly, Dee, if that's what is troubling you."

"How?"

"Need you ask? Gaming, of course! You know I have the devil's own luck at dice and cards!"

Deirdre's look of astonishment seemed to amuse him immensely.

"Oh, I know I can't hold a candle to you, dear sister," he said with a show of modesty, "but fortunately you will never be permitted to challenge me at any of the clubs I frequent. Shame, isn't it? But there's a rule against ladies being members."

"Good God!" she retorted indignantly. "They must be a lot of old dunderheads if you can best them at cards. I've still got a trick or two I have yet to impart to you."

Armand threw back his head and hooted with laughter. "I don't doubt it. Perhaps I should slap a pair of breeches on you

37

and take you with me to the less disreputable of my gaming haunts when next I am short of funds. With your aptitude and my luck, we should make a killing."

"Certainly not," said Deirdre, mildly reproving. "I have no objection to a contest of skill and wits, but gambling for profit is iniquitous. Reverend Standing would be scandalized to think I'd put his harmless knowledge to such a vile use."

"D'you still see the old boy?"

"Well of course. Who else am I to play chess with and so on? Now that you've deserted us, there is no one left at home to give me a run for my money, figuratively speaking."

"Is that the high point of your life now, Dee? What a dull time you must have in Henley! Don't you hanker after something different? After spending a year or so in the tropics, I would have thought your tastes might have changed."

"Nothing of the sort," she replied with some asperity. "I have my books and gardening and a few friends to keep me company. Besides, I manage the house and farm, such as it is. I have enough to occupy me for more hours than there are in the day." At least that was true, and not for the world would she admit to her brother the unmitigated boredom she suffered in the country, where the only acquaintances of her own age were married and apparently content with domestic bliss. The sum of their conversation was of husbands and babies with an occasional complaint about the scarcity of luxuries and fashions from France, an inconvenience occasioned by the interminable war. Deirdre found her spirits suffocated by their blatant provincialism, and their condescension to her single state was more than she could bear. She longed to accept her aunt's offer to travel on the continent, but anxiety for her impetuous brother crushed the impulse.

She looked at him for a long, considering moment. "Armand," she began hesitantly, "is this what your life is to be? Actresses and gaming and so on? What about the future? What will you do when your luck runs out? Don't you have an ounce of ambition?"

"Don't start that again, Dee." His tone was discouraging, and she lost the will to fight him. She stifled a sigh and after a thoughtful pause managed a smile.

"Why don't you come home to see us more often? Nurse misses you, you know. You always were her favorite. A few weeks' quiet rustication in the country wouldn't do you any harm."

Armand flashed her a wicked grin. "You'll have to do better than that, Dee! You can't come running up to town and box my ears, figuratively speaking, whenever I am a bad boy. Those days are gone forever!"

"Who says I can't?" Deirdre asked, an affectionate smile curving her lips.

Armand retrieved a cheroot from a porcelain box on the marble mantlepiece and lit it with a taper from the banked fire. He inhaled deeply, and turned to watch his sister with wary eyes.

At length he asked, "Why are you here, Dee? You've always had an aversion to town life since your first Season, so what brings you to town now?"

Deirdre resumed her place on the sofa and indicated by a motion of the hand that she wished her brother to be seated. When she saw that she had his attention, she began.

"Armand, I have decided that it is time I was wed."

"About time! And with your looks that shouldn't be too difficult. Then you can put an end to this excessive meddling in my affairs and set yourself to managing the poor sap who thinks to make himself your lord and master."

Deirdre disregarded this uncivil speech with a temperateness of long practice. "But Armand," she said coaxingly, "that's just it. How can I possibly snare a husband when my younger brother sets the ton on its ear? What eligible man in his right mind would wish to ally himself with a family as disreputable as ours? Why, any gentleman with a modicum of breeding must deplore the antics of my scapegrace brother!" She turned a limpid gaze on him. "Armand, don't you see how

39

much harm your mode of living may inflict on me at this crucial time? You could ruin my chances of ever finding a suitable parti and I will be constrained to remain single for the rest of my life." She shot him a quick, keen look from under her thick lashes to see the effect of her words. Armand's thin nostrils flared.

"I say, Dee! You can't really mean it!" he blustered. "Don't lay your lack of beaux at my door! As I recall, you were the one who turned down a score of offers any ordinary girl would be delighted to receive. It's your opinion of men that's kept you single, not my conduct! Who was it," he went on in an aggrieved tone, "who took your part against Mama at the end of your first Season when she wanted you to marry that Sir Adrian fellow? I remember your words! You said that all the eligible men you'd met were self-opinionated stuffed shirts who wanted women to be pretty, empty-headed dolls and you wanted none of it!"

"Did I say that?" Deirdre asked, smiling.

"You know you did! So why this change of heart?"

Deirdre considered. "Tempus fugit?" she asked wistfully. "Time, my dear boy, makes cowards of us all. I haven't much changed my opinion of men, but it came to me gradually that for a lady who has set her heart on mothering her own babes, it would be convenient, if not essential, if she should secure some suitable male and lead him to the altar preferably before embarking on a family. I'm conventional, you see."

"Really?" Armand asked doubtfully.

"Really!" said Deirdre firmly. "And the task, I hope, may not be beyond my capabilities."

"No, why should it? Even although you are my own sister, I own that you are a handsome filly, though a trifle managing for my taste. I don't think you'll have any trouble."

"Thank you. That is very generous of you," replied Deirdre, smothering a smile. "I wish I had your confidence, but you must remember that I am now four and twenty, past my first bloom. My dowry is almost negligible. I can scarcely hope for suitors to be lined up at the door." She shot him a deprecating smile. "You must not feel sorry for me, Armand. To be frank, I am almost reconciled to my single state. Should I fail in this endeavor, I shall take to wearing lace caps and declare to the world that I am a confirmed spinster. Perhaps my destiny is to be merely a maiden aunt. Of course, that has its compensations," she went on musingly. "When you settle down and set up your own establishment, naturally I shall make my home with you, mayhap keep house for you until such time as you find a suitable bride. I own to a few qualms about such an arrangement, being sensible of the fact that two women managing a household does not often lend itself to a tranquil . . ."

"Enough!" Armand barked out, aghast at the picture her words evoked in his mind. "What do you want from me?"

Deirdre smiled. "I knew that I could count on you," she said with a smugness which brought a foreboding glint to Armand's dark eyes. "And really, I have no wish to inconvenience you more than necessary."

"Oh, haven't you," he retorted with a touch of ill humor. "Just tell me what you wish me to do, in plain terms, if you please."

"Escort me to parties and so on?"

"Consider it done!"

"Gaming in those dreadful hellholes?"

"I'll confine myself to the regular clubs in the interim. Go on!"

"Naturally, your dueling must be curtailed."

"As you wish. Is that everything?" he asked with heavy sarcasm.

"And Mrs. Dewinters?" she intoned hopefully, coming at last to the very heart of the matter.

"What about Mrs. Dewinters?" Armand's tone was ominous and his eyes blazed a warning.

"Couldn't you give her up for the Season? Is that too much to ask?"

He sprang to his feet and glared down at her. "You don't know what you ask! You know nothing of such things, Dee! How should you? You have led a sheltered existence. Girls like you are totally ignorant of . . . well, never mind. I can't explain it to you. Suffice it to say that in this instance your understanding is limited, as it should be, and your meddling most inappropriate!"

This masculine condescension, coming as it did from a younger brother, was too much for Deirdre. Her temper flared to a white hot heat and all caution was thrown to the winds. "There's nothing wrong with my understanding," she snapped at him, "and from my observation, Rathbourne is no simpleton, either! If she prefers you, then why hasn't she given him his marching orders? I'll tell you why! Because he has the title and fortune and the 'lady'—I use the word loosely—knows which side her bread is buttered on! Furthermore," Deirdre went on, her voice rising in her ire, "I take exception to your arrogant assumption that I am a green girl still wet behind the ears. How dare you insult my intelligence by fobbing me off with such drivel! It may surprise you to know, my boy," she went on cuttingly, "that this big sister of yours knows a thing or two about the wicked ways of the world. D'you think just because I am gently bred, I haven't heard of the antics of those aging harridans, Ladies Besborough, Holland, Hertford, Jersey, and so on? Don't be a simpleton! D'you think we females are blind? Don't you suppose we know who Harriette Wilson is even although propriety forbids us to acknowledge her? Or that the lineup of the foremost peers of the realm at her opera box somehow becomes invisible to us? We see more than you men give us credit for!

"The truth of the matter is you must needs set yourself up as a lady's man, thinking in your youthful innocence that it somehow marks you out as a man of the world. Grow up, Armand! A man of Rathbourne's kidney can carry it off. He is a bona fide roué. But a boy aspiring to the follies of a libertine merely makes himself a laughingstock!"

Having delivered herself to this blasting diatribe, Deirdre caught her breath and waited for Armand's predictable invective to lash her. To her astonishment, he merely chuckled.

"You don't care much for him, do you?" he asked in an amused tone.

"Who?"

"Rathbourne, of course!"

"Oh him," she replied dismissively. "I assure you, I'm quite indifferent to the man. It is what he stands for that I abhor, and I have no wish to see my little brother emulate his scandalous example."

Armand grinned. "Haven't you? Well let me set your mind at rest, Dee. I have no wish to set myself up as another Rathbourne. I haven't yet sunk to that level! Give me some credit!"

"Well then, why won't you cut your connection with Mrs. Dewinters?" she pleaded.

Armand's brows knit together. "Dee, I warn you, this is one subject which we may not discuss! I mean it!"

"But if she prefers him to you?"

"Him!" Armand said with venom. "She is afraid of him! I have tried to persuade her to leave his protection to no avail. He seems to have some kind of hold over her, but he's only flesh and blood after all. I could deal with him if I had a mind to."

Deirdre gave him a quelling look. "I see!" she said stiffly. "And you will call him out in the interests of Mrs. Dewinters, a woman you have known for, how long is it, a month? But for the sister who has always had your best interests at heart, you will do nothing if it inconveniences you!"

"Dee, that's not fair! I didn't say I would call him out. Only that I cannot, will not give up Mrs. Dewinters. If he sees fit to call me out, then, as a gentleman, I have no choice."

She rose to her feet and looked beseechingly into his eyes. "And is that your last word, Armand? You will not do this for me?"

"Dee, understand," he said, grasping her hand, "I shall do all that you desire, within reason. But I cannot be held responsible for Rathbourne's actions."

She left him then, knowing that further argument would not sway him. She had won some concessions, but she was far from satisfied, for what did it matter who called out whom? A duel with Rathbourne was something that must be avoided at all costs. Other men might be depended upon to spare a young, inexperienced hothead little more than a schoolboy for all his posturing, but Rathbourne was unpredictable, and she was unwilling to trust to his generosity in anything which touched her happiness.

It suddenly occurred to her that Armand, by his foolhardiness, was putting into the Earl's hands the perfect opportunity to punish her, and the thought made her go clammy with cold. Once, she would have dismissed such a notion out of hand, but Rathbourne had become an enigma to her. Armand was right. A man did not earn the title "Le Sauvage" because of chivalry on the field of battle. She must find a way to shield him from the Earl's wrath. She must.

Chapter Four

Deirdre picked up her abigail at the front door and made her way north along Bond Street, the unsatisfactory interview with Armand robbing the morning of its pleasure. It was past ten o'clock, and the street was fast filling up with roving peddlers and flower vendors touting their wares from push carts or stout trays suspended by straps from their necks. Their cries of encouragement to the early bird pedestrians mingled with the rumble of the first horses and carriages rattling through the narrow, cobbled street. Tardy shopkeepers were hastening to unlock the doors to their treasure houses, and young lads in leather aprons were divesting the shop fronts of their iron grilles and hailing each other across the street with good-humored jests. Deirdre was deaf and blind to what was going on around her and missed the admiring glances which were thrown in her direction. Her mind was distracted by the problems presented by her brother and the interview which had just passed.

When it had come to her that the woman Armand had become enamored of was Rathbourne's mistress, the initial sense of shock had been followed by a tide of emotion—what was it, hatred? anger? pique?—so intense that it was only the greatest presence of mind which prevented her from giving vent to her fury. That Rathbourne's reprehensible conduct could be of any interest to her, she would have hotly denied, but her habitual poise had developed a crack, and Deirdre was shaken by it. Surely her outrage had been occasioned by nothing more than a natural antipathy to the indiscretions of a lecher and the follies of an inexperienced boy?

"How do you know him?" Armand had demanded, and she had cast her mind back fleetingly to her first and only Season, when she was a green girl and believed in the absurdities of chivalry and honor and all the nonsense which inexperienced young girls are apt to cherish before life turns them into cynics.

She had told Armand the truth when she said that she had met him at some party. But she did not disclose that the details were indelibly imprinted on her mind. She had been presented to him at the come-out ball of her friend, Serena Bateman, and had been instantly bowled over by the glamour of his casual good looks which any young girl would be hard pressed to resist. His brilliant amber eyes had flickered over her indifferently, dismissing her as another pretty chit unworthy of a second glance, and Deirdre's implacable dislike had taken root.

She never gave him a second thought until she wandered by chance later in the evening into the card room and was unwillingly pressed by her hostess to make up a table at picquet. When she saw that she was to play against Rathbourne, she almost took to her heels, but one glance at the bored set of his shoulders and his cynical expression and her spine stiffened. She determined to humble the pride of the man who thought her little more than a cypher.

For the first few hands, she deliberately played with the intensity of a novice and, when she won the first rubber, feigned such surprise and delight that she knew he put it down to beginner's luck, as she meant him to. She caught the exasperated glint in his bored eyes and she choked back a gurgle of laughter, pretending to be overcome by a spasm of coughing. When it was her turn to deal, however, she flexed her nimble fingers and sliced and cut the cards with the dexterity of a cardsharp. She heard his snort of disbelief and her bland glance lifted innocently to meet his suspicious gaze. Having nailed her colors to the mast, she feigned a disinterested ennui, and yawned behind the shelter of her fan, throwing out her cards without a second look. She trounced him, of course, and she silently blessed the Reverend Standing for his unworldly pursuit of the knowledge of games of chance and the many hours she had spent in his company mastering the art.

When she finally rose to excuse herself, she could not suppress the little gloating smile which played around the corners of her lips. Rathbourne's amber eyes glittered up at her, and the boredom, she noted with a stab of satisfaction, had left their expression entirely, to be replaced by a new respect.

She pivoted on her heel to leave, but his hand fastened around her wrist with crushing force, holding her captive.

"The winnings, Miss Fenton, go to the victor," he said in a lazy drawl.

So he had remembered her name! That surprised her. But she set it aside as of little consequence. She smiled archly and firmly withdrew her hand from his grasp.

"I don't play for money," she told him pertly, "only to defeat my opponents." And she put as much innuendo into her words as she could command.

In the weeks that followed, she had become aware of his veiled glances, those brilliant amber eyes following her when she was partnered in the dance or at supper, or in her aunt's box at the opera. His animal magnetism was almost impossible to resist. But Deirdre had resisted, warned by the other debs of his notorious reputation with women. He was a rakehell, so they said, holding nothing sacred but his own fleeting desires. But it was acknowledged, regretfully, that young ladies of quality had little to fear from the hellion Earl since he generally avoided their company like the plague and took his pleasures with those ladies of the demimonde who might bestow their favors more widely and liberally and with enviable impunity. And since it was common knowledge that he had decided on a whim to join Wellesley in Spain, he was permitted to run tame in the most fastidious drawing rooms. Besides, there was always the faint hope that his eye might be caught by some lucky girl who aspired to a coronet and the fortune to go with it, and such a well-bred specimen would know how to turn a blind eye to what every wife must endure.

Deirdre was at first dismayed and then repelled, and she soon developed a healthy contempt for him. She despised him as a hardened rake, and whenever she found herself captured by his bold amber gaze, her vivid green eyes would go icy with dislike and her lip would curl in open disdain, warning him off. But her obvious disgust only brought that sardonic smile to his face, and his mocking bow, she knew, was meant as an insult.

In the few weeks she had known him, he had scarcely spoken to her, but with those speaking eyes, she decided, the devil lord had no need of a tongue. And then he had appeared at her elbow at the Jerseys' ball at Osterley Park in Richmond, and had requested the pleasure of her company at supper. She had been so surprised that she had given her consent before she had time to consider.

When he led her through the Ionic columns of the grand portico to the dining marquee set out on the east lawn beside the man-made lake, she was aware of the envious glances of the other debs, and it somehow made her more determined in her dislike of him. She had been polite but distant, enduring his pretty compliments in stony silence, her smile as false as his flattering words.

After supper, she had placed her hand on his proffered arm and made no demur as he led her farther from the house to admire the beauty of the lake with its white swans floating in their lonely sentinel on the still water which reflected the brilliant lights set out to illumine the park for the admiration of Osterley's guests.

As far as she could remember, she had conducted herself

with commendable civility, concealing her dislike behind a wall of politeness.

At length, he shook his head and turned her gently to face him. "Why do you set me at a distance?" he asked softly, his tawny eyes strangely hypnotic. "Is it something I've said? Have I done something to offend you? Why do you punish me with this show of coldness? Other men have won your smiles and favors. Am I less than nothing that you barely conceal your contempt from me?"

She had been on the point of disclaiming, but some perverse impulse to humble him had goaded her to honesty.

"Do you think that I am flattered to be singled out by a man of your . . . reputation?" When he remained expectantly silent, she went on a little more boldly, "Surely, that does not surprise you? Your indiscretions are common knowledge; your intemperance, a cause for scandal. Can you really believe that any decent woman would wish to associate with you?"

"Oh, I assure you, many do," he replied with maddening reasonableness.

"Not this one," she snapped back at him.

When she observed his derisive grin, it suddenly became important to her to deflate his ego and her tongue became more scathing. "Your conceit is beyond belief. What do women see in you? You are a man who is known to be addicted to every sort of vice; your ambitions limited to the next wench you can coax into your bed, or possibly to cutting a figure on the field of honor. No one denies that your equestrian ability is exceptional, and on the ballroom floor you can pirouette with the best of them." She paused for effect. "Don't tell me, I know that in the privacy of your study you are addicted to Euripides—no, that will not suit. He is, after all, meant to be taken seriously. It would have to be Aristophanes. Like you, he is . . . comical."

There was a flash of something in the depths of his eyes, but it passed so quickly that Deirdre thought she had imagined it.

His voice, when he spoke, was as smooth as satin. "You

underestimate Aristophanes' comedies, but no matter. It is a common failing to miss the truth of the jest that is spoken in earnest. That argument I would be pleased to pursue with you, but not at present. Your opinion of me is another matter. You have taken my measure as a man. What can I say? I would be loath to disappoint a lady."

His fingers moved like lightning to wrap around her wrists. She was jerked to the iron wall of his chest, and his mouth, hard and brutal, smothered her lips. It was Deirdre's first kiss and a travesty of everything she had dreamed about. Devoid of tenderness, reverence, or love, it was a desecration, a violation of her innocence and meant to degrade her.

It was too much. Never before in her young life had anyone tried deliberately to debase her. For the first time, she became aware of her impotence as a woman in the face of a man's superior strength, and she tasted mingled fear and fury, dry and rasping, at the back of her throat. Hot tears scalded her eyes and coursed down her cheeks to the corners of her lips and she tasted the salt in them.

His mouth eased its bruising pressure, and Deirdre sobbed her relief, gulping in the cool night air from the lake. She remained rigid in his arms, her head averted, her thick eyelashes shielding her hurt and bewilderment from his steady gaze.

"Deirdre—oh damn!" he exclaimed softly. "I never meant to hurt you." She remained obstinately silent. "Look at me," he commanded.

Deirdre reluctantly raised her eyes. It was then that she heard voices, and she glanced over his shoulder to see other guests moving toward them. It gave her the courage she needed. In one swift movement, she wrenched out of his grasp and her hand came up and caught him a stinging blow on the cheek. His head snapped back, but before she could flee, her wrist was caught in a bone-crushing grasp. She stood shivering, straining to even her rough breathing, waiting for some kind of retribution. None came. He returned her to the house in silence and left her with her mother. Nor did he approach her again that evening, but she saw him flirt with every pretty woman in sight. From time to time, he caught her eye and quirked one quizzical brow as if he had caught her out in some social solecism, and Deirdre was incensed.

In the weeks that followed, Deirdre saw him everywhere—at the theater, in the park, on the streets of Mayfair, flaunting his lightskirts on his sleeve, and she was aware of his burning glances as they swept over her, or came to rest on her lips, or the exposed swell of her breast. In some small part, she had come to exonerate his insulting embrace at Osterley, acknowledging her own guilt in deliberately provoking his wrath. She was ashamed of her own behavior but could not bring herself to apologize to him, remembering the crushing fear which had choked her when he had punished her with his kiss. She forced herself to remain natural whenever they were in each other's company, but she distanced him with an aloof acknowledgment or a cool absent smile. And then, he found her alone at Vauxhall.

She had been with a party of friends, duly chaperoned, to see the famous gardens at night, but in the crush to take in the fireworks display she had lost her bearings and had become separated from them. Rathbourne had been there, but keeping his distance. But now he was at her elbow, appearing from nowhere, masterfully putting her hand into the crook of his arm, offering to lead her back to their companions. He hadn't, of course. He led her to a secluded part of the gardens which was poorly lit, and blind fear had made her furious as she demanded to know what he was up to.

His eyes had mesmerized her. There was not a trace of amusement in them, not a spark of his habitual sardonic humor. Their expression was soft and serious, devouring her. And she had stood transfixed, the breath suspended in her throat, her heart beating wildly against her breast like a bird beating its wings against a cage.

"Deirdre . . ." His voice was a hoarse whisper as his strong hands encircled her throat. "If I don't take my courage into my hands now, it will be too late. I've tried to fight your spell, but it's no use. You have bewitched me. I feel like a callow youth in the throes of first love." He gave a shaky laugh. "I know you are not indifferent to me. Don't deny it." His thumb brushed against her lips as if to silence her, but Deirdre was lost for words. Her senses were lulled by the satin smoothness of his voice and the soft breeze which warmed her skin in the darkness which shrouded them.

"Deirdre," he breathed against her mouth, his hot breath scorching her trembling lips, "I am on fire for you. Don't deny your heart. Take pity on me."

For a long moment she remained immobile in his grasp, his honeyed words allaying her instinct to resist. This somber, gentle man was not what she had expected, and she felt no fear. She stirred in his arms in a feeble attempt to shake off the lethargy that seemed to be seeping through her veins, but his head bent toward her and his lips slowly captured her mouth, choking off her halfhearted denial. He kissed her gently, and it registered dimly in her mind that he had been drinking. Then his hands slid down her shoulders to the small of her back and he drew her firmly against the length of him. His kiss was sweet and questioning, and Deirdre wanted it never to end. But it did. She half listened to his caressing voice as he told her that he had to leave for Spain on the morrow, that he wished her to join him as soon as possible, that their time together was too brief to be borne, that he had wanted her from the moment she had thrust herself into his life.

But she barely attended his words. She was lost in the sensation of his hands stealing over her back and shoulders, molding her to the hard contours of his body. She shivered, but whether in fear or anticipation, she could not tell. She had never before been held so closely by any man.

"Don't be afraid," he murmured thickly against her ear. "I swear I'll honor this night. Only let me love you, Deirdre."

And then his lips sought hers with a hunger which

frightened her. She wrenched her head away, but ruthless fingers twisted into the ropes of hair at her nape, holding her immobile. His kiss gentled, became persuasive, teased her lips to open to the sweet persistence of his invading tongue. With infinite patience, he soothed every halfhearted refusal, blocked each feeble attempt to evade him until she became pliant beneath his hands, allowing him the freedom of whatever he desired. Inevitably, he grew bolder. She felt his fingers brush aside the gauze of her bodice to release her breasts to his questing hands. His thumb caressed her swelling nipple and then his head came down and she felt a searing heat as he drew it into his mouth.

Some vestige of conscience, of shame, forced a weak protest from her lips, but he ignored it and his hands slid to the flare of her hips to arch her into the hard thrust of his loins. She felt the swell of him against her thighs and her quivering body melted into his.

The taste, the touch, the smell of him was like a drug, robbing her of rational thought, inducing longings she tried to suppress. She could not. Under the sweet torment of his hands and lips, her body became a thing apart from her with a will of its own. It welcomed him even as her lips tried to deny him. But he would not be denied and she was swept along on the irresistible tide of his passion, giving herself up to whatever he desired, heedless of who he was or what he was.

And then she felt his arms go rigid, and his head came up. She looked up at him, still dazed from the ardor of his embrace, but his glittering eyes were staring past her. She heard a feminine voice call his name and she twisted in his arms to look over her shoulder. Even in that dim light, Deirdre recognized the dark-haired woman in the scarlet costume. She had seen her in Rathbourne's company on several occasions, one of his lightskirts with the blatant sensuality which he seemed to prefer. The sight of her was like a douse of cold water bringing Deirdre back to her senses, and her arms dropped from Rathbourne as if the touch of him scorched her.

The brunette's amused smile was provocatively mocking as she took in the sight of the couple locked in each other's arms and she said something to Rathbourne which brought an angry retort to his lips. He thrust Deirdre behind him, and she heard the fury in his voice as he addressed the woman who seemed to have a proprietary interest in him.

But Deirdre did not wait to hear the lovers' quarrel. She felt cheap and ashamed, and turned blindly to run deeper into the shadows, her breath catching in her throat as she tried to hide herself in the dense undergrowth. She heard his quick tread behind her and fearful sobs racked her body. He caught her easily and turned her into his arms. The tears were streaming down her cheeks. She twisted her head from him to conceal the evidence of her wounded pride, but her jaw was held firmly by his lean fingers as his eyes raked her in the dim light. She felt his gentle touch brushing away the tears, but she flung his hand roughly from her and clawed at the hand which held her fast.

She heard his quick intake of breath and his soft appeal as he shook her gently, but she lashed out at him in fury. Then he swung her into his arms and his mouth, possessive, compelling, came down on hers as if to punish her for her rejection. His arms crushed her to his chest and Deirdre felt as if she was suffocating. She stilled, the fight knocked out of her, and he carried her unresisting form deeper into the shadows till he came to a stone edifice, a gardener's storehouse or some such thing. He carried her across the threshold and kicked the door shut behind him, setting her down in the velvet darkness, and his arms went round her like a vise.

She heard his murmured words of apology against her temple as he explained away the presence of the other woman, but Deirdre was in no mood to listen. She shook with cold rage, her emotions compounded of humiliation and revulsion at her body's betrayal to his lovemaking. She said angry, bitter words, demanding to be set free of his loathsome presence, but each word she uttered seemed only to incite him to a greater resolve and his grip tightened cruelly as she fought to free herself.

She tried to reason with him, but he was immune to her pleas, and she was defenseless against his strength. He was in the grip of some wild emotion, some raging fever, which threatened to sweep aside everything in its path. His lips burned her mouth and his hands slipped beneath her gown, searching her body with a relentless intimacy which left her shaken. She knew that she was beginning to yield to him, and she struggled within herself to marshal the vestiges of her bruised pride. She balled her hand into a fist and, with every ounce of her strength, struck him in the face, feeling the cut of the emerald on her finger as it smashed against bone.

He released her with a savage oath and she ran from him, sobbing with shock and relief. She dragged the door open and fled, unheedful of his command at her back, groping her way along the dark walk until she came to lights and safety. How she found her companions in her near hysterical state, she could never afterward remember. But not one of them remarked on her overbright eyes or the flush of her complexion, and she said nothing to enlighten them.

He came after her, of course, and she shuddered when she saw the blood-soaked handkerchief pressed hard against his cheek. He addressed her quietly, begging for a few minutes' private conversation, but she would not permit it. He tried to apologize, turning his back on her companions to shield her from their curious gaze, his voice urgent as he told her again that he would be bound for Spain on the morrow and that there was much that he wished to say to her. But her raging sense of betrayal would not allow her to accept his contrite words. She despised herself for surrendering so easily to his caresses when he thought her no better than the lightskirt whom he had callously abandoned in pursuit of bigger game. And before she could stop herself, those terrible words had been uttered, words she had regretted as soon as they were out of her mouth. "Go to Spain! I hope a bullet finds you and you never return!"

He had stood frozen, his brilliant tiger eyes narrowing to

slits, glinting with some dangerous emotion he could scarcely contain. Then he had swung away from her, and she had watched him with a sinking feeling in the pit of her stomach. She said his name under her breath and made to go after him to take back the vindictive words, but a figure moved out of the shadows to join him, her scarlet costume unmistakable. And his arms went round her, and Deirdre watched as he kissed her fiercely. She turned away, the tears stinging her eyes, and she dashed them away with her balled fists.

In the weeks that followed, she had flung herself into every pleasure that was offered in a vain attempt to banish him from her mind. When that failed, she had drifted into an engagement with one of the many suitors who clamored for her hand, no better, no worse, no different from all the other eligible men of her acquaintance. But it did not take her long to discover that the Earl had spoiled her for other men, and she broke the engagement.

At the end of the Season, she returned home, weary and heartsore. She soon heard of Rathbourne's exploits even in the quiet backwater of Henley. His daring conquests on the field and in the boudoir had made the dashing major something of a legend, and Deirdre congratulated herself on her lucky escape.

And then, tragically, the following year, her mother had succumbed to some fever that the doctors had never positively identified. Armand, in his first year at Oxford, had come home only infrequently, and Deirdre had become something of a recluse. It was her aunt, half out of her mind with worry, who had persuaded the lonely girl to accompany the Fentons to Jamaica for a year. The year had stretched to two and she had tried to forget Rathbourne in the pleasure of discovering a new land and in meeting new people. But she had never quite managed to free herself from his insidious memory. She permitted other men to court her, other arms to hold her, other lips to smother her with kisses, to no avail. She was like an ice maiden, untouched and unassailable, through no choice of her own.

Her one consolation was the knowledge that in resisting Rathbourne she had saved herself the fate of becoming just another string in his stable of women. That, she would never regret.

As Deirdre quickened her steps along the Oxford Road, she felt again the sting of tears at the back of her eyes, and she gritted her teeth in anger, determined that he would never again have the power to abase her. She felt for the rose on her redingote and tore it from her collar, crushing it in her hand and throwing it aside as if by that one angry motion she could be free of him forever.

Chapter Five

It was an equipage calculated to inspire envy in the bosom of any young fashionable hopeful of making his mark in society. The sleek, ebony black curricle, as flawless as a new minted penny, was hitched to a pair of incomparable matched bays. As Deirdre slowed her pace to her aunt's four-storied terraced residence which stood on the west side of the square, her glances, warm with mingled respect and approbation, were involuntarily drawn to the resplendent carriage and the finest horseflesh she had clapped eyes on since her sojourn in Jamaica. By slow degrees, the unpleasant memories of Rathbourne faded from her mind.

A groom of indeterminate years in the livery of some great house or other was standing at the heads of the horses, and she watched with growing pleasure as he gently stroked the necks of the restive beasts, his voice subdued and soothing as the animals snorted their displeasure at being kept standing by their dilatory master. They made an impressive picture, and it registered in some dim recess of Deirdre's mind that a gentleman of no small consequence was paying a morning call on one of her aunt's neighbors. She approved the restrained elegance of his sporting conveyance no less than the glossy thoroughbreds which the groom handled with commendable care.

With a polite word of dismissal, she dispensed with the services of her abigail, and crossed the cobbled street to the iron railing which enclosed the common gardens shared by the residents of the square. Tall stands of leafless English plane trees filtered the winter sun. In another month or so, it was to be hoped, with the advent of spring, that the delicate buds of narcissi and hyacinth would be pushing through the black earth. Deirdre breathed deeply. Spring was in the air, and at such a season, there was nowhere she would rather be than England. It was good to be home.

She extended one ungloved hand toward the neck of the nearest bay. "May I?" she asked the skeptical groom in her most persuasive accents, and flashed what she hoped was an endearing smile.

The lackey eyed her with faint suspicion for a moment or two as if calculating her trustworthiness to handle such a priceless treasure as his master's prime cattle. There was something in her poise, in her calm approach, however, that gave the unmistakable impression that the lady knew her way around horses. And she was a Beauty—a thoroughbred in her own right. It tipped the balance of the scales in her favor. His features relaxed into a less grimmer aspect. "Aye," he said cautiously. "I'm thinking there can't be any harm in it if you take care no to skitter 'em."

Deirdre voiced her thanks for the generous favor and advanced upon one of the bays with palm extended. She brought it to a halt a good twelve inches from his flaring nostrils. Watchful, coal black eyes surveyed the unfamiliar object for a moment or two, muscles tensing for instant flight, but as the hand remained immobile, just out of reach, curiosity overcame the bay's natural instinct for caution and he craned his head forward to nuzzle Deirdre's fingers.

"I learned on a horse farm in Jamaica how curious these animals are," said Deirdre with a hint of apology. Her hand moved across the corded sinews of the bay's neck, softly massaging, stroking him into submitting to her touch, and she murmured soft endearments under her breath.

At the liquid sounds of her soothing voice, the bay's ears pricked. Deirdre scratched them. "I presume your master knows your worth, you magnificent animal," she breathed against his silky neck.

"That he does," the groom interjected, his voice puffing with pride. "His lordship be knowing the worth o' his cattle, none better. He was born an' bred to the saddle, aye, an' can do an honest day's work in the stable when he has a mind to. He be a cavalry man an' no one o' yer flats w' nowt in their heads 'cept cuttin' a dash."

"I take it your master is one of those gentlmen who puts his cattle above people?" Deirdre was familiar with the type.

The groom shrugged. "He respects what he pays for."

"And yet he keeps them here standing," Deirdre needled with gentle malice, perversely hoping to open a crack in the lackey's blind devotion to this paragon of a master.

The groom's confidence was not to be shaken. "Nay!" he returned easily, disappointing Deirdre's hopes. "His lordship be putting the bit to a filly o' a different sort. He'll break her to bridle soon enough." A sly smile touched his lips. "He'll be having her tamely eating out o' his hand afore ye know it. The master has the knack o' gentling even the highest steppers. He knows how to be patient and so maun we."

"Are we talking of horses or females?" asked Deirdre primly.

"What's the difference?"

Deirdre was startled into a laugh. He was a bold one, and no mistaking. But he had a touch of the Irish in him. That would explain it.

"Rogue!" she flung at him with an impish grin. "I thank you for the warning. You may rest assured that in future I shall give both you and your master a wide berth, yes, and instruct all the ladies of my acquaintance to emulate my example. 'Break her to bridle,' indeed!" Laughter threaded her voice.

She gave the bay one last, reluctant pat and swung back toward the pillared entrance of her aunt's red brick town

61

house. She had taken only a step, however, when the door swung open and a tall, imposing figure in dark superfine and beige pantaloons molded closely to the hard muscles of leg and thigh stepped over the threshold. Deirdre caught a glimpse of the mahogany cast of the gentleman's ruffled locks before he jammed on his beaver and jauntily descended the few granite steps of the front portico.

"Rathbourne!" she exclaimed. Her green eyes shaded with surprise swept up to meet the golden glint of his steady gaze.

"Gareth," he corrected gently.

Before she knew what he was about, the Earl had grasped her firmly by the elbow and was propelling her toward the waiting curricle. "I have your aunt's permission," he warned when he felt the stiffening resistance beneath his fingers. "I assure you, Deirdre, it is quite acceptable for a gentleman to take a lady for a drive in an open carriage."

She might have known that the equipage belonged to him. The crest of red hawk emblazoned on its side should have warned her. But it had never occurred to her that Rathbourne would seek her out. Barely an hour had elapsed since they had spoken to each other on Bond Stret. What was he up to? Armand! Of course! He would wish to sound her out about her brother.

As she was solicitously settled on the cushions of the black leather seat, Deirdre looked around with a wrathful glint in her eye. Rathbourne had moved to the other side of the curricle to take his place beside her, and Deirdre, catching the speculative grin on the groom's face, bared her teeth in a ferocious grimace. She heard his strangled chuckle as he gave the ribbons into his master's hands. Then he deferentially touched his cap to her and with a surreptitious wink moved off down the street as if by prearranged signal, and she was alone with Rathbourne.

He flicked the ribbons smartly, urging the bays to a slow trot.

"Where are you taking me?" Deirdre demanded.

"Only to the Park. What did you think? That I meant to abduct you? Rest assured, that is not my intention." Amusement laced the soft sarcasm of his words.

Deirdre was stung by the smooth jibe. If he meant to show her up as a fanciful female, he was in for a disappointment. That he felt no real remorse for his unfeeling conduct at Vauxhall was obvious. No doubt *that* peccadillo paled into insignificance in light of his subsequent debauchery. It would feed his vanity if he ever discovered that what to him had been a passing flirtation had come close to blighting her life.

In the five years since her come-out, she had become adept at depressing the pretensions of overfamiliar coxcombs. Rathbourne's masterful manner might endear him to the likes of a Mrs. Dewinters, but Deirdre was confident that she had long since become inured to the hackneyed charm of a born flirt. He expected a blushing innocent. She would show him the face of a woman of the world.

"Naturally, I am disappointed. But don't let that weigh with you. I shall console myself with the thought that this afternoon I have an appointment with my mantua maker, and Madame Tremblay hates to be kept waiting. Perhaps some other time?"

She had expected to disconcert him, but when she flashed a glance at his profile, she soon discerned that it was impossible to depress the Earl. He was smiling broadly, and before Deirdre could make a recovery, he was on the offensive.

"It was never my intention to disappoint you, Deirdre. Your suggestion is well taken. An interlude of dalliance ought not to be compressed between appointments to one's tailor or one's dressmaker. How are you fixed for tomorrow?"

Deirdre retreated behind a veil of glacial politeness. "You had some business with my aunt, sir?" She was careful to avoid the use of his Christian name or title.

Rathbourne flicked her a satirical look. "A non sequitur if ever I heard one. Does this mean that we have sheathed swords? And just when things were beginning to get interesting." He gave a loverlike sigh which Deirdre ignored. "To answer your question," he continued affably, "I had some business of a private nature with Lady Fenton."

Deirdre waited, but the Earl had obviously no intention of satisfying her curiosity.

After an interval of silence she began on a new tack.

"How well you handle the ribbons." The exaggerated admiration was done to a nicety. Insult or compliment—let him make of it what he would.

"Don't!" he commanded.

She raised limpid eyes to meet the sudden blaze of his expression. "What did I do?" she asked innocently.

"You know perfectly well." He slowed the bays to negotiate a sharp corner, then went on more easily. "Don't play games with me, Deirdre, I won't allow it. And save those melting glances for the flats who are like to be taken in by them. You have my permission to act the grande dame, as only you can, with any other man of your choosing, but with me I insist that you be your own incomparable self. Between us, I expect a little candor. It was ever the quintessence of your charm."

She fell silent, watching resentfully from under veiled lashes as he skillfully maneuvered the bays through the Stanhope Gate and into Hyde Park. The odd rider had taken the opportunity of exercising his mount at a time when the park was certain to be thin of company, but there would be few carriages until later in the afternoon. Rathbourne brought the bays to a halt and slackened the reins, allowing them to forage on the winter brown grass at the edge of the drive. Deirdre felt a chill and dragged the folds of her redingote more tightly across her knees.

"Here!" He unfolded a traveling rug and draped it across her lap. "What happened to the rose?" His hand went toward the lapel of her redingote.

A faint flush stained Deirdre's cheekbones. "I lost it," she lied, suddenly ashamed of her ungenerous impulse.

"I'll get you another," he said softly, then on the next

breath, "You never married." It was a statement, not a question.

"No," she replied shortly. Two could play at being tight-lipped.

"Why?"

He had no right to ask. She owed him nothing. "Perhaps nobody asked me."

His measuring gaze wandered slowly over her, from the top of her jaunty blue ostrich feather to the toes of her new kid half boots, absorbing the slim but feminine figure with its promise of pleasure, the clear oval of her face, the fine-pored, flawless complexion. He grew pensive as he held those expressive green eyes which mirrored every fleeting thought and emotion. She would never know how easy he found it to read her. Even now, her eyes were narrowed in displeasure at his bold scrutiny. If only she would unbend a little and favor him with that slow, unconsciously alluring half smile that could transform her from passionless prude to Aphrodite incarnate. His gaze lingered on her lips, and he smiled.

"Oh, you were asked," he replied smoothly. "As I recall, you became engaged a fortnight or so after I left for Spain."

"And became disengaged a fortnight after that," she replied with an edge to her voice.

"So I heard. Then took off soon afterward for Jamaica. The question still stands. Why did you never marry?"

She tilted her head back to get a clearer view of his expression. Did he suppose that she had avoided marriage because of a forlorn tendresse for him? The thought came so uncomfortably close to the truth that she felt her anger rising.

"And take a master to lord it over me? You must be funning. I have yet to be persuaded that matrimony holds any material advantage for a woman." She caught his derisory grin and went on with biting persistence. "What, pray, does a woman gain by it? She merely passes from one man's dominion to another's. A guardian or a husband—what difference does it make?"

"If you don't know, I cannot explain it." Laughter flickered

65

in the depths of his eyes. "Suffice it to say that I find your education sadly lacking in some respects. But rest easy, Deirdre. You may depend on me to spare your blushes."

"Don't put yourself to the trouble. I don't blush easily. But deny if you can that marriage, for a woman, is like a game of chance. Whether or not her guardian or husband is benign or a tyrant is a matter of good fortune or bad. What protection has she if either proves intolerable? There is none."

"Not in theory, but in practice, surely, most women are cherished by their menfolk?"

"Do you think so? You may be right." She was not persuaded, but the subject was becoming too personal for comfort. She eyed him with frank curiosity. "But your case is not the same as mine. A man has nothing to lose if he takes a wife. Yet I don't see you rushing off to offer for some eligible girl. Answer your own question, Rathbourne," she commanded boldly. "Why have you never married?"

"Can't you guess?" he asked provocatively.

Deirdre did, and her composure was visibly shaken. "Yes, I can see that the question is irrelevant. What need of a wife when there are always dozens of women ready to throw themselves at your head? Don't trouble to deny it! The ondits of your shocking behavior in Spain were related to me, ad nauseam I may add, even as far away as Jamaica. And even before that . . ."

She fell uncomfortably silent, thinking that perhaps he thought she was fishing.

"And I had supposed that after Vauxhall, you never gave me another thought. I am flattered."

"Don't be. If I thought of you at all, it was with . . . indifference."

"Deirdre, why are you angry?"

"I am not angry," she said emphatically.

"But you are."

"I tell you, I am not," she retorted, visibly trying to control her fury.

66

He shook his head in mock disbelief.

"I am *not* . . . oh, this is silly." She would say no more.

"If there is anything you wish to know, you have only to ask me," he continued with maddening blandness. He cocked an inquisitive brow, but Deirdre was steadfastly looking away, pretending an interest in a lone horseman who was taking advantage of the deserted park to ride ventre à terre along the wide sweep of drive reserved for riders and their mounts.

"Is it my reputation?" he persisted gently. "I cannot pretend that I've been a saint all these years, but the stories that got about were grossly exaggerated. You can't mean to hold my past against me?"

"Why are you telling me all this?"

"I hoped we were to be friends."

"Friends? Why should we be?"

His laugh held a thread of self-mockery. "You have not an inkling, have you? No matter. I shall satisfy your curiosity when I judge the time is right. I rushed my fences once before . . ." He halted suddenly in midsentence as if he regretted saying so much.

"Is this an oblique reference to my brother?"

"Your brother?"

"He is only a boy."

"What?"

"Armand! You cannot feel threatened by him."

"I don't." He sounded surprised.

"He won't call you out. I have his word on it," Deirdre went on earnestly. "If you would just give me a little time, I hope to persuade him to give up . . . to come home to Henley with me."

He realized they were talking at cross-purposes. "That would not suit me at all," he said with a half smile gentling his expression.

The threat to her brother was unmistakable.

"Lord Rathbourne, Gareth," she began, and smiled engagingly into his eyes. The sudden intensity of his expression

67

almost unnerved her, but she forced herself to speak naturally and without hesitation. "Allow me to apologize for my brother's rash words when we met on Bond Street this morning. No one takes the boy seriously when he is in one of his takings. He really didn't mean to be insulting, you know. It's just that he speaks without thinking."

He looked at her for such a long, interminable moment that Deirdre began to think that perhaps she had offended him.

"Did he ask you to speak to me on his behalf?"

"Certainly not! Why if he knew that I was here with you now, he would be . . ." She faltered to a halt. The conversation had taken a turn she had no wish to pursue.

"He would? Pray continue?"

"It doesn't signify. I should never have mentioned it."

"But you did mention it, Deirdre, and I insist that you finish what you began."

But she wouldn't dare. She shook her head. "No, no! Let it rest."

"Deirdre, I am not a patient man. Either you tell me what I wish to know or I shall make a point of applying to your brother."

He must know the answer to that question. Why was he insisting that she bring up a subject which must give her considerable embarrassment? She would show him that she had more composure that he gave her credit for.

"Armand has taken you in dislike. That shouldn't surprise you. I gather that he imagines himself to be in love with a lady in whom you have a mutual interest."

"Indeed? You speak of Mrs. Dewinters, I presume?"

"Is there another?"

They might have been discussing the weather. They spoke with detachment, without rancor, and so rigidly correct.

"Not to my knowledge. Poor boy! Maria will make his life miserable!"

"But . . . don't you mind?"

"Why should I?"

"But isn't she . . . ? Everyone says . . ."

"You have been listening to gossip again, Deirdre, a regrettable failing. My interest in Mrs. Dewinters is strictly platonic." Then gently, "She means nothing to me."

Deirdre felt as if a crushing weight had been lifted from her chest. "Then Armand is safe? There won't be a duel?"

"I am not in the habit of dueling with children. But tell me, do you make it a practice to fight all your brother's battles for him?"

The hint of censure put her immediately on the defensive. "He is my brother, and under age," she said with crushing dignity. "It is natural for me to worry about him."

"Are you saying that you are responsible for him?"

"Not legally, of course. Armand has a guardian of sorts, but not so as one would notice. If I don't look out for his interests, no one will."

"Who is his guardian?"

"My late stepfather's brother, Giles St. Jean. But as a guardian, he is a useless article. Armand might as well not exist for all the attention he pays him."

"But you surely don't hope, on your own, to manage a young hellion like your brother? Ye Gods, you can't be much more than a year or two older yourself."

Why had she confided so much to him? It had been a mistake: Rathbourne was hostile to Armand, that much was obvious. His next words confirmed her observations.

"If I'd had him under my command, I would have whipped him into line soon enough. What that young man needs is a tight bit and a short rein."

The unfortunate metaphor had Deirdre bristling. "He is not a horse, but a boy who was deprived of a father's guidance when he had most need of it. But this is old history. I beg your pardon for boring you with details of what, after all, concerns nobody but myself. I'd be obliged to you if we could drop the subject."

To Deirdre's great relief, the Earl fell in with her wishes, and at her express request put the bays through their paces. He proved to be a notable whip which was no less than Deirdre had expected. She paid him the compliment of telling him so, in an offhand manner, of course, not wishing him to think that she would stoop to flattery. He thereupon casually offered to let her take up the ribbons for a short part of the way, an honor of which Deirdre was highly conscious. She was determined to show him that his confidence was not misplaced, and she was gratified when she aquitted herself, if not with distinction, at least with some credit. Rathbourne said as much, and Deirdre was satisfied.

Nevertheless, it soon registered that the Earl had set her at a distance. His air of preoccupation was feigned, she was sure of it. When he delivered her at Portman Square she wondered if she would ever see him again, except in passing, so coldly formal was his manner as he took his leave of her. Not that such a prospect troubled her in the least, Deirdre told herself resolutely.

Chapter Six

The Earl's air of preoccupation was to linger till he had flung himself up the steps of the front entrance of Rathbourne House, a spacious, sandstone edifice which stood on the north side of Piccadilly. In normal circumstances, he would have paused on the threshold to look back over his shoulder at the uninterrupted view of Green Park which lay directly across the street, an agreeable prospect in all weathers which never failed to bring him pleasure.

But on this occasion, he rapped smartly on the door with the brass knocker and, as it opened, pushed impatiently past the startled porter, who hastened to assist his master as he shrugged off his driving coat and stripped the gauntlets from his fingers. Rathbourne's eyes quickly scanned the open doors of several reception rooms leading off the main foyer with its immaculate white marble floor and yellow damask wall covering.

"Is Mr. Landron in, John?"

"I believe he's in the upstairs library, your lordship."

"And the ladies?"

"Shopping, sir."

Rathbourne took the stairs two at a time, leaving a slightly surprised flunky in his wake.

The Earl's secretary and man of business, Mr. Guy Landron,

who looked to be a summer or two older than his employer, was seated at a massive oak desk completely absorbed in the open ledgers and papers which were spread out in front of him. A tray set with cold, pressed meats, thick slices of bread and butter, and a silver coffee pot was pushed to one corner of the cluttered desk. At the Earl's entrance, Landron looked up, and a slow smile of welcome suffused his face.

His slightly disheveled appearance gave no indication of his many years under strict military discipline. But there was something in the quality of garments tailored with an eye for fit rather than fashion which marked him out unmistakably as no more no less than the true English gentleman. His thick, cropped brown hair, which was beginning to gray at the temples, was worn in the Brutus style, and emphasized the aquiline cast of his chiseled features. He made as if to rise, but the Earl crossed the short distance between them in a few swift strides and restrained him with a firm hand on the shoulder. Fine lines of pain which had begun to etch themselves on Landron's face immediately smoothed out.

"Don't stand on ceremony on my account, Guy. Just keep the weight off that gammy leg as the doctor ordered. How are things going?" The Earl indicated the open ledgers with a nod of his dark head.

Guy Landron relaxed against the straight back of the Hepplewhite armchair and looked up at the man who had been his commanding officer for five years. The impulse to stand in the presence of a senior officer was hard to resist, even supposing that officer had been closer to him than a brother since their madcap undergraduate days at Oxford, notwithstanding the wide disparity between them in rank and fortune.

Landron absently smoothed the soft knit fabric of his pantaloons over his lame leg. It had always been his intention to pursue a military career. Not that a younger son of a younger son had much choice in the matter, but a French shell had put paid to that ambition. His future prospects had looked bleak indeed till Rathbourne had come to the rescue with the offer of

72

his present position. Theirs was not the typical relationship of employer and employee, but of two comrades who had survived the grim necessities of war by their combined cunning and unwavering loyalty to each other. Their converse could never be, after their shared experiences, anything other than free and easy, and on occasion, frank to the point of rudeness.

"I'm beginning to get the hang of it, but I still think you would have been better served had you employed a bona fide accountant when Mr. What's-his-name moved on to better things."

The Earl grinned. "Your recommendation could not come higher."

"Which was?" asked Landron quizzically.

"My dear Guy, anyone who can keep a marauding band of undisciplined savages well provided with supplies and mounts when the main army is half starved and on foot must be something of a genius. Besides which," the Earl continued with a derisive grin, "I'm not forgetting that if it had not been for you and O'Toole, I would not be here now." Mr. Landron's look was blank and Rathbourne said in a wry tone, "What? Don't you remember last summer, at Belmont, when the Little Chapel went up in flames?"

"Oh that!"

"Yes, that! You needn't sound so disparaging! I assure you, in my poor estimation, the service you rendered then was quite remarkable. You saved my life."

"I shall never understand how you came to be so careless."

The Earl's smile held a suggestion of apology. "True. I can't think how I came to let that crossbeam fall on my head. And as for the thunderbolt which ignited the fire, well, I should have caught it and thrown it right back to Zeus on Mount Olympus."

"The gods had nothing to do with it! Two coincidences in one night is one too many to swallow."

"We've been through all this before, Guy. It was an accident. No one knew that I had gone to check on the roof the workmen were repairing. Besides, who, in my own home, would wish me ill?"

"You've made many enemies in the last five years."

"Yes, but they were French, and they don't know my identity. Besides, the war is over."

"I still don't like it."

"Forget it. I tell you it was an accident."

As Rathbourne brushed aside some papers to balance one hip on the edge of the desk, his eye was caught by the platter of cold meats, and he began to nibble on a thick slice of smoked gammon. "Have some, this is delicious."

"Thank you, no. I have had sufficient. But don't stint yourself on my account."

"I'm starving," Rathbourne admitted between bites. He poured himself a cup of coffee, but set it aside when he found it too tepid for his taste.

"As for my affairs," he went on idly as his eyes scanned the room for the decanter of brandy which had been displaced by the luncheon tray, "I have no doubts of your ability to handle them."

"Your confidence is staggering," said Landron with mock gravity. "Naturally, I am grateful for your patronage. I only hope you will never have cause to regret the generous impulse."

"I? Generous? You can put that notion out of your head. Self-interest has always been the driving force behind my every action."

Landron raised one disbelieving brow. "Does that apply to Maria Dewinters also?"

Rathbourne frowned, but Landron's mocking expression only deepened.

"You know the circumstances as well as I do," the Earl returned cautiously. "How could I abandon her? She would never have been accepted into Spanish society after the war."

"No, but you might have pressed His Majesty's government

to give Maria her just desserts for services rendered to the cause. Instead of which, you foolishly set her up in one of your own houses. Now that is going beyond the call of duty, unless, of course, the lady has come under your protection once again?"

"In a manner of speaking only! That part of my involvement with Maria was of very short duration, as you well know. But I still feel some responsibility for her welfare. I cannot forget, as others seem determined to do, that she was an invaluable agent behind French lines when we most needed one. I owe it to her, Guy."

"I'll not deny your words. I simply used Maria as an example to show that self-interest is *not* always the primary force which motivates you, as you assert. In fact, Maria Dewinters may well prove to be an embarrassing liability."

"Don't I know it!" Rathbourne pushed himself to a standing position and strode to one of the long windows which looked out over the busy thoroughfare of Piccadilly and to the park beyond. Landron sensed the sudden change in the Earl's mood and waited patiently for him to continue.

At length the Earl turned. "I have a job for you, one that is more in line with your specialized training."

"Cloak and dagger stuff?"

"If you care to put it like that. Nothing dangerous. This is peacetime, remember? I merely want you to find out all you can about a certain Giles St. Jean. He is the guardian of Armand St. Jean."

Landron gave the Earl a keen look. "Isn't that the brat whose name is linked with Maria's at present?"

"Yes, but that's not the connection that interests me." The Earl seemed reluctant to say more, but finally went on with slow emphasis. "He is half brother to Miss Deirdre Fenton."

At Deirdre's name, Landron's head went back and his expression became guarded but he said nothing. Rathbourne caught the sudden restraint in his friend's manner, and his smile became faintly self-mocking.

75

"What? Haven't you anything to say? No grim warnings about avoiding the vixen who left your friend a shell of his former self?"

Landron's voice was dry and chiding. "I've said it all before. I don't know why I bother. But I thought, in five years, you would be over her. Was I mistaken?"

The Earl answered with perfect affability. "Just because I happened to let slip a few details of my courtship of the lovely Deirdre whilst I was in my sickbed under the influence of laudanum does not indicate that I have, or ever had, any intention of taking you into my confidence in this matter."

"So you're not over her!" replied Landron flatly. "Pity."

"Why do you say that?"

Landron busied himself sorting the numerous bills and receipts which littered the desktop. "It's none of my business, of course," he said brusquely, "but from what you let slip . . ."

"I was delirious!"

". . . she sounded like a cold fish, one of those ungenerous types, of whom, thank God, we have generally managed to remain in ignorance."

"A prude?"

"If you say so."

"If it's true, and I don't admit it, that can be remedied."

"You've contrived to meet her again, haven't you? I've been expecting it. But why this interest in Miss Fenton's half brother and his guardian?"

"An unexpected complication which merits a thorough investigation before I decide on what tactics to employ. I want to be filled in on both the boy and his guardian; where their money comes from and so on, outstanding debts . . ."

"And any weaknesses that may be exploited as a last resort? Yes, I'm familiar with the formula, even supposing our days with Intelligence are over, or so I had supposed."

The two men looked at each other for a long, considering moment. The Earl spoke first. "If you find the task distasteful,

I can handle it without your assistance."

"That's not what troubles me."

"No? What then?"

"Your singlemindedness of purpose. In wartime, such a trait is invaluable in a soldier. The prize . . ."

"Is much higher this time. I'd be a fool not to use every means at my disposal to secure it."

The Earl's words won a reluctant smile from his companion. "Rathbourne, I hope you know what you're doing. Is Miss Fenton so exceptional then?"

The Earl shrugged. "You are asking me why I am partial to Deirdre, and I can't explain it. These things defy logic."

"You do realize that there are dozens, scores, of unexceptionable girls who would need little encouragement to pick up the handkerchief you care to throw down."

"Why do you dislike her so much?"

"I was the one who picked up the pieces after she had put the boot to you, or had you forgotten?"

"I hadn't forgotten how you coddled me, if that's what you mean. But that is beside the point. I never told you what happened between Deirdre and me, nor am I ever like to. If I hadn't been knifed in that low Spanish tavern . . ."

"Bordello," corrected Landron scrupulously.

". . . you would never have discovered any of this, and I would be feeling more comfortable."

"Yes, your tongue did rather run away with you at your first taste of laudanum. But what if the girl still refuses to have anything to do with you?"

"I am in no mood to accept a refusal. Shall we say that by fair means or foul, Miss Deirdre Fenton shall be persuaded to become the next Countess of Rathbourne?"

Rathbourne stalked to a side table where he had at last spied the brandy decanter and glasses. He returned with two generous goblets and thrust one at his amused friend.

"Shall we drink to it?" asked the Earl.

"Oh I have no objection to drinking to the next Countess."

"No, my friend. We drink to Deirdre, Countess of Rathbourne, if you please," replied the Earl with heavy deliberation.

"Do you know, Rathbourne, I can almost pity the poor girl? But on second thoughts, I shall reserve my pity for you."

The Earl looked questioningly at his friend over the rim of his glass.

"If she ever discovers how much she means to you, she will make your life hell."

Rathbourne was to think long and hard about Landron's glib prophecy.

78

Chapter Seven

The closed carriage bearing the Fenton ladies to one of the first soirées of the Season rolled to a halt before the blazing lights of Rathbourne House, and Deirdre peeped out. Majestic footmen in impeccable gray livery with silver frogging and epaulettes were stationed on the pavement on either side of the front entrance. As each coach disgorged its profusion of passengers, these vassals of the great house stepped forward as one, and with unflagging patience offered their assistance to the guests of their illustrious lord.

Deirdre threw herself back against the squabs and a low groan escaped her lips. Panic fluttered at the edges of her mind. This was the last door in London she had ever thought to enter. A lamb, she was a lamb daring to broach the lion in his den.

"Aunt Rosemary," she burst out on impulse, "what on earth possessed you to accept the Earl's invitation? I can't, I just can't go in there."

"Get a hold of yourself, Deirdre," the older woman exclaimed. "I told you, the Earl wishes to enlarge his sister's circle of acquaintances before she makes her formal bow to the world. This is not a grand affair by any means. You won't have to dance with the man, if that's what is troubling you. He merely wants his sister to meet some young people of her own age. How could I refuse such a reasonable request? On the contrary, I deemed it an honor to be included in the guest list. Had I known then that your antipathy to the Earl was so immovable, naturally, I would have offered some pretext to avoid his society. I've never seen you in such a taking. Now mind your manners, girl, and see that you don't disgrace me!"

"I hope you know me better than that," Deirdre managed, considerably subdued by the reproof in her aunt's tone of voice.

The carriage door swung open and the two ladies soon found themselves ushered into the wide foyer of the grand house. Deirdre absorbed the elegance of the gold and white color scheme and furnishings and reluctantly conceded that the primary impression was one of discrimination and restraint, although a trifle Spartan for her taste. Every stick of furniture, every well-chosen picture, every silver candlestick and carefully displayed objet d'art indicated that she had entered a house where money was no object. When she found herself surreptitiously examining the quality of Rathbourne's candles, she decided it was time to take herself in hand.

Comparisons were odious. Nevertheless, as the ladies ascended the wide sweep of the cantilevered staircase in the wake of some new arrivals, and as their feet sank into the thick pile of the Aubusson rug on the floor of the spacious saloon which was to serve as the ladies' cloakroom, Deirdre found it impossible not to contrast the magnificence of Rathbourne House with Marcliff, her own unpretentious domicile, a snug little Jacobean farmhouse with a hundred acres or so near Henley. She too was the proud possessor of an Aubusson, a diminutive one it was true, but the genuine article for all that. But she would no more think of laying it on the floor for hordes of unfeeling boots and slippers to trample than she would a painting by Holbein. It held pride of place on the dining room wall flanking the massive oak fireplace for honored guests to admire as they parleyed over dinner.

The Earl, as was to be expected, took a more casual attitude to his possessions. But then Rathbourne could afford to be indiscriminate in his use of money. Deirdre had become accustomed to looking at two sides of every penny before she spent it. Nor did she think herself ill-used in having to practice the most stringent economies to support those who were dependent upon her. On the contrary, she took pride in her accomplishments as steward of her small inheritance and put every spare penny into improving the farm. Armand's education at Harrow and Cambridge had been a drain on her resources for a number of years. That debt had yet to be retired. But with judicious management and the guidance of her guardian, who more or less allowed her a free hand, she could foresee no obstacles to a comfortable if rather lackluster future.

As they deposited their heavy wraps and mantles, Deirdre took stock of the finery of the other ladies present and noted with satisfaction that her own simple frock of gold sarcenet with ivory satin ribbons tied snugly under the bosom and at the sleeve needed no apology although it was four years old and recently refurbished. Her ensemble might not be of the first stare, but in this setting, and with Rathbourne's preferred colors, she could not have chosen better. The cream-colored rosebuds set adroitly in the ringlets of heavy gold hair which fell to her shoulders had been plucked from the bouquet which she had received that afternoon from the Earl. It would have been ungracious not to acknowledge his thoughtfulness in compensating her for the one rosebud she had so rashly discarded. Either way, he was bound to make some comment, and she hoped he would find the gesture placating and in some small measure be more kindly disposed toward her brother.

Deirdre fell into step behind Lady Fenton as they moved down the long expanse of corridor toward the grand saloon, which seemed to glow with the blaze of a thousand candles and where she knew their hosts would be waiting at the threshold to greet their guests. She tried to brace herself for what she saw must surely be a nerve-racking evening, and her spine straightened imperceptibly and the green of her eyes deepened to smoke. Then she caught sight of him, and she felt a pulse spring to life at her throat.

She had never denied that he was uncommonly handsome, although her personal preference was for men of a fairer complexion. His dark skin, sun scorched to bronze, and those mesmerizing eyes were too overpowering for comfort. She acknowledged that the sweep of his broad shoulders and the hard-muscled, lean length of him were made to be displayed in the current fashion of skin-tight breeches and coat. Few women, she knew, could resist that dark, rugged beauty and the charm of that engaging smile which he used with such unconscious effect. More fools them! Unexpectedly, his gaze traveled over the heads of his two female companions and his eyes locked with Deirdre's. For a fraction of a second, his smile faded. But the warmth of his admiring gaze reached out like a caress.

Deirdre was ready for him. Her long lashes fluttered down to shield her from that probing look, and when she next raised her eyes, she was careful to fix her gaze on the women who flanked the tall figure of her host.

Like the Earl, the Dowager Countess of Rathbourne and her daughter, Lady Caro, were tall and straight backed. Their elegantly coiffured tresses blazed unashamedly with the tawny hues of the Earl's locks, but less subdued, and Deirdre idly mused that future generations of the great House of Cavanaugh would carry the Earl's tawny imprint as a distinguishing feature. A fleeting impression of infants with soft red tresses playing at her feet and nursing at her breast flashed through her brain, shocking her into momentary immobility. A slow, faint blush of color suffused her cheeks. Her startled glance flicked to the Earl, but thankfully, his head was averted, his attention focused on the guests ahead of her.

She had always been cursed with a too lively imagination, and see the results of it, she told herself sternly. Nevertheless, as her slow, dragging feet brought her level with the receiving line, she could not suppress the fanciful notion that she was about to make her curtsy to a pride of lions. Three pairs of glowing amber eyes flecked with gold were turned upon her, and Deirdre forced herself to accept their unfaltering scrutiny with outward tranquility. She responded to Rathbourne's polite words of introduction and comment on the roses in her hair with a graciousness of long practice, but when she at last moved out of their menacing orbit, she breathed a long sigh of relief, then felt immoderately guilty when she caught her aunt's reproving frown.

Later in the evening, when Rathbourne had brought his sister to her and immediately departed with a muttered apology about a host's time never being his own, Deirdre was to wonder at that first impression, for the girl, with her long stride and tossing mane, seemed more in the style of a skittish colt ill at ease in an unfamiliar pasture. Caro's hands flexed nervously at her side, and her golden glances, wide and wary, roved the room as if anticipating some unfriendly overture from the throng of fashionables who graced her mother's best saloon. Deirdre, in a rush of sympathy, set herself to distract the girl from what she surmised was an understandable attack of nerves at her first public appearance.

After a turn around the grand saloon, they settled on a small white damask settee near the chamber reserved for supper. By dint of careful questioning, Deirdre soon had Caro holding forth on a number of topics which were of interest to any young deb on the threshold of her first Season, and at the end of ten minutes or so, she was amply rewarded for her pains when she noted that Caro's reserve had melted entirely and they were chatting like old friends.

"I suppose, since you are the only girl in the family, your mother has long anticipated your first Season?"

"True."

Deirdre sensed the restraint behind the noncommittal response.

"No doubt *you* anticipate the weeks ahead with as much

anxiety as ardor?"

Lady Caro's eyes showed a glimmer of interest. "How astute of you to notice. Nearly everybody expects me to be in high alt at the thought of taking my place in Society."

Deirdre resisted the impulse to smile. "But such a prospect, of course, puts you in the dismals? Now why is that?"

Caro's smile held a hint of reproach. "Can't you guess? Attending balls, routs, and so on, making small talk, and everyone pretending they have no notion of what is going on."

"What *is* going on?" asked Deirdre with a small frown of perplexity.

"You know! I am to find a husband, of course. Isn't that the object of this charade which is aptly named 'The Season'? Mama might as well have given me a shotgun or a line and reel to lug around, or put me on the auction block at Tattersall's. It's disgustingly embarrassing."

Deirdre was tempted to laugh at such a display of cynicism from a young slip of a girl, but concern for Caro's future acceptance by the high sticklers of the ton crushed the impulse. Such thoughts might well be common to some debutantes who were of a sensitive disposition, indeed she counted herself in their number, but it would never do for a gently bred girl to express herself so candidly, especially to a veritable stranger. For all that, Deirdre found the young girl's honesty refreshing.

"I know exactly how you feel," she began carefully, hoping to temper Caro's frankness with a modicum of discretion, "but it were wiser if you learn not to express such thoughts to all and sundry. Guardians and mothers, in my experience, are never swayed by the logic young debs articulate, however persuasive. My advice to you is to forget *their* ambitions and make the most of your opportunities. Enjoy yourself. Enlarge your circle of friends. I, for one, am very glad that I had this opportunity of making your acquaintance, and if there had been no Season, it would never have happened."

"That's true," said Caro, brightening a little. Then on the

next breath, "But of course, Gareth would have introduced us eventually."

Deirdre saw the object of their conversation approaching with a supper plate held aloft in one hand. "Speak of the devil," she said sweetly when he was within earshot.

The Earl smiled playfully down at her. "I am flattered that even when I am absent, you ladies think on me still."

Deirdre snorted. "What we think of you, Rathbourne, doesn't bear repeating."

"Here, brat," he said affectionately to his sister, "I've brought you some supper. Guy is right behind me, somewhere, I believe. Now mind your manners until he arrives to watch over you. Come, Deirdre," his soft baritone commanded with an imperious edge. "Permit me to rescue you from this precocious chit."

His warm hand covered hers and she was pulled to her feet before she could give him the dignity of a reply. She caught a glint of laughter in Caro's eyes, and managed to throw over her shoulder, "I'll be back directly."

"Oh no you won't," Rathbourne countered sotto voce in her ear as he steered a clear path for them through the crush. Deirdre noticed her aunt's gray head bent in conversation with Rathbourne's mother, and she smiled and nodded a greeting before the Earl had time to yank her through the open door to the room beyond. His mood was lighthearted, playful, like a young boy bent on mischief, and Deirdre wondered at it. She felt his hand briefly at the small of her back, and she frowned up at him, but nothing, it seemed, could shake him from his good humor.

A stoic footman heaped their respective plates with every kind of delicacy, and Rathbourne found a place for them in a deserted alcove half concealed by gold velvet curtains which could be pulled at will. If they had been alone in a small room they could not have been more private. Deirdre's lips thinned. Had Rathbourne made the slightest move to pull the curtains, she would have departed like a shot. As it was, she merely

85

sniffed, and ranged herself behind the low table opposite the Earl's place on the sofa. Rathbourne gave her a knowing grin and stretched his long legs to rest casually on the obstacle that separated him from his quarry.

"What did you think of Caro?"

Deirdre considered before replying. "I like her. She is so transparently honest."

"Frank to a fault, in other words?"

"That's not what I said," Deirdre protested. "She is frank, I don't deny it. But that is part of her attraction. Her lack of affectation is unusual in a girl of her age. She is a beautiful, winsome creature."

"And what do you think of her brother?"

"I beg your pardon?"

"Come now, Deirdre. My question is not ambiguous. I want to know where I stand."

She raised her glass of champagne to eye level and examined the bubbles as they floated to the surface. "As you can see, I am here," she began cautiously. "I have not spurned your offer of friendship. As for my brother, truly, I am doing my best to wean his interest from Mrs. Dewinters. It's no good taking a hard line with Armand. But I think I've hit upon a solution to bring him round my thumb." The slow smile she bestowed on the Earl verged on the self-congratulatory. "With a little cozening and a great deal of duplicity, I intend to prevent that scamp from causing you further embarrassment. He believes me to be on the hunt for a husband, you see," she went on in a confiding tone, "and has more or less promised to toe the line until such time as I've bagged one."

It suddenly occurred to her that the metaphor she had chosen to express herself was exactly as Caro had described her predicament, and Deirdre could not suppress a chortle of laughter. "Poor boy!" she finally managed. "Since I am most particular in my requirements, the chase could last indefinitely."

She half expected Rathbourne to share in her mirth, but

when she slanted a glance at him, she was dismayed to see an expression of bridled rage hardening his features.

He pushed to an upright position and looked at her from under the shield of his thick, dark lashes. "I don't appreciate the joke," he said coldly.

"What?"

"Good God, woman, do you really think I want you to help me stave off a quarrel with that blasted brother of yours?"

"I don't understand." Deirdre was bewildered at the line the Earl had taken. He should have been grateful for her assistance, not glowering at her as if she had committed some unforgivable gaffe.

"Can't you ever consider anything but your obsessive attachment to that ne'er-do-well? To think that you would stoop to such deceit . . . that you might put yourself in the way of some unscrupulous degenerate who may essay God knows what when he finds himself the thwarted lover—and all for what? What must I do . . . oh, never mind. Talking to you is like talking to a brick wall," he ended savagely.

His attention became fully occupied in selecting the next choice tidbit from the plate of tempting delicacies balanced on his knee. It was a task that he seemed reluctant to rush. "Deirdre," he drawled at last, not deigning to glance at her, "I don't give a tinker's cuss for that precious brother of yours. He's a nuisance, an inconvenience, a gadfly and nothing more. When he oversteps the bounds of what is permissible, as I don't doubt he will, I intend to deal with him in a way that will teach him to mend his manners, if he ever had any to begin with. It's perfectly clear to me that you have ruined the boy's character, indulging and petting him till he is beyond restraint." He gave Deirdre a straight, hard look and, ignoring the ominous set to her mouth, went on in the same controlled tone. "On this matter, Deirdre, I am not open to suggestion, nor will I permit you to protect that whelp from my wrath. Dare to meddle in this, and I swear I'll make you sorry. I shan't tell you again. Is that understood? And I'd be obliged to you if henceforth you'd refrain from dragging your brother's name into every conversation I try to initiate with you. In short, the subject of Armand St. Jean bores me to death."

His tone was soft and bland, so devoid of emotion that every word, to Deirdre's mind, was laden with a more frightening menace. That he should dare to threaten her inflamed her beyond reason.

She set aside her untouched platter of food and rose to her feet in a soft rustle of skirts. A bittersweet smile hovered on her lips. "Hail the Conquering Hero," she mocked with biting sarcasm, and bent her knees in a curtsy that dipped almost to the floor. "Mothers, hide your sons and daughters! 'Le Sauvage' rides abroad and eats babes for breakfast."

She saw the thunderous look that darkened his face, and the scar on his cheekbone, the scar of her making, stood out red and ugly. She had pierced his armor of indifference and she was glad of it, for her own anger, boiling and reckless, was past containing. It flowed out to scorch him.

"You dare prattle to me about character, you conceited oaf? Let me tell you that my brother has more genuine feeling in his little finger than you have in your whole body."

As she paused to marshall her wits to cut him down to size with her next shaft, Rathbourne set his supper plate carefully on the table in front of him.

"Touch one hair of Armand's head," she warned him, her lips contorted with fury, "and I'll damn well kill you myself. I'm an excellent shot, I promise you. And I don't give a tinker's cuss for the consequences."

She spun on her heel and made to stalk past him, but he was ready for her. His arm shot out like a coiled spring and she was dragged back to sprawl against the sofa. One hard yank and she was in his lap.

There was a cynical twist to his mouth as he lashed her with his scorn. "Genuine feeling? Coming from you, a woman who has a block of ice where her heart should be, I find that oddly amusing. But I'll never give you cause to question the depth of

88

my feelings again. 'My whole body,' I believe you said. How fortunate for you that your challenge was uttered in a room full of people, or I swear I would teach you a lesson you'd not soon forget."

She was lifted bodily and thrust into the chair she had so recently vacated, cowed by the fury flashing from his eyes and the leashed violence of the powerful hands that gripped her shoulders.

"Now pick up that fork and eat your supper," he told her curtly. "Perhaps when your jaws are busy eating instead of talking, your society will be a little easier to stomach."

That she dared not respond in kind to his blatant insults was a provocation she could scarcely endure. But caution, if not the implacable set of his stern features, held her in check. It was not the time to test the limits of Rathbourne's tolerance. And just when she was beginning to feel more comfortable with him, he had to spoil it all! Deirdre picked up her fork and ate.

Chapter Eight

They finished their repast in strained silence, apart from the occasional comment thrown out by the Earl. Deirdre thought that she discerned a slight softening in his expression, but so incensed was she at the indignity of being treated like a rebellious child that she responded to his civilities in only the coldest of monosyllables. Not that Rathbourne seemed to mind, and Deirdre found herself more infuriated by this show of indifference than she had been by the blaze of his anger. Pride demanded that she rise imperiously to her feet and demolish his arrogance with a few well-chosen words. Caution constrained her to remain passively in her place picking daintily at a dish of delectables she could scarcely swallow for bile. It was an intolerable situation and one which she would soon escape. He had only to return her to her aunt and she would plead a headache and shake the dust of his so-called hospitality from her feet.

As she entered the grand saloon on Rathbourne's arm, they were joined by Lady Caro, who seemed determined to pursue her friendship with the other girl, and before Deirdre's purpose could be accomplished, an event occurred which put the thought of flight entirely out of mind. Some late arrivals appeared at the far entrance to the main saloon, a diminutive woman flanked by two handsome young men, one as dark as the other was fair. Deirdre was only dimly aware of their presence until she felt the tug on her arm and heard Caro's voice, soft and husky, whispering in her ear.

"Who is that gorgeous man?"

Deirdre's eyes followed the direction of Caro's gaze, and what she saw made her spine stiffen. Armand, looking every inch the young chevalier in dark evening coat with a touch of white lace at the throat and wrist in the grand manner, had just entered and stood at his ease, his dark head bent toward the tiny brunette whose snapping dark eyes roved the assembled guests as if seeking a familiar face. Of the two men who flanked the pocket Venus, there could be no question as to which Caro's words referred. Armand was by far the handsomer. But Deirdre was in no mood to admire her brother's heart-stopping good looks. That he should dare to trespass on Rathbourne's hospitality filled her with dread. She threw an anguished look at the Earl, but his polite smile of welcome betrayed nothing.

"That," Deirdre managed in a choked undertone to Caro, "is my incorrigible brother."

Caro turned away to exchange a few words with a young acquaintance who hailed her by name and Rathbourne, without loss of stride, steered Deirdre purposefully to her brother and his two companions. As the Earl made the introductions, she was conscious of a silent message which seemed to be transmitted from Rathbourne to the woman at Armand's side, before the lady's name fully registered on her mind.

"How do you do, Mrs. Dewinters," she heard her own voice intone with smooth politeness.

By exercising the greatest presence of mind, she forced her attention to the fair-haired stranger whom she judged to be in his late twenties. His smile was friendly, but his eyes were frankly curious as she made her curtsy. Anthony Cavanaugh, as she remembered, was cousin to the Earl and heir to the title and estates until such time as Rathbourne should secure the succession by siring a son.

Conversation became general, and although Deirdre participated at one level of consciousness, another part of her brain was avidly taking in every detail of the woman who had captured the hearts of at least two of the men at her side.

Maria Dewinters was strikingly beautiful with a ripe sensuality which any redblooded male would recognize, so Deirdre mused with uncharacteristic petulance, from a mile off. Her hair was glossy and coal black, and swept off her face in a severe chignon, emphasizing her high cheekbones and wide-set eyes. Her gown was of scarlet satin, the perfect foil for the glow of her olive complexion. She was like some exotic bloom transplanted to an English country garden, and by comparison, Deirdre felt like a wilting wallflower, fading to oblivion in the bright blaze of the sun.

If she had not been so much on edge, Deirdre would have admired the masterly way Rathbourne detached Mrs. Dewinters from Armand's side with a few adroit moves to take a careless but determined leave of them. She noted with some unease Armand's tight expression. He had never acquired that virtue which the English extolled above all others—the capacity to be a good loser. He was so thoroughly French, ready to take offense at the least provocation.

Anthony Cavanaugh, "Tony" to his friends as he told Deirdre with a twinkle, had nothing of the Cavanaugh fire about him in either coloring or personality. So unaffected were his manners and so genuine his interest, that Deirdre soon found herself warming to the gentleman. It did not take Cavanaugh long, however, to sense the tension that stretched taut between brother and sister, and he took a celeric leave of them with the excuse that he wished to try his luck in the card room.

Deirdre lost no time in giving Armand the sharp edge of

93

her tongue.

"Are you tired of living?" she asked without preamble. "It was bad enough to barge in here uninvited, but what were you thinking of to bring that woman with you?"

Armand's eyes, alight with mischief, glinted down at her. "You are far off, Dee, if you think that I would dare such a thing. In the first place, I have my card of invitation here in my pocket, and in the second, I chanced to meet Maria on the stairs with Tony, so don't for pity's sake flay me with that tongue of yours when I have conducted myself with the utmost circumspection. I thought my presence at parties and so on was to be part of our bargain?"

"Rathbourne invited you?"

"That goes without saying, although I believe it is his mother's name that is on the card."

"I don't like it. What is he up to?"

"Playing cat and mouse, I don't doubt. From what I know of him, it's in character. Don't let it trouble you, I can take care of myself."

Armand's eye was caught by the slender figure of a girl with a mane of auburn hair which blazed to gold under the flickering lights of the crystal chandelier. As if sensing his eyes upon her, she glanced over her shoulder to look in his direction.

"Who is that angelic creature with the glorious hair?" he asked Deirdre in a hushed tone, his voice threaded with wonder.

Deirdre smiled. She had no high opinion of male constancy, but that Armand's interest had been piqued so soon after Mrs. Dewinters's departure, and by a chit of a girl so different from the one he professed to love, she found oddly comforting. She extended a hand in invitation to the girl who held Armand's steady gaze and Caro, seeing the gesture, moved to join them.

"Lady Caro, permit me to introduce the black sheep of my family, my brother, Armand St. Jean. Armand, this is Lady

Caroline Cavanaugh," then she added with a touch of sly humor, "the Earl of Rathbourne's sister."

Armand appeared to be struck dumb as his mind made the connection, but he recovered himself quickly, nor did the light in his eyes dim. An interest in the sister of the man he detested was out of the question, but as a connoisseur of women, he could admire, even if it was only from a distance, and Lady Caro was worth a few blighting looks from her top lofty brother.

Deirdre might not have existed for all the notice Armand and Caro paid to her. They had eyes only for each other, and she carefully wiped the smirk from her lips as she listened to them make a stab at conversation then fall into a bemused silence. If she weren't such a cynic, she might almost believe that she was witness to a bad case of love at first sight. Deirdre knew a sudden prick of disquietude. Rathbourne would no more tolerate her brother's interest in his sister than he would in his mistress. But the evidence of Armand's fickleness eased her fears a little. That he was still too young to form a lasting attachment was very obvious and some small consolation. Nevertheless, she had no wish to see Lady Caro fall under her brother's spell. That infatuation she would soon nip in the bud should circumstances warrant it.

Without conscious thought, she did a quick scan of the crowd, her eyes finally coming to rest when she spied Rathbourne. His back was against a window embrasure, his head bent in earnest conversation with Mrs. Dewinters, who reclined with stunning effect against the gold cushioned seats. They were oblivious to everyone but each other, as were the couple at her side, and for an unguarded moment, Deirdre could almost imagine that she was envious of the intimacy that a woman might share with a man.

It was a fleeting thought, easily suppressed. She had only to bring to mind her mother's humiliation at the hands of her stepfather to give her thoughts a different direction. Men of that stamp, and she included Rathbourne and Armand in their number, for all their charm and address, were to be avoided like poison. She had meant what she had told the Earl about marriage. It was a snare to entrap women and she meant to avoid it. She would be no man's chattel to be cherished or abused at his whim. Better to die an old maid than have the pride crushed out of her as she had seen happen to her mother.

Some childhood memory fluttered at the edges of her consciousness, but it was gone before she could grasp it fully. Her eyes narrowed as she watched Mrs. Dewinters stretch one dainty hand to lay it against Rathbourne's sleeve in a proprietary gesture. The Earl looked up at that moment and caught her unwary glance. Deirdre gave him her back.

Another hour into the party, and Deirdre had the worst headache she could ever remember. If it had not been for the fact that her brother insisted on lingering, she would have taken her leave of the Cavanaughs at the first opportunity. But she stuck to Armand like a limpet, and for once, he was content to permit it. She soon saw the reason why. Lady Caro, shepherded by her formidable mama who had yet to say more than two words to Deirdre, was doing her duty by making herself known to everyone present. As for Armand's second string, Mrs. Dewinters, Rathbourne monopolized that lady's society to the exclusion of all but the most persistent of intruders. Armand, however, had elected to give his rival a wide berth for the evening, to his sister's heartfelt relief.

She was quietly disposed in one of the window alcoves, reflecting on all that had transpired in the course of the evening, and having sent Armand to procure a glass of iced lemonade, when she saw him return with the Dewinters woman hanging on his arm. Deirdre's nerves were strained to breaking point, but a frantic survey of the room assured her that her host was elsewhere and in ignorance of this latest poaching on his preserves.

Mrs. Dewinters, Deirdre soon discovered, was not of pure English stock, which did not surprise her, but a Spanish hybrid, a hothouse variety by the looks of her, whose English mother had met and married her father when she was convalescing in Spain, the dry climate proving the perfect antidote to the constant lung infections which had so plagued the lady in the pervasive, freezing dampness of English winters. It was this circumstance which explained Mrs. Dewinters's command of the language and her proclivity for everything English, so she said. Dewinters, a stage name, had been her mother's maiden name.

In the course of the evening, Deirdre had taken the measure of the woman who had attracted the covert attention of every female in the room. It was with barely concealed amusement that she watched as Mrs. Dewinters returned the compliment. Those dark, flashing eyes swept Deirdre with veiled insolence as they made an overt inventory of every asset or lack of them which Deirdre possessed, and Deirdre conjectured that if questioned under oath, Mrs. Dewinters would be able to give an accurate account of every stray freckle, every refurbished bow and ruffle, every wilted rosebud which adorned her person. She must have passed muster, Deirdre reflected, for a spark of respect gleamed in the depths of her dark eyes. It was the latent hostility which Deirdre was at a loss to understand.

"Armand had told me so little about his unmarried sister, Miss Fenton—may I call you Deirdre?—and what little he imparted led me to expect . . . something different. You are much older than I had imagined." Her red lips pouted with studied effect as a child who has been denied a longed-for treat.

Deirdre was not slow to match exactly the glacial politeness of the other's tone. "You have the advantage of me, Mrs. Dewinters—may I call you Maria?—for no words of my brother could ever have prepared me for meeting you . . . in the flesh." She allowed her eyes to flick suggestively to the low décolletage of the actress's bodice. No wonder Rathbourne's head had been inclined so assiduously as he conversed with the lady throughout most of the evening. Even from her vantage point, Deirdre could detect the shadow of one dark, thrusting nipple as it rose to peak the soft satin of its flimsy confinement, and she wondered by what law of gravity the near bosomless bodice remained in place.

Mrs. Dewinters batted her long, curly eyelashes as she absorbed the shock of Deirdre's riposte. It did not seem likely that a demure English miss would have the will or the wit to engage in this dangerous sport of thrust and parry. A test was in order.

"Nor did Armand inform me that his sister was in the style of a veritable . . . Amazon. How I envy you your inches."

Deirdre acknowledged the hit with the ghost of a smile and immediately lunged with wit honed to rapier sharpness. "Thank you. It is very handsome of you to say so. But pray, just stay as you are. More of you could by no means be considered . . . an improvement."

The two women eyed each other with appreciative enjoyment. It had now become a game, a match which one must eventually cede to the other.

"And witty too?" Mrs. Dewinters exclaimed, her eyebrows elevating a trifle, as she smiled archly up at Armand. "Why did you not tell me, *querido,* that your sister is . . . a wag?"

An old maid, a giant, and now a quizz, thought Deirdre with growing admiration. Mrs. Dewinters was proving to be a worthy opponent.

She smiled with real pleasure. "We wags are used to cutting our adversaries down to size, but in your case"—her eyes swept over all fifty-eight inches of the actress's diminutive form—"I'll be merciful and forgo the pleasure."

Armand became restive. Why the ladies had taken it into their heads to spar with each other like two boxers feeling each other out before a match was beyond his comprehension, but it made him dashed uncomfortable. When Tony Cavanaugh saluted him from across the room, he made his excuses and escaped with unashamed alacrity.

"A charming boy," mused Mrs. Dewinters as she watched Armand's retreating back. She cocked a mischievous eyebrow at Deirdre. "He tells me you've been more in the style of a mother than a sister to him. I hope he accords you the respect your rank and years prescribe?"

"Certainly," said Deirdre smoothly. "I have no complaints about my brother. But his devotion is based on more than duty. I've no doubt that you've noticed, Armand is partial to . . . older, more experienced women."

She thought for a moment she had gone too far, then the Spanish beauty threw back her head and trilled with laughter. Deirdre soon joined in.

"Now I know what Rathbourne sees in you," confided Mrs. Dewinters. "You are not just another pretty face as I had at first supposed. For an English girl, you are quite out of the ordinary. If I can't win Gareth, I won't be too unhappy to see him go to you. But I warn you now, you will need all your wits about you, for this is one contest I have no intention of losing."

"Contest?" Deirdre repeated, although she was perfectly sure she had taken the actress's meaning.

Mrs. Dewinters bent a deprecating smile on Deirdre. "Have I been too blunt for you? I don't mean to give offense, now that I find I like you. But why dissemble? I intend to fight you for him. We are well matched as we have just proved. Shall we shake hands on it before we come out fighting, a quaint English custom which the gentlemen observe, as I collect."

"That won't be necessary. I don't know what Rathbourne has told you," Deirdre said in clipped accents, "but you are mistaken if you think I have any claim on the Earl."

"He hasn't told me anything." Mrs. Dewinters looked

faintly surprised. "There was no need to. D'you think I haven't been aware of the two of you slanting glances at each other all evening? I came here tonight with only one purpose in mind—to uncover the identity of Gareth's new interest. And now I know who she is."

"I assure you, Maria, I owe the honor of my invitation to my aunt, Lady Fenton. She and the Earl, although of only recent acquaintance, seem to have taken a fancy to each other."

"Balderdash. I probably shouldn't tell you this, but I am almost certain that Gareth cherishes a tendre for you. And knowing Gareth, he won't be content to admire from a distance. Do you mean to resist him? I should warn you that his charm is irresistible when he puts his mind to it, as no one knows better than I."

Deirdre couldn't help the complacent smile which tugged at her lips. "All it takes is a little practice. It's not as difficult as you seem to think. I'd be happy to give you a few pointers, should the occasion ever arise."

Mrs. Dewinters gave Deirdre a questioning look. After an interval, she spoke with something akin to pity in her voice.

"I think I understand. You are hoping for marriage. Naturally, a girl in your position must be adverse to what Gareth offers. I have no such scruples. I am content to take whatever I can get."

Deirdre, who a moment before had begun to wilt under the suffocating heat of the crowded rooms, felt a slow chill begin to seep to the marrow of her bones. An unfamiliar emotion, somewhere between pain and anger, held her in its grip.

"And what of my brother, Armand?" she asked quietly.

"Armand?"

"Doesn't Rathbourne object?"

"Object to what?" a soft baritone interrupted at Deirdre's ear.

She started violently at the sound of the Earl's voice. The length of his arm touched hers briefly and she flinched from

100

the contact. Bright laughter flashed in his eyes. He turned his gaze upon Mrs. Dewinters.

"Object to what?" he repeated.

Deirdre felt suddenly tired. She couldn't find the necessary stamina to continue fencing in such exalted company. She might be able to fend off one at a time, but together, Maria Dewinters and Gareth Cavanaugh would make mincemeat of her. She took the coward's way out.

"I see my aunt signaling. I must go. Perhaps we shall meet again, Mrs. Dewinters, I mean, Maria."

"I should like nothing better. Have Armand bring you to see me some afternoon soon." Deirdre did not doubt the sincerity of the invitation.

"Thank you, I should like that," she returned with equal candor.

Deirdre found the Earl's clasp firm on her elbow. "Permit me to escort you to your aunt."

As soon as they were out of earshot of Mrs. Dewinters, he turned a smiling face upon her, but his tawny eyes had lightened to an alarming amber, a sure sign that his temper was up.

"If I find you within a mile of Maria Dewinters's house," he drawled softly in her ear, "I shall make damn sure that you are packed off to that farm of yours in Henley. And save me the air of injured innocence," he went on with maddening arrogance as Deirdre opened her mouth to answer him, "for I know that *you* know perfectly well what I find objectionable."

"How dare you take that tone with me? You are not my keeper. And what possible objection could there be in calling on a lady I met under your own roof?"

"Maria is not here tonight by invitation," he said with asperity. "Short of throwing her out, there was nothing to be done but tolerate her presence with as much grace as possible. Don't think to make a particular friend of her, I warn you. The damage to my consequence is negligible, but association with

101

Maria could ruin you. Her crowd is one that you should avoid, as far as possible."

"But I really like her," protested Deirdre. "And furthermore, my brother will accompany me." She strove, without much success, to keep her voice down. "If Armand agrees to take me . . ."

He cut her off in mid-sentence. "I have not the slightest confidence in your brother. It doesn't surprise me that he would encourage you in this folly."

He propelled her firmly out of the saloon and down the long corridor to the ladies' cloakroom. For one wild moment, Deirdre thought that the Earl meant to fetch her wrap and throw her out on the street, but he swept past the open door with its frankly curious upstairs maid in attendance and half dragged her round a corner to an insignificant saloon at the foot of a short flight of stairs. He pushed her over the threshold, shut the door firmly behind him, and stood with his back to it, effectively barring her way.

Deirdre advanced to the center of the small room and turned to face him. There was no fire in the grate and the chill on her bare arms and shoulders brought an involuntary shiver to ripple along nerve ends already taut with something bordering on alarm. Out of the corner of her eye, she saw the grotesque flicker of her shadow which was cast by the glow of a brace of candles which stood behind her on the marble mantel. Deirdre forced herself to breathe slowly and deeply.

"If you are going to scream like a fishwife," he said with a calm that provoked her to renewed anger, "we had better be private."

Deirdre steadied herself to answer him in reasonable tones. She would not get angry, she would not raise her voice, she would not lose control whatever the provocation.

He pushed himself from the door and took a step toward her. "You were discussing me with Maria. What did she tell you?"

Deirdre stood her ground. "Nothing of interest," she

answered lightly, trying to match his air of nonchalance. "She seems to think that your charm is irresistible." A touch of flippancy shaded her voice. "I offered to give her the cure for her unfortunate malady, but sad to say, I don't think she was persuaded to try my remedy."

His eyes mocked her. "Instruct her by all means. I wish you success with the lady. But don't think for a minute that I have any intentions of permitting you to practice what you preach."

It took a moment or two before Deirdre could grasp the full import of his words. When his meaning finally penetrated, her green eyes, brilliant with fire, slanted up at him.

"As I recall, the last time you overstepped yourself, Rathbourne," she taunted, "I gave you something to remember me by. I would have thought that one scar marring the perfection of your handsome face would have been enough for you."

There was an awful moment of silence, and if Deirdre had not known better, she might have believed that a look of pain crossed the Earl's face. But it was gone in an instant and a mask of bitter contempt settled on his hard features.

"My God, Landron is right. You are a vindictive bitch, and I the sorriest fool in Christendom."

He jerked the door open and strode from the room without a backward glance, leaving Deirdre shaken and strangely remorseful in his wake. That she had the power to wound him had never crossed her mind. She had supposed that the Earl was toying with her, taking a sadistic pleasure in mocking her prudish ways as he pursued some game of his own. It did not seem likely that a man of his notoriety, an accomplished seducer of women, could be reached by the shafts of an inexperienced chit. Yet there had been something in his eyes in that one unguarded moment that told her she had cut him to the quick.

She sighed inaudibly and turned back into the room, taking a few moments to compose herself before she braved the scrutiny of the curious stares she knew would be waiting for her in the reception rooms. The sting of tears burned her eyes and she gave a watery sniff. She hadn't allowed herself to cry in years, yet a few skirmishes with Rathbourne and she was behaving like a green girl just out of the schoolroom. It was positively ludicrous, this effect he had on her. In the space of one evening, her feelings had run the gamut of every known emotion—all inspired by the whimsy of one solitary man. It was no wonder that she felt like a piece of laundry which had just been through the mangle.

She heard a quick tread at the door and turned aside to examine the mantel with feigned interest, embarrassed to be found by a servant in such a sorry state and in a part of the house she had no business to be in. Warm hands closed over her shoulders and she knew that it was he.

"My God, Deirdre," she heard Rathbourne's voice racked with strain at her back, "I don't know why I allow you to do this to me."

She leaned into him and his hands tightened on her shoulders. A soft sob of relief escaped her lips, and he wrapped her in his arms, cradling her against his chest with a fierce tenderness that she had never expected to find in him. It was this small gesture which unleashed her tears and they coursed unhindered down her cheeks.

He turned her to face him and she stood impassive in the shelter of his arms.

"I don't want to hurt you," he said gently as he traced the path of her errant tears with one finger. "I want only to love you. I am going to kiss you now. Don't fight me. For once in your life, Deirdre, just bow to the inevitable."

His eyes, warm and compelling, dared her to resist.

"Only a kiss, Deirdre. After a famine of five years, is that so much to ask?"

If he had laid a hand on her in anger, or tried to force her in any way, she would have fought him tooth and nail. But she was caught by the devastating tenderness of his hands and lips as they moved upon her with inexpressible yearning, dispelling her doubts and fears. It felt like the most natural thing in the world to relax against him and seek the promised solace of his embrace. The reverence of his caress was like a balm to wounds that had festered too long, exorcising that malevolent demon that seemed always to flare between them. The benediction of mutual apology and forgiveness was in that one, sweet kiss, a catharsis for every wrong and imagined wrong they had ever inflicted upon each other. For Deirdre, the bliss was almost too much to bear.

Rathbourne took a swift step backward and sank into the chair flanking the empty grate and Deirdre found herself tumbling into his lap. It broke the spell. She strained against the hard sinew of his muscled chest, struggling to free herself.

"Be still," he warned as he wrapped her closer, compelling her obedience with arms as powerful as bands of iron.

When she quieted against him, he brought his mouth down to cover hers, savoring her surrender with a slow sensuality. He gently coaxed her lips to open, pleasuring her with the slick invasion of his tongue, and Deirdre could almost taste the rising hunger which he kept in check. She stirred uneasily. It was all so achingly familiar, this quickening of the senses, the race of heartbeats, and the raging fever which would soon consume them. She felt his hand slip to her breast and she wrenched her head away.

"Don't spoil it," she entreated.

His head came up and he noted her alarmed expression with mingled exasperation and concern.

He cupped her face in his hands. "Spoil what?" he asked with strained patience. "Your maiden's dream of chastity inviolate? I don't intend to spoil what is between us. I want to make a woman of you." He felt her tense in his arms. "A kiss, only a kiss, Deirdre," he soothed.

She was burning, she was freezing; she wanted to resist him, she wanted to yield to him; she hoped he would stop, she willed him to go on; she hated him, she loved him. The fervor of his kisses threatened her sanity. Rathbourne sensed her weakening and pressed his advantage.

His hand slipped under the hem of her gown and brushed in a slow sweep along the smooth length of one silk-stockinged calf, languidly caressing, patiently stoking her ardor to a steady flame. When he felt her response, he shifted her in his arms. His hand parted her knees and moved higher.

Deirdre pressed her thighs together and grasped his wrist with both hands.

"Don't!"

Rathbourne resisted the pull on his hand. He could feel the rising heat of her desire, so close, so tantalizingly close. If he breached her defenses, he would soon rob her of the will to resist him. The ache to claim her fully went beyond the carnal need to slake his raging lust in her woman's body. He wanted nothing less than her unequivocal acceptance of his title to who and what she was. Let her try to disavow him, and he would soon teach her the error of her logic.

"A kiss, only a kiss, you promised," she hissed at him.

Still he hesitated. A few moments longer, that was all that he required, and by God, he would compel her to accept that she was destined for his full possession sooner or later. Wordlessly, his eyes locked on Deirdre's. He brought his free hand up and pried her fingers from his wrist.

"Gareth!"

It was a plea for his protection. And she had at long last given him his name. It touched something, some hidden spring within him. He growled deep in his throat, but he removed the offending hand and drew back his head, his half-hooded gaze lazily appraising. Passion was in her eyes but tempered, he knew, by her damnable caution. His hands grasped her head and brought her lips to within inches of his mouth. He spoke roughly.

"If a kiss is the limit of your generosity, girl, you had better make it memorable, or I swear I'll take what I want from you, and to hell with your blushes."

She held nothing back. He would not have allowed it. And when he had finished with her, she would have allowed him anything.

Chapter Nine

The weather turned unseasonably cold once again with flurries of wet snow turning to a dismal slush, a circumstance which inevitably curtailed the afternoon outings of the ladies of Portman Square. Warm outer garments which had been pushed to the back of the clothes press only the week before were now shaken out and hung on padded hangers at the front where they were easily accessible.

Deirdre and her friend, Mrs. Serena Kinnaird, had made plans to do a little shopping, but in view of the inclement weather, they had chosen instead to while away the hours of a dreary afternoon by sorting Deirdre's plethora of gowns which were spread out on every available flat surface of her comfortable chamber on the third floor. A fire crackled invitingly in the open grate and Deirdre was seated on a straight-backed chair close to the only source of warmth in the commodious room, a pencil poised between her slim fingers, ready to make notes. She looked at her friend expectantly.

"Well, what do you think?" she queried.

"You've done a remarkable job, considering you're such a skinflint," responded Serena as she regarded Deirdre's storehouse of treasures with a practiced eye. "Restrained colors, simple lines, and not a spare furbelow or ribbon to make your gowns memorable."

"I can't afford to be seen in memorable garments. There aren't enough of them to go round and I have no wish for snide jibes on the paucity of my wardrobe from the tongues of venomous dowagers."

"Deirdre! People would not be so unkind!"

"Oh wouldn't they? What would you know about it? Your case and mine are entirely different. You like to cut a dash in the higher reaches of polite society. My ambitions, like my purse, are more modest. I'm happy to merely pass muster. Now give me the benefit of your experience since you make it your business to keep abreast of the latest fashions."

"For a start, I suggest you have the skirts shortened a smidgen. We're showing a little more ankle this Season. And you could do with a few livelier colors. It's not as though you're a debutante who is obliged to wear pastels. I like the gold." She fingered the dress which Deirdre had worn to Lady Caro's party.

"In its former life it was a dusty rose."

"You had it dyed?"

"Of course. It's four years old, and even the vicar was beginning to remark that it was his *very* favorite frock of my entire wardrobe."

Serena looked to be impressed. "You are a resourceful chit, as I should have remembered. Very well then, if you want my advice, I'd get myself a gown in sea foam. The color is all the crack at present, and if anybody can wear such a vapid green, you can. It will do wonders for your eyes and fair complexion. It's not flattering to everybody, of course, although every lady and her dog seems to be wearing it this Season. Oh, and have it made up with long sleeves. They're coming back into fashion, even for ball gowns."

Deirdre plied her pencil. "And you?" she asked. "Do you sport this color?"

"Goodness no. With my mousy hair and sallow complexion, it would make me look like a sick monkey."

Although Serena Kinnaird was not a beauty in the current

110

idiom, her square shoulders and athletic build being a trifle boyish for fashionable taste, she was a striking young woman who had learned how to make the most of her attributes. She would never by any stretch of the imagination be deemed a pretty girl, but she had heard herself called "handsome" often enough so that she no longer repined for the impossible. Since her early years had been somewhat dampened by the epithet "ugly," she was more than satisfied with the universal acknowledgment that she was an arbiter of taste and, in her own right, an "original." Her long, slim hands, one of her best features, smoothed the folds of her scarlet kerseymere walking dress, which she surveyed with obvious pleasure.

Deirdre caught the gesture. "Actually," she mused, her voice taking on a wistful cast, "what I lust after in my heart is something in scarlet satin. But that's out of the question, more's the pity."

"Why do you say so?"

"Scarlet on me would not be flattering. I'd look like one of those vulgar beauties displaying her wares bold as brass at Vauxhall Gardens. Of course," she hastened to add, "on you it looks perfect."

"Scarlet suits almost everyone, if it's not overdone. Think of all those dashing young officers in their scarlet uniforms." She eyed her friend critically. "But you're right. On you, scarlet satin *would* be vulgar. Still, if you lust after it, don't deny yourself. Something restrained, claret velvet, might do. It wouldn't hurt to be a little more adventurous, Dee."

"I can't afford to be. Such a dress would be bound to be noticed, and I'd be obliged to wear it only occasionally."

"Suit yourself. Personally, I think you would look stunning in black. You don't by any chance have a doddering old uncle who's about to kick the bucket?"

A laugh was startled out of Deirdre. "Serena, where do you pick up such vile expressions?"

"From Reggie, of course. And that's the least offensive of my dear husband's cant. Horrid, isn't it? Grandmama is

111

forever decrying the tone of my conversation, as she says, an odd mix of baby talk and masculine crudity. That's what comes of eloping and acquiring a husband and two babies in quick succession." Her brown eyes, usually calm and sensible, twinkled at Deirdre.

"As I remember," Deirdre intoned with mock censure, "when we were at Miss Oliver's Academy for Girls, you attributed your low vocabulary then to a propensity for lingering with the grooms in your grandmother's stables."

Serena's eyes scanned the room for a chair. Not finding one unencumbered of garments, she finally decided to sit on the rug in front of the grate, and she brought her cold stockinged toes to rest on the brass fender, toasting them at the fire.

"So I did! Now I remember. Can I help it if I have the aptitude of a parrot? I should have been brilliant at languages. Why wasn't I?"

"Because you were too lazy to bother. You always allowed me to answer for you, yes, and made notes from my copybooks as I recollect."

"That demonstrates my prodigious intelligence. Why make the effort when you can find others to do the work for you? You, on the other hand, were always so eager to show off your bluestocking tendencies. Could I help it if you pandered to the streak of indolence in my nature and the streak of vanity in your own?"

"Serena, must you always flaunt your vices as if they were virtues? You haven't changed a bit since our school days."

After a comfortable silence, Deirdre slanted a glance at her pensive companion. "Do you remember," she began at length, "how uncomfortable the other girls at Miss O's used to become when we started to take each other down a peg or two?"

"Yes. Odd, wasn't it? Some people have no sense of humor. If one has a talent for caustic wit, one should be free to exercise it. What else are friends for?"

"Within reason, of course. Brummel went too far when he

called the Prince Regent his fat friend."

"Oh quite. But that was malicious, and he forfeited the friendship for that piece of spite."

"Serena?"

"Mm?"

"Do you know of any other girls who share our peculiar talent?"

"None whatsoever. We should have been men, you know."

"I've made the acquaintance of one. She was introduced to me at Caro Cavanaugh's party."

Serena stirred. "Now that's interesting. Who was the lady? Perhaps, if she's not too high in the instep, I can induce her to come to my dinner party."

"It was Mrs. Dewinters."

There was a moment of stunned silence.

"What was *she* doing there?"

"Looking over the competition. She heard that Rathbourne had a new interest and invited herself to his sister's party. She told me so herself."

Serena began to giggle. "I'll wager that his mother, the old battle-ax, was fit to be tied."

"You don't care for Rathbourne's mother?"

"Does anyone? Although the top lofty dame won't lose any sleep over my despite, no, nor anybody else's either. How did the old warhorse handle the presence of Rathbourne's ladybird? Oh I wish I'd been there to see the sparks flying."

Deirdre's face wore an arrested expression. "Lady Rathbourne didn't do anything. Perhaps she did look a bit granite-faced for most of the evening, but really, Mrs. Dewinters's presence passed without comment."

"What? No fireworks between the Earl and his hatchet-faced mother? Well, that *does* surprise me."

"How so?"

"There's no love lost between them. I thought you knew? It's common knowledge."

113

"Perhaps I did and I've just forgotten. It's nothing out of the ordinary, after all, for parents to be at odds with their offspring."

"Their aversion goes beyond what is natural, though. They say that Rathbourne joined up with Wellington just to escape the old harridan's intolerable meddling."

Deirdre's lips compressed into a thin line. "I don't doubt that the Countess had her work cut out for her with her delinquent son. But that doesn't explain why you dislike her so."

Serena's amused laugh was a trifle self-conscious. "Always the clever one, Dee? You are right, of course. She cut me dead after I had eloped with Reggie. We were at some gala event for the Prince Regent. Others were not slow to follow her example."

Deirdre reached out to grasp the other girl's hand in a comforting clasp. "You surely don't repine for the acquaintance of such small-minded people."

"No more than you do. Still, it hurt at the time. But when my grandmother finally became reconciled to my marriage, she made the push to have her friends receive me again. There are some drawing rooms, however, where I am still persona non grata. Fond mamas with young daughters to fire off are wont to look askance at a lady who tied the knot over the anvil at Gretna Green."

"But you had little choice in the matter. If your grandmother hadn't been about to announce your betrothal to that aging lecher who had nothing to recommend him except for his title, you would have married Reggie just as you ought."

"Nobody cares. It's appearances that are important in our circles, not morals. Now you know why I wasn't invited to Caro Cavanaugh's party. The Dowager Countess of Rathbourne is quite the stickler, although at one time she and grandmama were bosom bows."

"I would have thought that the mother of a son like Rathbourne would have little to crow about." After a considering moment, Deirdre went on, "Which reminds me, Serena. You knew when you wrote that letter that it was Rathbourne, didn't you?"

"What do you mean?" asked Serena evasively.

"Just what you think I mean."

A smile tugged at the corners of Serena's mouth. "Well of course I knew. But would you have come up to town if I had warned you in advance that the nobleman who was Armand's rival was your old flirt?"

"Why, Serena? Why go to the trouble?"

"Because you two are made for each other. Because I knew you hadn't put him out of mind in five years; because I was worried about Armand; and finally, because Rathbourne asked Reggie for your direction. Now dare slay me with that wicked tongue of yours, and I'll give you back as good as I get."

"Still the unrepentant romantic?" Deirdre asked with acid in her tone.

"Still the confirmed cynic?" Serena shot back with equal sarcasm.

Deirdre gazed at the fire for a long moment, watching absently as flames licked round one lump of coal, burning it by slow degrees to a cinder. Finally, she said with quiet conviction, "It won't work, you know."

"Why do you say that?"

Deirdre lifted her shoulders. "Many reasons. There is too much against us; Armand for one. And then, Rathbourne himself."

"But Rathbourne cares for you, I know it. He always did. You never gave him a chance."

"Forget it, Serena. That's old history."

"How can I forget it when I see my best friend throwing her life away, turning into an old maid before my eyes? You should be breeding children, not horses. No, don't eat me, Dee. You know I speak the truth. If you can look me in the eye and deny that you care for him, I'll never mention his name to you again, I promise."

115

Deirdre lifted her eyes and looked steadily at her friend. She made as if to say something but, after a moment, gave an exasperated shake of her head. Her smile was faintly self-mocking.

"You see?" asked Serena rhetorically.

"Don't refine too much upon it. It's a flame I intend to smother by one means or another."

"But why?"

"Don't you see?" Deirdre's tart tone gave evidence of her waning patience. "Not everything one desires is good for one. Didn't you just warn me off scarlet satin? Rathbourne is like that. For me, such a man would be poison, however much I may lust after him in my heart. If you want to play matchmaker, find me a beau like Reggie."

"Reggie?"

"A one-woman man."

"Ah, now I understand." Serena began to gather her things. She slipped on her nankin half boots and fiddled with the lacings.

"What is that supposed to mean?" asked Deirdre, laying aside her notebook and rising to her feet.

"Just what you think it means," retorted Serena, turning her friend's words back upon her. She lifted her face to plant an affectionate kiss on Deirdre's cheek. "I know too many of your dark secrets, my dear, not to understand what your antipathy is based on. Rathbourne is not your stepfather and you are not your mother. Remember that. But I won't come to points with you on your misguided notions. I've delayed too long as it is. Dinner on Thursday? You won't forget?"

"I'm looking forward to it. Will I know anyone there?"

"Yes, of course. But I daren't invite Mrs. Dewinters, at least not to this sort of gathering. Perhaps at one of my musical evenings when there are crowds of people. We shall see."

"Snob," teased Deirdre.

"Realist, more like," Serena flung over her shoulder as she swept out of the room. At the top of the long staircase, she

116

halted. "By the by, Dee, I've already invited Rathbourne and he has accepted."

"I thought you might," responded Deirdre with a careless lift of her shoulders. "Don't fret. I shall be as meek and mild as you could wish."

The two girls descended the staircase to the ground floor. At the bottom of the stairs, Serena laid a detaining hand on Deirdre's arm. "I've also invited Henry Paget. You don't mind, I trust?"

"The Earl of Uxbridge?"

"The same."

"I'm surprised. I thought he had put himself beyond the pale. Is he received in society then, a man, I forbear to use the word 'gentleman,' who deserted his wife and children to elope with another man's wife? You can't mean to have him under your own roof?"

"How cruel and unfeeling you have become, Dee. It isn't like you. That happened five years ago. After his wife divorced him, he married the lady he had eloped with."

"Yes, and what a shady business that was, having to run off to Scotland so that his wife could divorce him under Scots Law. It shouldn't be allowed."

Serena turned a look of wounded outrage upon her friend. "Some of us have occasion to be grateful for the enlightenment of Scots Law. It allowed me to marry my Reggie, and it permitted the Pagets to go their separate ways. Why shouldn't a wife be allowed to divorce a husband for adultery? It's barbaric that in England only a husband has that privilege. Besides, there was talk of Caroline Paget and the Marquess of Lorne. That Uxbridge allowed his wife to remain the innocent party in view of the gossip says something about the man's character."

Deirdre's cheeks were pink with embarrassment. "Serena, forgive me. I spoke without thinking. I meant no offense. You are innocent of what I impute to Uxbridge."

"And that is?"

117

After a moment's reflection, Deirdre said firmly, "Immorality."

"Have it your own way. I can't uninvite him. Do you mean to call off then?"

Deirdre hesitated. "No." She gave a slight shake of her head. "Of course not. Just don't expect miracles. I shall be civil to the man but I can never like men of that kidney."

"I'm not asking you to. Just try to keep an open mind. Till Thursday then." And with a firm tread, Serena descended the steps to the front door to make a dignified exit.

On the following Thursday evening, at Serena's elegantly appointed table in her house in Burlington Gardens, it was with no little relief that Deirdre found herself seated between two unexceptionable gentlemen, the Viscount Wendon and Mr. Guy Landron. She flashed a quick look of gratitude at her hostess as that obliging lady indicated to the two notorious Earls, Rathbourne and Uxbridge, that she wished them to take their respective places of honor on her right and left hand. For some reason, however, Deirdre found that her attention wandered and was inexplicably drawn to the two men she was most determined to dislike. Furthermore, that her friend was looking ravishing in scarlet satin, she found vaguely irritating, and as dinner progressed, her mood became more aggravated as she covertly watched her hostess listen with rapt attention as Lords Rathbourne and Uxbridge argued the strategic intricacies of boring battles that had taken place centuries before.

As Serena's footman filled her glass with the obligatory champagne, Deirdre's eyes narrowed on the Earl of Uxbridge. It was hard to believe that a man of his rank and background could have embroiled his family in a scandal that had rocked court circles, or that a gently bred girl like the Lady Charlotte Wellesley should have been so lost to all sense of decency that she had deserted her husband and children to elope with a married man. What did she see in him? Uxbridge looked to be in his mid-forties, and although handsome enough in a stylish sort of way, there was nothing about him as far as she could tell to warrant giving up everything for the dubious pleasure of sharing his bed.

They had both paid dearly for their unhallowed passion. Neither the Earl nor his Countess were received in polite society, and Uxbridge's preferment in his chosen profession had come to an abrupt standstill. What did he expect? He had run off with no less a lady than the wife of Wellington's youngest brother, and his deserted wife of thirteen years was very highly connected. The former Caroline Villiers, the Earl of Jersey's sister, and now married to Lorne, the Duke of Argyll, was not to be cast off without some sort of reckoning.

It did not sit well with Deirdre that Serena should encourage the pretensions of such a degenerate, even supposing that Uxbridge was her next-door neighbor. She supposed that Reggie's work at the War Office obliged him to have some contact with the man who was popularly believed to be the finest commander of cavalry in England. But she deplored her friend's unquestioning admiration for the man at her side. Lady Uxbridge, she understood, had become something of a recluse, hiding herself for the most part at Beaudesert, Uxbridge's estate in Staffordshire. Deirdre could not find it in her heart to be the least bit sorry for a jade who had brought such a fate upon herself.

Deirdre picked up her dessert spoon and began to toy daintily at the froth of pink syllabub in her porcelain dish, her eyes sweeping surreptitiously over the score of guests at Serena's board. It was very evident that Lord Uxbridge's credit with the company, especially the gentlemen, all of them cavalry types with the exception of her host, had lost nothing by the scandal in his private life. Rathbourne looked to be on the friendliest terms with the older man. But then, his private life didn't bear close scrutiny either. Neither Rathbourne's mother nor sister was present, but whether their absence was occasioned by the former misconduct of Uxbridge or Serena, Deirdre had no way of knowing.

119

Her eyes were caught by an eloquent look from her aunt, who sat next to Rathbourne at the far end of the table, and she hastily marshaled her wandering thoughts and gave her attention to the Viscount on her right, who had made some innocuous compliment about the repast they had just consumed. Deirdre hastened to answer and searched around in her head for some comment to further the conversation, as etiquette prescribed.

"I have the feeling that we have met recently, and yet you say you've been with Wellington for the last five years?"

"Yes, with Rathbourne and Landron here, and formerly with Uxbridge, of course. But you are correct in your thinking. I was with Rathbourne at the White Swan the day that you walked in." His look was faintly curious, and Deirdre gave her full attention to her dessert.

"Indeed," she intoned discouragingly.

"Quite a coincidence, really. Rathbourne had just asked me if I knew anything about an Armand St. Jean when you entered the dining room. I had no idea, then, that you were St. Jean's sister."

"Rathbourne was interested in my brother? For what purpose?"

"Can't say as I remember," Wendon returned easily as he leaned back in his chair, his hooded eyes lazily observing as the lovely at his side touched her tongue to her lips to remove the sticky traces of the sweet dessert.

"Are you a particular friend of the Earl?" she asked more for something to say than any real interest.

"You might say so. We went to the same school and university." He sipped his champagne and studied Deirdre with veiled pleasure. Perhaps it was her glorious blondness which attracted him, so alluringly different from the dark-skinned Spanish women he had enjoyed briefly during his soldiering on the continent.

"And you? Do you know the Earl well?"

Deirdre's smile was a trifle strained. "I scarce know him. He

120

is a friend of my aunt." It was close enough to the truth to suppress any twinge of conscience she might feel.

Her answer, unaccountably, seemed to please the Viscount. "Good," he said with evident satisfaction.

Deirdre looked at him questioningly, but he only smiled and shook his head. What was it Serena had said about the Viscount's being on the lookout for a wife? She toyed with the idea as she absently stirred her spoon in her dish. She would keep an open mind on the subject. He seemed pleasant enough, and she certainly did not feel threatened by him. She tried to analyze why this should be so and came to the conclusion that it was not only because his manners were so refined and respectful, but because she wasn't intimidated by his physical presence. He was a fine enough figure of a man, but with nothing of Rathbourne's towering height or massive shoulders. Nor did she think the Viscount's temper would be as unpredictable as the Earl's. Her gaze shifted to Rathbourne and she caught his look of amused tolerance, as if he had read the direction of her thought. Her chin lifted a fraction, and when she heard the remark of the gentleman on her left, she turned her luminous green eyes upon him and gave him her sweetest smile.

Guy Landron had not missed the byplay between his dinner companions. He had no personal interest in the woman who had captured his friend's heart, but when he caught the smile on her lips as she turned to him, he was willing to acknowledge that Rathbourne might be excused for his hot pursuit of the cold-hearted vixen. Her smile was positively bewitching, an odd combination of innocence and coquetry, promising more than she could possibly realize. It was just as well that she rarely smiled. The men would be on her tail like a pack of rutting wolves. He wouldn't like to be in the Viscount's shoes if he set himself up as Rathbourne's rival.

"You farm near Henley?" he repeated as he appraised her over the rim of his glass.

"Yes, but only on a small scale, enough to make us self-sufficient. For the most part, I breed horses."

Landron looked interested. "How did you get started on that?"

"By accident, more or less. It began when my neighbors purchased horses I had bred for my own use. I seemed to have the knack for it. When I couldn't keep up with the demand, I increased my stock, by degrees, you understand. Then I spent some time on a horse farm in Jamaica and I decided I could make more money from my few acres at home by turning my hobby into a business. This is a new venture for me."

"Who is your stud groom?"

"You wouldn't know him. He's Irish, but I found him in Jamaica. I more-or-less bribed him to join me with the promise of exorbitant profits that have yet to materialize."

Landron suffered a momentary pang. As a female with heart, Deirdre Fenton he judged to be wanting, but as a survivor in a man's world, she was without par. He had made a thorough investigation, and believed he knew as much about her background as anyone in present company, more perhaps than she knew about herself. This was a rotten game they played. He could almost feel sorry for what he had to do next.

Good God, she was about to become a countess and have more worldly wealth than she ever dreamed possible. In the end, everything would work to her advantage. Still, he had learned something about her pride, and he felt vaguely dissatisfied at the route Rathbourne had chosen.

"Why didn't the profits materialize?"

"Lack of capital," she stated unequivocally.

"I find that hard to believe. I number among my clients many gentlemen who would be interested in investing their money in such a venture."

"I'm sure you do. But not, generally, where the promoter of the enterprise is a female."

"Not generally, no. But there are always the exceptions." His hand went to his vest pocket and he extracted a card.

"Here is my card. If you are interested in discussing this

further, I should be happy to call on you. I'm well known in the city, and Lords Rathbourne and Uxbridge can provide references should you require them."

He let the matter drop, knowing that to appear eager would defeat the purpose. Let her make inquiries. She would find his credentials unimpeachable. His connection with Rathbourne, he had already hinted at. He would be caught out in no lie. The first rule of intelligence work was that one should never tell a lie if it could be avoided. He made some observation to the lady on his left and let Deirdre reflect on his offer.

When the gentlemen joined the ladies after dinner, Rathbourne somehow managed to deflect Wendon from his purpose, and he slipped smoothly into the empty place on the sofa beside Deirdre. Wendon, after a moment's hesitation, went to sit beside his hostess on the striped satin sofa close to the piano.

Deirdre felt the heightened color across her cheekbones and did her best to ignore it. She unfurled her fan and proceeded to ply it as if she found the room a trifle warm for comfort. She tried to put out of mind the last time she had been in Rathbourne's presence, but one quick look at his laconic expression and she knew that he did not mean her to forget. Her brows knit together in a frown.

"Deirdre, be kind to me," he murmured in her ear under the pretense of removing a cushion from his back. "Won't you favor me with one of your smiles? You weren't so niggardly with Landron. What does he have that I haven't got?"

"Manners," said Deirdre shortly, and bared her teeth at him.

"That was a grimace. You can do better."

The laughter in his eyes nettled her, but she was determined that he should never know it. She batted her eyelashes and flashed him a smile of pure bovine vacuity.

"Now that is more like it. Where did you learn that trick?"

"From Bessie, my prize cow. It's the look she reserves for Squire Townsend's rampaging bull when we lead her home

123

from pasture of an evening." She flicked him a derisory grin. "He's tethered, you see, and I swear Bessie knows it." Her eyes wandered the room as if she had lost interest in their conversation.

Rathbourne raised one black brow. She was playing her games off on him again, pretending to a worldliness he knew perfectly well was unnatural to her. She could never resist the temptation to put him in his place. A slow smile touched his lips. But then, he would not rest either until he had Deirdre Fenton in the one place he had long since reserved for her—his bed. She really didn't stand a chance, although he knew she would never admit to it.

"Is Bessie a milker?" he asked innocently.

"The best."

"Then perhaps Bessie's look conveys a message that is beyond your ken, my dear Miss Fenton."

She had an answer for him on the tip of her tongue, but she dared not utter it. She had gone her length and he knew it.

"Why don't you say what's on your mind?" he goaded.

"Because I am a lady." There was more heat in her tone than she wished to convey.

"I take leave to doubt that."

"And you, sir, are no gentleman."

His eyes held hers. "I meant it as a compliment," he said softly. "I'm not much interested in 'ladies.'"

"And I have no interest in men."

"Not even Wendon?" he quizzed lightly. "A safe, quiet, biddable sort of a chap, wouldn't you say?"

A quiver of some unknown emotion disturbed her equilibrium. He could not possibly know of her stated preference in a husband. Only her aunt had been taken into her confidence and she would not have breathed a word of it to the Earl. But she didn't trust his knowing smile.

"Wendon is a gentleman," she said with slow emphasis.

He made no attempt to conceal the heat of desire which glowed in his eyes. "Deirdre, a gentleman is only a gentleman until he meets the woman who excites his senses."

To this blatant effrontery, Deirdre could find no ready answer, and as one of the guests approached, she looked up with unabashed relief. When she recognized Lord Uxbridge, her smile, already strained, became a little tighter.

"Trust you to corner the prettiest girl in the room, Rathbourne. How do you do it?"

"Practice," said Deirdre without thinking, and immediately regretted the unfortunate remark.

Rathbourne turned away to hide a smile, but Uxbridge, with the aplomb of the practiced flirt, treated Deirdre's sally as a challenge.

"In the art of dalliance, I take leave to tell you, Miss Fenton, Rathbourne is still a greenhorn. I suppose it's time I gave these younger beaux a chance with the ladies, but mark my words, in my salad days I'd have had these striplings looking to their laurels."

Deirdre drew herself up a little straighter. A raging sense of ill-usage suddenly washed over her like a rising tide. There was nothing that could shame the sensibilities of such hardened degenerates. Hadn't she discovered that with her stepfather? Such men flaunted their indiscretions as if somehow it gave proof of their virility. She rose to her feet in one unhurried, fluid movement and the tight smile on her lips became a sneer. There was a warning look in Rathbourne's eye which she refused to acknowledge.

"You gentlemen have so much in common," she managed in a dulcet tone. "I shall leave you to reminisce about all your conquests . . . on the battlefields and elsewhere."

Rathbourne came to her side before a half hour had gone by. One moment she was engaged in quiet conversation with Mr. Landron, a gentleman Deirdre found very easy to talk to since he never once paid her gratuitous compliments or made remarks which might be construed as flirtatious, a courtesy which she appreciated, and the next instant without being aware of how it had come about, Rathbourne had changed places with him.

"Was that necessary?" His voice was soft and devoid of anger, but his eyes held a dangerous glint.

"I don't know what you mean," Deirdre parried.

"What makes you think you are such a paragon of virtue? You have slighted the best damn cavalry officer in the British Army, who also happens to be my good friend. I hope you are satisfied."

Deirdre's eyes wandered to Uxbridge, who, at that moment, was the center of attention of some of the younger ladies. Every banality he uttered was met with a gale of girlish giggles. It was obvious to Deirdre that Uxbridge was basking in their open admiration.

"Women have no sense," she said with disgust. "Look at them! Beguiled by a handsome face and a pair of broad shoulders, and I don't doubt that the gentleman's salacious reputation is an added attraction."

"You refine too much upon it. Uxbridge has an eye for the ladies. What of it? They're as safe as houses with him. He happens to be head over heels in love with the Countess."

"Which one?" she asked with ill-concealed contempt.

"That was uncalled for. You know perfectly well that I meant his wife."

"Yes, and everybody else's wife to boot, I don't doubt. Men of that stamp always run true to form."

"What is that supposed to mean?"

"You're his bosom bow, you figure it out."

"I never imagined you could be so petty or unforgiving. So he was a bit of a libertine in his salad days, what of it? Marriage to the woman he loved put paid to his former follies. Why should you care?"

"Why do you defend him?"

"Because I know Uxbridge and esteem him."

"As a gentleman or as your commanding officer?"

"Both."

His answer should not have surprised her, but somehow she

was disappointed that he should show such unquestioning loyalty to a man who had forfeited her good opinion. It confirmed her worst suspicions of his own character. What had she expected? No doubt Rathbourne would deal with his own countess in much the same manner. He and Uxbridge were two of a kind.

She meant to keep her own counsel, but found she could not prevent herself from uttering one last cut.

"Then don't let me detain you, my lord. Birds of a feather, so they say, flock together. Like your friend, I'm sure you would rather be exercising your prodigious charm with ladies of a more receptive disposition."

Rathbourne said not a word, but he removed from her side immediately and did as she had bade. And for what was left of the evening, Deirdre had the pleasure of seeing Rathbourne make a cake of himself over every pretty chit in sight. A few curious looks were bent in her direction, but as Lord Wendon made himself as attentive as she could have wished, she hoped that Rathbourne's rapid desertion for greener pastures would invite little comment.

Chapter Ten

The row of overhead lamps suspended from the decorative wrought iron railings above the front entrances of the few houses which made up Burlington Gardens cast a dim though welcoming light in the early morning darkness of the moonless night. Lords Rathbourne and Uxbridge were the last of Serena's guests to take their leave, and they lingered on the steps of Uxbridge House exchanging a few desultory civilities before going their separate ways.

There was a storm brewing. Rathbourne could feel it in the air as the stiff breeze whipped at the capes of his heavy greatcoat. He pulled the folds of his mantle more securely about him, morosely reflecting that the violence of the black night exactly matched his mood of contained fury which had simmered, barely checked, since Deirdre had dismissed him with haughty disdain in the Kinnairds' drawing room. Her galling rudeness to Lord Uxbridge, no less than to himself, gnawed at his insides like the effects of a slow but deadly poison.

"Uxbridge," the younger man began on a cautious note, "I can't tell you how sorry I am that you were subjected to that piece of impertinence from a chit who has the manners of a guttersnipe. Were she in my charge," he went on, his voice hardening, "it would give me the greatest pleasure to beat her to within an inch of her life."

Uxbridge gave his friend a curious look. "I never gave it another thought until you mentioned it just now. Was she impertinent? I really hadn't noticed. You're making too much of it, Rathbourne. Besides, there's no need for you to apologize for the chit's remarks. It's not as if you are related, or about to be, is it?"

Rathbourne heard the laughter in his companion's voice and his harshly handsome features relaxed into a faint smile. He was relieved that the Earl would pass over Deirdre's unprovoked malice with such obvious lack of rancor. But Uxbridge was known for his amiability. It was a virtue that amounted almost to a fault.

"*Are* you about to become related to the lady?" Uxbridge persisted.

Gravely, Rathbourne countered, "Not to Miss Fenton's knowledge."

"Oho, so that's the way of it?"

Rathbourne said nothing but turned up his collar in a defensive gesture as he came under the close scrutiny of a pair of piercing blue eyes. He was faintly regretful of having given so much away with his unguarded words, and Uxbridge, sensing his friend's embarrassment, let the subject drop.

After a moment, Rathbourne remarked idly, "There's a storm brewing. I'd best be getting along."

"You're sure I can't persuade you to come up and crack a bottle with me? Then I'll let you go." A look of frank speculation gleamed in Lord Uxbridge's eyes, but he turned away without comment and ascended the shallow steps in a slow, measured tread, giving Rathbourne the impression that he was reluctant to bring the tête-à-tête to an end.

Suddenly, on reaching the front door, Uxbridge turned and called Rathbourne by name. "I couldn't be happier for you, Gareth, you know that, don't you? It's about time you got on with your life and put that other episode behind you once and for all. Bring her up to Beaudesert when the thing is settled, why don't you? Char will love her."

Rathbourne could think of no ready rejoinder and he touched his walking cane to his curly-brimmed beaver in a polite but distant acknowledgment and turned on his heel toward Bond Street and home.

He could scarcely tell his friend that Miss Deirdre Fenton and "that other episode" were one and the same. Only Guy Landron had ever been privy to that confidence and he had stumbled upon it by accident. Rathbourne was aware that during his early years on the Peninsula, his complete disregard for life and limb on the battlefield had roused wild speculation among his comrades-in-arms, and it had become tacitly assumed that a woman must be behind the almost suicidal audacity of their ferocious commander. By slow degrees, he had mastered his emotions until he could think of Deirdre Fenton with something like contempt and had congratulated himself on a lucky escape from the clutches of a harpy. That fiction he had been able to sustain only intermittently, and when he had received the surprising intelligence that Deirdre had not in fact married, as he had supposed, but had accompanied the Fentons to Jamaica, he could not deny the wild surge of elation which had swept through him, leaving him visibly shaking as if he had been a green recruit on the eve of his first battle.

From that moment on, the torment had been replaced by a new emotion, a cold and unshakable determination to bring the woman he desired above all others, the only woman he had ever wanted, to heel. But still, even yet, she thwarted him!

He could not remember when he had last been in such a towering fury. Bridled rage mixed with frustrated desire throbbed in his veins. His hand clenched hard on his gold-tipped cane and he swung it in a savage arc in front of his face. A wild desire to strike out at somebody, anybody, assailed him like the buffeting gale, and he wished with grim fervor that some foolish footpad would make the attempt to waylay him on this night of all nights. Only the week before, he had been accosted as he had walked through Green Park to his own front door. There had been only two assailants then, and they hadn't stood a chance against him. Five years with Wellington had tuned his senses to such a degree that a sixth sense warned him of danger long in advance. On that particular night, he had been in a generous mood, permitting the ruffians to crawl away after he had beaten them senseless. Such was not the case tonight. His rage was so great that he wanted to do murder.

How dare she judge him and find him wanting after the hell she had put him through since their first chance encounter? How dare she bracket him with Uxbridge, or any other man for that matter? She had taken his measure and found him wanting. So be it. He would give the prude something to gloat over. What he needed was a night of whoring, and he'd make damn sure the report of it got back to the stuck-up bitch.

"Char will love her." Lady Uxbridge would never be given the chance to touch the hem of her gown, if Deirdre had her way, Rathbourne raged in silent fury. That he could still desire such an unsympathetic and prune-faced baggage heated his blood to boiling point. But he had known what she was like from the moment he had first set eyes on her, when her vivid green eyes, openly assessing, had swept over him as they were introduced at Serena's come-out five years before. How often he had regretted not obeying his first sure instinct to avoid like poison the "butter wouldn't melt in her mouth" debutante who looked at the world with clear and uncompromising vision. Damn her! What did she have to be so superior about?

She had rejected him without knowing the first thing about him, without giving him a proper hearing, and that had hurt. It had hurt because he had been captivated by everything about her. What a contemptible specimen he was to let her acquire such power over him. What did she have that she had this hold over him? He had known more beautiful women; women, moreover, who were of a frankly passionate nature as he preferred them. Did she think she was the only intelligent chit to match wits with him? There were dozens he could name and much more alluring into the bargain. Then why did he have to fall under the spell of such a clear-eyed, cold-hearted witch?

His mind was suddenly filled with the vision of Deirdre as she had last been in his arms, her lips swollen with his bruising kisses, her green eyes dazed with surprise and deepening to emerald with the passion he had roused with such patient deliberation. Damn! His body was on fire for her! Did he think to gammon himself? Her beauty was matchless; her intelligence incomparable; her company uncommonly delightful; no woman had ever crossed swords with him to such devastating effect; her air of unattainability was a spur to his bridled desire; and the passion which she rigidly suppressed, which she denied him even when he had brought her to the point of surrender, was more alluring than the sensuality of the most highborn sluts who graced the finest drawing rooms of Mayfair no less than the camp followers of those transient bordellos which invariably followed an army on the move. He contemplated Deirdre's outrage should she read his thoughts and an unholy smile of amusement touched his lips.

She resisted him with a strength he might have admired in other circumstances. And yet, she was fragile, although she had shouldered burdens that a lesser woman would long since have sloughed off. She needed a man to protect her if only from scoundrels like himself. The thought of Armand, whom he regarded as a parasite, brought a frown to his eyes and a sharp expletive to his lips. That Deirdre should lavish her devotion on such a worthless creature was like a thorn in his flesh, a constant irritant that kept his temper on a short fuse.

Damn right he was jealous! Armand St. Jean's scandalous career was the result of overindulgence, a surfeit of female affection which had cushioned his life from the cradle. The follies of Rathbourne's youth were no worse than her brother's. Yet Deirdre forgave her brother everything while she treated him like dirt beneath her feet. What did she know about the loneliness of his childhood, the unfulfilled longing for recognition and affection that had driven him to a despairing kind of indifference to whether he lived or died? She knew nothing about him. He didn't wish her to know. He wasn't looking for pity, only for recognition that he was a man with a man's strengths and weaknesses. And that he was man enough for her—that went without saying.

Rathbourne lost the rhythm of his stride as a thought came to him, revolving in his mind with tantalizing slowness, bringing a devilish smile to his lips. What Deirdre Fenton needed to cure her unending ministrations to Armand St. Jean was a babe in her arms. And that, he promised himself with grim conviction, would be *his* pleasure. He had been a prize fool to let her turn him off once before, respecting her wishes, her scruples, with unaccustomed gentlemanliness. Well, the war had taught him something—that gentlemen, beneath that thin veneer, were really savages, with primitive instincts that civilization could never obliterate. She was his woman, he would make it so, and if she didn't know it yet, she would soon learn it. Time was running out for Miss Deirdre Fenton, and the sooner she became reconciled to her future, the better. She had cheated him of five years, and he had reached the limit of his patience.

As he turned the corner of Bond Street into Piccadilly, the threatening rain came down in a deluge and he lengthened his stride, savoring the battle with the elements as wind and rain lashed him mercilessly. A slate was torn from a roof by a ferocious blast of wind and came to a splintering crash a yard ahead of him. He laughed, a primitive sound of defiance and exultation. Rathbourne House was just ahead, the house which he would share with Deirdre. His house, his bed, his heart, and there was nothing in this world that would prevent it. Nothing! His mood lightened, the projected night of whoring scarcely remembered. It was time to procure that Special License. She would probably cavil at the suddenness of their marriage, but he would make it up to her. But he refused to tolerate another month without her. Miss Deirdre Fenton

had better make up her mind to a very hasty marriage or he
would take her without it.

She awakened to the muffled sounds of deep-racked sobbing.
It took a minute or two before she could force her slumberous
thoughts into focus. She put a hand to her face. Tears
drenched her cheeks. Deirdre brushed them aside, her lashes
slowly fluttering open as she absorbed the shadowy forms in
the darkened interior. Like a sleepwalker slowly awakening
from a dream, she turned her head slightly in the soft feather
pillow, and her eyes shifted to the silhouette of the dressing
table which stood against the long window in her bedchamber
in Portman Square.

The steady beat of the rain soothed her tumultuous
thoughts. She concentrated on its rhythm as it drummed on
the slate roof and coursed its way to overflow the guttering
which ran the length of the stone parapet. A gust of wind
rattled the windowpanes. Deirdre pulled herself to a sitting
position and her unbound hair tumbled loosely around her
face and shoulders. Her erratic breathing slowed by degrees to
a more regular pace.

A childhood memory, long suppressed, beat against the
fringes of her mind like the breakwaters of the rising tide,
blotting out her awareness of her surroundings, swamping her
senses with the vivid imprint of forgotten fragments of her
nightmare. Rain, she could almost feel it still, the force, the
pungent smell of the driving rain drenching them as her
mother paid off the hackney which had conveyed them to the
unfamiliar street, to some godforsaken tenement in the slums
of London. Deirdre was all of eight years old, yet she had clung
to her little brother as if she would protect him from the worse
storm that she sensed was to follow.

She touched her tongue to her lips as if she could still taste
the rain fresh in her mouth, and vestiges of her dream came
rushing back. Sounds—a woman sobbing; words—her mother

pleading; curses—her stepfather shouting; and finally the heady scent of the other woman as she entered the room to gloat over the deserted family.

A long, involuntary shudder convulsed her body. After an interval of forced quiet, she gave up the attempt to control the bleak misery that had been the aftermath of her dream. With impatient fingers, she threw off the bedcovers and groped on the bedside chair for her dressing gown. She shrugged into it, belting it tightly at the waist, taking some comfort in the warmth of its voluminous folds. Her fingers found a sliver of a match on her bedside table. She carefully dipped it into its companion bottle of acid, and the acrid fumes of sulphur assailed her nostrils. Shading the flickering flame with one hand, she lit the candle which stood on the rosewood table inlaid with ivory. The soft glow reassured her as the shadows receded.

After a few desultory paces around the room, she crossed to the undraped window to gaze out at the velvet black of the dark night. She watched the faint outline of the trees as they swayed grotesquely in the force of the gale, then she rested her face against one of the small windowpanes which had misted over with the outpouring of her warm breath as she had dreamed the night away. The cool touch beneath her feverish brow was oddly comforting.

What had brought that painful memory to mind? What ungodly catalyst had invoked that demon of her childhood to stalk her dreams? She knew the answer before the question was fully formed on her mind. Rathbourne! He had stirred the dregs of long-forgotten memories to rouse this slumbering nightmare.

She flung the window wide and kneeled on the bare floorboards, her face turned up to meet the wind and rain as if in accepting the fury of the elements as they beat against her, she could somehow confront the specters of her lost childhood and forever lay them to rest. She allowed the familiar emotions to wash over her, dragging her into their irresistible eddies, and

136

she took a quick, indrawn breath of air as if she would save herself from drowning in the flood of remembered pain.

The child that she once was quivered with mingled fear and shame as she climbed the interminable stairs behind her mother to the top floor of the foul-smelling tenement, her hand securely clasped in Armand's. Some primitive sense had given Deirdre wisdom beyond her years. To Armand, at four years old, the outing was a strange adventure and, blessedly, soon to be forgotten. But Deirdre understood the significance of her mother's tears; she knew instinctively that Armand was the bait to lure her mother's errant husband from the arms of a new love. And she was afraid.

And then—the confrontation. Bitterness rose like bile in her gorge as Deirdre remembered, as if it were yesterday, how she and Armand had been subjected to the most intimate details of their parents' lives, hearing things in that passionate quarrel that children ought never to hear.

The fury of a woman scorned was a sad fiction, as Deirdre had discovered. The picture of her mother, pathetic, like a whipped dog, as she begged the man she loved not to desert his wife and child rose in her mind, burning her with the intensity of the impression, filling her with a revulsion she could no longer hide from herself.

Deirdre felt her skin cold and clammy under her drenched night attire. She rose to her feet and stepped out of her robe, leaving it in a sodden heap on the floor. There was little letup in the storm. She slammed the window shut and turned back into the room, gliding toward the washstand to find a towel to dry the dew of mingled perspiration and rain from her skin. She sat on the edge of the bed, becoming involved in the simple task, her thoughts still sifting through the flotsam of childhood memories.

The year that had followed her stepfather's elopment with his mistress was not a time that Deirdre cared to remember. The deserted family had become the object of their neighbors' pity—a cruelty harder to endure than open ridicule, even for a child—those hushed conversations and covert glances which seemed to follow her as she trailed her mother in the village shops or sat in their pew in the parish church. Only Armand had been blissfully ignorant of the pall of suffocating pity that had enshrouded them. And Deirdre had watched helplessly as her sensitive mother had become a poor, spiritless creature under the crushing weight of tendered sympathy.

And then her mother had become a respectable widow when St. Jean was carried off the following year by one of the frequent outbreaks of typhoid in London. The news should have made her happy, but Deirdre could still remember the emptiness that had filled her heart, and with her child's logic, she had blamed her stepfather for this final desertion also.

He had left his wife destitute, and only the interest from Deirdre's small portion left to her by her own father stood between the small family and utter ruin. Her guardian had managed her affairs, supplementing their small income with gifts from his own purse, although he had an extensive family of his own to provide for and had yet to ascend to the higher reaches of his chosen profession.

Then, out of the blue, when Deirdre was thirteen years old, the fates had smiled on them. A small competence and the house and farm of Marcliff had been left to her by some maiden aunt, a distant relation she scarcely knew. It provided a roof over their heads and a livelihood for their future. By the terms of the will, she was also left an amount sufficient to pay for a seminary education and a Season in town when she reached the age of eighteen. There was no doubt in her mind that the object of the latter was to enable her to make a suitable alliance.

Her mind shied away from the direction memory had taken her. She crawled into the tester bed and resolutely pulled the covers up to her chin. But thoughts of Rathbourne were not to be so easily repressed.

She was not her mother, she reminded herself sternly. She would never be an object of pity again. She leaned over and blew out the candle on her bedside table, and lay with unblinking eyes for a long moment.

Damn men! Damn Rathbourne! And damn her woman's heart for being so susceptible to his potent charm!

The tip of the cigar glowed red in the darkened room. The man who smoked the cigar, still in evening clothes, lay full length on top of the covers of the bed and listened absently as the storm raged outside the window. His night's work, he reflected, had gone quite well. He inhaled deeply. Things looked to be coming to a head—a word here, a word there, was all that was necessary. But it wouldn't do to get overconfident. Rathbourne was a slippery fellow.

He stubbed out the cigar in the brass ashtray on the bedside table, and he drank back the dregs of the brandy from the glass in his hand. It was bad luck really, he mused, that the war had ended before a French assassin's hand could do the deed for him. Still, there was more than one way of skinning a cat. And this cat, he thought smugly, had come to the last of his nine lives.

Chapter Eleven

My Lord Rathbourne looked up from his absent perusal of the front page of his daily *Times* and gave his full though somewhat guarded attention to Mr. Guy Landron as that gentleman struggled out of his greatcoat and threw it with unaccustomed violence over a shield-backed, brocade side chair at the door.

"It's done?" queried the Earl.

"Right and tight." A note of grim displeasure threaded Landron's words.

The Earl stretched out his hand and grasped a slim document which his secretary had thrust under his nose.

"She has no suspicions?"

"None whatsoever. Why should she? My references are impeccable. Miss Fenton took one look at my honest face and decided I was to be trusted." He threw himself down on a wing-back armchair and winced as a pain went shooting through his leg. "Damn! That was stupid. I keep forgetting about this gammy leg."

The Earl filled a crystal glass from a decanter on the console table by his elbow and reached it across to his companion.

"Here, drink this. Perhaps it will improve your temper."

Landron, who had been carefully massaging his lame leg, looked up and accepted the proffered glass. After a moment's appraisal of Rathbourne's impassive features he remarked, "You'll make money on this venture, Gareth, if you let it ride. Miss Fenton knows what she is about."

Rathbourne's amber eyes regarded his friend with lazy interest. "I don't doubt it. I have every respect for Deirdre's capacity to make a success of whatever she undertakes."

"As long as scoundrels like us don't send her to the roustabouts!" The quiet words were challenging and slightly contemptuous.

"My, my, your opinion of 'the Fenton bitch,' as I remember you were used to call Deirdre, has undergone a drastic change, has it not?" Rathbourne folded the newspaper in his hands with a snap and threw it carelessly on the table. "May I be permitted to know the reason for this turnabout?"

"To know the lady is to love her," said Landron with blatant provocation.

"Indeed? I cannot quarrel with you on that score."

There was a thoughtful pause, then Landron cleared his throat. "Gareth, I wish you would take me into your confidence."

"Do you?"

"You cannot mean to ruin the girl, surely?"

"Certainly not."

"You do intend to offer marriage?"

"Can you doubt it?"

Landron's intelligent brown eyes rested thoughtfully on the Earl. "I don't trust you," he said baldly.

Rathbourne's features relaxed into the ghost of a smile. "I give you my word, Guy, that I shall approach Deirdre in the ordinary way. Does that satisfy your sense of fair play?"

"Then why this elaborate plot?"

"I don't know what you infer. To invest five thousand pounds in the girl's enterprise is hardly a plot merely because I choose to remain anonymous."

Rathbourne took a pinch of snuff and offered his box to Mr. Landron, who declined the invitation and sat pensively chewing on his bottom lip. After a moment Landron began with unaccustomed vigor, "There are things about Miss Fenton you know nothing about."

"Pray continue."

"She is a misanthrope."

"I beg your pardon?"

"She hates men. Oh not milk and water fops who pose no kind of threat to her, nor indeed those, such as myself, whom she regards in an avuncular light. But let any man worth his salt try to breach that glacial shield of civility and she immediately takes flight. No doubt, you've noticed that she holds our gender in low esteem."

"With the exception of Armand St. Jean."

"Naturally. St. Jean is her brother, and a younger one at that. He evokes only Deirdre's mothering instinct. A suitor—now that is a horse of a different color."

"I think I get the drift of what you are saying." The Earl crossed one booted foot over the other and drawled, "You haven't told me anything I don't know already."

Landron took his time as he savored the mellow taste of his employer's fine sherry. "Excellent," he murmured appreciatively. "You always did like the best, Gareth, which brings me back to Miss Fenton. Did you know that Deirdre's antipathy to men can be laid at the door of one particular man?" He leaned back in his chair with a satisfied grin when he observed that Rathbourne's habitual expression of indifference had fled.

"Who?"

"Her stepfather."

There was an electrified silence. Mr. Landron gazed at his friend's startled face with shocked comprehension. "Good God, Gareth, it's not what you are thinking! You mistake my meaning! I meant only that her stepfather was a wastrel. Deirdre was a mere child when he ran off with some woman and left her mother to fend for herself and two infants. That's why Deirdre mistrusts our sex. And from what I can gather,

143

her mother, until her death, confirmed every vile opinion of men that Deirdre ever entertained."

Rathbourne relaxed his grip on the slender stem of his sherry glass. "That piece of information is highly enlightening. No wonder Uxbridge . . . never mind. It's of no consequence. To be forewarned is to be forearmed."

"Don't be so sure of yourself. You're not dealing with an impressionable girl. Deirdre is not like other women. You read the dossier I prepared? Well then, you must understand that she is used to ruling the roost. By God, if she hadn't, I don't know where that family would be today. She grew up in a hurry, what with an improvident stepfather, a mother who took to her bed at every minor crisis, and a brother who depended on her support and protection from the time he was in leading strings. That small farm and competence which was left to her was a godsend. One wonders how she would have contrived otherwise. I daresay she would have become a governess or some such thing. Who knows? She is a resourceful girl. She might have turned her hand to any number of things."

The Earl rifled through some papers he had taken from a drawer. "Isn't there some sort of allowance that goes to St. Jean from his father's estate?"

"Merely an appearance of it. The money comes from Deirdre's own purse. Armand was told nothing of the circumstances surrounding his father's desertion. As far as he knows, the elder St. Jean left a small competence to provide for his schooling and a moderate allowance until he reaches his majority. He's been a drain on Deirdre for years. I believe she wanted to protect him from the ugliness of the economies she has been forced to endure. One must give the girl credit for what she has done."

"Can you doubt that I do?"

Landron drained the last of his sherry. "And I don't doubt that you'd like to shoulder her burden to boot."

"And if I do?" Rathbourne's look was questioning.

"The price might be too high," explained Landron. "I think Miss Fenton is a confirmed spinster or close enough that makes no difference."

For the first time since Landron had entered the room, Rathbourne permitted himself a genuine smile. "You've done your part well, Guy, and I thank you. I have every confidence that I can handle things from here on." When Landron said nothing, the Earl spoke with growing impatience. "Don't waste your sympathies on Deirdre. I have already told you that I mean her no harm. Now leave it be. In a month from now, you'll look back at this and laugh at your scruples."

Landron looked doubtful. "I take leave to tell you, Gareth, that I'd far rather face Boney's armies than face Deirdre if you make use of the weapon I've just put into your hands. Dammit all, the girl trusts me!"

"Well, of course she does. Doesn't everybody? That's why you made such an excellent agent. Now stop worrying. What have I done that's so reprehensible? I repeat, I've merely invested five thousand pounds in Deirdre's horse breeding venture. The next move is up to her."

"How much does St. Jean owe you?"

"His vowels amount to five thousand, give or take a pound or two."

The confrontation with Armand St. Jean had been one that Rathbourne had relished. He had set up the boy quite shamelessly, knowing how the arrogant young cub prided himself on his invincibility at the gaming tables. He had prevailed upon the services of his cousin, Tony Cavanaugh, to gain admittance for himself and St. Jean at Watiers where the stakes were notoriously high. Armand had been none too pleased when late on in the evening Rathbourne had insinuated himself into the game, but pride had kept the boy riveted to his place. When only the two of them remained at play, and Armand had begun to lose to the older man rather heavily, it was the same pride that compelled him to continue and finally accept his immense losses with a nonchalance that did not deceive the Earl for one minute.

There was a discrete knock on the door and at Rathbourne's command a liveried footman bearing a tray with a gilt-edged visiting card upon it entered and impassively presented it to his master. The Earl read the name on the card and a satisfied smile that came very close to gloating spread over his handsome face.

"Where is Mr. St. Jean?"

"I had him wait in the blue room, your lordship, as you instructed."

"Thank you."

When the lackey had departed, Rathbourne stretched like some jungle feline and slowly eased himself to his feet.

Landron gave a slight shake of his head. "I didn't think she'd be fool enough to give him the money."

"Oh didn't you?" drawled Rathbourne. "Haven't you learned yet that Armand St. Jean is Deirdre's Achilles' heel?" As he reached the door, he turned slightly and said over his shoulder, "You'll conduct that other business for me? Thank you. I don't think Giles St. Jean will be too hard to persuade. A man like that always has his price. I shouldn't wonder if he'd be glad to be shot of young St. Jean. Deirdre said that as a guardian the man was useless."

When Rathbourne entered the blue room, he was met by a very frigid and stiffly correct young man who was obviously ill at ease.

"Sit down, St. Jean, and make yourself comfortable. I really hadn't expected to see you this soon."

Armand looked uneasily at the tooled leather chair the Earl had indicated and after an infinitesimal pause he accepted it with an ill grace which the Earl seemed not to notice.

A moment later, a glass of amber liquid was thrust into his hand. He had never meant to accept Rathbourne's hospitality. How he came to be sitting in Rathbourne House and sharing a glass with a man he detested, he was at a loss to explain. A frown gathered on his brow. He decided to take his lead from his host.

"We have some business to transact, sir," he reminded Rathbourne with a show of civility. "I have on my person a bank draft for five thousand pounds. If you would be so kind . . ."

"Your vowels," supplied Rathbourne easily. "Of course. I had supposed that you might be asking for more time in which to redeem them. You are fortunate to be able to lay your hands on such a large sum of money, and so quickly."

"I have friends," was the quiet rejoinder.

"And a lovely sister," added the Earl gratuitously.

Armand's head snapped back, but Rathbourne's expression remained innocent.

"As you say, a lovely sister who is under my protection."

At the veiled threat, Rathbourne's lip curled. "That must be a great comfort to her, I'm sure."

It was very evident that the Earl was in no hurry to conclude their business for he made no move to return the vowels for which Armand so anxiously waited. It puzzled and rather irritated the boy to find himself drawn into a conversation in which he inadvertently laid bare the details of his early life and schooling. But the Earl, he was coming to see, exerted an oddly persuasive influence once he set himself to please. Armand, more than once, had to remind himself that Rathbourne was an enemy, a detested member of the English aristocracy, "Le Sauvage," whose cruelty to the French was legend.

"Have you ever considered making a career for yourself in the diplomatic corps? With your talent for languages and grasp of politics surely Sir Thomas could find a place for you somewhere."

"I'd die of boredom."

"Then your sister's enterprise, breeding thoroughbreds? Does that hold no interest for you?"

"What, mucking out stables and birthing foals at some ungodly hour of the night? I'm not a groom nor a midwife. I prefer to confine my interest in horseflesh to Newmarket and so on."

The answer was facile, and Armand was rather ashamed of his flippant remarks. The truth of the matter was that he was rather embarrassed to have to explain himself to a man of Rathbourne's kidney. In his own circle, such comments would have been greeted with guffaws, if not approval. But under the Earl's stern eye, he was made to feel like an errant schoolboy. He shifted uncomfortably in his place. Rathbourne was beginning to sound remarkably like Deirdre. He looked keenly at the Earl.

"I wonder at your interest in my affairs," he observed coldly.

"I have no interest in your affairs except insofar as they touch upon my own." The Earl extracted some scraps of paper from a bureau that stood against the wall. "Your vowels," he said curtly as he put them into Armand's hand. "You're not a bad player. Your mistake was in not knowing when to withdraw. Why didn't you when you saw that you were outmatched?"

"A matter of honor."

"Honor!" retorted the Earl. "Your honor has cost you dearly, my boy, but who am I to cavil when I am five thousand pounds the richer for it? Do you mean to make your fortune through gaming?"

"And if I do?"

"Then be advised, either sharpen your play or be prepared for debtor's prison."

Armand's eyes smoldered with hostility at this careless warning, but before he could utter a word, the door opened to admit an enchanting vision in white spotted muslin. Lady Caro's eyes skimmed over her brother and came to rest on his young companion.

Armand rose to his feet, his dark eyes softening as he made his bow. Not a word was said between them, but the silence was potent.

Rathbourne was conscious of it, and stirred himself. "You

wanted something, Caro?" he asked gently.

Her eyes slowly focused on the Earl and she seemed to come to herself. "It's Mama, Gareth. You're wanted urgently," she managed with some composure.

Rathbourne bit back an unkind rejoinder. "Perhaps you would be good enough to see Mr. St. Jean to the door?"

He left them in the foyer, not without some reluctance, and swiftly mounted the stairs to his mother's apartments.

Armand lingered, easing his York tan gloves over his long fingers. He studied Caro's face. "You're looking rather pale," he finally observed.

"You mean ghastly, don't you?" she asked artlessly. "I've been couped up for more than an hour with Mama in her dressing room. It would appear that I am a long way from knowing how to conduct myself as a lady. I always get one of my headaches when Mama takes to scolding me. I feel as if a bell is tolling in my head."

Armand's rakish smile made her heart skip a beat. "What you need is some fresh air."

"Yes, and the park is just across the street," she said encouragingly.

"I'd be happy to accompany you."

"Would you?" She held her breath.

"You know I would."

"I'll have to fetch my pelisse."

"I'll wait."

"And my abigail?"

"I should say so! And don't forget to leave word of your direction."

Caro flashed him a brilliant smile. "Nobody will miss me for ages. Mama has been saving up a million things to say to Gareth."

"Nevertheless, you'll do as I say."

"Shall I? I thought you didn't give a rap for the proprieties?"

"Not for myself, no. But you are an entirely different case."

149

Deirdre caught sight of them as they strolled through the gate of Green Park a few minutes later. They were within hailing distance and she called to them but neither of them spared a glance for her, so patently unaware were they of anyone outside their own charmed circle. Deirdre suffered a pang and she glanced involuntarily to Rathbourne House on the other side of the street.

A footman in the Earl's livery was descending the front steps to the pavement. His glance fell on Deirdre and she quickly looked away, but not before she had seen him summon a sedan. It was a ridiculous notion, but she could not dismiss the thought that Rathbourne's lackey had been sent to spy on her. She called to her abigail, put down her head, and fled toward the refuge of Hatchard's book shop, doing her best to melt into the fashionable shoppers who thronged Piccadilly.

A good half hour later, having given in to the temptation to purchase a copy of *Mansfield Park* by the unknown lady whose novels were approved by no less a dignitary than the Prince Regent, Deirdre stepped outside the door of the book shop. She was cross and feeling a little guilty for having squandered a sum of money that she ought to have reserved for her next pair of silk stockings. It reminded her forcibly of the straits to which they had come with Armand's latest peccadillo and her spirits sank even lower.

They rose slightly when her eyes lifted to the splendid equipage that stood before Hatchard's. Her glance slanted to the groom who held the heads of the lead horses and she recognized him instantly. She took a quick step to the left with some wild notion of escape and practically fell into the arms of the Earl of Rathbourne.

"It took you long enough," was Rathbourne's only comment before he whisked her to the curricle and handed her up.

She could tell that it was no use to protest or struggle. He was in one of his masterful moods. She righted her wilting bonnet, ignored the frankly speculative look of his lordship's

Irish groom, and took refuge in silence.

The groom was dismissed, as Deirdre knew he would be, as was her abigail, and the Earl gave the bays the office to start. The curricle bowled along Piccadilly and Deirdre held on to her hat.

Rathbourne made a few commonplace remarks which Deirdre did her best to ignore. But when the curricle missed every gate that led to Hyde Park, she was constrained to demand where the Earl thought he was taking her.

He seemed in an uncommonly mellow mood. "Only to Chelsea," he informed her gravely. "My bays need the exercise, you see. And I have something of a particular nature I wish to say to you."

"Indeed. What may that be?"

"Only that I think courting is damnable. I'm no good at it. You must marry me, Deirdre, and soon. You know that, don't you?"

"Oh," said Deirdre faintly, and fell silent.

It was as if she were reliving a fantasy, an unattainable dream wish that persistently haunted her last conscious thoughts before she was claimed by sleep—that in-between time when the will is temporarily suspended and imagination, unfettered and reckless, comes into its own. At such times, as is the way of dreams where all things are possible, Deirdre had become another person, transformed, possessing a rare beauty and endowed with a noble title and no mean fortune. Not unnaturally, with such attributes, Lady Deirdre was the most sought-after marriage prize in London, and the Earl had fallen under her spell. But she remained proud and unattainable, scorning his soft words of supplication, spurning his offer of hand and heart.

She realized dimly that what she experienced was a revenge fantasy, but when she cast about in her mind for old scores which she wished to pay off, nothing of significance presented itself. Until now! Until the Earl had coolly relieved Armand of the five thousand pounds which was to stock her stables, thus jeopardizing their very livelihood. For all Armand's faults, she did not think they were to be compared to the ruthless way Rathbourne had used him, a mere boy.

She assumed the cool half smile which the dream Deirdre of her fantasy habitually wore.

"I think, Lord Rathbourne, that I explained my views on marriage to you once before. I have not changed my opinion, nor am I like to. I am sensible of the honor you do me, but my answer is, must be, no."

"In other words, you don't trust me to treat you kindly? I haven't forgotten the farrago of nonsense you spouted. In spite of what you think, Deirdre, a woman needs a man. You would gain far more than you would lose by marriage with me."

"I have no interest in your rank and wealth."

"That is what I like in you. But you would have my protection. That is not something to sneer at."

"I have my brother. I need no other's protection."

His bark of laughter grated on Deirdre's nerves. She clenched her teeth and said with commendable restraint, "My refusal is not personal, I assure you. A wife's first object must always be to please a husband. Such a task would be beyond me."

"Don't let that weigh with you. I intend to teach you all that is necessary to please this particular male."

The amused tolerance in his tone brought her patience to an explosive end. "I wouldn't marry you if you were the last man on God's earth! How dare you entertain such a notion? Your women, your gaming, your whole mode of living is repugnant to me. I have told you so before."

"I thought that there was nothing personal in your objection to my suit?"

If Deirdre thought to have the upper hand in this contest of wits, she soon saw her mistake. This unrepentant roué was not the crushed lover of her fantasy.

"I see nothing personal in the wish to avoid association with any man who keeps a stable of women. Your protection must

152

be very extensive, my lord. How many women, in your long, lecherous career, have had the honor of naming you their protector?"

"Not half as many as rumor would have it."

"As many as that?" Deirdre shot back, stung by his levity.

"Oh, a different one for every night of the week and two on Sunday. Deirdre, this is a ridiculous conversation. If every man who had a past were to forgo the pleasures of marriage, there would be no such institution. You are being irrational. Forget the past. Look to the future—our future."

A silence fell between them. Deirdre would not admit the truth of what he said, but she was unwilling to argue the point further, knowing that he would deride her logic as naiveté. She flicked him a look of displeasure.

His sordid bedroom exploits were as celebrated as Wellington's glorious victories in battle, yet this did not detract from his appeal to other women. They were not burdened by her scruples. She had not been blind to the lures thrown out to him by the beauties who flocked to his side given half an invitation. She wished she had a hundred lovers that she might throw in his face—anything to shake him of that insufferable complaisance.

"We have no future," she said with what she hoped was crushing dignity. "I shall never marry. A woman should look to her own protection. I need no man to perform that office for me."

"It's as I expected," he replied as if she had just told him the time of day.

"Then why did you ask me if you knew what my answer would be at the outset?" Try as she might, she could not quite match his tone of bland indifference.

"Merely to oblige a friend. I told him this approach would be useless."

"A friend? You asked me to marry you for the sake of a friend?"

"I've shocked you. I beg your pardon. I should never have

allowed myself to be persuaded into a course of action I foresaw was doomed to failure. I shall wait for better odds next time."

"Then you shall wait for a very long time, sir."

His eyes mocked her. "My dear Miss Fenton, this is merely a skirmish. The battle has yet to be joined."

With that, he gave his horses their heads and they took off at a spanking rate along the Chelsea Road. Deirdre was compelled to hang on to the sides of the curricle as it jostled her about in a most undignified way. That his lordship drove to an inch with four in hand brought no amelioration to her sense of outrage. For a thwarted suitor, he looked to be remarkably carefree. She was glad that he meant to offer for her again. Next time, next time, she promised herself grimly as he took a particularly sharp bend at a dangerous speed, sending her sprawling, next time she would administer the coup de grâce.

Chapter Twelve

Deirdre was nervous. Even the tedious, hour-long drive in the closed laudaulet that Armand had procured for the evening did little to relieve the weakness that seemed to have spread to every part of her anatomy. Her knees knocked, her teeth chattered, and she stared sightlessly through the carriage window at a landscape that was shrouded in almost total darkness.

The coach crested the rise of the Richmond Bridge and butterflies fluttered alarmingly in the pit of Deirdre's stomach. She should be home, safe in her bed, not gallivanting to some gaming den in the wee hours of the morning tricked out as the lightskirt of the handsome young blood who sat stern and silent beside her.

"Folly Lane," said Armand as the landaulet made a sharp turn toward the Thames.

The name seemed appropriate, but Deirdre said nothing. On their left was Marble Hill House, the former residence of Mrs. Fitzherbert, the discarded mistress of the Prince Regent. In the deepening gloom, however, nothing was to be seen of its Palladian grandeur.

The right front wheel struck a pothole in the muddy lane and the coach lurched. Deirdre grabbed for the leather strap overhead to save herself being flung to the floor. Armand's hand at her elbow steadied her.

"How much farther?" she asked in a wavering voice that she scarcely recognized as her own. She could see only the chiseled outline of her brother's profile in the darkened coach, and she sensed that his nerves were as taut as a bowstring.

"Not long now. There's still time to turn back if you have changed your mind."

"Don't be ridiculous. We've been through all this before. This is the only solution, and you know it. My flair and skill at cards surpass yours. I am sorry if your vanity has been bruised, but you know I speak the truth."

There was no further conversation between them. They had done all their talking in the days before, when Armand had confessed to Deirdre his gaming debt to the Earl of Rathbourne. He had sworn that he had tried every avenue open to him to raise the monstrous sum, but it had availed him nothing. His credit, even with the notorious three percenters, had inexplicably dried up. It was a chastened Armand who came to Deirdre, laying the whole sordid business before her. The debt was a matter of honor, doubly so since Armand's creditor was a man he held in the utmost contempt. Deirdre understood this. She gave him the funds to settle the matter immediately. Never once had he blamed the Earl for his predicament, and for that Deirdre had been thankful.

If it hadn't been that she faced financial ruin because of Armand's peccadillo, she might even feel grateful to the Earl for precipitating the crisis. Armand had changed. He had said very little, but Deirdre could sense that the threat of disgrace had forced her proud brother to face some unpalatable truths about his mode of living. She wondered idly for a moment if Caro had a hand in the new maturity she sensed in her brother, but that thought she shied away from.

It was a notion too horrible to contemplate. Rathbourne would never permit the impoverished son of a French émigré to pay his addresses to his sister. Far better if Armand continued his pursuit of the elusive Mrs. Dewinters. But of late, he had said very little about his interest in that quarter, and Deirdre had come to the conclusion that the infatuation had run its predictable course. So much for undying love, thought Deirdre with a cynicism that had become almost second nature to her.

"We're here."

As the coach was slowly negotiated between the massive stone pillars of the ornate entrance to Winslow House on the banks of the River Thames, Deirdre drew in a deep breath to steady herself, and she wondered wildly what had possessed her to this night's folly. It was madness to expose herself in this manner; even a rakehell like Armand said so. But then Armand knew nothing about the mortgage on Marcliff that had paid for his gentleman's education. He knew nothing about the money she *must* retrieve and invest to stock her stables in the next month or so. She could lose everything if she failed to recoup her losses tonight. But that intelligence she had withheld from her brother. He thought her comfortably enough situated. It suited her to let him think so. But even he, reckless and careless as he was about money, had agreed that five thousand pounds was a loss that a small farm like Marcliff could not easily sustain. For that reason, he had been persuaded to accept Deirdre's wild scheme to bring their fortunes about.

The coach halted, and Deirdre drew on a black velvet demi-mask, an article that was de rigueur for the patrons of Winslow's establishment. She fluffed out the folds of the new gown she had chosen with particular care, indulging a whim she had long cherished. It was a diaphanous slip of scarlet satin and admirably suited the harlot's part that she was forced to play. But she took no pleasure in having proved to herself that in scarlet satin she looked as common and cheap as a tart on the London docks.

Armand offered his hand and Deirdre's fingers held on

157

tightly as she alighted from the coach, her eyes sweeping over the magnificent columned entrance of Lord Winslow's Georgian mansion. Beyond the uncurtained, small-paned windows of the house, she could see other masked ladies and gentlemen moving about under the brilliant chandeliers. No lady coming to this elegant den of vice, so it seemed, far from the madding crowds of town, had the least inclination to make her identity known, a circumstance which suited Deirdre perfectly.

She wandered with Armand through the various apartments, ignoring the intent crowds at the faro banks and rouleaux tables which she dismissed as mere games of chance, and finally found what she wanted. The picquet tables were set up in a comfortable saloon at the back of the house overlooking the river, and Deirdre's steps slowed. She moved from group to group as if in idle curiosity, discreetly observing play at first one table and then another. Only Armand, a constant shadow at her side, was aware of her true intent. Having summed up the caliber of the opposition, Deirdre was impatient to get down to business. She felt like a wolf in sheep's clothing. Not for the first time, she reflected that if Reverend Standing could be persuaded to give up his calling and pursue the less exalted profession of gamester, he would make a fortune. She could not know that the heavenly minded man of cloth whom she revered had learned his arts as a young rakehell bent on mischief in just such dens of iniquity, and had forsworn it all without regret when he had tumbled into love with the beautiful daughter of an itinerant preacher.

The bold, assessing stares of many of the gentlemen present she ignored with a cool, dampening detachment, having been warned in no uncertain terms by Armand that although gaming was the primary purpose of Lord Winslow's house which became a gaming establishment on Wednesday evenings, many of the gentlemen expected to go home with more than their uncertain winnings from the gaming tables. If the tonnish Almack's Assembly Rooms, which met on the same evening of the week, were aptly named "The Marriage Mart," Winslow House had no less deservedly earned the sobriquet "Courtesans' Court." Still, she was unprepared for the openly lascivious caressing that many of the couples engaged in, and she was careful to smile often at Armand to ensure that the watching world knew that her "protector" was close at hand.

Her chance came when a gentleman with a smile lurking in his eyes gestured an invitation after his opponent, obviously a sore loser, threw down his cards and made for the faro bank. Deirdre had been aware of the stranger's friendly interest since she had first entered the picquet room. His glances had lacked that ravening, hungry look that were brazenly bent on her by some of the other gentlemen, even supposing Armand stuck to her like glue. His interest bordered on the avuncular, in Deirdre's opinion, although he was an extremely handsome man with blond hair shot with silver at the temples. Behind the mask, the kindest blue eyes that she had ever encountered gazed at her with a roguish twinkle. There was something vaguely familiar about the gentleman, but since his approach lacked nothing of civility, Deirdre had no hesitation in accepting the place his late opponent had vacated.

"I'm keeping this spot warm for a friend," he offered by way of explanation. "I expect him directly. If you don't mind changing partners in the middle of play, I'd be happy to stand in for him till he returns."

Deirdre indicated politely that she had no objection to this arrangement.

At first she played cautiously, undismayed by the outrageous stakes since Armand had already warned her how high they might reach. Her prodigious memory served her well, for she never forgot an opponent's discard and played her own hand with unerring calculation. The gentleman said so and Deirdre thanked him. Within half an hour, her winnings amounted to a cool one thousand pounds. Deirdre was almost ecstatic, and she shuffled the cards demurely, bestowing a smile on her kind adversary that came close to being an apology. His blue eyes twinkled merrily back at her, and Deirdre, feeling a twinge of guilt for relieving him of such a considerable sum, prayed silently and fervently that the gentleman was well breeched.

That soft and confiding smile was remarked by a broad-shouldered gentleman in black form-fitting evening coat and white satin breeches, arms negligently folded across an expansive chest, who reclined with careless grace against an Ionic marble column at the entrance to the card room. He was joined by a diminutive, dark-haired lady, but he seemed not to notice. His lazy, tawny glance had become riveted to a green-eyed lovely in a diaphanous slip of scarlet, the badge of a lightskirt, that was frankly suggestive. A frown gathered with ominous portent on Lord Rathbourne's broad brow.

His eyes narrowed to the soft mounds of Deirdre's white breasts bared almost to the nipple. A patch placed strategically on one swelling contour drew the steel in his eyes like a compass to a magnet. He flexed his strong fingers as if contemplating the pleasure he would experience should he be so fortunate as to lay his hands on the slender column of her throat, which rose, swanlike, to support a mass of dark tresses embellished with one scarlet ostrich feather. His eyes slowly traversed its provocative curl as it came to rest against one dewy cheek, drawing attention to the perfect oval face which was barely recognizable with its concealing demi-mask and layers of powder, rouge, and paint. That the lady was in no wise distinguishable from the motley crew of fair Cyprians who graced Lord Winslow's noble, albeit notorious, establishment, dampened the heat of his simmering anger not one jot.

An Exquisite with quizzing glass dangling by a black velvet ribbon from one limp finger was seen to approach the tall forbidding figure of the Earl. Rathbourne's eyes shifted to take in the extravagantly costumed person of Sir Geoffrey

Balnaves, and a faint smile of derision briefly touched his lips. Balnaves's coat was of claret velvet and heavily embroidered with gold thread. Silver buckles adorned his high-heeled shoes in which he was obliged to walk with small, mincing steps. His neck he kept very erect, a necessary inconvenience, since the starched points of his collar brushed the diamonds at his ears. The intricate folds of the fine linen neckcloth at his throat were a wonder to behold and gave the impression of a small, stuffed cushion on which Sir Geoffrey might rest his weary chin.

He made an elegant leg to the lady who stood restively at his lordship's side. Mrs. Dewinters smiled and gave the gentleman her hand, which he kissed with a flourish. It was evident that the fop and the actress were well known to each other and on the best of terms.

Balnaves made a turn around the column against which Rathbourne inclined and came to stand at the Earl's elbow, slightly to one side.

"Tempting morsel, ain't she?" he lisped in a languid undertone. His quizzing glass was trained on Deirdre. "Gad, if Uxbridge ain't an insatiable fellow. 'Twas to be expected, I suppose, with Lady Char at Beaudesert."

The Earl seemed not to like the tone of the baronet's remarks. He pushed himself to an upright position and said in a voice like flint, "The lady has an escort."

Balnaves's quizzing glass shifted to take in Armand. "What? That young whelp standing at her elbow? He don't signify. Russell has his eye on her. Thought you ought to know."

His eyes met the Earl's in perfect comprehension. He inclined his head gravely and strolled away. After a considering moment, Rathbourne offered his arm to Mrs. Dewinters and they advanced upon the picquet table where Uxbridge and Deirdre were engaged in play.

An unsuspecting Deirdre glanced up when a handsome couple came into her line of vision. Her fingers froze, and the

161

cards she had been in the process of shuffling spilled on the table in front of her. In spite of the black demi-masks, there could be no mistaking the Earl of Rathbourne and his beautiful companion, Mrs. Maria Dewinters. Deirdre felt Armand's steadying hand at her shoulder and she mumbled an incoherent apology to her companion, who had already risen to his feet to greet the newcomers.

He said a few quiet words in Rathbourne's ear which Deirdre could not catch, then very politely and firmly took his leave of Deirdre with a grave bow. My Lord Rathbourne took his place and Deirdre rigidly controlled the shudder of unease that rippled through her. She retrieved the spilled cards, shuffled them rather ineptly in the manner of a female, and slowly and deliberately dealt a hand to each of them.

For a moment she was persuaded that if she kept a cool head she might carry off the deception, that the Earl might not recognize the lady under the harlot's guise. One glance at those cat's eyes soon put that misguided notion to rest. There was steel there and a blaze of anger that was almost frightening in its intensity. Deirdre carefully lowered her lashes to cover her shock, her mind furiously grappling with what his presence might portend. He knew! He had come here on purpose, had lured her to this very table to accept a challenge from an accomplice, knowing that if she had once caught a glimpse of *him,* she would have taken to her heels. The manner of his bringing about such a dastardly plot troubled her only slightly. But his *purpose* in singling *her* out, that was more than a little frightening, and eluded her completely.

There was no retreat. Already he had picked up the cards she had dealt him and was looking at them intently. There was nothing for it but to brazen it out. She glanced at the array of cards in her hand but found it hard to concentrate. Her eyes kept wandering to the actress who hovered behind the Earl. Mrs. Dewinters's gown was a modest but beautiful creation of blue sarcenet with white underdress and white satin ribbons adorning the bodice and puff sleeves. She looked every inch the lady, and Deirdre, highly conscious of the picture she herself presented, squirmed uncomfortably in her place.

Deirdre was at a loss to say why, but she was almost certain that Mrs. Dewinters, unlike the Earl, had not penetrated her disguise. She watched in fascinated interest as the actress batted her long, silky eyelashes behind Rathbourne's back and threw out lures to Armand. What was she up to? There was no time to reflect further, for the Earl had commenced play.

For the first rubber, she played very cautiously, more as a reconnoitering measure. When she won it quite handsomely, some of her confidence returned. It was obvious to her that the Earl's play had changed little since she had first trounced him at picquet almost five years before. Since Wellington's officers were known for displaying a fine leg on the ballroom floor rather than for their sleight of hand at the card table, she became bolder. Her eyes sliced to Rathbourne, and she relaxed even more. The Earl was seething, if she was any judge of character.

His eyes locked with hers. "I propose we raise the stakes, if you have no objection, miss?"

"Madame X," supplied Deirdre unhelpfully, giving him back stare for stare. "What is your wish, sir?"

A negligent shrug of the shoulders was her answer.

"Five hundred pounds a rubber?" she threw at him daringly.

"Make it a thousand and I might be interested," was the cool rejoinder.

Deirdre tried to cover her dismay. She sought Armand's guidance. Not finding him behind her chair, she scanned the room quickly and saw him disappearing through a pair of French doors with Mrs. Dewinters on his arm. Deirdre's first presentiment of disaster was strengthened and a flutter of panic shimmied along every nerve ending. Rathbourne was toying with her! Her eyes narrowed and she brought the pack

163

of cards in her hands together like the crack of a whiplash.

"Deal!" she fairly snapped at him.

She paid dearly for that piece of recklessness. Two rubbers down and she had reluctantly formed the conclusion that the aristocratic Earl of Rathbourne, for all his fine posturing, was an out-and-out cheat! There was no other explanation. How it was done, she had no way of knowing. Cheating at cards had never been any part of Reverend Standing's instruction. But it was perfectly obvious to her that the cards were marked.

"Double or nothing?" she heard Rathbourne's smooth question as if from a distance.

An interested crowd had gathered around the table to watch the play of the two grim-faced antagonists, but Armand was not among them. If she meant to withdraw, now was the time to do it.

"A glass of wine in the interim?" Rathbourne suggested with insulting negligence, and before Deirdre could frame a blistering refusal, he raised one hand to attract the notice of one of the many footmen who dispensed champagne in crystal glasses from silver trays.

Deirdre accepted with a show of indifference and quietly took stock of her situation as she slowly sipped the fizzy beverage. She was more than badly dipped. She was cleaned out, and she was certain that the Earl knew it. But if she won the next rubber, and she was sure she could do it if she could put a halt to Rathbourne's cheating, she would walk away from the table with a very handsome profit.

"Why not?" she flung at him brightly. Then with a challenging look at her contemptible opponent, "A fresh pack, I think, and my turn to deal?"

It was the closest she could come in company to telling the man that she had divined his despicable game. Rathbourne merely returned a smile.

The cards were placed in Deirdre's impatient fingers and she gave them her most careful perusal. It did little good. She hadn't the least notion of what she was looking for. If only Armand were at her side, he would advise her. She could not believe that her brother would desert her without good reason, and it had better be good, she thought fiercely, for when I catch up with that rapscallion, I'll flay the skin off his back. Sudden knowledge blazed in her eyes and her accusing glance sliced to the Earl. That unscrupulous gentleman, as if reading Deirdre's chagrin, merely raised one questioning black eyebrow and intoned mildly that he was ready if the lady wished to commence play.

Throwing off all caution, Deirdre shuffled and dealt the cards with a dexterity that gave rise to the speculation in the minds of more than a few curious bystanders that the wench had been born and bred in a gaming house. A hum went round the table and wagers were laid, soto voce, on the identity of the mystery woman who had the temerity to cross swords with the implacable Earl.

It soon became evident to Deirdre that by procuring a fresh deck of cards she had thwarted Rathbourne's devious game, but her triumph was to be short-lived. The Earl was not the careless player she had worsted five years before. In the intervening years, he had learned a thing or two, and had become a very formidable opponent. Her former easy win at the start of play she now saw had been a base trick to lull her suspicions and make her careless. He would not deceive her again.

She won the first hand, although he played her to close finish. Confidence returned, and she remarked tauntingly, "I see, sir, that not only did your stint with Wellington improve your leg on the ballroom floor, but your ability to play your cards has sharpened quite handily. I wonder where you found the time for battles and so on?"

Rathbourne opened his box of snuff, took an infinitesimal pinch, and sniffed delicately. "For that piece of impertinence," he said with unruffled composure, "I shall demand unconditional surrender when you cede me the final victory. Now deal, if you please."

Feminine giggles and masculine hoots of laughter greeted this sally. Deirdre joined in the general amusement, conscious that to appear outraged would gratify the Earl's vanity. But she deplored the innuendo, and her eyes glittered like shards of ice.

From then on she was given no quarter. They played in a silence that stretched taut as if the fate of the world turned on their cards. Deirdre had never played better in her life. It availed her little. As the hours flew by, Rathbourne took her measure and played every winning hand she held to a halt. She had met her match and he was determined that she should acknowledge it. She lost two consecutive rubbers and took little pleasure from knowing that it had been a close game.

She watched with horrified fascination as Rathbourne made a notation on the tally card. He raised his head and said without emotion, "Six thousand pounds, by my reckoning. Do you wish to continue?"

Deirdre could scarce take in the extent of her losses. Her eyes met his in silent appeal. She could see that she had roused some emotion in him, but it was not the one that she wanted. There was a gloating look about his eyes, and his mouth curved in a smile that boded ill for her. No, in victory, the Earl would not be generous. But Deirdre was no coward either. She was not about to let herself be intimidated by the man who had wronged her.

"Do you wish to continue?"

Deirdre's eyes dropped to the cards on the table. "What would be the point?" she asked in a voice which betrayed nothing of the anger that seethed within.

The scrape of the chair warned her that Rathbourne had risen to his feet. She felt his presence at her back but could not bring herself to look at him. Her chair was pulled back roughly and Deirdre rose with a show of unconcern. A possessive hand encircled her waist and a titter went round the spectators.

Hectic color heated her cheekbones. There could be little doubt that popular opinion had already decided how her debt was to be canceled. My Lord Rathbourne had much to answer for.

He led her purposefully from the card room. "Shall we discuss terms, Madame X?" he asked in a mocking undertone.

A footman appeared with her wrap and Deirdre allowed the Earl to draw it around her shoulders. Her expression was frigid. Rathbourne regarded her for a long moment, a frown gathering on his brow. "Are you all right?" he asked softly.

Her eyes blazed an answer, and Rathbourne patted her shoulder as if she had been a child. "That's better. You had me worried for a moment."

With his hand firm on her elbow, she walked stiffly but without protest until she saw that it was *his* coach that was drawn up at the entrance. Deirdre rounded on him. "What have you done with my brother?" she demanded in a voice vibrant with emotion.

"Don't trouble yourself about him," he replied with an offhandedness that did not endear him to Deirdre. "I've had him put to bed. When he wakes tomorrow, he won't recall a thing. I haven't hurt him, Deirdre, if that's what is in your mind."

The carriage door was opened by one of Rathbourne's coachmen and Deirdre was hustled inside. As the Earl settled beside her, she shrank into the corner and deliberately lifted her skirts out of his way as if she feared contamination from any part of his person. It was only a small act of defiance, and Rathbourne affected not to notice. It was as if by tacit agreement there would be no scene until what they had to say to each other could be said in absolute privacy.

Their journey was short, and when the carriage drew up before a small, terraced house in a dimly lit street that formed one side of a square common, Deirdre looked to the Earl in some surprise.

167

"Why are we stopping?"

"Have you forgotten that we have yet to discuss terms?" His voice was mild and unthreatening. "Or do you perhaps have a draft for six thousand pounds in your reticule with which to discharge your debt?"

Deirdre said nothing. She allowed him to help her alight.

"Where are we?" she asked, forcing herself to speak calmly.

"In Richmond. I thought we should be private. This is a house I am in the process of letting."

There was nothing of the lover in his clipped accents. She sensed that his anger was on a tight leash and the thought was oddly comforting. He might ruin her financially, but she doubted if she would suffer any serious injury at his hands. The Earl was, in spite of everything, an English gentleman. Her confidence was pinned on that hope. Having disposed, in her own mind, of her most pressing fear, she gave free rein to her righteous anger, at least in the silence of her personal reflections.

He pushed her ungently ahead of him through a dark vestibule and up a steep, narrow flight of stairs. He found the door he wanted and thrust her over the threshold. Deirdre took one look and shrank back against him.

A small card table set for two with white damask covers stood in the middle of the room. Two French gilt-edged chairs were placed by the table, and on a rosewood console against one wall were various covered silver serving dishes filled, so Deirdre guessed by the inviting aroma, with all manner of delicacies. The lighting was subdued. A brace of candles stood on the table, another on the white marble mantlepiece. Everything was in crimson from the velvet drapes, which were drawn tight, to the crimson satin hangings on the massive Queen Anne four-poster, which stood between two long windows. The atmosphere was one of decadence and Deirdre was outraged. She whirled on her captor.

There was so much she wanted to cast in his teeth; his

treachery at placing her in such a shocking position; his high-handed removal of her brother's protection; Mrs. Dewinters's connivance in his unscrupulous plot; the smooth way everyone and everything had been manipulated to his base ends. But one thing infuriated her above all else.

"Cheat!" Her voice shook with anger. "Filthy, low, conniving, unscrupulous, abominable cheat! How dare you use me so? You took advantage of me. It was no coincidence that you met me at Winslow's. Did you set your spies on me? How dared you play against me with marked cards! I shall never permit you to get away with this outrage! I'll have you blackballed at White's or wherever it is you disgrace with your vile presence. Snake! Did you cheat Armand too? I'll ruin you if it's the last thing I do! Don't you dare touch me," she cried as Rathbourne lunged for her.

He caught her by the arms and spun her round to face the mirror above the mantelpiece. "Take a good look at yourself, Miss Fenton." He dragged the wig from her head and Deirdre winced with the pain as the pins pulled free. "Don't talk about trying to ruin me. I have only to let slip the name of the doxy who partnered me at Winslow's and you will be ruined for life."

Deirdre was not best pleased at the unwelcome reminder of what her disguise was meant to portray. She had never seen so much naked bosom in her life. Her eyes shrank from her own reflection and sought his gaze in the mirror. "You are despicable," she said through gritted teeth.

Rathbourne let her go and she put some distance between them.

"Sit down," he said curtly, but with so much menace behind the words that Deirdre obeyed, albeit with some reluctance. "I knew that you would try something but this is beyond belief. What was St. Jean thinking of to allow you to expose yourself in this way? That boy needs his head examined!"

The question was rhetorical and Deirdre sat mute, regarding

him stonily. She listened to his spate of invective with only half an ear. It had finally registered in her mind that she was alone with a man in his bedchamber—and such a chamber! No threat, no objection of hers could sway the man who stormed at her. She needed all her wits about her if she was to persuade him to let her go.

When his anger had run its course, she addressed him in more mollified accents. "Lord Rathbourne, come now, you can't hold me here indefinitely. I don't know what your game is, but I am willing to overlook this . . . practical joke, if you return me to my family forthwith. I admit that I was at fault, and I promise to mend my ways. But let us be done with this charade. If you care to call on me at Portman Square tomorrow, or at your convenience, I am certain that everything can be settled between us quite amicably."

He had moved to the console table as she spoke and seemed to give her words due consideration, but his answer brought a flutter of alarm to the pit of her stomach.

"You will be returned to your family in due course. However, I think it imperative that we conclude our business tonight, but not before we have eaten. I thought it better to forgo the pleasure of dining in Winslow's. You might have let slip something to reveal your identity and I had no wish to expose you to further risk." He removed the covers and heaped a platter with a sample of each serving dish. More than anything she wanted to spurn his hospitality, but she was afraid to try his temper to the limit.

She made a show of eating, but she scarcely swallowed a morsel and she drank sparingly of the wine he pressed on her. That Rathbourne placed no such restraints upon himself but drank down three glasses of Burgundy in quick succession disturbed her more than she cared to admit. She wished that she had had the foresight to conceal a weapon on her person. She absently twisted the emerald ring on her finger, but immediately desisted when she observed the Earl's knowing smile.

As the meal progressed, his looks became darker and every nerve in her body screamed for her to make the attempt to escape, although outwardly she was careful to appear poised and in command of the situation. She mentally reviewed the options open to her and decided that her best course would be to follow his direction until she discovered what he intended. She put her knife and fork together on her plate to signify that she had finished and pushed her chair slightly back from the table.

"Drink your wine, Deirdre, you'll feel the better for it," he said in a voice that was not unkindly. Somehow, she found this unlooked-for solicitude more distrustful than his habitual temper.

She kept her voice pleasantly modulated. "I'm sure this elaborate abduction has some point to it, my lord. May I know what it is?"

"Did you forget that we have yet to discuss terms?" he asked softly, regarding her over the rim of his fourth glass of Burgundy with an impenetrable expression.

"I have not forgotten. By all means, let us discuss terms."

"Six thousands pounds is no mean sum. How do you propose to raise it?"

"Does it matter? You, I am persuaded, have it in mind to dispose of every suggestion I put forward until I hit upon the one you are determined upon. What do you propose, my lord?"

He raised his glass as if in salute. "You cannot raise such a sum unless you sell that farm of yours, and since it is mortgaged to the hilt, that won't answer."

"You seem to be remarkably well informed about my affairs," she said coldly.

"Remarkably," he concurred. "But then, that was to be expected since I have of late invested a tidy sum in your horse breeding venture."

He let the words sink in, waiting, perhaps even hoping, he was willing to admit, that her unshakable composure would develop a crack. But she only stared at him, and nothing betrayed how his words had affected her.

"Five thousand pounds, to be exact," he added gratuitously.

Her eyelashes flickered down, and he went on with cruel deliberation, "You are destitute, Dee. I've made sure of that. There are no alternatives. Marry me and I shall undertake to meet all your obligations, both present and future. You will find me a generous husband, even although you are in no position to dictate terms."

"I see." The fingers on the stem of her wineglass shook slightly, the only sign that she was not in full control of her emotions.

"You may remember that I told you I would renew my offer when the odds were more in my favor. Don't be frightened, Deirdre," he added gently as he noted the unnatural pallor of her complexion. "You should be flattered to think I would go to such lengths for you. I would not have done as much for any other woman."

Deirdre knew that she was in shock. Her thought processes seemed to have ground to a halt. She wanted to shout her outrage, but the words would not form on her lips. She saw that he was watching her with those habitually indolent eyes, and pride goaded her to speak with an icy hauteur.

"But I am not flattered. You want me only because I have refused you, a unique experience for you, no doubt."

"True."

"Your consequence, your vanity has been wounded by my refusal, nothing more."

"That too."

"Once I surrender myself, you will soon lose interest and regret that you ever thought of marriage."

"You do yourself an injustice," he returned dryly.

"I am a realist," she shot back.

"A cynic, more like," he countered. After a strained interval, he went on more gently, "Deirdre, I know my own mind, and I know yours also, whateve: you might say to the contrary."

She was silent, and Rathbourne seemed to come to the end of his patience. He cursed softly and began to gather together the remains of their supper on a tray. He moved to the door, pushed it open, and deposited the tray on the floor outside. He then shut the door with a snap.

So the servants were not to be given even a glimpse of her, Deirdre reflected. In a night of unmitigated disaster, that Rathbourne should try to protect the remnants of her reputation was a very small consolation.

He turned back to face her, putting himself deliberately between Deirdre and the door. "Well? What is your answer, Miss Fenton?"

"If I refuse?" The question was pointless and she knew it. There was no arguing with a man who had proved that he would stoop to the tactics of a felon.

"That would not be acceptable."

To quarrel with him when he had been drinking and in such an unpredictable temper was unthinkable. Not that she would ever consider marrying such a domineering man. She hated him with a passion. But now was not the time to tell him so. She was in this position only because he had deceived her. She had no qualms about returning the compliment. Once she was out of his clutches and on safer ground, she would raise the money to repay him somehow. She determined to play her cards with a cool head.

She became conscious of a subtle change in him. His eyes, behind an assumed languor, were watchful; his posture, tense. Her eyes were drawn to the faint scar on his cheek and she remembered Vauxhall.

"Then I accept your offer," she said with a grace she was far from feeling.

173

She pushed herself from the table and looked about for her cloak. It was on the quilted crimson bed. Keeping a wary eye on her abductor, she moved to retrieve it, but held it in her arms in front of her, fearful that if she put it on, he might regard the action as some sort of provocation. "May I go now?" she asked, despising the break in her voice.

He laughed without mirth. "You accept? Without argument? And I am free, I suppose, to send the notice of our betrothal to *The Times* and approach your guardian and make all the necessary arrangements and so on?"

"Of course." The thought that she might have made at least some show of resistance came to her belatedly. Her compliance was not in character. But then, what did this arrogant man know of her? No doubt it was no less than he expected.

He came to tower over her and Deirdre forced herself not to drop her eyes from his unnerving stare.

"Just like that?"

"You give me no choice."

"And you will honor our bargain?"

"Naturally."

"Deirdre, you will run to earth as soon as you are shot of my hateful presence. You would like nothing better than to make a laughingstock of me. In short, I don't trust you!"

She looked at him coolly. "What do you suggest, then? That I put my promise in writing and sign it in the presence of witnesses? Would that satisfy you?"

One careless finger tipped up her chin, and she felt his hand warm and firm on her shoulder. "What I suggest, Deirdre, is a pledge of your good faith, a down payment, if you like, of what you promise for the future."

"A pledge?" she echoed foolishly.

"Something that will bind you to me forever. A week from now our vows will confirm the consummation of your promise."

For a long moment they stood unmoving, and Deirdre half

174

believed that she had mistaken his meaning until his hand slid lightly to her fingers and, before she knew what he was about, he had removed the emerald ring. She heard it clatter as he threw it on the nearest table.

"Merely a precautionary measure," he said with a challenge in his eyes as he bent to take her lips.

Chapter Thirteen

Her hands splayed out and she pressed them hard and urgently against his chest to fend off the embrace. The heat of his skin through the fine fabric of his shirt sent a tremor of shock through the tips of her fingers, impelling her senses to a vivid awareness of the jeopardy this man presented. "Don't! You can't!" There was a catch in her voice and in her eyes was the sheen of helpless rage.

Rathbourne felt a small pang of conscience, but it was easily stifled. She was in his arms, where she belonged. To be swayed by her scruples now would be to lose the advantage. Deirdre would never permit him to get close to her again, and that wall of reserve which held him at bay would become impenetrable. Dammit, he had not wanted it this way, but she had left him no choice. She saw the uncompromising set of his mouth and tensed for flight.

"I can and I will," he stated flatly. She surged against him, catching him off guard and he staggered sideways. One lunge took her to the door. She twisted the knob and dragged hard upon it. Nothing happened. She sobbed, a sound of pain and fury, and she strained every muscle to open the door. It would not budge. She wheeled to face him, pressing herself back as far from him as possible.

"I locked it," he said gently, as if he regretted the deception.

He calmly removed his jacket and neckcloth and draped them over the back of a chair. His eyes never left Deirdre's.

Involuntarily, her hands fisted and unfisted in the folds of her gown. She felt as if all the breath had been knocked out of her body. "My brother will kill you," she finally managed, her voice dry and rasping.

"We both know that you will never tell him. Oh, not for my sake, but for his."

His hands moved to the collar of his shirt, and Deirdre's breathing became more labored as he undid the buttons, one by one, slowly, agonizingly, easing the shirtfront open to reveal the mat of dark hair that curled against his chest. He shrugged out of it, and Deirdre closed her eyes against the persuasive virility of his sleek torso with its powerful shoulders and arms. She knew then why she had always felt Rathbourne's presence as a threat. If she had known what he concealed under his fine-tailored clothes, she would never have come within a mile of him—no, nor ever would again. When she opened her eyes, he was kicking out of his shoes.

"If you do this, I shall never marry you—never! I swear it." Her voice wavered and the threat sounded weak and empty.

"I am of the opposite persuasion. You will never marry me if I don't."

His hands moved to the waistband of his breeches and a small animal cry of fear was wrung from her. "Gareth, no!"

He laughed softly and shook his head. "You deign to give me my name at the oddest moments! Do you think *that* will persuade me? Before this night is over, I promise you, my name will come very naturally to your lips."

It was his calm purpose that unnerved her. He was beyond reason, beyond tears. Nothing could sway him now. His fingers undid the top button of his breeches and she stood, frozen, staring at him for a long moment, then she took a quick sideways step toward the window. He moved with catlike speed and caught her easily, his hands warm and compelling on her shoulders. "Deirdre." His voice was gentle and almost pleading. She jerked away from him with such violence that she would have fallen had he not been there to catch her.

She was lifted in his arms and held high against his chest. "Our first bedding needn't be a battle," he said softly against her temples. "Don't force me to be cruel. You won't admit it, but you want this as much as I do."

Her answer was to beat wildly at his chest and head. In two strides he was at the bed and he flung her roughly down, throwing himself beside her. He rolled on top of her and held her wrists easily with one hand. And then the slow assault on her senses began.

Resistance was useless. The press of his weight hindered every movement, and to draw each shaky breath became a struggle. Her head thrashed on the pillows and silent sobs of fury choked in her throat. He shifted his weight slightly, and Deirdre drew a steadying breath. Then his mouth, open and hot, closed over one nipple through the fabric of her gown, and Deirdre bucked madly against him. He reacted swiftly to her rejection. One arm fell heavily across her chest, pinioning her shoulders to the mattress. He ignored her soft whimper of distress and bent his head to suckle deeply. Her breasts seemed to swell, becoming heavier, straining against the silk of her bodice. She gritted her teeth and willed her body to feel nothing, but when his deft hands stripped her to the waist, freeing her sensitive nipples from the compressing tightness of her stays, an involuntary moan of something close to relief escaped her lips. That one faint sound of surrender stoked her receding anger to boiling point.

She wrenched violently away and succeeded in freeing one hand. Her nails found a target and she raked his shoulder, flaying him remorselessly. She took grim pleasure in his growl of pain before her wrist was slapped away by a stinging blow from the back of his hand. His body covered hers, pressing her deeper into the soft feather mattress and his hands went round her throat, his thumbs pressing lightly against her pulse points. It was an unspoken threat of how easily he could subdue her if he tired of her resistance.

He took her lips slowly, flicking them sensually with his tongue until she opened them under his demanding pressure. Her mouth was filled with him, and his tongue surged and receded in a feverish assault, each rhythmic plunge sending her senses higher until they began to reel.

One hand trailed to her waist and in a slow, sweeping motion he pushed her garments to her hips. His hand slid between her tightened thighs, pushing to the core of her femininity. She shied away from him. He stayed her frantic movements with one leg, and brought the flat of his hand to her abdomen, tracing the muscles that strained taut and hard against him. He kneaded slowly, increasing the pressure, kissing her deeply again and again, smothering her soft whimpered protests until she lay trembling beneath him. He parted her thighs and she made no move to halt him. His fingers found her and lingered, sliding and probing with slow sensuality, deliberately heightening her awareness of the pleasure that would follow with his body. Deirdre turned her head into his shoulder in a telling gesture. Rathbourne drew a ragged breath.

He pushed to an upright position and he released her completely. Deirdre made no move to escape him. He breathed deeply and touched his hand to her hair. He was shaking! He quickly stripped her of her garments and divested himself of his breeches, then he lay full length beside her, propped on one arm.

"Take down your hair for me, Deirdre," he breathed against her mouth. He waited, willing her to obey this simple request. It wasn't enough that she should accept him passively, like a whipped cur terrified of its master. He wanted her vibrant and responsive in his arms. He wondered what she had been taught about the intimacy of the marriage bed. It was irrelevant. He would be her teacher now and bring her alive with a passion to match his own. "Deirdre . . ." he said hoarsely.

She raised herself on one elbow and he breathed his relief when she took the pins from her hair. He helped her unbraid the heavy strands and he ran his fingers through the soft, blond swathe, fanning it out behind her as he pushed her back on the pillows. His eyes dropped and he drank in the tantalizing perfection of every feminine hollow and contour. His hands shook as they moved upon her, taking slow possession of what she had so long denied him. He had robbed her of the will to resist. The thought brought the blood thundering to his brain.

Her eyes swept up and his gaze locked with hers. Her eyes were soft and languorous with the passion he had kindled, but he detected a hint of reproach in their emerald depths.

"There was no other way," he said simply.

He thought that she shook her head in slight negation, but he could not be certain. Then he gave up all thought as he sought the delirium of her honeyed lips. The taste of desire was in her mouth and it fanned the flames of his passion to a conflagration. He burned for her.

His head dipped to tease one rosy nipple and Deirdre cried out her pleasure, lifting herself to him. He parted her legs and she opened for him. He entered her with his fingers and her hips writhed an invitation he instantly recognized. He stilled, feeling his control slip. His breath burned in his lungs and his heart hammered wildly against his ribs. She wanted him as much as he wanted her.

He found her hand and put it to his chest. Her fingers fanned out, obedient to his tutoring. He initiated her further, guiding her hand down the length of his hard-muscled abdomen. He felt her restraint when he curled her fingers over the hard swell of his arousal. Her eyes were wide and questioning as he taught her his pleasure.

"Touch me, love. I have hungered for your touch," and he thought his heart would burst when she began her own exploration of his body.

Never in her wildest fantasies about Gareth Cavanaugh, and there had been a few, had Deirdre ever imagined such intimacy. Where his hands touched, she melted. He said a word, and she obeyed. His power over her body should have

181

shamed her. But she was past rational thought. She was dazed with sensations and emotions she had never before experienced. Tomorrow would be time enough for regret. Tonight, his touch made thought incoherent. Tonight, she knew only a mindless need for him. She reached out to him.

He kneeled between her legs, his arms bracing his powerful torso above her. "Put your arms around me. Kiss me, Deirdre."

Deirdre raised her head slightly from the pillow to reach his lips. Her fingers tangled in his hair. She felt him twist and thrust above her and a burning pain seared her loins. Her cry of anguish was smothered as his mouth closed over hers. She shuddered convulsively, shrinking from him, straining against his shoulders as she tried to escape the source of her torment. Her protest went unheeded. He pressed deeper, surely, relentlessly, until he was fully sheathed in her soft woman's flesh, their bodies locked together, their hearts beating in feverish rhythm.

"Damn you!" she expelled on a shaky breath.

He kissed her with infinite tenderness, tasting the salt tears as they coursed into her hair. "No more pain," he promised as he withdrew and inch by slow inch entered her again. His movement stirred some powerful sensation in the center of Deirdre's being.

"Gareth!" she said faintly, but with so much feeling behind the word that his pulse raced out of control.

His kisses became fierce and hungry; his thrusts, an urgent demand, driving her passion higher. Deirdre felt something build within her, some wanton, mindless craving that he was deliberately fueling, that only he could answer with his driving body. He was compelling her to surrender everything to him. Her muscles tensed and every nerve grew taut against him. Her hands fell away from his neck; she shut her eyes tight and gritted her teeth. He felt her resistance and strained to delay his own release. His hands slid to her hips, lifting them to meet his need. His voice was raw and uneven. "Deirdre, don't fight me. Deirdre!"

Some final remnant of pride or self-preservation gave her the will to shut her ears to him. She had little hope that he would accept her passive refusal. Nor did he. His hand slid between their joined bodies in a voluptuous caress. At the exquisite pressure, something seemed to dissolve within her. She surged against him, crying his name. His lips sought hers fiercely, frantically. He pressed deep within her, quickening his rhythm, and wave after wave of pleasure shook her to the very core. His body tensed and he took his own shuddering release, his powerful thrusts possessing her completely. By slow degrees, the tension left him and he relaxed against her.

His weight was crushing and Deirdre shifted under him. His forehead rested lightly against hers.

"I ought to beat you," he said finally.

Deirdre tensed, but his lips descended in a warm, languid kiss. He rolled from her and pulled her onto her side, keeping her in the circle of his arm. He continued to stroke her with leisured possessiveness as if he could not believe that she was real and in his bed.

"Was it so hard to surrender yourself to me? I thought, at the last, that you meant to thwart me." His head rested on one hand and his smile was faintly mocking.

"Thwart you?" She drew the coverlet up to hide her nakedness. His smile deepened and he proceeded to draw it down to her waist.

"You fought me at the end. Why?"

Her eyes fell away from his compelling gaze. "Self-defense?" she asked lightly.

He pressed his lips against hers. "I am your defender, now. Remember it."

"But who is there to defend me against you?"

His expression became seriuos, and the hand stroking her hair stilled. "Am I not forgiven, then?"

"I'm not scratching your eyes out." Some demon compelled her to add, "Perhaps it was time I took a lover."

"No, it was time you became my wife." He bounded from the bed and in a moment was back with two crystal goblets filled with ruby red liquid. Deirdre hauled herself to a sitting position and accepted the glass he held out to her. She saw the smug smile on his face broaden into a grin.

"You look awful," he told her baldly. She stiffened and his grin widened. "Was all that paint on your face really necessary for the harlot's diguise?"

He set his goblet on the bedside table and went to the washstand. In a moment he was back with a basin of cold water and a washcloth. Deirdre submitted to his ministrations in silence, but when he moved the coverlet so that he might wash between her thighs, she grasped his wrist.

"No, please!" she said in a mortified tone.

He brushed her hand aside. "My privilege! The proof of your virginity, and my virility—you will be much more comfortable when the evidence of our . . . joining has been removed."

She looked down at her naked thighs and saw the streaks of blood and something else. She could not meet his eyes and was furious at the slow flush that suffused her cheeks. His amusement at her expense was intolerable.

He washed her in spite of her strangled protests. "My shy little innocent," he teased unmercifully.

Deirdre took a gulp of wine. "An observation that I cannot reciprocate," she said with an edge to her voice. "I, on the other hand, was tutored by an expert."

He shrugged carelessly and dried her with a towel. "You have benefited from my experience. You should be grateful."

"How so?"

Again that wicked grin creased his face, giving his features an attractive, boyish aspect. His hand reached out to lift her chin. "My gift to you was the ultimate in pleasure a woman can experience. I was not . . . happy that at the last you would try to reject my offer."

Her eyelashes flickered down to conceal her expression. "You didn't offer, you compelled, my lord, whether I would or no."

The basin and towel were laid aside with deliberation. Again he grasped her chin. "Deirdre, look at me!" he commanded.

Her eyes swept up and she could not conceal the spark of defiance that lurked in their depths.

There was a disbelieving edge to his voice. "You think you can prevent me bringing you to pleasure anytime I wish?"

"It won't happen again," she promised, stung to a reckless anger by his show of male arrogance.

His eyes were stormy. "That fiction we shall lay to rest for all time."

His hand slid between her legs, forcing them apart, and his fingers entered her easily. Deirdre jumped, spilling the wine from her goblet over her breasts, belly, and thighs. He dashed the goblet in her hand to the floor.

"You taste headier than any wine," he murmured, and his mouth began a slow descent of her body, licking and savoring the droplets of burgundy. Deirdre whimpered and tried to raise herself, but she was pushed firmly back into the pillows.

She tried to slow her breathing but it was beyond her power. Her body had a new awareness of its purpose, and responded to his lightest touch, trembling in anticipation of the next rapturous caress.

His hands kneaded her gently and she writhed. She was beyond pride. She opened to him and lifted herself to his fuller possession.

"Gareth, please!" she cried softly.

"Soon, love, soon," he promised, understanding her need perfectly.

She wanted him to fill her, to bring her the release her woman's body craved. She shook with the ache in her loins. She held her breath. Her hands clenched into fists and her head thrashed from side to side. "Ga . . . r . . . eth!" Her cry, low and keening, filled the room and he swiftly put an end to her agony with his own driving body.

They lay entwined for a long time afterward, saying nothing.

Presently, Deirdre sighed and tried to push out of his arms.

"Why so pensive?" he asked in an amused tone, but he did not release her.

"Why not?" she said, making no attempt to conceal the rancor in her tone.

He was over her in an instant, arms braced on either side of her shoulders. "You're a poor loser," he murmured, and took her lips in a slow, proprietary kiss. "Admit that I am master of your body."

Green eyes flashed fire at him. He saw her defiance and a sigh of exasperation escaped his lips.

"Don't you realize yet, Deirdre, how much power you wield over me?" He brought her hand to his arousal. "See what you do to me?" His voice held a thread of self-mockery.

His hand guided hers to touch and caress him so that she could not mistake his need.

"You cannot mean . . . you cannot want . . ."

"Oh, but I do mean and I do want," he said with gentle malice. "The other was for you. This time, you will pleasure me."

He pushed himself to a sitting position, his back hard against the headboard and drew her to kneel over him. His hands splayed out over her hips. He lowered her gently until he was completely buried inside her. "For me, Deirdre," he coaxed hoarsely, and arched her back so that her breasts were thrust out to his descending mouth.

But he lied. His pleasure had become of secondary importance. He wanted to drown her senses with the feel and taste of him so that one touch would be enough to evoke the passion they had shared. He wanted to kindle a fire in her that would never be put out.

His tongue licked round one tender nipple, and he smiled as it hardened under his caress. Deirdre tensed.

"Ride me gently, love," he said, his voice thickening, and he beat back the wave of desire that brought the blood surging to his temples. He controlled her rhythm with his hands on her

186

hips, stilling her from time to time as he felt himself losing control. He would not take his release until he had brought her to the ultimate peak.

When he heard her breath rasping, deep in her throat, he rolled her onto her back.

"No!" Her cry was a wail of protest, but at his soothing entry, she subsided.

"Until you are more used to my body . . ." but he never finished the sentence. He felt her tense beneath him, and he surged against her, burying himself deep as he took her over the edge. Her cries of pleasure filled his ears and he groaned harshly in his throat. She was his, completely and irrevocably, and he would never let her forget it.

The return to Portman Square was made in the coach Armand had procured for the evening. Rathbourne had every hope that no one would notice, in the hour just before dawn, that the gentleman who escorted Deirdre home from the night's revelries was not the one who had called for her earlier.

Deirdre did not care. She dozed, curled in his lap, murmuring unheeded protests as he plied her with warm kisses and pressed his hands on every part of her person. He whispered a lewd suggestion in her ear, his hand lifting the hem of her skirt. Deirdre slapped it away, and he laughed.

He wakened her as the coach turned into Park Street, and admonished her to tidy herself. Deirdre could scarce keep her eyes open, and allowed him to arrange her voluminous hooded wrap into a semblance of order. The ostrich feather which had adorned her coiffure was gone forever—no one knew where, and the wig itself had been thrown away by the Earl with an unmentionable comment.

As the carriage drew to a shuddering halt, Deirdre stifled a yawn and tried to focus her thoughts on what Rathbourne was saying.

"That will give you a day's grace in which to inform your relations or anyone else you care to."

"What will?" she asked stupidly.

He smiled patiently and touched one gentle finger to trace her lips, rosy and swollen from his passionate kisses. "For God's sake, don't let anyone see you like this," he said, laughter lingering in his voice. "The announcement of our betrothel—it will be in the *Gazette* and *The Times* on Friday, I think."

His words banished the vestiges of sleep from Deirdre's mind. "No!" she said quickly—too quickly. His hands tensed on her shoulders. "It isn't necessary, was all I meant," she amended, searching frantically in her mind for some plausible excuse to cover her reluctance. "I need time, Gareth, to persuade my relations to this marriage. And then there is Marcliff. I must go home to put my affairs in order. What need is there of a betrothal announcement? The news of our nuptials will be in the papers. That should suffice."

He studied her for a long, considering moment.

"Please!" She laid a hand on his sleeve. "I must go home to Henley. There is much I must see to. Surely you see that I am in the right?" In her eyes was the film of tears and faint regret as she looked steadily at him.

His kiss was gentle but his words were unyielding. "Deirdre, you are mine. Do you understand what I am saying?"

She shook her head dumbly.

"You gave me your promise. We exchanged rings." He brought her hand to his lips and gently touched them to the Rathbourne ruby and pearl betrothal ring which encircled her third finger. On his own hand was Deirdre's emerald. "We pledged our troth with our bodies. I will hold you to that pledge, come what may. Now do you understand?"

No words were necessary. She had taken his meaning and he was satisfied. He made no move to follow her as she alighted from the carriage, but he detained her with one hand on her wrist, turning her back to face him.

"Go to Henley. I shall spend a few days in Belmont. I can always find something to do there, and I'd like you to see your future home at its best. In one week, I shall join you. We might as well be married from Henley as anywhere. Don't look so crestfallen. What have we done that is so wrong? We have merely celebrated our nuptials one week in advance."

There was no answering smile and he was constrained to say in a rougher tone, "Don't be too hard on me, Deirdre. I promise you'll never have cause to regret this night."

"I don't regret it," she said in a low voice, and swiftly turned from him, running lightly to the house in a rustle of skirts.

Rathbourne leaned back against the squabs, his eyes closed, turning over in his mind the source of the irritation which gnawed at him. He didn't trust Deirdre's air of preoccupation. She was up to something! Not that it mattered a rap, of course. There was nothing she could do to deflect him from his purpose. But it angered him that she would still try to hold him at arm's length after what had passed between them. Any other woman would have been in a fever of impatience to have the banns called, but not his Deirdre! Damn her! She should be insisting that he marry her on the morrow, not fobbing him off with excuses about "persuading" her relations to the match. Good God! Didn't she know what a catch he was? They should be ecstatic! But that wouldn't weigh with Deirdre, not one jot. And he loved her for it.

"I don't regret it," she had said, and the ring of truth was in her words. A slow smile touched his lips. Let her try to deny that she wanted him, loved him, and he would use his body as the instrument to subdue her. That avenue of thought brought a rush of heat to his loins and he regretfully turned his mind to more pressing problems.

He rapped smartly on the roof of the carriage. "Bond Street, O'Toole, if you please." It was time for his interview with St. Jean. Perhaps it was as well that Deirdre would be out of town until they were wed. She would miss the fireworks when her spoiled brat of a brother learned what his new guardian had planned for his future. Rathbourne was prepared to be very patient with his bride. He would be as generous a husband as she could wish, except in one particular. He would not permit her to spend herself on a brother who cared not a fig for what straits he brought her to. The burden of Armand St. Jean was too heavy for Deirdre's slim shoulders, and belonged more properly to her husband.

He would make a man of St. Jean or break him in the attempt. That the boy should bring one more moment of unease to Deirdre was intolerable. Deirdre would not like it, but she would accept it. As her husband, he would give her no choice.

Chapter Fourteen

Deirdre shut her ears to the hum of the bustling servants as they prepared to close up the house for the duration of the Season. She sat in the breakfast room, solitary and silent, and gloomily stirred the small silver spoon in her cup of coffee, the third she had consumed that morning in lieu of breakfast. Since her aunt's departure for Brussels was imminent, Deirdre's own valises had been packed in the preceding days for the journey that was to take her home to Henley. But Henley was far from Deirdre's thoughts on this particular windy March morning as she sat quelling her impatience until her aunt should make an early appearance as was her custom.

The door of the breakfast room opened and Lady Fenton entered, pausing as she took in the droop of Deirdre's shoulders and the dark circled eyes in a face that was unusually pale. She sat down at the breakfast table in a rustle of skirts and her shrewd eyes examined Deirdre closely.

"That must have been some reception you attended last night with Armand. What time did you come home, young lady?"

"Late," said Deirdre noncommittally, and flashed her aunt a smile that was meant to divest her abrupt answer of any incivility.

Her aunt reached for the silver coffee pot and poured herself a demitasse. "Then why are you up so early? I thought you would sleep till well past noon. Your trunks, I know, have already been brought down for the trip to Henley, so why the haste?"

"I'm not going to Henley," said Deirdre firmly. "I have decided to take you up on your offer to accompany you to Brussels, if it still stands."

"Of course. But may I ask why?" Lady Fenton's eyes narrowed fractionally.

"Because I am bored and like being with you," said Deirdre, striving to keep her voice light.

The older woman heaped a generous portion of marmalade on a small, gold-rimmed side plate, spread the merest smidgen on one corner of a piece of dry toast, and nibbled daintily. After a moment, she said, "It's Rathbourne, isn't it?" At Deirdre's startled look, she went on more kindly. "Can't you confide in me, my dear? I am not blind to what is going on under my nose. What has he done now to provoke this fit of the dismals?"

"N—nothing," stammered Deirdre, and blushed to the roots of her hair.

"Nothing? But you want to run away and hide from him? I was afraid something like this might happen. I warned him not to rush his fences."

Under Deirdre's astonished gaze, Lady Fenton delicately spread another smidgen of marmalade on her dry toast. "Delicious," she said placidly as she nibbled upon it. "Try some."

"Aunt Rosemary," said Deirdre with a faint note of impatience, "how could you possibly know?"

"That he paid his addresses to you? Because he asked for my permission, as if my refusal would have made a jot of difference to a man like that." She chuckled. "And you think that by putting the English Channel between you, you can keep him at a distance? For how long?"

"It's that or the wilds of Scotland," said Deirdre desperately. Her aunt looked a question at her. "I have a friend who lives in Aberdeen. She would love to see me again. I haven't seen her since school days, although we keep in touch. She tells me that the climate there is very healthy and bracing."

"I don't doubt it. That explains why you prefer Brussels. But Deirdre, do think what you are about. A man like Rathbourne has a lot to offer and I am not talking about his title or fortune."

"What Gareth Cavanaugh has to offer, I don't want," Deirdre responded gently but very firmly, and there was no doubt that she meant what she said.

She had spent a long, sleepless night, reliving every moment of their hours together. She could not deny that he could bring her bliss, but he could also bring her anguish, and she was a fool if she thought otherwise. His ruthlessness of purpose terrified her. He had tried to relieve her of her beloved Marcliff, taken away her virginity, and now thought to rob her of her freedom of choice. Did he think they were still living in the middle ages? And these were the least of his iniquities. The consummate skill of his hands and body as he had brought her to pleasure, in retrospect, was a grim reminder that Gareth Cavanaugh was no novice as far as women were concerned. He had never tried to deny it. How many women had he taken as he had taken her last night? The thought made her stomach turn. She had told him that she didn't regret it. That was no lie. He had made a woman of her, and she could not be sorry for it, although some vestiges of conscience provoked a vague sense of guilt when she remembered how actively she had participated in her own downfall since he had brought her body alive to passion. She had reveled in his lovemaking, but it was an experience she had no wish to repeat. She would not tie herself to such a voluptuary for the rest of her life, to condemn herself to wretchedness wondering where he spent his nights and who his next conquest might be. She had watched her mother go through that hell. It was a fate she had no intention of letting overtake her. But she knew that she was already in hell—this wanting, without having; this loving . . . She balked at the direction her thoughts had taken and brought the subject ruthlessly around.

"Aunt Rosemary, I don't want Rathbourne or anyone to know that I am going with you. I know he'll find out soon enough, but I prefer to put some distance between us for as long as possible."

"You sound as if the man had threatened you."

"He has."

Deirdre's calm statement was met with shocked silence. "He's very persistent," she explained patiently.

"But as a gentleman, he must accept a lady's refusal."

"He isn't a gentleman. He is a nobleman. And what Gareth Cavanaugh wants, he takes. Don't you know that by now?" She sounded weary beyond words.

"Deirdre, has Rathbourne dared to . . ."

"No! Certainly not!" She fought back the guilty rush of color. "But there's no telling what a man like that might do. I would feel safer under Uncle Thomas's protection." Her eyes were tear bright and the hands on her coffee cup were white at the knuckles. "Aunt Rosemary, he is hounding me and I cannot bear it."

Lady Fenton rose and laid a motherly arm around Deirdre's shoulders. "I warned him how it would be," she said soothingly. "The beast! The unmitigated impertinence of the man, to frighten you like this. I've no doubt there's a lot more you're not telling me. Of course you may come with me to Brussels. We'll find a way to throw him off the scent, if we put our heads together. And if he dares show his face, he'll have your uncle to contend with, not a defenseless slip of a girl and an old woman."

By the time the ladies had disposed of their meager breakfast and decided on a course of action, Deirdre's spirits had risen a trifle. She was, however, anxious to see her brother and made her excuses to her aunt, having sent for a hackney by one of the footmen. She had hardly stepped out of the house when she spotted O'Toole, Rathbourne's groom. He was on foot and lounging against the railing at the far side of the Square in conversation with some vendor or other. Deirdre's lips tightened. So that was how the Earl knew of her every movement! He had set spies on her. It was just as she had suspected.

When she was dropped at Armand's door, she lingered in conversation with the hackney driver and it was not long before, out of the corner of her eye, she caught sight of O'Toole. He was mounted on a glossy bay gelding. And to think she had liked him! With a flounce of her skirts, Deirdre entered her brother's lodgings. She found him in the bedroom engaged in packing a large valise and one leather grip which lay open on the bed. She had barely crossed the threshold when he rounded on her.

"Dee, how could you?" he accused fiercely.

"How could I what?" she parried, momentarily taken off guard and blanching at the thought that Armand had divined what had transpired between Rathbourne and herself the previous evening. His next words reassured her.

"Marry him, of all people! Stop gaping at me. I know it's true. He was here just before dawn, hauling me out of bed to inform me of the happy event." He jammed some neckcloths into the leather grip, unmindful of the wrinkles his rough handling produced. They were crushed beyond redemption, but Armand was past caring for such trivia. "That man, and my own sister!" he bit out, his jaw clenching with helpless rage.

"I'm not going to marry him, calm down!" Deirdre said quietly, and moved to stand beside him. "What are you doing?"

"Packing. What do you mean you're not going to marry him? He informed me that I was to have the privilege of giving you away at Henley before our removal to his estate at Belmont."

"I can see that you are packing, but where are you off to?"

"For God's sake, Dee, tell me what happened last night after

195

I was drugged into oblivion."

"I thought it was something like that. But how could you, Armand? To leave me . . . alone, and with *him!*"

His neck flushed scarlet and he rubbed it with one hand. "Dee, you must understand . . . when Maria said she had something she wished to say to me in private, and that it would take only a minute, I could see no harm in it. Besides," he went on defensively, "I could tell that Rathbourne had recognized you and that he was annoyed to see you in such a place. I thought you would be safe with him watching over you."

"Safe? With Rathbourne?"

"I've seen the way he looks at you! I thought, I *knew*, for the few minutes I'd be gone, that no one would get near you with him as your watchdog. Good God, his eyes flash warnings at me sometimes, and I'm your brother."

"Armand, his eyes flash warnings at anyone who gets in his way."

"He ripped up at me something awful for taking you to such a den. In this instance, he had the right of it. Dee, I'm sorry, truly. I should have known better."

"You were not to blame, Armand. I was the one who insisted."

"Nevertheless, Rathbourne . . ."

"He has no right to interfere," she interrupted, suddenly incensed that Armand had been taken to task by the Earl. "Rathbourne takes too much upon himself. If it weren't for him, everything would have worked out fine."

"Then what went wrong?"

Deirdre chose her words with care. It would be fatal for Armand to suspect the truth. "Need you ask? Rathbourne beat me at cards and I owe him a considerable sum, which, of course, I cannot pay. He suggested that in lieu of payment, he would accept me as his wife. Generous, isn't he?" she concluded dryly.

Armand sat down at the edge of the bed and raked both hands through his disheveled hair. "I don't understand. Why would he go to such trouble? Why not simply ask you?"

"He did, and I refused him. You need not look so surprised."

He recovered himself quickly. "I'm not. It's only that . . . well, you remember, from the moment I first saw you together, I wondered, and you insisted that you didn't care a button for the man, but later . . ."

"Armand, please! I don't want to go into all that."

Something in her voice warned him not to pursue that particular avenue of reasoning, so that after a moment, he asked in a matter-of-fact tone, "How will you pay off the debt?"

Deirdre turned and took a few steps to the window to steady herself. Bond Street was choked with pedestrians and coaches of every description. She spotted O'Toole lounging in the door of a draper's shop. She didn't think much of Rathbourne's spying methods, or any of his methods, come to think of it.

"I have no intention of paying. He cheated! The cards were marked! Can you imagine? That's why Mrs. Dewinters distracted your attention. It was all a ploy so that he might play on my inexperience."

"Bitch!" he growled, then patiently pursuing the thread of her story, "But if Rathbourne has your vowels . . ."

"He doesn't have my vowels. I didn't sign anything."

"That doesn't sound like Rathbourne." He was watching her intently.

She managed a convincing laugh. "Put it down to overconfidence. I am merely a female. He doesn't expect me to fight back. How little he knows me!"

"What do you intend to do?"

"I told you I won't marry him. I am running off to Brussels with Aunt Rosemary. If necessary, I shall throw myself on Uncle Thomas's protection. Now will you tell me why you are packing?"

Armand put his head between his hands. "God! What a coil we are in. He wants *you* for his wife, and *me* for his ward. I think he must be mad."

"His ward?" She looked at him blankly, then sudden

197

comprehension jolted her. "Do you say that Rathbourne is your guardian?" She sat down as if she had been struck.

"Ironic, isn't it?"

"How? Why?" Deirdre asked, trying to bring her spinning thoughts into some semblance of order. The sudden conviction that Rathbourne would always be one step ahead assailed her. She tried to shake it off, but as she listened to Armand, the conviction grew stronger.

"Why is he doing this? Isn't that obvious now? To keep you in line. If he puts the thumb screws on me, he knows that you will be the one to suffer. How did he manage it? Bribery, I suppose. It's no secret that all the St. Jeans have pockets to let. I don't doubt that Uncle Giles, damn him to hell, is now lording it over his neighbors with some bit of blood whose mouth he'll ruin in less than a fortnight. It's all legal, though not above board, and there's not a damn thing I can do about it."

"There must be. We just haven't thought of it yet. I'm not going to escape his clutches so that you can fall into them. Get me a sherry, will you, Armand? That or something stronger. I feel the need of a lift."

She was not about to run off and leave her brother to Rathbourne's tender mercies. In just under six months, Armand would reach his majority, then Rathbourne couldn't touch him. No one could. She sipped her sherry. If she weren't so frightened she might be flattered at his tenacity in pursuing her. But she was frightened, terribly frightened. Why couldn't he leave her alone?

Tired. She was so tired. And nothing had gone right since he had come back into her life. She shut her eyes and tried to concentrate. Think. Rathbourne had found the one weapon that could really hurt her—her love for Armand. She did not doubt for one moment that he would use it to compel her obedience.

"Armand, if what you say is true, that Rathbourne intends to use you to force me to fall in with his wishes, then we have no choice. You must stay out of his reach until he either forgets about you or you reach your majority."

"Easier said than done, Dee. He has set one of his watchdogs to guard me—discreetly, of course—and tomorrow morning we make for Belmont. I shouldn't think I'd have much chance of evading him once he gets me into his own neck of the woods."

"I'm surprised you let yourself be bullied by him. It isn't like you, Armand."

"There was no alternative. He gave me to understand that if I failed him, you would suffer the consequences."

It was some time before she could frame a reply. She was more upset than she wished Armand to know. Anger and fear had been displaced by a new emotion. She was deeply hurt to think that the man whom she was beginning to suspect she was half in love with could be so callously indifferent to the anguish and terror he was putting her through. She had no doubt that Rathbourne's threats were never idle.

"He hasn't won yet," she said in a rush of confidence that had its basis in hope rather than conviction. "I am not going to marry him, and you are not going to become his ward."

Armand's reply mirrored his skepticism. "What's to be done? He'll only find me and bring me back. He has the resources to do it."

"You are coming with me, to Brussels. It won't be so easy for him *there* to have everything his own way, and if he makes a move against us, well, we'll cross that bridge when we come to it."

"He isn't about to let us slip through his fingers at this date. We'll never pull it off."

"Perhaps not, but we must at least make the attempt." She drained her sherry glass and set it aside. "He thinks that we are not up to his weight. He may be right. But I don't intend to make it easy for him. What do you say, Armand?"

His grin was infectious. "I say that Rathbourne has met his match in you. I'm game if you are, sis. What have we got to lose?"

199

Later that afternoon, Rathbourne's agent, stationed outside the Fenton House in Portman Square, observed a hired chaise pull up at the front entrance. An affecting scene followed as a young woman whom he thought to be Deirdre took a tearful farewell of her aunt. Her brother Armand, wearing a frock coat of the finest blue superfine over an unusual striped blue and gold waistcoat, was also in attendance. He helped the driver of the chaise stash several bandboxes and one heavy valise. As soon as the coach pulled out of Portman Square, Armand and Lady Fenton entered the house. Rathbourne's agent then moved toward the mews to collect his mount. Within half an hour, having followed Deirdre's chaise for several miles, he ascertained that its probable destination was Henley, and he turned aside.

A second agent remained at his post. His quarry was St. Jean. He watched with narrowed eyes as a sedan approached. Armand descended the stairs, his face obscured as he lowered his head to don a curly-brimmed beaver. The blue superfine and striped waistcoat, however, remained unmistakable. He entered the sedan and was conveyed to his lodgings in Bond Street, Rathbourne's agent following at a discreet distance.

When the Fenton coach arrived to convey her ladyship and her abigail to Dover to catch the last packet that evening for Ostend, there was no one to observe the footman whose straight carriage and spritely gait belied his silver locks. He took his place on the box beside her ladyship's coachman and almost at once the six bay geldings harnessed to the coach made for the Dover road at a frantic pace, with outriders front and rear. Inside the coach, Deirdre and her aunt conversed in terse comments, betraying all the strain they felt at the precariousness of their situation.

"We've done it," said Lady Fenton triumphantly.

Deirdre was less assured. She rapped on the roof of the coach. "Armand, is anyone following?" she shouted. His negative reply was barely heard above the thundering hoofbeats of the galloping horses.

Almost at the precise moment that the Fenton coach rumbled into Dover, in Rathbourne House on Piccadilly, Lord Rathbourne was entertaining a former colleague who was attached to the War Office. The tidings that he received were as disquieting as they were urgent.

"Napoleon has escaped from Elba," repeated Smythe-Jones tersely. "The news will be all over London by tomorrow. I've come expressly to ask for your help."

Rathbourne whistled softly and uttered a soft imprecation. "The Devil he has!" After a moment's consideration, he went on as if speaking to himself, "It could not have come at a worse time."

Smythe-Jones grimly agreed. "How true! Our crack units are still in the Americas. We've secured peace on one front, only to have hostilities begin in another." He noted the Earl's questioning look, and said by way of explanation, "Hadn't you heard? The war with America is officially over. Still, it will take some time to bring our men home, and there are thousands of veterans like yourself who have taken up their former lives in England. No, it could not have come at a worse time, I agree."

"That's not what I meant," interrupted Rathbourne, and paced to one of the long windows which looked out on Green Park. Buffets of wind shook the trees, and he idly noted that the weather was blustery and typical for March. "I have a personal life, you know," he went on after an interval. "You've come at a critical time. In another week or two . . ." His voice trailed off as he became immersed in private reflections.

Smythe-Jones shifted uncomfortably but said nothing. The Earl had always been something of an enigma to him. They had never been on intimate terms, despite their long association. But of one thing he was certain. Rathbourne knew his duty.

"Where is Wellington?" asked the Earl at last.

"In Vienna for the moment, but he'll soon be making for Brussels. Our armies are amassing in Flanders."

"I see."

"It might come to nothing, you know," said Smythe-Jones hopefully.

Rathbourne's emphatic words were touched with derision. "I don't believe that and neither do you."

The Earl was restless. Smythe-Jones watched him with a puzzled frown as he paced the length of the library like a caged tiger. The older man cleared his throat and resumed the conversation where it had left off.

"Napoleon, I suppose, has a certain charisma, if that's what you're getting at. Our commander agrees with you. Wellington expects that the French will flock to his standard in droves."

"And you want me to find out who and where Boney's elusive friends are?" The question was rhetorical, and faintly cynical. Smythe-Jones did not dignify it with an answer.

"Where is he now?" asked Rathbourne, coming finally to a standstill. One hip edged onto the desk and he folded his arms across his chest. The relaxed stance made Smythe-Jones feel only marginally more comfortable.

"Last we heard he had landed in France, in the Golfe Juan, with a handful of men."

"In a month, they will number in the thousands, in two months, a hundred thousand."

"What of Marshalls Ney and Soult? Will they remain loyal to the French king, d'you think?"

"I wouldn't count on it," said Rathbourne. "What is Louis to them? They served their former master for fifteen years. Napoleon Bonaparte will always have their first loyalty."

"Perhaps not. It's early days yet for that sort of prediction."

"Have it your own way. I need two days in which to set my affairs in order. In three, I can be in Brussels. Let it be known that I have been asked to rejoin my regiment. Who will command our cavalry?"

"Wellington has asked for Combermere, but he'll get Uxbridge. I suppose the Iron Duke is still smarting about the scandal with Uxbridge and his sister-in-law."

"I doubt if that would influence Wellington. Both men are

first rate, but I won't be sorry to serve under Uxbridge."

"You've served with him in Spain, of course, with the Seventh? Officially you will be Major Lord Rathbourne and one of Uxbridge's aides-de-camp."

"Thank you. I'm familiar with the set-up."

Within minutes of Smythe-Jones taking his leave, Rathbourne was issuing orders for his carriage and a team of his fastest horses to be readied by first light to make the dash to Henley so that Deirdre might be escorted back to London. He calmly informed his mother and sister that they were to prepare themselves for his marriage, which was to take place in twenty-four hours at Rathbourne House.

He then closeted himself in his study with Guy Landron, arranging his business affairs as befitted a man on the eve of his marriage and he a soldier with battles before him. Deirdre's future security was well provided for under the terms of his new will.

"It will be strange not having you with me on this assignment," Rathbourne remarked at the conclusion of their business, "but I want you here with Deirdre, looking after things."

"She may wish to go with you to Brussels, you know. There's no real danger yet. It will be some time before our old enemy is in a position to make things uncomfortable for us on the continent."

Rathbourne looked to be slightly discomfited. "I shall insist that she remains in England."

Landron grinned. "I can see how you wouldn't want your bride hovering over your shoulder when much of your information comes from the loose tongues of wives and daughters of suspected traitors."

"She might form the wrong impression," agreed Rathbourne readily with an answering grin.

After a restless night, he rose at dawn and set about arranging for his journey and for those who were to accompany him. The air of leashed excitement about Rathbourne House and stables was almost tangible. Bonaparte's escape from Elba was on the tongue of every man, woman, and child in London. When Rathbourne arrived at Mrs. Dewinters's house in Chelsea, she greeted him as if she expected him.

"It will be like old times," she said rather wistfully as her watchful eyes swept over Rathbourne's magnificent set of shoulders.

"Then you will come?"

"Did you doubt it?" she asked with a hint of surprise in her husky voice.

"You're a good agent, Maria," he said in a kindly tone, which had the desired effect of deflating any hopes she might have entertained.

She forced her voice to a convincing lightness. "Much as I admire you, Gareth, my involvement in this fight is a personal one. You know what happened to my family in Spain. I shall never forget it, nor ever want to."

"A personal vendetta then?"

"You need not sound so superior. What about your own motives? Are they so disinterested? I've often wondered what led you into this line of work."

"A vested interest. I have an aversion to the grandiose schemes of a little man who would make himself Emperor of Europe. Today France, tomorrow England. But then, you are part French, Maria. I do not expect you to see things in the same light as I."

"And that makes you suspect? You forget that my husband was Spanish, as was my son." Some memory twisted inside her and she averted her head. Knowing that she would scorn a facile sympathy, Rathbourne picked up his gloves and made as if to leave.

"What about Deirdre?" she asked quietly as he reached the door. "What will she think?"

He turned back and his gaze was very steady as he regarded her. "Not a breath of scandal must touch her; nothing from the past and certainly not a suggestion of the roles you and I will be constrained to play in the next month or so till this is over."

"I understand," she said softly, and tried, without success, to conceal the pain his words had given.

When the Earl entered Rathbourne House, he sensed that some calamity had befallen him by the chill of his mother's smile as he met her on the stairs, but short of telling him that his groom, O'Toole, awaited him in his study, she gave no hint of what the smile might portend.

Guy Landron approached the study as O'Toole was leaving and heard the groom's vehement imprecation, "Damn and blast all women to hell, the deceitful bitches! And to think I liked her!"

Landron opened the study door cautiously and paused on the threshold, thoughtfully regarding his friend's rigid back as he stood in his familiar pose at the window. He entered and shut the door softly.

"Gareth, what happened?" he asked, trying to erase from his voice the concern he felt at the unexpected turn of events.

"She tricked me royally!" Rathbourne said without emotion, then with a bitter laugh, "and to think His Majesty's government relies on my intelligence networks. God! What a fool she made of me!"

"Where is she?"

"On her way to some godforsaken place in Scotland, so Lady Fenton's abigail told O'Toole. It was she who took the chaise to Henley."

"What about St. Jean? Doesn't he know anything?"

"He can't be found. I don't doubt that he bolted with Deirdre to Scotland."

"What are you going to do?"

"What can I do? Nothing!" Then with more vehemence, "I hope I never set eyes on her again!"

The silence stretched uncomfortably. Rathbourne's face was a mask of impassivity when he finally turned to face his friend. "Destroy the will I made, Guy."

"Of course."

"But add a codicil to the original to the effect that if Deirdre . . ." He faltered, turned back to the window, and spoke over his shoulder. "If Deirdre should be delivered of a child within the next twelvemonth or so, I want everything that is not entailed to be settled on my son or daughter."

There was a shocked silence. When Landron finally found his voice, it was harsh with anger. "What the hell did you do to her, Gareth?"

The words unleashed all the pent-up fury that Rathbourne had been laboring under. Two strides brought him to stand before Landron. His face was contorted with passion, his eyes glittered like coals of fire. "I didn't do a damn thing to her that she didn't want me to do, although why I should be telling you is beyond me. You're not my confessor! And what you left out in your dossier on Deirdre Fenton was that that damned bitch has no heart at all. She doesn't know how to love. *Can't* love. It is an emotion that is beyond her ken." He struggled to gain command of himself and finally managed to say in more reasonable tones, "Now write that codicil to my will and don't ever again ask me to answer for my actions in regard to Deirdre Fenton."

Landron's face registered all the shock he felt at this outburst. The words, the tormented expression, the passion were so forcibly reminiscent of another night—the eve of their departure for Spain five years before. He had not known Deirdre then, though.

"The girl cares for you. I know it," he said with quiet assurance.

Rathbourne's answer was to sweep the decanters and glasses on the nearby side table to the floor with a vicious swing of one arm. Crystal shattered and the carpet drank up the blood red wines and liqueurs. He stood looking down at the senseless destruction, then drew a tired hand over his eyes. "Let it be, Guy. I don't want to talk about it anymore. She's gone, out of reach again. Last time it was Jamaica; this time it's Scotland. I haven't the time to pursue her, nor do I have the inclination. At the moment, my destiny lies in Europe."

Landron looked as if he was trying to frame the words that might comfort his friend. Finally, he said, "I'll join you in Brussels as soon as I may."

"What? Of course. There's no reason why you cannot come with me now. That's one consolation."

Rathbourne fell silent, and Landron withdrew with the softly spoken comment that he would have the will ready for signing by first light.

Outside, the shadows lengthened. At the front entrance, footmen standing on precarious ladders were attempting to light the lanterns at each house. Rathbourne looked out blindly, a sudden moistness blurring his vision. A wave of longing, like the blaze of a smelting furnace, surged through him. He smothered it ruthlessly.

He had gambled and lost. Ironic that the game hadn't been worth the candle, but he had not had the sense to recognize it. He knew it now, but it did not lessen the sense of loss. It seemed that the pain of wanting had been a constant throughout his life. Anything he had ever truly coveted, he had forfeited. Better never to want at all.

He thought of Andrew for the first time in many months. Andrew, his younger brother by two years and the apple of his mother's eye. He had never been forgiven for being the one to come back from that climbing holiday. He was not certain that he had forgiven himself. Andrew—blythe, impetuous, fool-hardy, and at sixteen on the threshold of manhood. What a waste—not of one life, but two.

At the time of the accident, he had long since become inured to his mother's indifference. Perhaps he had always been a rather solitary and difficult child, as he was accustomed to hearing. But his protective shell had developed a crack at the stream of abuse she had shrilled at him on the very day of Andrew's funeral. She was distraught, of course. But after that, there could never be a reconciliation between mother and son. And with a vengeance, he had set himself to live up to every scurrilous condemnation of his character, every damning prophecy for his future that she had flung at him. His subsequent notoriety was as predictable as it was deserved. It had brought him a kind of satisfaction until he had wearied of the game; wearied of everything; wearied of himself.

Andrew . . . his mother . . . Deirdre . . . Could she be with child? The possibility was there, although admittedly rather faint. But she had taken out of his hands the power to give his name to any issue that might result from their union. This final rejection was the greatest wound of all. No other woman would have conducted herself with such disregard for the consequences of their night of lovemaking. Damn her! He would never forgive her. Never!

He was at breakfast next morning when an envelope bearing the single word "Rathbourne" was brought to him. The script was not particularly feminine, nor was there even a hint of scent about the small packet. But intuitively, he knew that it was from her. He excused himself abruptly and removed to the privacy of his dressing room. When he tore open the seal, a small ruby and pearl ring rolled into the palm of his hand. The message on the single enclosed sheet was terse and to the point.

My gaming debt, I consider paid in full. Your investment in Marcliff will be repaid with interest after a twelve-month, as arranged with Mr. Landron. Don't try to find me.

Deirdre Fenton

In the back room of a dingy tavern in a rundown street in Soho, two men sat at a small table spread with a filthy rag of a cloth of indeterminate color while another, a huge bear of a man in workman's rough clothing, stood guard at the door. The steady tramp of boots ascending and descending the stairs to the girls' rooms overhead gave evidence that the tavern served more than one purpose.

"He's already in Brussels, as I understand," said one of the men at the table, and he stowed a wad of banknotes in the pocket of his ornate coat. His companion bent a long, contemptuous look at the fop's extravagant attire. The dandy was aware of that look but ignored it and said easily, "I should prefer if the deed were done as soon as possible."

"What's your hurry, *mon ami?*" The question was asked gently, but there was no doubt that the man who asked it wanted an answer.

"No hurry," said the dandy. "I know from experience that our quarry is elusive, nothing more."

"Ah, I think I understand." There was a moment's silence as the two men gave each other an appraising look. "You want us to succeed where you have failed?"

The dandy got to his feet and reached for his greatcoat. He threw it negligently over his shoulders. His expression was faintly haughty, but he said nothing.

His companion slanted a look at him, and smiled, but there was no humor in the look he bent on the man who had betrayed the identity of the English agent who had bedeviled his compatriots for close on five years. He detested traitors of any description. "You must contain your impatience, *monsieur*. These things take time. He may lead us to others."

"Have it your own way. But my advice to you is not to underestimate him. He's as slippery as an eel. There's no telling what damage he may do if you let him slip through your fingers."

"Your devotion to our cause is most gratifying."

The dandy smiled, and there was a glint of genuine amusement in his eyes. "Don't patronize me, old boy. Lost causes have never been in my line. Don't get me wrong. I admire your Napoleon. His victories, before Elba, were stunning. But then, he's never had a match against Wellington, has he?"

The man at the table made a gallic gesture, shoulders

haunched over and arms upraised. "My apologies," he intoned with soft sarcasm. "How could I know that you were a military man? You have served under Wellington perhaps?"

"That would be telling," replied the gentleman non-committally.

"Or is this a personal vendetta?" persisted the other.

"What do you care? Not only have I given you the name of the man who is your most bitter enemy, a man who does believe in causes, I take leave to tell you, but I've also supplied enough evidence to convict him of that charge before any French tribunal. I think it better if we leave motive and such like out of this. Don't you?"

When he had taken a courteous if sardonic leave of his hostile companions, the one at the door swore softly. "*Cochon!*" he said under his breath. "Do you wish me to go after him and slit his throat in some dark alley?"

"Let him go," was the thoughtful rejoinder. "That one takes no chances. And he's right. Ours is not to reason why."

"You trust him?"

"*Mon dieu!* Trust that slime? *Jamais!* But his information is genuine. It's been gone over with a fine-tooth comb by our own agents." He went to the window and looked out, but in the gathering gloom, there was little to be seen. He turned back into the room and said wearily, "I don't doubt that our enemy uses the same methods we do. God, I feel filthy after treating with scum like that."

"You feel sorry for the man he betrayed?" There was a note of surprise in the big man's voice.

"Sorry? No, I can't be sorry. We're all soldiers. Like the rest of us, he must take his chances. But it makes me sick to see a pig like that topple a man whose boot laces he's not fit to tie. Now let's get out of here before we're rumbled."

In the closed carriage, the dandy carefully removed the wig and makeup which disguised his identity. As the hackney rolled into Mayfair, he tapped with his cane on the roof of the cab. It took him only a moment to divest himself of the dandy's

attire which concealed his own immaculate dark coat patterned
after the style of that arbiter of masculine fashion, Mr. George
Brummel. He stowed his disguise under the coach seat and
drew his great coat over his shoulders. When he had paid off
the hackney driver, he made his way along Picadilly to St.
James Street. He had money in his pocket and he felt lucky.
When he thought of Rathbourne, there was no regret to rob
him of his pleasure.

Chapter Fifteen

Spring came early to Brussels in that year of our Lord 1815. The creeping scent of violets, sweet and heavy, hung in the air, and the gardens and parks displayed the small purple flowers in splendid profusion. The capital teemed with people, and most of the visitors, as was to be expected, were English sojourners who had flocked to the comparative security of the city behind British lines when the news of Napoleon's escape from Elba became general. Scarcely a house was to be had since the citizens were compelled to quarter the staff of the combined allied forces and their large contingent of auxiliaries. No Bruxellois was exempt from this edict, even the members of the Belgian aristocracy had to turn over large parts of their grand houses and châteaux for the use of the defending armies. No one complained, for to do so would have been considered unpatriotic, and in a city rife with rumors of traitors and spies, and where many Bruxellois had formerly fought for Napoleon, to have one's loyalty called into question was a hazard that few were prepared to chance.

As a result of the scarcity of private accomodations, many visitors were forced to put up at the hotels. The Fenton ladies were at first dismayed when Sir Thomas informed them that the only lodgings he had been able to secure were rooms in the Hotel d'Angleterre in the Rue de la Madeleine, but it did not take them long to perceive the advantages of such a situation. Their apartments were spacious and comfortable, but more to the point, they found themselves in the hub of things. The public rooms and corridors were brilliant with a plethora of uniforms, and many of Wellington's officers were domiciled at the d'Angleterre, and there were more members of the ton in residence in the hotels of Brussels than were to be found in London—and this at the height of the Season. The atmosphere was gay to the point of being frenetic, and the threat of Napoleon at their doorstep, perversely, seemed only to add to the general air of excitement.

More visitors arrived daily, as if attracted like magnets to the irresistible pull of the momentous drama that had begun to unfold; two of the greatest generals the world had ever spawned, Wellington and Napoleon, were about to square off in a battle that would change the face and history of Europe forever. In years to come, to have been even on the periphery of this fateful occasion would be more than a thrilling bedtime story to tell one's grandchildren. Brussels had suddenly become the center of the universe. To be there at the critical moment was to grasp at one's share in destiny. There were few who elected to make for home and safety, and many more who arrived to swell the ranks of the general populace.

Deirdre soon found that her days in Brussels followed a similar pattern to her days in London. There were carriage rides in the park, and morning calls to make and receive with families which had the approval of Lady Fenton. Invitations to parties and balls began to arrive, and there were the obligatory shopping expeditions to while away any spare hours that were left over from a full calendar of engagements.

There were, however, important dissimilarities which she found entirely to her liking. Modes and manners were far more relaxed in Brussels than were to be found in England, and the circle of her acquaintances as a consequence became much less exclusive than formerly. It could not be otherwise for it was impossible not to strike up a casual conversation with strangers in the situation in which they found themselves, and to exclude from one's society a young man who might soon be called on to make the supreme sacrifice for King and Country merely because one did not know his father seemed the cruelest kind of snobbery.

As March slipped into April, Deirdre threw herself into every amusement that was offered, and there were many. This excess of frivolity had the desired effect of bringing her to the point of exhaustion every night so that when she crawled between the sheets of her solitary bed, she fell asleep almost as soon as her head touched the pillow. Her dreams, however, were not susceptible to the will of iron that governed her thoughts in the daylight hours, and she was subjected to the most distressing fantasies of the one man in the world whom she was determined to banish from her life.

Dismay quickly followed upon distress when, on several occasions, she thought she caught sight of Rathbourne in the distance or someone who looked very like him. The first time she saw him, he was on horseback, in the blue and silver regimentals of an office of the 7th Hussars, and he was riding in the park with no less a personage than the Duke of Wellington. She thought she saw him again, shortly thereafter, in the Hotel d'Angleterre foyer, although she could not be sure that it was he. She had just turned the corner of the stairs and had paused on the half landing when she remarked a pair of broad masculine shoulders that looked very familiar. He was at the front desk in conversation with one of the clerks, but there was a press of people which made it impossible for her to get a clear look at him. She had almost decided to turn and flee to her room for safety when the hotel clerk looked up and caught sight of her. Within moments, the man who resembled Rathbourne strolled out the front door and down the steps. He was not in regimentals.

On applying to the desk clerk for the identity of the stranger, she learned that the gentleman was a certain Mr. Dennison who was making inquiries about his brother from whom he had become separated when they entered the city. Deirdre was somewhat reassured, although a little shaken, and chided herself for a fanciful disposition which had been a troublesome affliction since childhood.

Nevertheless, as the weeks progressed, she could not shake herself of the conviction that Rathbourne was in Brussels. She half fancied that she was being watched when she rode in the park or waltzed under the blaze of candles in the ballrooms of those fortunate enough to be domiciled in private homes. When she confided her suspicions to Armand, he laughed them off and half convinced her that she was suffering from a mild case of dementia, which was not to be wondered at considering what she had been through in the last weeks. Furthermore, he pointed out, if Rathbourne were in Brussels, an unlikely event since Lady Caro was in the throes of her first Season in London, he would lose no time in rejoining his regiment, and with events as they were and the future unpredictable, there could be little time in a soldier's life to pursue matters of a purely personal nature.

Deirdre saw the sense of what Armand said and she tried to quell her fears, but she warned her brother to be on his guard. He agreed so readily and with such negligence that Deirdre was left in no doubt that he completely discounted the Earl as a threat. It troubled her, not least because Armand had distanced himself from her in the weeks they had been in Brussels. He had fallen in with a group of young men who, so she thought, led a rather rakety existence, following the pattern he had established in town. It had not taken Armand long to discover that the gaming houses in Brussels, no less that in London, could be a lucrative source of income for a young man who was compelled to earn his living by his wits. When he moved out of the Hotel d'Angleterre to share lodgings with a Mr. Stonehouse, a likeable young man but of a similar bent, Deirdre's misery was complete.

She was alone in the hotel lobby mulling over how she might bring her scapegrace brother to a sense of his iniquity when the rumble of carriage wheels at the hotel entrance caught her ear. There was a slamming of doors and shouts of good-natured masculine laughter from several voices. The hotel lobby was almost empty of hotel guests, and Deirdre, who had been sitting idly and feeling rather conspicuous in a leather armchair against one wall as she waited for her aunt to descend so that they might set off on a shopping expedition, shrank back and reached for the first periodical that came to hand, pretending to read it assiduously.

A wave of young men surged into the hotel, some in colorful regimentals, others in the height of fashion. They proceeded to the hotel desk where they demanded loudly, though in pleasant enough tones, that they be shown to the rooms which had been bespoken for Lord Uxbridge. At the familiar name, Deirdre chanced a quick look over the top of her paper. Her breath caught in her throat and her cheeks colored hotly then blanched to match her white muslin walking dress. *He* was there—unmistakably and indubitably—the Earl of Rathbourne. She did not think that he had recognized her and she had the presence of mind to turn her back upon the group of noisy arrivals. Not for the world would she hazard a second glance in his direction. She waited with baited breath until the din of their departure receded up the stairs. One shaking hand went to her temples and she expelled the breath she had been unconsciously holding.

The low, familiar voice at her back made her start to her feet, and the periodical fell from her nerveless fingers. My Lord Rathbourne bent to pick it up.

"I did not know that you were conversant in German," he said mildly.

"What?" Deirdre could scarcely take in the misfortune that had befallen her.

An amused smile touched his lips. "This newspaper is in German," he explained patiently, "and I remarked that . . ."

"Yes! I know what you said. It's a language that I hope to master," she ended feebly.

They stood lost in thought, staring at each other for a long, protracted moment, then Rathbourne made as if to speak, but a voice from halfway up the stairs rudely interrupted him and wakened Deirdre from her reverie.

"Rathbourne. There you are! I wondered where you had run off to. Oh, I say, am I interrupting something?"

The stranger who came to stand beside Rathbourne was of a slighter build, and Deirdre judged him to be younger, but only by a year or two. His face was pleasant rather than handsome, but his eyes, quite his best feature, were a startling shade of blue and Deirdre admired their directness and the lively intelligence she observed in their depths. He was garbed in the scarlet and gold regimentals of a British staff officer and Deirdre correctly supposed him to be one of the aides assigned to Lord Uxbridge. A lock of fairish hair fell over his forehead. He pushed it back carelessly, and regarded Deirdre with a steady though somewhat speculative expression.

"Gareth?" he prompted, and smiled disarmingly at Deirdre.

"Miss Fenton, permit me to present Captain Roderick Ogilvie of the Horse Guards," drawled Rathbourne with a discouraging glance in his friend's direction.

Captain Ogilvie raised one quizzical brow at Rathbourne's speaking look, but made no comment other than to intone politely that he was charmed to make the lady's acquaintance.

"Did I hear correctly?" asked Deirdre after an awkward pause. "Does Lord Uxbridge take up lodgings here? I had supposed, since he is second only to Wellington, that he would be quartered in more stately and private apartments."

"You supposed correctly," said Ogilvie. "Our commander arrived in Brussels yesterday and was most suitably settled in a private house, but when he heard that the Belgian Marquis and Marquise who owned it had been forced to remove to the upper floors so that he might be comfortable, he elected to seek accommodations in one of the hotels."

"And selected the d'Angleterre by chance?" Deirdre asked, flicking a quick glance at the silent Earl.

"Quite!" interposed Rathbourne adroitly.

"But Rathbourne, didn't you advise . . ." began the captain unwisely.

Rathbourne cut him off politely but firmly. "Captain Ogilvie, would you be so kind as to tell the others that I shall be along directly? They must be wondering at the delay."

"Are you pulling rank on me, Major?" asked Ogilvie quizzically.

Rathbourne smiled. "What do you think, Captain?"

"What I think is that next time I chance to meet Miss Fenton, I shall ensure that there are no superior officers in sight to give me my marching orders. Ma'am." He sketched a bow, gave her a regretful smile, and left them alone.

"Sit down, Deirdre." Her look became mutinous and Rathbourne said more firmly, "I said sit down."

She obediently sat down and said in a rather offhand manner, "I wasn't mistaken then. It was you I saw about town these many weeks past, and in the hotel foyer and so on?"

"And I thought I had been the soul of discretion," he responded easily. "I have been in Brussels only intermittently. No, don't make conversation. What I have to say won't take long. It's only this. You have made your sentiments perfectly plain to me. Don't be alarmed. I have not pursued you here, if that is what you are thinking. I am here to rejoin my regiment. You won't be troubled again with a renewal of offers which are obviously repugnant to you. I tell you this because we are bound to fall in each other's way in the next month or so, and I don't wish our chance encounters to become a source of embarrassment for either of us. As for our betrothal, I told only a few intimates of it and their discretion may be relied upon. It was fortunate that you forbade the publishing of the banns. I suppose I should thank you for it. But I presume that *that* act of premeditation was to save yourself from becoming an object of ridicule rather that with any thought for the figure I might cut amongst my friends and associates."

His tone had gradually become rougher and she interrupted

miserably, "Gareth, please! People are staring."

"Then walk with me." She looked at him uncertainly and he went on in a more controlled tone, "I have no objection to saying what I have to say to you before an audience if that is what you wish."

She colored slightly and obediently laid her gloved hand upon his arm and allowed him to lead her into the street. He resumed the conversation almost immediately.

"I make no apologies for making love to you. You wanted me to and I obliged you."

"You obliged me?" she asked, her voice threaded with incredulity.

"Certainly. Your resistance was token and we both know it. What I regret is that you chose *me* to make a woman of you. You used me as a man uses a woman of the street. You took your pleasure, then discarded me."

"I see," said Deirdre frigidly. "Then it is I who should be apologizing to you?"

"I accept your apology."

"You accept my—"

"However," he went on, ignoring Deirdre's frozen expression, "you did me a favor, albeit unconsciously. You cured me of an infatuation that has been the bane of my existence since I first set eyes on you. You look surprised, but I assure you, it is true. I have imagined myself in love with you for a very long time now. It had become almost a habit. But thankfully I am broken of it. You are not the woman for me. A man wants more than passion in a wife." His tone remained pleasant although his words were scathing. "That is very easily come by for the price of a few trinkets. What cannot be bought is a woman's respect, her confidence, her loyalty, and above all, her heart. You are a beautiful woman, Miss Fenton, but I take leave to tell you that within that comely form there beats a heart of iron."

Under this hail of vituperation, Deirdre's remorse had gradually given way to outrage, and she halted in her tracks and looked up at him with eyes glittering like crystal prisms.

"Then you should thank me, Lord Rathbourne, for bringing you to a sense of your folly. It would seem that you have had a a lucky escape."

"Have I?" he drawled, and forcibly took her by the elbow, compelling her to continue their walk. "That is one point on which I need some reassurance. Should I choose to marry in the near future, I must know that you have no claims upon me."

At the end of the pavement was a small walled garden which belonged to the hotel. He led her through the gate toward a stand of trees which were just coming into leaf. Deirdre noticed with some unease that Rathbourne and she were quite private.

"I make no claims upon you," she said coldly, trying not to show that she had been affected by the remark that he might soon marry. "How could I? The engagement was broken."

She suffered his intent scrutiny for a moment or two, then repeated, "I make no claims upon you."

A small, cynical half smile tugged at the corners of his mouth, but his eyes remained watchful, searching, and never wavered from Deirdre's puzzled expression. "Not even a little one? I am prepared to pay for the consequences of my pleasure should there be any," he baited.

Intelligence dawned in Deirdre's eyes, and a slow flush suffused her cheeks. "No, I am not pregnant," she said bluntly through clenched teeth, "and even if I were, do you think I would throw myself on *your* mercy?"

"Even the intrepid Miss Fenton might balk at being saddled with my by-blow," he responded with infuriating calm.

"Your by-blow? Do you mean your bastard? How many unfortunate women have been faced with the disgrace of bearing your bastards?"

His eyebrows elevated in mild surprise, as if slightly pained by her use of such strong language, but he smiled with amused tolerance and said amiably, "None, to my knowledge."

Deirdre found his air of studied detachment offensive in the

221

extreme, and sought for some way to shake him from it. "In my case," she said, injecting as much scorn as she was capable of into her words, "you need have no anxiety. You might well have fathered a child on me, but do you suppose that I would ever have allowed you to be a father to any child of mine? I'd sooner give myself to the first man who would have me and let him think he had sired your bastard than allow you to gain control of my child."

His whole body went rigid with fury and his hands fisted at his sides. She thought for a moment that he meant to strike her, and knew herself to have been sadly wrong to provoke him to such lengths. It was something in his expression, however, which shattered her mood of anger.

"That was unforgivable. I beg your pardon," she said in an altered tone. Her knees had begun to buckle and she extended a hand against the nearest tree to steady herself. "I didn't mean it, Gareth. I hope you believe me. But you baited me so unmercifully that I retaliated in kind."

"I should beat you for that," he said tersely.

"I thought you meant to."

"Next time—"

"But you provoked me beyond endurance."

"I meant every word I said."

She came erect at the insult. "Thank you," she said tonelessly. "And now that you have ascertained that you are free of obligation toward me, there can be nothing more for us to say to each other." She made as if to stalk past him but he detained her easily with one hand.

"There is one obligation I am honor bound to execute, and that is my guardianship of your brother, or had you forgotten that he is my ward?"

She turned back to him, making no move to escape his loosened grasp. "But that cannot signify now, surely? What possible motive could you have for wishing to be Armand's guardian?"

"None whatsoever, now that you are not to be my wife.

However, the thing was done in good faith, and in good faith I will fulfill my responsibilities. In this you have no ordering. I warn you now, I shall not tolerate your interference."

"But the boy is no—"

"He is not a boy. He is a man. Oh don't look so stricken, Deirdre. There is a war going on and I have more than enough to occupy me at present. Who knows? Perhaps I shall not survive the forthcoming battle, then all your troubles will be over. But if I do, make no mistake about it, St. Jean will find me a very hard taskmaster."

That Rathbourne thought she could wish for his death seemed the worst insult of all. It brought to mind the careless words she had flung at him before his departure for Spain, "I hope a bullet finds you and you never return." If he meant to punish her, he had succeeded admirably.

"You can be very cruel," she said in a chastened voice.

"I might have known that you would take that attitude. St. Jean has been coddled past redemption. Too much petticoat government, I don't doubt. Any discipline I impose must be regarded as one more evidence of my depraved character."

"That's not what I meant," she protested. "You are always determined to misunderstand me. Please, take me back to the hotel. My aunt must be wondering what has become of me."

Rathbourne returned her to the hotel foyer, but as there was still no sign of the dilatory Lady Fenton, he determinedly seated himself beside her and continued their conversation under the speculative glances of the desk clerk and a few of the English hotel patrons who were returning from their morning constitutional.

"I shall keep the emerald. I think I earned it." Deirdre remained silent. "Think of it as payment for services rendered. I've often given such trifles but never been in a position to receive one before." He extended his left hand as if to admire the large stone glittering on his finger. "Cat got your tongue, Miss Fenton?" he asked soto voce, leaning over so that his warm breath fanned Deirdre's cheek.

Deirdre struggled to hold on to her temper. "Keep it by all means," she said with as much nonchalance as she could muster. "The ring means nothing to me."

"Who are Marie and Alexandre?"

Deirdre looked at him blankly for a long moment, then comprehension slowly dawned. "You've read the inscription. Armand's grandparents, I suppose. Why?"

Rathbourne looked faintly surprised. "I thought you said the ring belonged to your father."

"I was used to think of my stepfather as my father before . . . before I came to know that my own parent had died when I was a babe."

"Strange," he mused, his tawny eyes resting on her thoughtfully. "I understood that you despised your step-father."

Deirdre was shaken. She had confided her feelings on the subject of her stepfather to only two people, her aunt and her friend Serena. The circumstances of his desertion were almost forgotten except by a few who had been closely connected with the events of that dreaful episode. Even Armand had been kept in ignorance. She wondered how much the Earl knew.

"You are mistaken," she said with crushing finality.

Deirdre came under the hard scrutiny of eyes alert with intelligence. "Don't gammon me, my girl. I know the whole story," he said flatly.

After a moment, she managed to speak with some composure. "You have been prying into what does not concern you, my lord. If your vulgar curiosity must be satisfied, then let me tell you that Papa, Armand's father, gave the ring to me when I was a child. I never pretended that I did not love him or that he was cruel to us children. In many respects, he was an exemplary father. Unfortunately, he had the taint which is natural to your gender. Passion overcame every other obligation when his mistress gave him an ultimatum. He deserted us and he never gave us another thought. The ring

224

means nothing to me now. I should have discarded it years ago."

Her expression was not encouraging, but he did not let that deter him. "You are determined to let a wretched episode from your childhood destroy your life. Grow up, Deirdre. The man was only human. I've no doubt he was as wretched and remorseful as it is possible for a man to be. I know the hell Uxbridge went through when—"

"Enough!" she cried, putting her hands over her ears. No one in her life had ever spoken to her so before. That he had the temerity to pass judgment on her and make excuses for the cruel neglect of the man who had robbed her of a childhood was more than she could endure.

"I might have known where your sympathies would lie," she said tersely, lowering her tone. "Your unsavory reputation does not bear scrutiny either. I won't argue the point with you about Lord Uxbridge, although there is much I might say. Frankly, I don't wish to converse with you at all."

She rose in one fluid movement and made to glide past him, but he was up before she had taken a step. She stiffened, shrinking back slightly from the menace of his towering form. Her eyes swept over his broad shoulders and she was forced to tilt her chin to meet his eyes. She was immediately reminded of the last time they had been in such proximity, and her breasts rose and fell rapidly as she remembered the masculine power that was concealed beneath his fine cambric shirt.

Rathbourne read her expression correctly and a glint of satisfaction flickered briefly in his eyes. "Nevertheless, Deirdre," he said with deceptive mildness, "you will converse with me on any and every occasion we happen to be thrown together. Not to do so would cause comment and the kind of speculation I am sure you would wish to avoid. Someone of my—how did you phrase it?—unsavory reputation can weather such vulgarity with impunity, but you are a different case entirely. Well," he added with quiet menace when

225

Deirdre said nothing, "do I make myself clear?"

"Perfectly." Her voice shook a little, and her eyes slid away from the threat she read in his.

He stepped aside to permit her to pass, his mocking grin deliberately adding insult to injury. Deirdre's withering look from the safety of the staircase only seemed to increase his amusement.

She went in search of her aunt and found her in her chamber, reclining on a sofa with unshod feet negligently propped against a small table, and in her hand, a cup of chocolate, a beverage Deirdre knew her aunt detested.

"Oh for a nice cup of tea!" Lady Fenton complained wistfully. "But these foreigners have no notion of how to boil a kettle of water. Is it any wonder that the tea leaves float on the surface like dead bodies? No strainers either, of course. What do they expect us to do—strain the leaves with our teeth? And if one complains, they only tell one to try the coffee."

Deirdre had heard this complaint from many of the English patrons, and she merely smiled with fond forebearance. "But you are partial to coffee and you detest chocolate, Aunt Rosemary."

"What of it? I wouldn't give them the satisfaction of fobbing me off with their famous Belgian brew! As if it could compare to a cup of good English tea."

"Uncle Thomas would not approve of such prejudice," Deirdre teased. "Relations between Bruxellois and the English are sensitive at the best of times. Such unguarded comments might be considered seditious in some quarters."

"Here, take this dreadful stuff away from me and hand me my shoes, Deirdre. You certainly took your time with Lord Rathbourne."

"You saw us?"

"Certainly. When I descended the stairs, I saw you leave the hotel together and I thought it prudent to allow you to sort out your differences without interference."

226

"Did you know that Rathbourne was in Brussels?" asked Deirdre suspiciously, setting aside the cup and saucer on the carved oak mantlepiece.

"As a matter of fact, I did. But he particularly asked me to say nothing to alarm you until he had the opportunity of speaking to you himself."

"You spoke to him?"

"Didn't I just say so? And found him most reasonable. Really, Deirdre, I think Sir Thomas is right. Two females on their own are apt to let their imaginations run riot. What ninnyhammers we were to let our groundless fears chase us out of London as if the devil himself were after us. Rathbourne is a gentleman. We should have trusted to that fact. You have made your feelings very obvious by running away from him. He won't trouble you again."

"And yet he has contrived to become Armand's guardian," Deirdre pointed out with quiet persistence, irritated to find that Rathbourne had somehow won her aunt's confidence.

Lady Fenton dismissed Deirdre's suspicions with an impatient wave of her hand. "He explained that circumstance to Sir Thomas's complete satisfaction. And no bad thing, either! Armand needs a firm hand. Sir Thomas was only sorry that he had not thought of the scheme himself."

"Sir Thomas approves? But I had hoped that he would use his influence to have the guardianship set aside."

"What would be the point in that? A court case could take months to decide, perhaps longer. Armand would reach his majority before the thing was settled. No, Sir Thomas is satisfied that Rathbourne will deal firmly but fairly with the boy."

Deirdre stared at her aunt in disbelief, watching idly as she drew on her gloves and picked up her parasol in readiness for their shopping spree. It was impossible to argue with such logic. Rathbourne was the epitome of the best that England had to offer. There was no higher compliment than to give a man the simple epithet "gentleman." His unsavory reputation with women of a lower order counted for nothing in her circles, as long as he was discreet. Deirdre pursed her lips together. She could destroy his character with a word, but in so doing she must expose her own conduct to censure. Her lips were sealed and he knew it. Gentleman indeed! She knew better!

Chapter Sixteen

Deirdre and her aunt were not present when Lord Uxbridge and his aides arrived late in the afternoon to take up their lodgings at the Hotel d'Angleterre, but the gentlemen's presence on the floor above soon made itself felt, for the ladies were forced to tolerate the incessant tramp of spurred boots on the ceiling overhead well into the early hours of the morning. This aggravation was dismissed as of little consequence by the aunt, a sentiment not shared by her niece, and Deirdre was hard pressed to conceal an irritation that she could scarcely explain to herself.

She awakened the following morning feeling cross and rather out of sorts, but she came to herself gradually as she sipped the excellent cup of coffee which was brought to her by a chambermaid. Private parlors were no longer to be had at any price, and the ladies were in the habit of taking a solitary breakfast on a tray in the privacy of their bedchambers. Occasionally, Sir Thomas was in attendance, but very infrequently, since the press of work at the Embassy necessitated long stretches in his office where a cot had been set up for the odd times when he might snatch a few hours' sleep. As a consequence, the ladies scarcely saw Sir Thomas except at official functions, and they were obliged to make their own way in society without reference to anything or anyone but their own personal preferences, a circumstance which discommoded the ladies in no wise.

Lady Fenton was at her morning ablutions when a note was delivered with an invitation, which included Deirdre, to share a bite of breakfast with Lord Uxbridge in his private parlor. Her ladyship accepted with alacrity and lost no time in dressing and walking the length of the corridor to Deirdre's room to apprise her niece of their good fortune.

"How does he come to have a private parlor?" asked Deirdre pettishly as she struggled into a white muslin morning dress which buttoned high at the throat.

"How should I know?" asked Lady Fenton sharply. "Who cares?" She adjusted Deirdre's dress across the shoulders and fluffed out the gored skirt. "I really must make a push to engage an abigail as long as we are in Brussels." Her critical eye surveyed Deirdre from head to toe. "How old is this dress?"

"It's new."

"I thought all your new frocks had long sleeves?"

"Oh that," said Deirdre dismissively. "That was Serena's doing. I've altered all three of them. Serena is always ahead of herself. Nobody here has caught up with that particular fashion yet."

"Oh well, take a silk shawl with you, or something. And do be quick. Lord Uxbridge is the man of the hour and we mustn't keep him waiting."

"I thought Wellington was the man of the hour."

"Really Deirdre! What's got into you? One would think you didn't like Lord Uxbridge, and that can't be so. Everybody likes him. He's the most amiable young man."

"He's middle-aged!" retorted Deirdre.

"Don't let him hear you say that. He's a regular beau, and in his prime. But you young people are all the same. Let me tell you, Deirdre, that age is relative. I suppose you think that I am in my dotage?"

Deirdre dimpled. "You, dear aunt, are the epitome of all that is elegant," she responded handsomely.

Lord Uxbridge, looking every inch the Commander of Cavalry, cut a very fine figure in his dark blue dolman with its yards of gold lace braiding across the chest. Deirdre quickly scanned the faces of the other gentlemen present and the muscles which had knotted tight at the base of her neck relaxed by degrees when she ascertained that Rathbourne was not among them. She made a curtsy to Uxbridge's aides who, in their tunics of scarlet and gold, made no less favorable an impression than their commander. In the presence of such masculine finery, Deirdre thought that the ladies, in their pale muslin frocks, came a very poor second best. So taken was she with the color and cut of the gentlemen's scarlet jackets that she formed the notion of making up a short kerseymere spencer in the same color and with gold frogging for her own use. She mentioned as much to Captain Ogilvie, who had beaten out the competition to sit next to her at the table, and he warned her, in a bantering tone, that it would be disastrous to don such a piece of apparel in Brussels, for she might be mistaken for one of the aides and be forced into running errands for any number of generals and commanders.

Conversation at the table never once touched upon anything of a serious nature. It was as if the gentlemen were determined to enjoy a short respite from weightier matters by making light of every trial and tribulation, and rumor had it that there were many.

"Do you recall, Thornhill, what the Duke said in Spain when you and Rathbourne presented yourselves as two fresh young officers just out from England?" a voice asked derisively from the end of the table.

"Certainly I remember," said Major Thornhill gravely. "He paid us the highest compliment it is possible for any commander to pay an officer."

The hilarity was general, and Lady Fenton asked diffidently, "What did Wellington say?"

"I remember his words exactly," drawled Major Thornhill. "He looked us over with that supercilious expression that no one has quite managed to emulate, and he said in his usual bored way, 'I only hope that the enemy trembles as much as I do when he learns the names of my newest officers.'"

"And why did he say that?" asked Lady Fenton innocently. But no one gave her a satisfactory answer, although there was much innuendo and laughter at Major Thornhill's expense.

They were such splendid young men, all of whom had served under Uxbridge in Spain and looked forward to serving with him again, that Deirdre at one point in her reflections blinked rapidly to dispel the gathering tears. By the time breakfast was over and the ladies had retired to their own rooms, Deirdre was forced to the conclusion that Lord Uxbridge's credit with his men, both as a man and as an officer, could not have stood higher. It caused her estimation of his character to shift slightly in his favor.

Lord Uxbridge's presence in the hotel made a great difference to Deirdre, for a goodly contingent of gentlemen and officers (among them, Rathbourne) came to wait on him and they filled the hotel with their laughter and jests. Uxbridge went out of his way to show every courtesy to the Fentons, and in the ordinary course of events made them known to many fellow officers. Deirdre could not forget the threat of war that gradually crept closer and she treated each with a sisterly affection which more than one aspiring suitor deeply regretted. Only Major Ogilvie, quiet yet doggedly persistent, refused to accept the brotherly role which Deirdre attempted to cast him in and, within a fortnight of having made her acquaintance, was on such a familiar footing with Deirdre that he was forced to endure much good-natured raillery from his colleagues.

The notion of making up a form-fitting spencer in the color that she preferred above all others had taken a firm hold on Deirdre's fancy. She enlisted the advice of Lady Fenton, who, though not as au fait with the current fashions as her friend Serena, was no dowd and thought Deirdre's idea a splendid one. They spent several pleasant hours designing the garment and deciding on the placement and quantity of brass buttons. When a slight difference of opinion arose over how much gold frogging would be appropriate, Deirdre always tending to understatement, they sent for Armand to give the benefit of the male point of view. He sided with the older woman, saying with crushing finality that Deirdre's dress sense verged on the mediocre, "modest and unmodish," and that she was saved from becoming a complete nonentity only because she was such a handsome creature.

Deirdre, slightly cowed by her brother's frankness, gracefully submitted to the dictates of her self-appointed mentors. The four yards of scarlet kerseymere (the softest and finest wool twill that was to be had), one dozen brass buttons, and yards of gold braid were duly purchased. It was Armand who found a seamstress to make up the garment, but Deirdre did not question him too closely on how he had come by that piece of information.

It was with some relief that she discovered that Mrs. Dawson was a perfectly respectable Englishwoman whose husband was a lieutenant with the 95th Rifles—that crack regiment which had covered itself with glory in the Peninsular Campaign. The Dawsons, with their three young children, were billeted in two rooms in a private dwelling only a stone's throw from the Hotel d'Angleterre. Deirdre found herself drawn to a woman who, though not much older than herself, had seen a side of life that was far from Deirdre's experience. Mrs. Dawson was an army wife who had made up her mind early in her marriage that she would not be separated from her husband as he pursued a military career. Deirdre had often heard the expression "follow the drum," but she had never understood its full significance or the hardships and sacrifice such a life entailed till she met Mrs. Dawson.

She took to dropping in of a morning with treats for the children, who soon came to recognize her step on the landing, and she would insist in relieving Mrs. Dawson of the care of the baby while the kettle was put on the boil for a cup of good

English brew. In normal circumstances there could have been little converse between women of such disparity in station, for the Dawsons at home would have been considered "genteel" rather than "gentry," and their paths would have been most unlikely to cross except by accident. Nor would the wife of a lieutenant have deemed it proper to sell her skills as a seamstress, but such niceties were overlooked in the situation in which they found themselves. Moreover, the Dawsons were putting aside every spare penny to buy Lieutenant Dawson his captain's commission, and Mrs. Dawson was determined that their growing family (she was again breeding) should not stand in the way of her husband's preferment.

Deirdre was by turns aghast and admiring of the life that wives who chose to "follow the drum" were obliged to endure.

"You were there, at the Battle of Salamanca?" Deirdre tried to cover her incredulity without much success.

"Certainly," responded Mrs. Dawson calmly. "We women weren't in the thick of it, you understand, and mostly the officers' wives were sent to safety far behind the lines. But the wives of those enlisted men who had won the lot were never far from the battlefield."

"Won the lot?"

Mrs. Dawson took the baby from Deirdre's arms and settled him in his basket. "Didn't you know? Five enlisted men in every company are allowed to take their wives overseas with them. They draw lots to choose the lucky ones. Officers have no such restrictions placed upon them."

"And these women were actually present when the battle took place?"

"I think that I have offended your sensibilities."

"Not at all," Deirdre hastily disclaimed. "It's just that I find it so incredible and, to be frank, rather foolhardy and pointless."

"I cannot agree. There are many stories I could tell you of wives saving their husbands' lives after a battle—yes, and the lives of other wounded as well. You needn't look so shocked,

Miss Fenton. It is only when the smoke has cleared that the women venture upon the field of battle to look for their loved ones."

"Yes, but what if the battle were lost? What happens then?"

"That is something I never think about." She picked up Deirdre's scarlet spencer and became engrossed in setting in one sleeve. Deirdre sipped her tea pensively.

Her thoughts drifted back to that memorable night in Vauxhall Gardens, and some words she could not quite recall that Rathbourne had spoken. He had wanted her to follow him to Spain, but as his wife or as his doxy had been left in some doubt. If things had been different, *she* might have spent five years "following the drum." She wondered if she would have had the stamina for it. But then, Mrs. Dawson had been the daughter of a country parson. There was nothing in her early life to predict the pluck she had demonstrated under the most trying circumstances.

"I think," said Deirdre, lightening her tone, "that if I were Wellington, I would award medals to the brave wives who act as unpaid auxiliaries of the British Army."

Mrs. Dawson flashed Deirdre a grateful smile. "Thank you. But we only do our duty. You mustn't think that we are braver than we are. It is the French girls who run the most appalling risks."

"I cannot conceive of anything that could possibly surpass what you have just told me."

Mrs. Dawson carefully maneuvered a length of scarlet thread through the eye of her needle. "There are many who would dispute what I am going to tell you, but I know for a fact that many French girls go into battle with their husbands and sweethearts."

Deirdre carefully replaced her cup on the saucer. "How do you know?" she asked skeptically.

"Because after the battle, the dead are stripped of their uniforms, and I've seen, with my own eyes, the bodies of young French women where they have fallen, yes, and sometimes

235

entwined in the arms of a dead lover." She glanced cautiously at Deirdre and decided against telling her that it was looters of the victorious army who stripped the dead of anything of value and left them naked where they lay. She was beginning to regret that she had told this gently bred and sheltered girl so much, but she had done it with a purpose. There was a favor she wished particularly to ask of her.

"Miss Fenton," she began diffidently, then hesitated, unsure of how to frame her request. "Miss Fenton," she began again with more resolution, "before the battle begins, you will be sent to Antwerp for safety."

"No one has told me so."

"Believe me, I know. The wives and families of diplomats and senior officers are rarely to be found in the vicinity of the battle. No, don't protest! Whatever you might wish, you will have no say in the matter. My place is with my husband—but the children . . ." She faltered to a halt and looked expectantly at Deirdre.

Deirdre's expression was stricken. "You cannot mean to tell me that, in your condition, you mean to follow the army to the battlefield?"

"Certainly! I had hoped to find someone to take my children to a place of safety, but if I fail, I shall take them with me."

Deirdre used all her powers of persuasion to try to deflect the young woman from her purpose, but nothing she said had the least effect. She felt helpless in the face of so much immovable determination. Mrs. Dawson was more fortunate. She secured the promise from Deirdre that when the time came, she would convey the Dawson children to Antwerp and safety.

This was no hardship, since Deirdre was fond of children and had taken a particular liking to the two little Dawson girls, Sally and Sophy, who at three and four years old respectively, were very well brought up infants. She formed the habit of taking them to the park for outings over the halfhearted protests of their mother, so that Mrs. Dawson, who had no maid, might be relieved of their care for an hour or two. It was with great relief that Deirdre discovered that her aunt's new abigail, Solange, a young Belgian girl of sixteen years or so, was inordinately fond of children since much of the care of the youngsters would fall on her shoulders once the time to remove from Brussels arrived.

Rathbourne, mounted on a handsome gray charger, happened upon her one afternoon when she was sitting on a park bench with baby William resting contentedly in her lap. Solange was playing a game of ball with the two little girls, and their squeals of pleasure carried delightfully on the air. Deirdre was deeply contented, her imagination running riot as she dreamily gazed down at the infant in her arms. Rathbourne took in the scene at a glance, checked his mount, and cantered toward Deirdre. It was a moment before she recognized him.

"A prettier portrait of domestic bliss, I have yet to see," he remarked pleasantly.

Deirdre straightened instinctively and blushed as if he had caught her red-handed in some nefarious plot. "I happen to like children," she said defensively.

"So I see. Whose children are they?"

"They belong to Lieutenant Henry Dawson of the 95th."

"I remember the fellow. His little girls were born in Spain. That would be Dawson's son in your arms and the hope of his family, I collect?"

Deirdre replied that it was and fell silent, not knowing what to say next. An awkward pause ensued, with the Earl making no move to disengage himself. She stole a quick glance at him and thought that he looked very grave.

"They might have been ours, if things had been different— but I am forgetting your sentiments on my capacity to be a worthy father."

There was bitterness mingled with injury behind those words and Deirdre was moved to say earnestly, "Gareth, I already asked your forgiveness for expressing that stupid lie. I would have said anything then to wound you. I swear I did not mean it. Can't you forget that I ever said it?"

His expression softened. "Children become you," he said quietly. "I am delighted to see that you have at least some of the instincts that are natural to your sex."

If he had meant the sentiment to be conciliatory, he failed miserably. Deirdre's head went back.

"And you, sir, have all the predatory instincts that are natural to a man. I regret deeply that I ever questioned your aptitude for fatherhood. How can I say what sort of father a man of your stamp might make? But as a husband, I make no mistake that you would fail miserably."

Baby William, as if sensing the anger between the two adults, began to whimper, and Deirdre soothed him by laying her hand against his cheek and crooning words of comfort.

Rathbourne's jaw clenched. "And you, Miss Fenton," he ground out, "had best resign yourself to maidenhood, I beg your pardon, spinsterhood. You have the capacity for passion, I grant you, but the softer virtues of *your* sex are beyond you."

He dug his spurs into his horse's flanks and rode off at a furious pace, leaving Deirdre deeply mortified and searching in vain for the words that would cut the feet from under the detestable Earl.

She made up her mind that the next time they met, since she had yet to win a contest of wits with him, she would give him the cut direct. After mulling over the form of retaliation such an insult might provoke, her resolve wavered and she determined merely to go out of her way to avoid him. Further reflection convinced her that this was the coward's way. No, she would heap coals of fire on his head. She would show him how much his thoughtless words had wounded her. This humiliating pose, however, was naturally distasteful to Deirdre since it forcibly brought to mind her mother's air of martyrdom, and she soon discarded that particular means of bringing the Earl to heel.

As it happened, she might have saved herself much needless deliberation for it was some time before she was to see Rathbourne again. She heard from Ogilvie that the Earl had left Brussels, but when she asked for particulars, he became evasive, and she let the subject drop.

They were at a small dinner party given by Lord Uxbridge on the eve of his departure, along with his staff, for Ninove where cavalry headquarters had been established.

"I shall miss you all," said Deirdre wistfully to Ogilvie, her eyes lingering on Uxbridge and his aides.

"Don't sound so forlorn. Ninove isn't so far away, and we are under orders to fraternize with the general population. You'll be wishing yourself shot of us before long. Still," he went on with mock reproach, "it is rather lowering to find oneself only one among many whose absence you regret."

"What will you do when all this is over?" she asked, ignoring his quiet cajolery.

"I'm a professional soldier," he answered. "I have no settled domicile, so to speak." He took her gloved hand and gently turned Deirdre toward him. "My sword and my heart are my fortune, fair lady."

Deirdre felt a pang of dismay at the gravity of his expression and, fearing that he was on the point of making a declaration, made an effort to turn the subject. "Everyone has a home," she said flippantly, "even soldiers. Where were you born and bred?"

"In a place you've probably never heard of," he said with an inaudible sigh, releasing her hand as she moved slightly apart from him. "In the hills of Scotland, a place called Aboyne, near Aberdeen."

"Aberdeen? Why, I might have been there now visiting a friend, if my aunt had not invited me to come with her to Brussels."

"Then it must have been fate that brought you to me," he said quizzically.

"You were telling me about Aboyne," she reminded him.

"How can one describe the beauty that is Scotland to a native of England—mountains, mists, and barren peaks? You English prefer a gentler landscape—your verdant valleys and gently rolling hills with forests of trees—pretty, I grant you, but give me the loneliness of our moors and the mystery of our mountains."

"It sounds to be something like the Lake District."

"True, but beautiful as the English Lake District is, it is only a shade of what is to be found in Scotland."

"Pooh!" said Deirdre derisively. "Don't speak to me of mountains. I am a farmer and horse breeder. Can mountains raise wheat or barley or provide pasture for my beasts? What good are they?"

"Mountains, you little ignoramus, are for climbing and conquering. For a man to pit his skill against the elements of nature, that is a true test of endurance and character."

"I think, Captain Ogilvie, that you like to flirt with danger."

"Well, it is dangerous, but I've only once been involved in a climbing accident. Did Rathbourne ever tell you about it?"

"No. What happened?"

"The worst thing possible. Rathbourne's younger brother, Andrew, lost his life. We were at Harrow at the time—boys really. I suppose I was to blame for getting him all fired up about climbing. He came for a holiday and brought Gareth along with him. Rathbourne was a natural. We tried the easy peaks first—nothing too hard for beginners. But Andrew wouldn't rest with that, not daredevil Andrew. Rathbourne and I did one of the more difficult climbs. My father's gillie wouldn't allow Andrew to attempt it. Andrew didn't like that and protested loud and long. It didn't do a bit of good. Robertson stood in place of my father when I went climbing, and when he made up his mind, nothing could sway him. Andrew broke one of the cardinal rules of climbers. He went out alone early the next morning before anyone was about. I suppose he wanted to show us how we had misjudged him. We knew immediately what had happened, of course, but we were

240

too late."

"That must have been ghastly for you," said Deirdre in stricken tones, laying a comforting hand on his sleeve.

"Certainly it was. But for Rathbourne especially. I understand there was a rift with his mother over the tragedy. Damn fool woman! As though Gareth did not blame himself already for what had happened. He was distraught. I think he was always in the habit of looking out for Andrew, and now Caro, of course."

Deirdre felt a rush of sympathy, the first time such a gentle emotion had ever touched her with respect to the Earl. It was hard to imagine him as a young and vulnerable youth. He always gave the impression of being so much in command of himself and every situation. Ogilvie's revelation did not fit in with the impression she had taken of Rathbourne's character. It puzzled her that he should feel so little empathy for her position with respect to Armand when, if Ogilvie was correct, he had experienced some of her own anxieties for a younger sibling.

This new softening toward the Earl was not fated to last long. It died a very sudden death when Deirdre next set eyes on him at one of the receptions given by the British Embassy.

There were many such parties which, for all their frivolity, concealed a more serious purpose—or so Sir Thomas said. Confidence between the Belgians and their allies had never stood very high, and most Bruxellois were known to tolerate the English only marginally better than they tolerated the French. It was hoped that these informal assemblies would ease that very natural and mutual distrust which lay just below the surface.

The conversation that evening, as ever in diplomatic gatherings, was of Napoleon Bonaparte and his amassing armies, which were reputed to outnumber the British by two to one. It was known that his former generals, to a man, had offered him their allegiance without firing a shot, and that the unpopular Louis had fled Paris only in the nick of time. The latest rumor which circulated was that the workshops of Paris were turning out huge quantities of guns and ammunition night and day. It might be supposed that such an intelligence would have put a blight on the festivities, but the officers, looking very handsome in their dress regimentals, laughed it off with a show of unconcern and merely remarked that it was ever the fate of the British Army to be outnumbered and outgunned. This calm indifference from veterans who had chased Napoleon's armies out of Spain did much to relieve the tension, and if anything, the gaiety became more extravagent.

"How typical of the English," said Armand to Deirdre in slightly contemptuous accents. "Their confidence is insufferable when one considers that some of their best units are across the Atlantic—yes, and have taken an ignominious beating at the hands of the despised colonials. Who do they think they are? They underrated the Americans and paid for that error. Now listen to them laugh off the threat of Napoleon and his 'froggies.'"

Deirdre's eyes nervously swept over the throng of dancers. "Keep your voice down," she said severely. "And you're wrong about their confidence. They know perfectly well what they're up against. I think that they are the bravest, most gallant fellows I've ever encountered."

The words were scarcely out of her mouth when her eyes were drawn to the powerful figure of a man who had just entered the grand saloon. My Lord Rathbourne, magnificent in full dress regimentals of red tunic with gold epaulettes and lace across the throat, the uniform of a staff officer, stood at his ease, one white-gloved hand negligently resting on his hip. It was the first time Deirdre had ever seen the Earl in regimentals and her heart constricted painfully. Until that moment, the war had seemed remote, a thing apart that could not touch her or hers. In one blinding moment of revelation, that illusion was destroyed forever.

His eyes searched the room and found her. She stared at him, incapable of speech or movement, her breasts rising and falling slightly with her quickening breath. There was a movement behind him, and the spell was broken. Mrs. Dewinters inclined her head slightly in Deirdre's direction, and said a few words in Rathbourne's ear. They shared an intimate smile that pointedly excluded Deirdre.

She swayed slightly and found Armand's comforting hand at her back. He turned her toward him.

"I had hoped to spare you the knowledge of their liaison," he said softly. "She's seen everywhere with him, but I never thought he would introduce her into the circles you move in, Dee."

The orchestra played the opening strains of a waltz, and Deirdre said miserably, "Dance with me, Armand."

They danced well together, Armand taking up the slack in the conversation until Deirdre should come to herself. When she finally made a response to some innocuous comment he had made, he said, "That's better! Now smile," and Deirdre obliged.

"And I thought you didn't care for him," Armand quizzed gently.

"Are you softening toward the Earl?" she asked, a trifle breathless as Armand swung her neatly to the crescendoing rhythm.

"Oh, I don't know. He's a hard man, it's true, but one picks up things, you know."

"Like what?"

"This and that," was the maddening reply. "I daresay much of what I heard is exaggerated. He doesn't care much for me, however, that I do know."

The Duke of Wellington put in a brief appearance, and Deirdre could well imagine why he was reputed to inspire such confidence though little affection in the rank and file of his men. Tall, of aristocratic demeanor, contemptuous of praise and censure alike, he moved from group to group exchanging a few pleasantries. In his wake appeared Uxbridge, by far the more approachable of the two men. His graceful manners and

243

easy address made friends for him everywhere. But it was Lord Rathbourne who was easily the most sought after.

He was the epitome of the young warrior: handsome, erect, and of brooding demeanor until his wandering eye should alight on some breathless female. Then his lazy, persuasive smile would come into play, and every feminine heart in the room would beat a little faster. That he was an accomplished though inconstant flirt was quickly established, but to be taken up by him, notwithstanding the propriety airs of his companion, Mrs. Dewinters, lent a lady a degree of glamour that was the envy of her less fortunate sisters.

Deirdre was not sorry that she did not lack for partners and her vanity would have been soothed if she had known that her beauty was remarked by many a young officer who waited on the sidelines to capture her hand for the next dance. It was the first time Deirdre had worn the sea-foam creation which Serena had persuaded her to have made up. It drew an inordinate number of compliments from her partners, but she grew rather impatient with their inanity when she heard for the upteenth time that her eyes were like pools of liquid emerald that a man could lose his soul in, or words to that effect.

It was left to Lady Fenton to deflate any conceit that Deirdre might have entertained as a consequence of her success. "So Serena was ahead of herself, was she, with the fashion for long sleeves?" she asked dryly, nodding in the direction of Mrs. Dewinters, whose gown of gossamer lavender drew the admiring eyes of every lady. The sleeves, Deirdre noted, sheathed her arms to the wrist.

"Mark my words," observed Lady Fenton, "in another week or so, long-sleeved gowns will be all the crack."

Deirdre was claimed by Lord Uxbridge and her ruffled vanity was somewhat soothed by the stares, some speculative, some spiteful, of many a young woman who aspired to be his flirt for the evening. When he sat out the following dance with Deirdre and impatiently waved away the young bucks who thought to break up their intimate tête-à-tête, the suspicions of the room were roused against them. In fact, Uxbridge and Deirdre were enjoying a discussion on a subject which was close to the heart of each of them—horses. So spirited did the argument become at one point that Lord Rathbourne was upon them before they were aware of it. He spoke briefly to Lord Uxbridge in an undertone which made it impossible for Deirdre to catch what was said.

"Miss Fenton," Lord Uxbridge said, taking her gloved hand and placing it in Rathbourne's extended one, "I beg leave to be excused. A soldier must ever be ready to make sacrifices in the course of duty. Believe me, nothing less would drag me from your side. Rathbourne will stand in for me. I know you to be old friends and have reason to believe that you will not mind the substitution."

Rathbourne held out his arms and Deirdre moved stiffly into them, studiously avoiding looking directly into his eyes. It had seemed to her that in the course of the evening he had danced every dance with only the prettiest girls in the room, but not once had he made the slightest move to engage her interest. It galled her to think that it was only by the direct order of his commanding officer that he was dancing with her at all.

She placed one hand gingerly on his shoulder and picked up her demi-train. When she felt the pressure of his hand, splayed out at the small of her back, bringing her closer, unexpected and unwanted recollections brought her senses alive, and her eyes swept up to meet his searching gaze.

"That's better," he said, and immediately spun her round with such violence that she momentarily lost her balance and clung to him to save herself falling. He laughed and spun her around again. Two spots of color showed on Deirdre's cheeks.

"You are making a spectacle of yourself," she said caustically.

"Am I? I rather thought you were the one who held that distinction this evening. You have attracted quite a bit of notice. And flirting with Uxbridge, too, of all people. Pray, tell me, when am I to wish you and Captain Ogilvie happy? Oh very good! That look of pained surprise is most convincing. I assure you that in the officer's mess the announcement of your engagement is no longer a matter of conjecture."

Deirdre spluttered, but before she could get a word in edgewise, he whirled her into a series of fast turns that made her head spin. "Gareth," she said weakly. "Don't."

"Don't what? Don't congratulate you on your performance as a lightskirt? Or was it a performance? Now that I have introduced you to passion, do you think to repeat the experience? I'd be happy to accommodate you, if it's only a man you want."

Deirdre could not believe that this conversation was taking place. "You cad . . . you blighter . . . you seducer," she began, her voice rising as she warmed to her subject.

"Hush!" He gave her a slight shake. "People are staring."

Deirdre, recalled to a sense of decorum, showed the world a mouthful of perfectly even white teeth as she bared them at her unsmiling partner. "Hypocrite!" she said in a pleasantly modulated voice. "Your mistress is becoming suspicious."

Rathbourne followed the direction of Deirdre's glance. Maria Dewinters, in the arms of Captain Ogilvie, bowed slightly in their direction.

"You are jealous," he said to Deirdre, not without some degree of satisfaction. "You don't like to think of me making love to another woman, do you? You're such an innocent, Deirdre. But I've told you that before, haven't I?"

"I am not jealous," she protested hotly. "I happen to like Mrs. Dewinters."

He was silent for a long moment, then spoke in more moderate accents. "Deirdre, you are mistaken. Maria is not my mistress. She just happens to be desperately in need of friends at the moment. You are in a position to do her a good turn, if what you say is true."

"What good turn?" she asked, her suspicions roused.

"No doubt you have noticed that Maria is on the fringes of

society. If you were to take her up, befriend her, others would soon follow your example."

Deirdre digested his words slowly. "That is not the advice you gave to me in London. As I recall, you warned me off forming a friendship with the lady."

"Circumstances have changed," he asserted without hesitation. "Maria is aiming at respectability. And I should like to do everything in my power to assist her to achieve her object."

She absorbed the shock of his words without a flicker of emotion, but inwardly, she felt herself reel as if the ground had been cut from under her feet. She recalled the occasion in the hotel gardens when he had intimated that, should she make no claims upon him, he might soon marry. In the light of these observations, his sudden desire to lend Mrs. Dewinters an air of respectability was easily understood. It was a long moment before the lump in her throat dissolved and she was able to speak with some composure.

"My aunt may object."

"Leave her to me." He was watching her closely, trying to read her expression. "*Are* you jealous, Deirdre?" he asked softly.

She shot him a withering look. "Bring Mrs. Dewinters to see me tomorrow. If it is possible for a wanton such as I to lend countenance to another of the same ilk, then by all means, it shall be as you wish."

"Thank you," he said with a chuckle, and smiled in that lazy, gloating way which she detested. "I am sure Maria and you will deal famously together."

Chapter Seventeen

Rathbourne's earnest suggestion that Deirdre ease Mrs. Dewinters's way in polite society seemed, on more sober reflection, as impracticable as it was unpalatable. The more she debated the propriety of such an action, the more ineligible Deirdre deemed the enterprise. Setting aside a personal distaste, which appeared irrational in light of her avowed cordiality toward the actress, she did not see how her aunt could be persuaded to such a course, quite the reverse, as she soon discovered.

In the carriage on the way home from the reception, there could be little doubt that Rathbourne had lost his credit with Lady Fenton. Deirdre, still reeling from the shock of Mrs. Dewinters's presence in Brussels and all that it might signify, sat mute and miserable as her aunt voiced her outrage at Rathbourne's want of delicacy in consorting openly with such a woman. Lady Fenton's parting shot at the door of her bedchamber as Deirdre made to move off down the length of the corridor, "You're well out of it, my dear, well out of it," expressed the very thought that had taken hold of Deirdre's mind. Had she been persuaded to marry Rathbourne, *she* would be stuck at his estate in Warickshire while *he* would be cavorting in Brussels doing whatever it was he was doing with Mrs. Dewinters. The thought was the perfect antidote to the morass of self-pity that heaved with distressing effect in the pit of her stomach. A surge of pride, hot and angry, brought a quickness to her step and a determined jut to her chin. If she was discomposed by Rathbourne's misconduct, and she was not prepared to admit that it was more than that, *he* at least would never know it. She would kill Rathbourne and his lightskirt with kindness before she let him think that he could evoke in her breast anything stronger than an imperturbable tolerance.

For the next day or two, Deirdre pushed Rathbourne from her mind. She had an unwitting ally in Lord Uxbridge, for on the morning following the reception, Sir Thomas arrived at the hotel with a note from the commander. Uxbridge requested in the politest terms possible that Deirdre allow him the honor of providing a mount for her for as long as she intended to stay in Brussels. He had done as much for his sister, Lady Capet, who had arrived with her family, as arranged, in the previous week. Furthermore, he taunted brazenly, he was sure that once Deirdre had put her spurs to Lustre, she would be forced to concede what she had disclaimed in their tête-à-tête at the Embassy, namely that, in spite of her preference for Barbaries and Turks, there could be no finer horseflesh than the English thoroughbred, especially when such a specimen could claim Eclipse for her grandsire.

Deirdre was thunderstruck. She looked at her uncle for confirmation.

"I gave my permission," he said with a twinkle. "Uxbridge's groom awaits your pleasure."

Deirdre picked up her skirts and dashed down the stairs with little ceremony and halted abruptly when she was blinded by the bright light of day. She shaded her eyes with one hand then let out her breath on a rush. A mounted groom held the reins of a glossy, blood chestnut. She stood about sixteen hands high, long and clean limbed with powerful quarters and an eye that sparkled with intelligence.

"Give me five minutes," breathed Deirdre to the groom, and

spun on her heel to go racing back the way she had come. She met her aunt and uncle in the hall.

"Will someone tell me what all the fuss is about?" asked Lady Fenton plaintively. "It's only a horse after all."

Deirdre pushed impatiently toward her chamber. "You tell her, Uncle Thomas. I must change into my riding habit."

Sir Thomas obliged. "That little filly has a pedigree, my dear, that even Prinny cannot match." He saw that his words had made little impression on her ladyship. "Her grandsire was Eclipse." Not a flicker of intelligence registered in Lady Fenton's eyes. "She is related to Wellington's Copenhagen and Napoleon's Marengo. They share the same grandsire," he concluded patiently.

"Oh, is that all? Well, I'm sure that's very agreeable for Deirdre and most civil in Uxbridge. Now what was it you particularly wished to say to me, dear?"

Sir Thomas's pained grunt of resignation was lost on Lady Fenton. He held the door open for her, and at the thought of the coming interview, he purposefully squared his shoulders.

Deirdre returned to the hotel in high alt. Uxbridge had provided the sweetest little goer that she had ever been privileged to mount. Bred for stamina and speed, and with a mouth that was sensitive to the slightest pressure of the bit, Lustre had proved herself an incomparable. Not for this filly a sedate jog in the park to take the fidgets out of her long, clean limbs, but a hard gallop in the open terrain around Bois de là Cambre, where any equestrian worth his salt was to be found exercising his bloods.

As she walked back from the mews to the hotel, Deirdre pondered on the one blight in an otherwise perfect morning. She had chanced to meet Rathbourne's groom, O'Toole, when she had checked Lustre on the rise of hill. He was directly below her, mounted on the Earl's magnificent gray. Her cry of recognition had gone unheeded, although she was certain that he had seen her. He had, she mused, given her the cut direct. She would not have believed him to be so petty, but she concluded that the groom bore a grudge for the way she had duped him in London. It seemed absurd for a lady to be put out by the crotchets of a servant, but Deirdre freely admitted to herself that such was the case. She had lost O'Toole's good opinion and it troubled her.

O'Toole and his petulance were forgotten as soon as she entered her aunt's chamber. So charmed was Deirdre with Lord Uxbridge's gift that she could not help exclaiming at length on his generosity no less than his unerring eye for horseflesh. It did not take her long, however, to become conscious of the strained atmosphere that prevailed between Sir Thomas and Lady Fenton, and she faltered to a halt, looking expectantly from one to the other.

"Prepare yourself for a shock, Deirdre," said Lady Fenton, her mouth thinning ominously.

"Rosemary!" snapped Sir Thomas, his voice and expression flashing a warning. He addressed his niece directly, and his tone softened. "Deirdre, my dear, Lord Rathbourne has applied to me in person, as head of this family"—here he looked toward his wife with a riveting eye—"as I say, as *head* of this family, to grant a favor which, much as I wish to, is only partially in my power to confer. Do you know what this favor is, Deirdre?"

She glanced at her aunt's glowering expression. "Yes," she said without prevarication. "He wishes me to cultivate Mrs. Dewinters and promote her entry into society."

"And you agreed to this preposterous proposal?" demanded her aunt, her voice querulous and rising.

"Certainly I did," returned Deirdre steadily, "as long as I have your permission, of course. Why should I not? Mrs. Dewinters's manners are unexceptionable." After an infinitesimal pause she concluded with less confidence. "And I happen to like her."

"He means to marry her then?" questioned Lady Fenton of Sir Thomas.

"Possibly."

"Well he can do it without my patronage! I have no intention of lending my support to the woman with whom he openly consorts, and I forbid Deirdre to be a party to this . . . this infamous affair."

Sir Thomas, as a rule not given to outbursts of temper, shouted, "Silence!" with such volume that two pairs of shocked eyes simultaneously came to rest upon him. "I beg your pardon," he said apologetically. "I did not mean to startle you, but this sort of wrangling is not only senseless but irrelevant. The matter has already been settled. I gave Rathbourne my word on the condition that Deirdre had no objections. Do you object, Deirdre?"

"No, sir."

"Good girl. One thing more, madam wife, before you start spitting fire at me. Rathbourne is not the only one who is championing the cause of Mrs. Dewinters. The man obviously has friends at Court. Without divulging more than I ought, it only remains to be said that, as long as Deirdre is not averse to the scheme, you will do everything in your power to comply with the Earl's wishes. Do I make myself clear?" Lady Fenton could not deny that he had.

Deirdre deliberated long and earnestly on her uncle's disquieting disclosures. It was evident to her that some sort of pressure had been brought to bear on Sir Thomas. That should not have surprised her, she told herself with bitter self-mockery, for she more than anyone had reason to know how desperate and ruthless the Earl could become whenever he set his mind on some purpose. This lack of constancy in his regard was no surprise either. It merely confirmed that rank tendency she had long observed in the male animal. One might admire a man's strength and fortitude, his intelligence and humor, even his virile beauty though its potency was vaguely menacing, but this sad want of particularity with respect to the darker side of his nature was an offense against every feminine sensibility.

Such were Deirdre's thoughts when a day or so later she was called by her aunt to the window of her chamber which overlooked the front of the hotel to witness the arrival of Mrs. Dewinters and her extensive entourage. The ladies watched mesmerized as three carriage loads of baggage and scarlet-coated dragoons, with Mrs. Dewinters the center of attention, disgorged on the front steps of the hotel. A laughing Lord Rathbourne dismounted from a massive gray gelding and did the honors of leading the lady, over the protests of his vociferous comrades, into the hotel foyer. To Deirdre's deep chagrin, Roderick Ogilvie formed one of the actress's admiring cisebeos.

"The whole of the bloody light cavalry seems to be in attendance," observed Lady Fenton with blighting vituperation. "And to think that is the useless article that stands between Napoleon and England. Someone should tell Lord Uxbridge."

"Mrs. Dewinters looks to be taking up residence at the d'Angleterre," said Deirdre, her spirits sinking.

"It will be interesting to see where Lord Rathbourne decides to billet." Lady Fenton's mouth twisted with cynical disdain.

When, however, an hour or so later, the grande dame received a note requesting the pleasure of her company in the private parlor of Mrs. Dewinters, she assumed a tranquil and faintly smiling demeanor. "Take your cue from me, Deirdre," she admonished her niece, then as an afterthought, "How the devil does she come to have a private parlor?"

"Influence, I suppose."

"Sir Thomas shall certainly hear of this." The smile slipped infinitesimally.

It was Lord Rathbourne who lazily uncoiled himself from the depths of an armchair and came to do the honors as host. "Maria is changing," he said by way of explanation. "May I get you ladies a glass of something to drink?" He seemed in fine fettle.

"Sherry will be fine," said Lady Fenton with perfect amity, her supercilious gaze damning the gentlemen for their partiality to strong spirits.

Captain Ogilvie took a step toward Deirdre but halted irresolutely when the lovely turned aside and gave him a perfect view of her back. Lord Rathbourne choked on his brandy. It was then that some of the younger gentlemen, observing that a dampener was about to descend on their jollity, made their excuses and left.

Deirdre and her aunt sat straight and primly on the edge of the white and gilt damask sofa awaiting the pleasure of their hostess. As was to be expected, Mrs. Dewinters made a grand entrance, the gentlemen all rising politely, the ladies' eyes sweeping assessingly over every inch of her diminutive form.

"Oh no," said Deirdre enviously to her aunt. "Scarlet satin and long sleeves!"

"All she lacks is a rose between her teeth and castinets in her fingers," returned her aunt without moving her lips.

Deirdre's eyes widened and she looked askance at Lady Fenton. Never in all her life had she ever observed such uncharitableness in the lady, and she wondered if it was provoked by the uncharacteristic despotism of a husband who, to her knowledge, was used to doting on his wife.

Mrs. Dewinters, catching sight of the ladies through the crush of red uniforms, approached with outstretched hand. She flashed a singularly triumphant smile in the direction of Lord Rathbourne and curtsied deeply, holding the pose for several moments.

"Come now, ma'am," said Lady Fenton briskly, "we're not royalty, nor is this the theater. Come and sit beside me and tell me how you are getting along in Brussels. Deirdre won't mind taking a turn about the room, will you, dear?"

Mrs. Dewinters trilled a laugh and obeyed the summons gracefully. "I like it well enough," she intoned in confiding accents, "but my circle of female acquaintances is almost nonexistent."

Deirdre did not doubt it, and bit down on her tongue to stifle the comment that would have betrayed a childish resentment.

Rathbourne, glass in hand, strolled toward her. He took a

long swallow of his drink, his eyes resting on the beauty reclining elegantly on the sofa. "Beautiful woman, isn't she?" he asked Deirdre casually. "And blessed with all the female virtues to boot." His eyes were alight with mockery.

"Oh, a paragon, indubitably! She'll make you a marvelous Countess, Rathbourne." Her tone was cold and clipped, and Deirdre regretted that she could not inject more warmth into her remarks.

Rathbourne, however, seemed inordinately pleased with her answer. "Do you think so? I'm very glad to hear it."

Deirdre's eyes followed the direction of his gaze. Mrs. Dewinters's dark dramatic beauty could not be eclipsed. It was very evident to Deirdre, however, that the actress, beauty and paragon of every feminine virtue as Rathbourne professed, would never be blessed with babies with downy soft hair in the hue which she herself preferred above all others. The thought was oddly comforting, and Deirdre smiled.

"A penny for your thoughts," said Rathbourne in a soft undertone, and Deirdre colored slightly.

"Oh no, Rathbourne! I'm not going to let you inside my head!"

His injured look was faintly reproving and his voice sank to a whisper. "I'd be satisfied, Miss Fenton, if you'd let me inside your—"

She cut him off in a rush. "Don't you dare say it!" Shock registered in her eyes.

"—circle of intimates," he concluded mildly, but he could not control the burst of laughter which was loud enough to drown all conversation in the room.

All heads turned in their direction. "Miss Fenton will explain the joke," he said with maddening calm, and left her blushing and tongue-tied to face a sea of curious eyes.

"It w—was n—nothing," Deirdre stammered lamely, and blushed more hotly when the curious eyes turned speculative.

Justly incensed with Lord Rathbourne for making her the

center of unwelcome attention, she retired to the isolation of a corner chair where she covered her confusion by drawing a young and homesick ensign into conversation. His family farmed in Yorkshire and Deirdre, far from jogging the lad out of his melancholy as she had intended, found herself more homesick by the minute. She wondered when her aunt would signal that it was time to withdraw. Rathbourne and Ogilvie, she noted dourly, were hovering assiduously over the beautiful actress, giving Deirdre a perfect view of their backs. She munched on a macaroon and ground it into little bits between her teeth.

When her aunt rose to leave, Deirdre started to her feet with alacrity. She took Mrs. Dewinters's hand and intoned a polite farewell.

Mrs. Dewinters's sloe eyes, cordial and without affectation, looked directly into Deirdre's. "Miss Fenton . . . Deirdre, thank you," she said simply, and there could be no denying the sincerity of her expression.

Deirdre felt chastened. If only she could bring herself to dislike Mrs. Dewinters, this irrational and uncharitable urge to put a rub in the way of Rathbourne's ambitions for the woman would seem less spiteful. But it was not in Deirdre to spurn a friendly overture. "Not at all," she said, and smiled reassuringly, though a trifle wanly.

At the door, Rathbourne commented regretfully, "I hope you did not take it amiss, Miss Fenton, when I did not include you in the invitation to drive with me tomorrow, but Maria does not ride and my curricle accommodates only two comfortably."

Since Deirdre had not heard the invitation, and she was sure that Rathbourne knew it, she looked at him questioningly for a moment or two trying to divine his purpose.

Lady Fenton, irritated to find her niece cast into the shade by a woman she had no hesitation in disliking, and to whom Deirdre had lost all her beaux besides, took it upon herself to become Deirdre's champion. She rushed into speech before Deirdre had a chance to frame a suitable reply to Rathbourne's question.

"Of course Deirdre does not mind, Lord Rathbourne. Why should she when Lord Uxbridge has mounted her? Yes and I'm sure that Deirdre has the handsomest seat of all the ladies in Brussels."

Deirdre risked a quick glance at Rathbourne, certain that her aunt's innuendo would cause another outburst of laughter. She was taken aback at the blaze of anger which was directed toward her before his expression became shuttered.

"Indeed?" he queried with glacial politeness. "Miss Fenton is fortunate to have attracted the notice of Lord Uxbridge."

"Which of his mounts did he give you for your use, Miss Fenton?" asked Ogilvie.

"A handsome filly that goes by the name of Lustre," answered Deirdre artlessly. "Do you know her?"

Ogilvie looked at Rathbourne. "Lady Capet particularly asked for Lustre but was refused. The filly is something quite out of the ordinary. I believe our commander said that she was to be reserved for Lady Uxbridge's exclusive use should she make the trip to Brussels."

"Oh dear," crowed Lady Fenton, by no means put out by the reflective looks the gentlemen exchanged. "I do hope Lady Uxbridge is not of a jealous disposition. There's no telling what construction she might put on his lordship's excessive civility to Deirdre."

Deirdre did not dare look Rathbourne in the eye. The smile on her face became fixed and she meekly followed her aunt out the door. Only a few steps took them to Deirdre's chamber, and several more beyond that to Lady Fenton's door at the top of the stairs, but the Earl insisted on escorting them. Deirdre sensed that he hoped to maneuver her alone to give her the sharp edge of his tongue. She was careful not to give him the opportunity, and sat for the next hour in Lady Fenton's chamber until she saw him from the window ride off on his gray.

They were destined to meet again the following morning. Rathbourne and Mrs. Dewinters were in the open curricle with O'Toole sitting up behind. Deirdre, in form-fitting green riding habit with matching cap perched jauntily at a slight angle over one eye, was mounted on Lustre. Armand, astride a handsome roan, unwittingly had chosen to don a riding jacket that matched Deirdre's habit exactly. Brother and sister, one darkly and negligently handsome, the other radiant with a translucent, porcelain beauty, drew many admiring glances. Rathbourne noted it with little pleasure as he checked his team. The two of them looked to have been born and bred to the saddle so easily did they sit their mounts and control their movements. Lady Fenton had not exaggerated. Deirdre had the handsomest seat he had ever seen in a woman.

They drew alongside each other and halted. "Will you ride with us in the park, Miss Fenton?" asked Mrs. Dewinters. "I should be glad of your company."

"Thank you, no. Some other time, perhaps? Lustre is accustomed to something a little more strenuous in the morning. She knows the way to the Bois de là Cambre, you see, and would show a most unladylike side to her nature if I changed her schedule."

Rathbourne's smile was not far removed from a snarl. "Very commendable. But I trust that you will make yourself available this afternoon? I escort Maria to Grand' Place to help her pick out a new gown or two, and your presence has been promised by Lady Fenton. Shall we say about two o'clock."

Even Mrs. Dewinters looked to be pained by Rathbourne's ill-natured display, but before anyone could say a word, the Earl had flicked the ribbons and had given his team the office to start.

Mrs. Dewinters might be only mildly ruffled, but Deirdre, the object of Rathbourne's spite, was provoked to the limit of her endurance. "Philistine!" she grated through tightly clenched teeth. She looked to Armand for confirmation.

He stood in his stirrups, gazing steadfastly after the curricle as it bowled along the street. After a moment, he flashed a quick smile at his sister. "Amazing!" he exclaimed, his eyes dancing with devilment. "He can't even hide it!"

"Hide what?" demanded Deirdre.

Armand shook his head, then laughed ruefully. "Why his temper, of course!" he replied evasively. "D'you know, I had the strangest feeling that he wanted to do me an injury?" He laughed again. "Come along, Dee. Let's get these fidgets out of our horses."

She held back. "Armand, you'll come with me this afternoon to Grand' Place?"

His eyes opened wide. "You must be funning! I have no wish, yet, to meet my Maker. But don't worry, Dee. You, I am persuaded, are more than a match for the irascible Earl. Now come along!"

Deirdre took particular pains in dressing for her outing with Rathbourne and Mrs. Dewinters. She eschewed the pristine white muslins and elected to wear the new daffodil crepe walking dress with its white satin stitch roses embroidered lavishly at the bodice and hem. The loss of the long sleeves, which she had removed only the week before, she refused to lament, and purposively draped a white shawl over her arms and shoulders. As she critically surveyed herself from head to toe in the long, gilt-edged looking glass, she thought that she looked very pretty, and wondered why she should be plagued by vague feelings of discontent.

Rathbourne, Deirdre was relieved to note, had recovered his equilibrium, and his mood verged almost on the playful. Mrs. Dewinters was her usual elegant self in a gown of startling peacock blue, and Deirdre felt a stab of envy when she observed the long sleeves with matching satin ribbon gathered at shoulder, elbow, and wrist. Mrs. Dewinters, she decided, was a fashion plate whom even Serena would be hard pressed to emulate.

The pleasant walk to Madame Lecquier in Grand' Place, the heart of the shopping district, was delayed by frequent chance encounters with many of the young ladies whose acquaintance Deirdre had made in the previous month or two. After the introductions had been made, Rathbourne, at his most charming and urbane, skillfully brought Mrs. Dewinters forward. She behaved very prettily and demurely, and Deirdre had the pleasure of hearing many invitations to parties and musical evenings pressed upon the actress and her dashing escort, with herself included almost as an afterthought.

At Madame Lecquier's, Rathbourne was in his element. "I want all the lady's gowns put on my account," he said with a wicked grin to the modiste, whose expression remained impassive. Mrs. Dewinters looked to be acutely embarrassed, and Deirdre did not know where to look.

"Have them made up in pastels, whites, pale green, and one in this color," he said, indicating Deirdre's new walking dress.

"Gareth," said Mrs. Dewinters patiently, "those are Deirdre's colors and suit her admirable. They won't do for me."

"Nonsense," he replied with a show of gallantry. "Mayhap Deirdre lacks the panache to carry off vibrant tints such as scarlet and so on, but I am persuaded that any color would look divine on you." He raised her hand to his lips, but his eyes, blazing with mockery, locked on Deirdre's.

She remained stony-faced and silent, and Rathbourne, with a faint shrug of his shoulder, turned back to the modiste. "And as for style, no long sleeves, if you please. I like them short, and feminine, like these." Again he indicated Deirdre's gown.

"Really, Gareth," Mrs. Dewinters's patience was sorely strained. "This is the outside of enough. Long sleeves are coming back into fashion. In another week or two, they'll be all the rage."

261

"That's very true, sir," interrupted the modiste. "Soon all the ladies will be in long sleeves, even at balls."

"Deirdre has three new gowns, and to my knowledge, not one of them has such sleeves." He turned for confirmation to Deirdre. "Isn't that so?"

Deirdre was at a loss. It seemed that the Earl had made a study of her wardrobe, and it annoyed her as much as it puzzled her. Her unexceptionable gowns were not meant to excite notice.

"Isn't that so?" he repeated when she remained obstinately mute.

"Yes, as you have remarked."

"Why?" he asked baldly.

"Because," she replied mendaciously, "my shoulders and arms are my best feature and I wish to show them off."

Before Deirdre knew what he was about, he had removed her shawl, and his eyes measured her slowly and tauntingly.

"Possibly! How can I tell?" he said with blatant provocation. "If it's true, why do you hide yourself behind this monstrosity?" He held up the shawl with one negligent finger.

Mrs. Dewinters spoke sharply. "Gareth, leave the girl alone, and take yourself off for a good half hour or so, if you please. I haven't come here to order a full wardrobe of clothes, as you very well know. What I require is a gown for the Duchess of Richmond's ball and I *will* have it made up with long sleeves and in the color of my choice." Her eyes happened to wander to the window and she exclaimed, "Oh look! There is Lord Uxbridge crossing the square. Didn't you—"

Deirdre whirled to face the window, caught a glimpse of Lord Uxbridge on the pavement outside, and dashed out of the modiste's before Mrs. Dewinters could finish the sentence. She had, of course, written to thank Lord Uxbridge for the loan of her mount, but she had not seen him in person since the night of the Embassy reception. He looked up as she came flying down the front steps of the shop, and caught her in his outstretched arms, swinging her off her feet. Rathbourne, a thunderous expression on his face, watched it all from the window. When Uxbridge planted a kiss on Deirdre's cheek, Rathbourne spun on his heel and strode after her.

Lord Uxbridge's arms dropped from Deirdre's slim waist when he caught sight of his friend's black expression. Good God, he thought to himself not without some amusement, does Rathbourne really regard me as a rival? Perversely, he felt his spirits soar.

"Ah Rathbourne," he said easily, ignoring the dangerous glitter of tawny eyes narrowing upon his person, "I was just telling Miss Fenton how honored I am to provide a worthy mount for her. Pretty little filly, isn't she?" he asked obliquely, the vivid mockery in his eyes returning Rathbourne's challenge.

"Yes, very," said Rathbourne stiffly, then by degrees, relaxed his grim expression. "Very!" he said again, and choked on an embarrassed laugh.

"Pretty!" said Deirdre, betraying her disappointment at the meager econium. "This filly is one in a thousand! To be mounted on her and riding ventre à terre is"—she cast about in her mind for an extravagant compliment—"heavenly," she concluded creditably.

"Quite," said Lord Uxbridge, keeping a straight face.

The eyes of the two men met over Deirdre's head and Uxbridge could hardly contain his mirth for what he read clearly written in Rathbourne's piercing expression. Bedamn if the whelp wasn't warning him off, and no mistake about it! It made him feel ten years younger and a very fine fellow indeed.

Lord Uxbridge, however, fearing that his welcome was about to wear out, did not linger. He was scarcely out of earshot when Rathbourne turned the full force of his anger upon Deirdre.

"You seem to be on very friendly terms with Uxbridge."

"Hardly that! But I cannot deny that he has been very civil to me, for whatever reason."

"Oh, I think we can safely assume the reason for his civility," he answered her. "Flirting with him at the Embassy, permitting him to mount you quite publicly, and mount you in private too, for all I know."

Deirdre stared at him open-mouthed, her breasts heaving. She shut her eyes for a moment as if the sight of him disgusted her. When she opened them, green lightning flashed from their emerald depths. "Your male crudity is beyond anything," she stormed at him. "I have done nothing to be ashamed of! Good God, the man is old enough to be my father! And I thought you were his friend? Who was it told me that Uxbridge was madly in love with his wife? Who was it upbraided me for being rude to him? Who was it—"

"Hush! I know what I said. But if you throw yourself at his head, you'd better be prepared for the consequences. You're not the innocent you once were. You know perfectly well what can happen if you tempt a man beyond endurance!"

"Ooh!" Deirdre choked. "How neatly men turn the tables! Now I am the one to blame for your . . . your . . ."

"Pray continue! My what?" he taunted.

"Your lechery!" Her tone was blistering.

Rathbourne observed the delightful flush of color high on her cheekbones, the rosy lips tremulous with emotion, and the softly heaving bosom.

"Compose yourself, Deirdre," he remarked gently, the heat gone out of him. "If anyone should see us now . . ." He glanced quickly around as if to ascertain that they were unobserved. Deirdre took the hint and brought her emotions under control.

She allowed him to return her to the modiste's, where Mrs. Dewinters had just completed her purchases. On the way back to the hotel she replied civilly if a little coldly to every comment he addressed to her, but she refused an invitation to partake of a small glass of sherry in Mrs. Dewinters's rooms. That Rathbourne wished to talk to her privately was very evident, but she forestalled him by saying lightly that Armand would be waiting and she daren't test the patience of a brother as if he were a beau.

In her own mind she had determined that the time for words was past. She was not prepared to accept the Earl's apology for the insults he had inflicted, and there were many. She had no idea of making him jealous. She did not think that was in her power. But neither was the ordering of her life in his power. It was a lesson Gareth Cavanaugh needed to learn.

Chapter Eighteen

In the Hotel d'Angleterre, in the apartments which had once been occupied by Lord Uxbridge and his staff, my Lord Rathbourne took a long swallow of his fine French cognac and looked over the rim of his glass at his pensive companion, Lieutenant Colonel Colquhoun Grant, chief of Intelligence Operations and responsible only to His Grace, the Duke of Wellington. He absently shut his box of snuff and replaced it in his coat pocket. The chamber was lit by several branches of candles which were scattered throughout the room. The grate was empty for it was already June, and although a summer storm blazed outside the open window, the air inside was hot and humid.

It was Lord Rathbourne who broke the comfortable silence. "My impression is that Napoleon cannot afford to wait. The attack must come soon. Everything points to it."

"That is debatable. With conscription in France reinstated, it makes more sense for him to wait till August. By that time he could double the strength of his army."

"Very true, but so could we. He knows that he outnumbers us already, and he fears our units will have returned from America if he delays overlong."

"This Louis Bourmont fellow, you trust him?"

Rathbourne shrugged. "I should like to say 'implicitly,' but

267

in our line of business, I've learned not to trust my shadow."

"It seems strange that one of Napoleon's own generals should be willing to aid us."

"He is not aiding us. His loyalty is to France first and foremost. He sees the little Corsican as a scourge on the country he loves."

"Damned near impossible to sift the wheat from the chaff. My desk is littered with reports, all of them contradictory."

"What does your nose tell you?" asked Rathbourne, lazily observing the forked lightning as it streaked across the sky. The ferocious clap of thunder overhead made not the slightest impression on either man. The Earl's eyes shifted to his companion, an officer whose judgment he held in the highest regard.

At five years his senior, Lieutenant Colonel Colquhoun Grant had made Wellington's Intelligence Service a formidable organization. Though held to be very young for such a responsible position, his uncanny nose for sifting fact from fiction had become almost proverbial.

He stroked that aristocratic object with his index finger. Rathbourne noted the gesture and the slight flare of his nostrils, and the Earl smothered a smile.

"In the Emperor's own words, one French soldier is equal to one English soldier, but worth two of any of our allies. I'm inclined to agree with you. He knows that we are vulnerable and he won't give us time to even the odds. Damn those Yankies for the trouble they have caused!"

"I would rather damn the politicians for being so shortsighted. These differences with the Americans should have been settled by the diplomats. Fortunately, we have our cavalry intact. That's one consolation."

"Naturally, *you* would say so! I'd settle for more guns and ammunition."

"There's always Congreve's rockets, or had you forgotten?"

"Oh those!"

"Don't be so disparaging! I assure you, the French are

already quaking in their boots at this latest scientific invention of modern warfare."

"How did that come about?"

Rathbourne's lazy smile was telling. "A policy of misinformation to the enemy which I was at pains to foster. They are not to know that Congreve's missiles are a source of terror to our own ranks as well." When he noted Grant's questioning look, he explained. "Maria Dewinters is very friendly with a Belgian count whom, all unsuspecting, we know to be a collaborator with the French. She passed the information along. It was confirmed later by my sources close to Napoleon's staff."

Grant gave his companion a long, level look. "You are playing a very dangerous game, as I've already told you."

"Why? Simply because my identity has become known to the enemy? It has its advantages, so long as they don't know that I know they know, if you know what I mean." He quirked one sardonic eyebrow.

"I don't see the advantage if you're dead," said his companion soberly.

"You refine too much upon it. No one values my life more than I do. I'll be careful. Have you discovered how they came by the information?"

"Not yet, but it's only a matter of time before I do." After a moment's considering silence, Grant asked, "How are things progressing with Mrs. Dewinters?"

"Couldn't be better. By the way, I must thank you for your tactful intervention. Maria is accepted everywhere."

"So I heard. Has the ploy been useful?"

"You've seen my reports! I gather information, Maria dispenses misinformation. It's a strategy that works well. She is known to be close to me. Those who think to pick my brains without my knowledge try to get at them through Maria. Naturally, it's done with great finesse, and Maria is clever enough to let them think that she has been duped."

"You trust her then?"

"Better than I trust my own shadow."

"From you, that's saying something!"

"Don't worry, I never leave anything to chance. As far as possible, I get confirmation from others in my network."

"Which brings us to the Belgians. You are convinced that they will take to their heels as soon as hostilities begin, then?"

Rathbourne held his glass up to the light and gently eddied the amber liquid. "Perhaps not as soon as that. It's not that they are cowards, you understand. It's simply that they don't regard this as their fight. They'd like to be shot of the lot of us."

"I can't say as I blame them. I've cautioned the Duke, although, to be frank, I think it's what he expected." After an interval, Grant queried, "So, what am I to tell His Grace? Where and when can we expect the attack, in your opinion?"

"Within the next week or two, I should say. The French border has been cut off for days, not by us, but by Imperial loyalists, and you know what that means. The enemy has tightened security. Almost nothing can get through. I think Napoleon will soon be on the move."

"Your sources of information have dried up then?"

"Not quite. Guy Landron is our man on the front line. He's one of Bourmont's secretaries. Ironic, isn't it?"

"What about his gammy leg?"

"Oh that! He has trouble walking, but he can still push a pen. Says that the blue regimentals are more to his taste than our garish redcoats, and the French girls likewise."

"Tell him he will have his fill of French girls when we march victoriously into Paris."

"I will. I'll be checking with him in a day or two."

"Of course. You always did like to be in the thick of things, just like Lord Uxbridge. I, on the other hand, take my cue from Wellington."

"A more detached approach?"

"As it should be in a professional soldier. You haven't told me yet where you think the attack will come."

"I don't believe that Napoleon has made up his mind, or if he has, he's not telling anyone. But you may be sure, when he does, he'll attack with the speed of a thunderbolt."

As if to emphasize Rathbourne's words, a bolt of lightning blazed across the sky, giving the uncanny impression that night had suddenly turned into day. A moment later, torrential rain beat against the windows, signaling the end of the storm.

"It will be like that with Napoleon," said Grant musingly. "One last burst of glory, then gone forever."

"But sending so many to an early grave," Rathbourne interjected. He bolted the contents of his glass and helped himself to another shot from a crystal decanter.

Both men became lost in private reflection. "To return to the problem of where the attack will come," said Grant finally. "The Duke prefers a defensive strategy if Napoleon's attack is imminent. He thinks that at present, going on the offensive would be a hopeless proposition. He's looked over the terrain and favors the Charleroi Road as our best defensive position. Pity it's impossible to place Napoleon exactly where we want him."

"Oh, I don't know. Stranger things have happened. By all means, let us quietly let it be known, in the right circles, you understand, that Wellington has grave misgivings about defending the city."

"He thinks that it's going to be a very close-run thing."

"Such optimism is most heartening."

"You think we shall lose?"

"No! I share the Duke's opinion."

"Where does Deirdre Fenton come into all this? Is she part of your network?"

A look of surprise crossed Rathbourne's face. "She knows nothing. Nor do I wish her to know! It's safer that way."

"Good God! And she let you browbeat her into accepting Maria Dewinters? I was under the impression that there was some sort of understanding between you and the girl."

"And if there is?"

"She must be something very out of the ordinary to put up with the gossip that is circulating about you and Maria Dewinters. No, don't roast me! I presume you know what you're doing."

"Thank you."

"And the girl's brother, St. Jean?"

"What about him?"

"He's your ward, I believe, and half French?"

"What of it?"

"He seems to be having trouble deciding which side he is on. There have been several reports about him which, so far, I've discounted."

Rathbourne took another long swallow of his brandy. "Go on," he said levelly.

"He has a loose tongue. He admires Napoleon and doesn't mind who knows it."

"In my experience," intoned Rathbourne carefully, "it's those who profess a dislike for the little emperor who are the most suspect."

"Very true. It's probably only youth speaking. Wellington, after all, professes an admiration for the man as a general, but as a gentleman utterly despises him. Nevertheless, you will keep an eye on the lad, won't you? It would be a pity if we had to hang him as a traitor."

"Thank you for the warning. I'll take care of it."

"Good. I knew I could rely on your discretion."

Rathbourne was to have the opportunity of tearing a strip off his tempestuous ward, a pleasure he had long anticipated, toward noon of the following morning when St. Jean returned with Deirdre from their daily jaunt to the Bois de là Cambre. It was a grim-faced O'Toole who informed the unsuspecting young man that his lordship would be obliged with a few moments of his ward's time on the instant. Such a peremptory summons, Armand dared not refuse.

Deirdre followed behind, but when she made to ascend the stairs to Rathbourne's rooms, she was turned aside by the unyielding groom. Armand, striving to appear natural, though his serious demeanor betrayed something of his disquietude, adjured his sister to wait for him in her chamber. Deirdre reluctantly complied.

Once there, she could not settle to do a thing, but strode about the room in a fever of impatience. It was soon evident that the interview between the two men was taking place in the room directly above. The din of raised voices, though muffled enough so that Deirdre could not hear what was said, was distinct enough to inform her that they were in the throes of a violent argument. A sudden commotion overhead shook some plaster from a cornice on the ceiling. Deirdre froze. There followed a few moments' silence, then she heard the clatter of boots as they descended from above on the flagstones of the back stairs, which in normal circumstances were used only by the hotel staff. Deirdre ran to the gib door which gave onto the service stairs and fumbled with the key as she tried to turn it. By the time she had dashed onto the landing, Armand's back was disappearing around the corner. She called to him, but he gave no indication that he had heard. She dashed back into the room and ran to the window. Armand emerged from the back door of the hotel and flung away as if the devil himself were after him. Deirdre noted the white handkerchief with red splotches which he held to his mouth. A surge of anger, hot and reckless, shook her to the core.

She raced up the hard stone steps which Armand had recently descended, found the door she wanted, and threw it open. Rathbourne, his back toward her, turned at her entrance. From the corner of her eye, she saw O'Toole pick up the pieces of a small, shattered side chair. He took one glance at her white-mouthed expression and looked to his master.

"Leave us," said Rathbourne in a voice that was barely audible, "and O'Toole, shut the door behind you."

The click of the latch as the groom made his exit was the signal for Deirdre to advance upon the powerful figure of the Earl. She halted when she was only a step away from him.

273

What she intended to do or say, Deirdre had yet to formulate, but a glance at his contemptuous and faintly challenging expression and Deirdre's temper exploded. She wanted to humiliate him in the most insulting way she could think of. She looked him straight in the eye and spat in his face.

She fell back at the blaze in his eyes, but strong hands caught her in a viselike hold, and she was hauled, struggling and kicking, till he had positioned her, head down, over his muscular thighs.

"My father used to say whenever he beat me that this hurt him more than it hurt me. I, Miss Fenton, do not share his sentiments. This is a pleasure I will long remember."

He removed one of the slippers from her wildly bucking legs, and plied his arm with ferocious vigour. Deirdre, mortified at the indignity of her ignominious position, gritted her teeth and tried to weather his retribution with an indifference which she hoped would show her utter contempt for the man. She bit down on her lip to stifle her cries, and tears of pain and frustration squeezed from under tightly closed lids.

At the sixth blistering stroke of the slipper, a strangled groan was torn from her aching throat. She had every intention, when the shaming ordeal came to an end, to spit in his face again, but she was turned and held with infinite tenderness against his chest.

This gentling she found more humiliating than his former fury and she strained against him in a vain effort to free herself. Arms, corded with muscles she had never suspected existed, grasped her securely and she gradually stilled, though she held herself tense and ready to take advantage of the first sign of weakness.

"Deirdre, why do you persist in making me lose my temper? Don't," he threatened when he saw that she was about to spit on him again, "or I'll blister your backside till you can't sit down for a week."

"You would!" she sneered, her eyes glistening with tears.

"You know you deserved it," he reasoned patiently, as if he

274

were speaking to a willful child. He found his handkerchief and carefully brushed the tears from her cheeks. His voice altered. "Deirdre, look at me."

His eyes locked with hers and a pulse beat frantically in Deirdre's throat. She had seen that look in his eyes before. He bent his head to take her lips. For an unguarded moment, she wanted to melt into him, to give herself to the gentleness and strength of arms which would shield her from every adversity, relieve her of every worrisome burden. She thought of Armand and her feelings of tenderness died stillborn. She tore herself from his arms, half falling on the floor in her frantic haste. He let her go and she put some distance between them.

"Why did you thrash my brother?" she asked him, straining for some semblance of calm.

He looked at her for a long, dispassionate moment. "Because I am a sadistic savage? Isn't that what you'd like to think?" He drew out his snuff box and helped himself to a miniscule pinch. The negligent gesture was almost insulting.

"Why do you hate him so?" persisted Deirdre.

"I don't hate him. That implies strong feeling. I am indifferent to him."

"I don't doubt it! You use him to punish me because you know how much I love him."

"Is that what you call it? Love?" he sneered. "Love is when you seek another's highest good. The maudlin sentiment which makes you blind to all St. Jean's faults should not be dignified by so lofty a word."

"I do love him," protested Deirdre, stung by his open contempt. He looked credulous, and she repeated more forcefully, "I do!"

"Then prove it! When next he comes crying on your shoulder to help him out of his latest peccadillo, let him suffer the consequences."

"It's not like that!" she cried, and wondered why she wanted to make him understand. "He is all I have. We're family! It's only natural for us to be loyal to each other. You had a younger

275

brother once." She saw his head come up and quickly explained, "Captain Ogilvie told me. You of all people should understand my anxieties on behalf of a younger sibling."

"I do understand," he said patiently, "none better. But if your brother doesn't mend his ways, he is in a fair way to throwing away his life."

"I . . . I don't understand."

"Don't you? He has not told you, then, that his sympathies in this coming confrontation lie with the French? I find that very hard to believe since he has made no effort to conceal his views from all and sundry. Now why wouldn't he tell you?"

"Armand doesn't mean anything by it."

"I'll remind you of that when they hang him as a traitor."

The words made her brain reel. "D—don't be ridiculous!" she stammered. "Armand isn't the only one to express such sentiments. Even the Duchess of Richmond has said as much. No one takes *her* seriously. You're just trying to frighten me."

"So you did know of St. Jean's indiscreet words? I thought as much. As for Her Grace, I hardly think that is relevant. She is not French, nor without friends at Court. You should be glad I am your brother's guardian, else he might be languishing in some godforsaken cell by now awaiting a much severer punishment that the one he provoked today. I can see, however, that you have no intention of thanking me."

He moved to the gib door and held it open. "It was foolish of you to burst in on a bachelor establishment unannounced," he said with a devilish smile lightening his expression. "It might have proved very embarrassing. I see that I shall have to keep my door locked in future."

Deirdre's cheeks flamed. She, none better, knew what scene of seduction she might well have interrupted. She quelled the ache in her chest, and lifted her chin a fraction. "In the middle of the day, my lord?" she asked archly.

As she sailed past him to the service stairs, she heard his burst of laughter as he shut the door behind her. "Oh Deirdre, you're such an innocent!" And her cheeks flamed even hotter.

Her anxiety for Armand increased during the days that followed. He became abrupt and moody and refused to discuss what had taken place between himself and the Earl. Their morning rides continued, however, and Deirdre found herself looking forward to them more than ever since a pall had descended on the engagements Rathbourne forced upon her in the hours that remained each day. She soon came to see herself as little more than a chaperone as Rathbourne squired Mrs. Dewinters to every social event of any note. His excessive gallantry toward the lady, whether in his box at the theater, at small private dinner parties among close friends, in his borrowed open carriage which was large enough now to accommodate a silent and subdued Deirdre, and on any and every occasion, was enough to bring a curl of contempt to Deirdre's usually tranquil expression. When she quizzed him lightly about the nature of his duties as Lord Uxbridge's aide which allowed him so many hours of leisure while others were obliged to remain at Ninove, he answered evasively that his role was more in the line of liaison officer.

In retrospect, Deirdre came to acknowledge that it was her own reckless behavior at the Château de Soignes, the ancestral home of the Marquis and Marquise de Soignes, which brought matters to a head between herself and the Earl. Perhaps she had been guilty of imbibing too many glasses of champagne; perhaps she might have behaved with her habitual decorum if Lady Fenton had been in attendance instead of laid upon her sickbed with a ferocious megrim; perhaps if Armand had not encouraged her so outrageously but had tempered her precocity with a look or a word; and perhaps if Deirdre had not heard that the Earl's liaison with the actress was generally accepted, she might have remained collected behind her usual protective wall of reserve. But she did overindulge in champagne; Lady Fenton was not present that evening; Armand made no attempt to restrain her; and she did hear the latest titillating ondit about the Earl. As a consequence, Deirdre went a little wild.

She had turned dizzy and slightly sick when Lady Mary Ingram, a young friend, an acquaintance really, had whispered outrageously behind her fan as the Earl and Mrs. Dewinters waltzed past locked in each other's arms, that she wouldn't mind changing places for one night with the sultry actress who was fortunate enough to be tutored in the ways of amour by such a delectable protector as the wildly exciting and rather dangerously good-looking Earl. Since Lady Mary was a well-brought-up and sheltered young deb who had little notion of what she imagined she knew, and Deirdre could not claim such innocence, it was not to be wondered at that it was Deirdre's cheeks that flamed to a pretty shade of pink. Lady Mary silently remarked the phenomenon, and made a mental note that Miss Fenton was probably a confirmed spinster and much too nice in her notions for her taste.

It was from that moment on that Deirdre's personality seemed to undergo a transformation. As if she had been sheltering in the protective warmth of a cocoon until that evening, she emerged, a rare butterfly, a thing of beauty and utterly enchanting, flitting from one handsome partner to another, sampling but never remaining with one for long, unless it was with Armand, who took her into supper and whose eyes seemed almost as feverish as her own.

La crème de la crème of Brussels society was present at the Château de Soignes that evening, and many a watchful, experienced gentleman remarked the English beauty whose escort gave her only the most cursory attention.

The Conte de Wetteren kissed her in the conservatory where they had gone to observe a rare orchid which had been cultivated by their proud host. The Marquis de Nivelles kissed her on the terrace where they had strolled to view the lake. The Baron de Gembloux offered her carte blanche in the library where he had escorted her to view, so he said, a very rare manuscript, a letter written by the scholar Erasmus. Armand surveyed it all from the sidelines, his lazy, watchful eyes flicking to Rathbourne, whose brooding expression had become more thunderous as the hours slipped by.

When word buzzed round the assembly that the Conte de Wetteren and the Baron de Gambloux had ridden off to the Forest of Soignes to fight a duel over the dainty morsel, Armand made his move.

"I think a storm is brewing!" he said languidly to his sister, and he nodded surreptitiously in the Earl's direction. Rathbourne was moving swiftly toward them.

Deirdre crowed, as if her brother had said something uncommonly witty, but she was not so lost to all sense of her jeopardy that she did not understand the urgency of leaving the premises with all dispatch. They bolted for their carriage like a couple of mischievous children and fell back against the squabs convulsed in hoops as if they had just done something terribly wicked and clever.

"You're foxed, Dee," Armand accused without rancor.

"No more than you!" protested his sister with great dignity. "Where to now?" she asked as the coach picked up speed for the six-mile drive back to the city.

Armand regarded her pensively. "I'm meeting some of my friends at the Café Royale, but I don't think it's quite the thing for you to come with me."

"Why not?" she pouted.

"Rathbourne won't like it," said Armand decisively.

"Oh, won't he? He's not *my* guardian," she coaxed. "And what I choose to do is none of his business. Oh Armand," she went on, her brittle air of gaiety slipping, "I couldn't bear to go home and think right now. If I were a man, I should drink myself into oblivion. Please don't make me go home to my own thoughts." She saw that he was weakening and ended on a rush. "Especially when *his* rooms are right above mine. I don't think I could bear it."

Armand expelled a soft expletive. "I don't understand. I could have sworn that he . . . oh never mind! Don't repine, Dee. I'll take you with me. Half of my friends are in love with you already, and the other half are dying to meet you!"

Shortly after four o'clock in the morning, when the sky was beginning to lighten over Brussels, Deirdre trudged wearily into the hotel. She gave a muted belch as she passed the night porter, and elevated her brows a trifle as she tried to focus on him. She had been imagining all evening that Rathbourne's groom, O'Toole, had been doggedly following her about. She hoped she had been mistaken, for she did not wish for one word of her night of dissipation, ever, *ever* to get back to the Earl. She thought of the "ladies" who had accompanied Armand and his friends on their round of Brussels nightlife, and she shuddered. Her aunt would give her the worst scold she had ever had in her life, and Rathbourne would positively *kill* her. She was sure she did not know which was more to be feared. She favored the night porter with a frown and passed on.

She struggled up the broad staircase and fumbled in her reticule for the key to her chamber. When she could not find it, she dug deeper and gave a triumphant crow when her fingers closed about it. She turned the corner of the stairs and took one step into the long corridor. The key dropped from her fingers, and Deirdre giggled. As she bent to retrieve it, she became conscious that the door at the far end of the hall which gave onto Mrs. Dewinters's private parlor had opened. Deirdre slowly drew herself to an upright position. Rathbourne, his back to her, was silhouetted against the open door. Mrs. Dewinters was in his arms. Deirdre could not tear her eyes away as the Earl crushed the actress to him in a passionate embrace. One hand closed over a thrusting breast and slid below the taut bodice of the gown. Deirdre did not wait to see more.

She whisked herself around and went racing soundlessly down the carpeted stairs, her head miraculously clearing of the effects of her night of overindulgence. She heard the heavy tread of footsteps in pursuit and she picked up her skirts, giving the stunned porter a clear view of her drawers and neatly turned ankles. Her name was called in a compelling voice at her back, but she ignored the summons. Her one thought was to reach the safety of her room. She dragged open the door to the service stairs and half threw, half dragged herself up by the iron railing, a stitch knotting painfully in her chest. She heard the door open behind her, and she sobbed aloud and stumbled, recovering almost on the instant, and pressed forward. The key to her chamber was clutched convulsively between her fingers. She pushed it home, turned it quickly, and sobbed again when she heard the reassuring click of the door give way beneath her shoulder. Before she had taken a step, however, she was spun around and flung, head down, over Rathbourne's broad shoulder, as if she had been a sack of potatoes or a side of beef, and he one of the porters at the early morning market in Grand' Place.

He went up the stairs two at a time as if scarcely aware of the weight on his back. Deirdre was not afraid, only desperately angry, but she restrained the impulse to kick or struggle, biding her time till he should put her down and she would be in a position to do some damage. The instinct for flight which had governed her actions only moments before had changed to a primitive desire to inflict punishment on a hated enemy.

He kicked open the door to his suite of rooms and lowered her gently to the floor. The moment her feet touched the ground, Deirdre spun on him. In the flickering light of the lone brace of candles on the mantlepiece, she gave the appearance of some mythical creature, a Valkyre, a warrior maid of the North with a curtain of flaxen hair tumbling in wild disarray about her shoulders. Her eyes were stormy and reckless with unbridled rage, and a feral snarl distorted her lips. He knew, in that instant, that if a dagger were put into her clenched hand, she would plunge it into his heart without a moment's hesitation. She was magnificent in her anger, he thought on one level of consciousness, while another gave him the wit to move out of her way. His spirits soared.

He had deliberately baited her with the sight of another woman in his arms. A slight twinge of conscience provoked him to remember he owed Maria Dewinters an apology for his

281

callous and impulsive use of her. But the actress was dismissed from his thoughts as he circled the snarling spitfire who faced him. His smile was blatantly triumphant.

"You're jealous."

Deirdre lashed out at him, catching him a glancing blow on the cheek as he dodged the full force of her ferocious backhand.

"Not fair!" he taunted. "Gentleman Jackson would disqualify you for that inadmissable blow."

"I hate you!" she stormed at him. "I hate you!" Her foot caught him hard on the hip, missing her target by only inches. He lunged for her wrist and sent her spinning.

She lay panting on the floor, fighting to regain her breath. She heard the soft click of the door latch as he shut it, and his tread on the rug as he advanced toward her. She scrambled to her feet and stood glaring up at him, a blaze of defiance reaching out to scorch him.

"Touch me," she said between her teeth, "and I'll scream the house down."

He held up his hands, palms open. "I won't come near you! I won't touch you, not unless you touch me first. But I won't let you go till we talk this thing out."

She relaxed slightly, but her eyes were watchful as he neared her.

"I promise, I won't touch you unless you touch me first," he repeated. And, he promised himself fervently, he would make damn sure that she did touch him, and not in anger either.

She forced her hands to unclench and said tonelessly, "You have no right to keep me here! Please let me pass."

"I have every right," he said curtly, "and you know it. But we won't go into that at present, if you please." He looked her over for a full minute and said very softly, "I've never seen you so beside yourself. You're angry, Dee, and I want to know why."

"I'm angry because you dragged me here against my will," she cried out.

"That's not the reason," he said, and moved closer.

"Stay away from me!" She took a quick step backward and came up against a tall escritoire. He was only a pace away now.

"You're angry because you saw me with Maria, and you did not like what you saw. Dee, you're jealous! Admit it!"

She managed a shaky laugh. "Jealous!" she exclaimed, and injected as much scorn as she could command into the word. "I was embarrassed! Who wouldn't be? I tried to be discreet and remove myself before you became aware of my presence. What was I to think when I heard you thundering at my back? I know you for what you are! Naturally, I was frightened!"

His confidence seemed to be slightly shaken, and Deirdre pressed her advantage. "Let me pass, Rathbourne, please?"

"And it means nothing to you if I go to her now and finish what I began? You don't mind if I hold another woman in my arms and touch her intimately and join my body to hers?"

"Stop it! I won't listen to more of this!" His face was only inches from her now. "You stink of her scent! Carnations!" she spat at him, and turned her head away.

"Then drench me in yours. It's what I want."

"I have an antipathy to perfume. I never wear it!"

"That's not what I meant."

The silence stretched taut. His eyes locked with hers and held them. The soft quickening sounds of their mingled breathing beat a disturbing tempo on Deirdre's senses.

"Do you want me to go to her?" he asked in a whisper, and his breath warm and sensual, fanned Deirdre's lips.

"A threat, Rathbourne?" she queried.

He groaned. "No! An ultimatum, damn you! I won't go on with this unnatural celibacy whilst you flirt and do God knows what with every buck who comes sniffing around your skirts. How do you think I felt tonight when you flaunted yourself like a lightskirt with every lecherous roué whose jaded palate revived at the thought of savoring you in his bed?" His hands came up and he braced them on either side of her head. The heat of his body seemed to penetrate every pore of Deirdre's skin. "You knew how much I wanted you," he went on raggedly. "You knew! Yet you deliberately tormented me. You belong to me, Deirdre. I'll kill any man who says otherwise. Now touch me, damn you, touch me."

He strained against his arms, keeping the press of his weight only inches from her body, making rational thought an impossibility for Deirdre.

"Deirdre!" he groaned. "I need you. I love you."

Instinctively, she put out her hand and covered his lips with her fingers. "Don't, oh don't," she whispered.

Her touch jolted him. She felt him go rigid. He inhaled deeply and relaxed the press of his arms till his body slowly covered hers. His hands tangled in her hair, forcing her head back, and his mouth, with gentle savagery, cut off her soft whimper of protest when she realized the enormity of what she had done.

Chapter Nineteen

His passion had the ferocity of a full-blown tropical hurricane. Nothing could stand in its way. Deirdre did not try. He kissed her again and again, deeply, compellingly, his mouth and tongue urging her to open herself fully to him. His hands caught her hips, and he ground himself into her, the hard press of his arousal blatantly communicating his ultimate purpose. She answered instinctively, melting into him, and she raised her arms, giving him freer access. At the age-old gesture of invitation, he pulled back.

His eyes were fever bright, the pupils by turn dilating and contracting, as if he were laboring under the effects of some powerful narcotic which had been pumped into his blood.

"You'd better make up your mind to what this means," he told her. "I won't be turned away again, not ever."

She gave a soft cry and pulled his head down, offering him her lips. He took them hungrily, then pulled back. She was spun round and propelled firmly to the door of his bedchamber, his fingers deftly working on the buttons of her gown, stripping it from her in one quick movement and discarding it on the floor where she stepped out of it. He pressed her down on the bed and stood over her, tearing off his clothes in a frenzy of impatience.

Deirdre was not intimidated, only surprised and a little

dazed by the intensity of his ardor. She watched the soft rise and fall of his bare chest, the rough tempo of his breathing the only sound in the silent room. When he told her to undress, she sensed the tenuous control behind the thickened words. His urgency was almost tangible. She could taste it, smell it, feel it, see it.

Her fingers were too slow for his desperate haste. He threw himself down beside her and ripped the garment from her back, his hands covering her shoulders and breasts with deliberate possessiveness. He dragged the hem of her chemise around her waist, and Deirdre gasped when her fine linen drawers were violently wrenched from her.

"Gareth," Deirdre protested, and made a slight movement to escape the torment of his fingers. She tried to raise herself on her elbows, but he spread one hand against her breasts, pushing her down. He took her mouth again, kissing her deeply, coaxing her into submission. Her thighs gradually relaxed against the pressure of his hand, yielding him the freedom he desired.

He knew that he was going too fast but he was helpless to stop himself. He parted her legs and positioned himself above her. Her hands flexed against his chest as if to restrain him, but they both knew that she might as well try to turn back a tidal wave. He drove home, exulting in the feel of her warm, enveloping flesh, and he threw back his head and groaned his pleasure, instantly recognizing the triumph of the primitive male in him laying claim to his mate. He went perfectly still and looked down at Deirdre. He had taken her with all the instincts of an animal! He drew a long, shuddering breath. "Did I frighten you?" he asked softly.

"Yes," she pouted.

"Liar!" He kissed her with slow languor, savoring the novelty of her body open and receptive to him. "Don't move," he warned as she shifted her weight beneath him. He eased himself slightly to allow her to draw breath. Her muscles tightened around him and on an urgent breath he warned again, "Don't move."

"I thought you were in a hurry."

"Mmm," he ran his teeth over one taut nipple, indifferent to Deirdre's quick intake of breath, deliberately intensifying her distress by slowly drawing the hardened bud into his mouth. "I was in a hurry to join my body to yours, not to hasten the end of our pleasure," he murmured. "How long has it been?" His lips, hot and open, moved to pleasure her other breast and Deirdre gave a soft cry. "Three months? It seems like an eternity. You might have guessed how it would be once I finally got my hands on you."

He raised himself on his arms and his eyes dropped to their joined hips. He levered himself higher, easing himself more deeply inside her. This was his territory that he and only he would ever chart. He told her so, and thrust deeper as if to convince her of that fact.

She was like velvet beneath him, and he luxuriated in the feel of her soft, tender flesh. He set a slow pace, patiently bringing her to fever pitch with each sensual movement of his hips. His lazy eyes surveyed her through a haze of passion as she moved beneath him. The flush of desire was on her skin; her eyes were dark and dazed with the need he was building in her loins; her lips were soft and open to him, and her strawberry-tipped breasts rose and fell at each labored breath. When her head began to thrash on the pillow, he withdrew completely.

Deirdre's eyes flew open and she lifted her arms to draw him back. He read the confusion in her drowsy expression.

"I would be drenched with your scent, love," he whispered beguilingly, and he drew himself out of reach. Softly, with feather-light kisses, he began a slow descent of her body, his lips and tongue searching out each pulse point, tasting, savoring the dew on her heated skin. The coaxing pressure of his fingers spread her inner thighs. He moved lower, but Deirdre's soft whimper of distress brought him back to take her lips in a reassuring caress.

287

"Deirdre, love, don't be frightened. I won't do anything you don't want me to do." He lavished kisses on her eyes and throat and took her lips again, seducing her senses with ravishing tenderness. "Let me, love, oh yes, let me . . . yes."

She abandoned herself to the deep need she sensed in him, surrendering to every sensual caress, every murmured expression of his love and longing. He heard her soft cries of pleasure as permission for the intimacy he urgently craved.

She felt the soft brush of his hair at her thighs. Her senses heightened and focused on the sweet, drugging torment of his honeyed tongue.

Her fervent moans shattered his tenuous control. He reared over her, taking her with one sure thrust. He drove deeper, controlling her writhing movements with the press of his hips, delaying their pleasure until he thought he would die of love for her.

At her cry of mingled outrage and rapture, unexpectedly, he laughed. He captured her lips, soothing her bruised pride, inhaling her moist breath with lungs burning with the erotic incense of her exhalations. As the waves of ecstasy slowly receded, he locked her in his embrace. The sheen of suppressed tears was in his eyes as he nuzzled her with infinite tenderness, his hands pressing her almost convulsively into the shelter of his body.

For a long time afterward, they said little, as if each was reluctant to let the outside world intrude on their perfect communion. By slow degrees, coherent thought finally returned to Deirdre. Her thoughts became restive, and she wondered at the vague feelings of disquietude that had begun to tease her mind. He had explained nothing of his reasons for coming from Mrs. Dewinters's quarters at four o'clock in the morning. Had he taken his mistress first, as the main course, then taken her later, as dessert? His appetite was insatiable. Of that there was no question. The picture was not flattering.

He had said that he loved her. Was that merely another cheap ploy, part of his bag of tricks to break down a reluctant female's resistance? He had told her often enough that she was an innocent. It was the truth. She was no match for him in this game of love. Did he tell all his women that he loved them?

She pushed herself to a sitting position, exposing the full swell of one satiny mound with its strawberry ripe nipple. Rathbourne groaned and fastened his lips to it, pressing her back into the depths of the soft feather mattress. Deirdre tried to resist, but his compelling hands and mouth gave her no quarter.

Much later, she flung herself out of bed before he had a chance to stay her movements. He raised himself on one elbow, and one eyebrow quirked as she stalked about the room in naked splendor, examining first one ruined garment then another. As he heard her wails of protest, his face creased in an unrepentant grin.

When she caught sight of his expression, she stood very much on her dignity. "How am I to explain these torn garments to my aunt's abigail?" she demanded, shaking the torn drawers at him. She dropped to the floor and let out a cry of anguish. "Look what you've done to the strings of my stays," she accused, holding the article in question under his nose.

To be truthful, the garments meant nothing to her, and one way or another, she was sure that she would hit upon some plausible explanation to satisfy Solange without rousing her suspicions. But she was close to tears, bedeviled by doubts and confusion. The destruction of her underthings was only an excuse to vent her feelings on the real object of her frustration.

She threw the drawers and stays at him and said dolefully, "You're the great lover, the master of clandestine intrigue. You fix them!"

Rathbourne gave up trying to keep a straight face, and a great gust of laughter convulsed him. "If you could only see yourself now!" he said, looking over her naked torso with a long appreciative stare.

Deirdre shimmied into her crushed silk gauze and said with

awesome dignity, "Now that you've had your way with me, I am the one who is left to suffer the consequences."

"Now that I *what?*" he expostulated, and immediately dissolved into another fit of laughter. When he had dried his streaming eyes on the bed sheet, he ventured, "I thought it was you who had your wicked way with me." Deirdre did not rise to the bait, and he went on in a more conciliatory fashion. "Don't fret, love, I'll buy you dozens of replacements for the things I ruined, and not so serviceable either," he concluded as he examined more closely the threadbare drawers and stays which flaunted not one piece of fancy lace or ribbon.

Deirdre, who had been looking under the bed for her best silk shawl, brought her head up and glared at him. "In the meantime, what am I to tell Solange when she comes to collect my drawers and stays for the laundry? I can't possibly say that I've lost them! To lose a shawl is one thing, but drawers?"

"How the hell should I know?" He raised himself further to get a better view of the ripe twin globes which were falling half out of her brief bodice. "Tell her to mind her own bloody business. If my valet were to pry into every shirt or pair of drawers I'd lost, I'd soon send him packing."

Deirdre rounded on him, her mouth forming a perfect O. My Lord Rathbourne became conscious that he had stepped blindly into a treacherous quagmire. "All I meant, love," he said hastily, trying to retrieve his position, "is that such things have never mattered to me before. The ladies I have bedded in the past never had the need for chaperones and abigails and such like."

Deirdre gnashed her teeth and Rathbourne figuratively kicked himself.

"Where did you learn to make love like that?" she demanded, her hands splayed ominously across her hips. The question had hovered at the back of her mind since he had first initiated her into the mysteries of love.

"Like what?" he asked mildly, desperately playing for time.

"Like a depraved maniac who hasn't a shred of decency left

in him."

"I had an expensive education," he shot back, his ego bruised at the aspersions on what had seemed to him the most natural and perfect expression of his love and reverence for her.

"In the brothels of London, I don't doubt," she jeered.

"Paris, to be exact," he retaliated with equal vigor.

"Oh yes, the Grand Tour—finishing school for the young, rich drones who make up the spear side of our depraved society."

"Come, Deirdre. One's education is never finished, as you well know. You should thank me for making you the beneficiary of my years of diligent study—and practice!" he added venomously for good measure.

She looked completely taken aback and, for one unguarded moment, totally vulnerable. He swept the bedclothes aside, meaning to gather her into his arms and put an end to their absurd quarrel. She stopped him with a deep, insulting curtsy which she held for several moments.

"My Lord Rathbourne," she intoned with crushing civility, "pray accept my thanks for a memorable evening. Your generous hospitality is something quite beyond the ordinary, the likes of which I am sure I shall never meet with again, no, nor ever hope to."

He bowed stiffly, feeling rather ridiculous in his nakedness, but he would not allow her the last word. "Don't mention it, Miss Fenton. I should be the last to raise false hopes, but I take leave to tell you that you may expect to be the recipient of my generous hospitality—with regular frequency!" His voice rose with menacing effect on the last words.

She picked up the torn drawers and stays, arranged them neatly on her arm, and sailed majestically out of the room, the picture of wounded innocence.

"Resign yourself to that fact!" he called after her, but Deirdre did not dignify his parting shot with a reply.

She wakened with the first hangover she had ever experienced in her life. Her head ached, her stomach churned, and every muscle in her body was in torment. The slight tenderness between her legs, she discounted. The blame for that discomfort, she was perfectly sure, could not be laid to the many glasses of champagne which she had so freely consumed both during and after the reception at the Château de Soignes.

Lady Fenton, quite recovered from her own distressing malady, was beside herself with worry. Deirdre looked awful, and as she told her abigail, it could not be put down to a woman's monthly trial, for the girl had never suffered overmuch during that particular affliction. It was deemed expedient to send for a doctor.

Chancing to meet Lord Rathbourne in the corridor, her ladyship unburdened herself in his sympathetic ear, quite forgetting that she was out of charity with the reprehensible gentleman. She was relieved when he took command and within the hour, a physician, a personal friend of the Earl, came to examine the patient.

Dr. Shane McCallum was no fool. As a member of the army's medical corps, he had on many occasions witnessed the ailment which had laid Deirdre by the heels. In fact, he told her ladyship breezily, with a sly wink at Deirdre, he had occasionally fallen victim to it himself, but only occasionally. Deirdre was merely suffering the effects of an overindulgence in a cuisine that was unfamiliar to her. He prescribed a small glass of brandy to settle the stomach. Deirdre sipped it slowly, and within minutes her stomach heaved and she was retching into the chamber pot which the doctor held for her. Moments later, she owned that she felt much better and wished to get up. Dr. McCallum, after telling her to eat and drink sparingly for the rest of the day, withdrew to pay a call on Lord Rathbourne, who, he told a stricken Deirdre, was waiting most anxiously for news of the patient.

She knew that she was in Lord Rathbourne's black books the moment she left the draper's shop where she had gone to buy supplies to repair her stays and drawers. She caught sight of the empty curricle with O'Toole standing at the heads of his lordship's horses. The Earl joined her as she crossed the square of Grand' Place, and she felt his proprietary hand on her elbow.

"Get into the curricle," he said curtly, and Deirdre obediently complied. O'Toole was dismissed and Rathbourne climbed in beside her.

"I'm not feeling very well," she told him, and managed a creditable, die-away whine in her voice.

"By the time I've finished with you, madam, how you feel now will be only a pleasant memory! How dared you put yourself at so much risk by exposing yourself in the stews of Brussels?"

The queasiness returned to Deirdre's stomach. "Gareth, I can explain everything."

"Do so."

"What did I do that was so wrong?" she parried, and she cast around in her mind for a plausible explanation for a night of folly that shocked even herself.

Rathbourne was not slow to itemize her misdeeds, beginning with the abortive duel which was prevented only at the last moment by his intervention, to the round of cafés in the society of a class of women, not to mention rackety ne'er-do-wells, she should be ashamed to give the time of day to.

"It was O'Toole spying on me, then, wasn't it?"

"He was there at my command to look after your interests, not to spy on you. Good God, even he is shocked, and that's saying something."

Deirdre's back straightened imperceptibly. "What it has suited you to leave out, Lord Rathbourne, is the most scandalous part of the whole affair, when you carried me off to your room."

He chuckled. "True. But then it's not likely that I would look upon *that* in the same light, now is it?"

A thought suddenly occurred to Deirdre. "Does O'Toole know about that too?"

"Possibly. He's very acute. Naturally, I've told him nothing, but there's not much he misses."

"Oh no!" Deirdre's mortification was transparent.

"Is that all you worry about? O'Toole's good opinion? Let me tell you, if I'd had the foresight to collect you in a closed carriage, I'd have blistered your backside by now for these wild escapades of yours." His anger cooled somewhat, and after due consideration, he gave a low laugh. "That's not true, and we both know it. If I'd had the foresight to bring a closed carriage, I'd have had your skirts up to your waist and your drawers—"

"Gareth Cavanaugh!" Deirdre screeched.

"I beg your pardon," he said without a pretense of regret. "We shall consider that last remark unsaid, if you prefer it." He cocked a wicked eyebrow at her, but Deirdre's expression was not encouraging. Two flags flew in her cheeks, and her bosom rose and fell with the effort to maintain her shaken composure. He thought she made an adorable picture. He was tempted to say more but decided against it, and he recalled his wandering thoughts to a topic he had yet to broach.

"Have you seen your brother today?"

"No. Why?" She became alert and wary.

"He seems to have run to earth. That doesn't surprise me. He knows that I hold him responsible for your misdemeanors. He won't escape retribution for this. I have my men out looking for him now. After what has passed between us, I expected better of him. He holds a grudge, I see. I wasn't blind to the way he encouraged you last night. He knew how I felt, oh yes, he knew!"

"Don't be absurd, I'm older than he is. When I make up my mind to do something, Armand knows better than to try to change it. Don't lay my misdeeds to his account."

"You always make excuses for him!"

"You never listen to reason where Armand is concerned."

He said nothing for some moments, his attention occupied in negotiating his team between two stationary wagons loaded with fresh produce which were parked on opposite sides of the narrow street leading out of the square. After the difficult maneuver was complete, he said cautiously, "I've received a letter from home which gives me some concern. It mentions your brother."

"From whom?"

"I'm not at liberty to say. Has St. Jean confided in you?"

"I wish you would call him Armand," she said testily. "What has he done now?"

"I thought you might tell me."

She fell into a troubled silence, searching her mind for some clue.

"No, don't look like that, Dee! It's not that serious. Armand and I shall settle this little problem very easily between us. Now there, I gave him his Christian name. Does that please you?"

But Deirdre had the distinct impression that Armand was in a more serious fix than Rathbourne was willing to reveal, and it vexed her when he would not be drawn on the subject.

When he drew up at the hotel entrance, he held her wrist in a loose clasp and said in a serious tone, "I shall be out of town for a few days. When I return, God willing, there is much that must be settled between us."

"Gareth . . ." she said uneasily.

"No Dee, your wishes no longer come into it. If need be, I shall put the whole matter before your brother and Sir Thomas. Now be a good girl until I return. I leave O'Toole to look after you. See if you can win back his good opinion. Expect me on the fifteenth. I shall be at the Duchess of Richmond's ball. And Dee"—one finger tipped up her chin— "make damn sure you save all the waltzes for me—yes, and I had better be the one who takes you into supper, too." And he kissed her very swiftly before helping her down.

Lady Fenton observed it all from her chamber window. She staggered back into the empty room, her expression thunderstruck. "Well!" she said to herself. "The sly chit! She has fooled us all!" She plumped herself down on the brocade settee, and fell into a brown study. She heard Deirdre's footsteps pass her door on the way to her own chamber. "Well!" she said again, and absently smoothed the pair of long satin and gauze sleeves on her lap which had once adorned Deirdre's new sea-foam ball gown. A modiste had been engaged by her ladyship to reset them in Deirdre's dress for the Duchess of Richmond's ball.

Solange entered with the laundry, and unobtrusively began to put things away.

"Long sleeves aren't everything," said Lady Fenton.

"Madame?"

Her ladyship came to herself. She rose and handed the sleeves of Deirdre's ball gown to her maid. "Dispose of these," she said regally. She gave the young maid an affectionate pat on the cheek and intoned sagely, "Make a note of it, Solange, where the gentlemen are concerned, long sleeves aren't everything, no, not by a long shot, long sleeves certainly aren't everything."

She half expected Deirdre to make her entrance with the happy announcement that she would soon become Rathbourne's Countess. But the door remained closed. Lady Fenton was not unduly put out, thinking that his lordship might first wish to consult with Sir Thomas. Perhaps they might even wish to make the betrothal public at the Duchess of Richmond's ball. The thought of the ball gave her mind a new direction, and she was soon looking through her wardrobe for a gown which would not disgrace her position as wife of a high-ranking diplomat of His Majesty's Government.

The ball was far from Deirdre's thoughts as she threw herself down on her bed and looked up at the ornate ceiling. She could hear the tread of footsteps overhead, and wondered where Rathbourne was off to again, and why he was always so secretive. Sometime later the room overhead became silent. She heard a door open and shut down the long corridor. She imagined the Earl taking his leave of Mrs. Dewinters. Surely not now—not after what had passed between them last night and what he had said to her in the curricle. The thought nagged at her like the pain of a persistent toothache. She had to know if her imagination was running riot again, or if she had grounds for her suspicions.

She rose and opened her door slightly, then shut it again. This was ridiculous. She must learn to trust him. She took a turn or two around the room and was drawn once more to the door. She opened it and stepped into the corridor, thankful that it was deserted. Step by guilty slow step, she advanced to Mrs. Dewinters's rooms. On the other side of the door, she could hear voices, but not distinctly enough to make out to whom they belonged. She was on the point of turning away when the door handle turned. Without conscious thought, Deirdre whipped herself round the corner of the half landing and pressed herself against the wall.

"I shall see you at the Duchess of Richmond's ball then," she heard Rathbourne's voice say, low but distinctly. And then, adding insult to injury, "I've left O'Toole to look out for you. Be a good girl till I return."

Deirdre's hackles rose. Without a second thought, she swept out of her hiding place and turned the corner, running full tilt into Rathbourne. He was holding Mrs. Dewinters's fingers to his lips. Deirdre's eyes took in the loose robe that concealed nothing of the actress's voluptuous figure. It was clear that Mrs. Dewinters had received the Earl in her night attire. The intimacy of their relationship was self-evident.

The suddenness of Deirdre's appearance must have startled them, she thought, because Rathbourne's face registered an emotion that was very close to horror, and Mrs. Dewinters's eyes were enormous. Deirdre gave a convincing laugh and winked conspiratorially at the Earl.

"Don't forget to tell her to save all the waltzes for you," she said roguishly over her shoulder as she began a slow glide into the long corridor. "And, of course, you'll be the one to take her into supper." A few more steps and she would be at her own door. The Earl seemed rooted to the spot.

She wagged a mischievous finger at him. "Have a safe

journey, Rathbourne, and don't do anything I wouldn't do."
She whisked herself into her chamber and bolted the door. She
didn't wait to find out what Rathbourne's reaction might be,
but took off down the back stairs. Once outside, she dodged
behind a milk cart and raced out of sight of the hotel. She
found herself in an alley that ran down toward Grand' Place,
and she sheltered in a doorway till she regained her breath, her
heart pounding in her chest. She remained motionless for
several minutes, tensing for sounds of pursuit. When none
came, she relaxed and gradually become conscious that she was
attracting the stares of tradesmen who were making deliveries
at the back doors of the homes and shops that lined the Rue de
la Colline. She gave herself a mental shake and returned a
serene smile for every raised eyebrow, as if it were the most
natural thing in the world for a slightly disheveled lady to be
found traipsing in the back alleys of the city. When she purred
a *"Bonjour"* in a faint English accent, her eccentricity became
comprehensible, and shrugs of disdain and rude Flemish jests
soon took the place of curious stares.

She set out in the opposite direction from the hotel, deciding
on impulse to go and search out Armand. It would help pass an
hour or two until Rathbourne had gone, and she wanted to
quiz her brother on Rathbourne's disquieting disclosure that
he was in some kind of trouble at home.

She returned to the hotel at dusk, and made her excuses to
her aunt saying that her morning's malady had returned in full
force and she wished to make an early night of it. Lady Fenton
was sympathetic. It was very evident that Deirdre was not
shamming. She offered to send for the doctor but was quietly
refused, though Deirdre did accept the proffered glass of
brandy to settle her stomach.

A physician would have been able to tell at a glance that
Deirdre was suffering from exhaustion and shock. Lady

Fenton had no way of knowing it, for Deirdre said very little before retiring to her room, not even to the extent of acknowledging her aunt's comment that Lord Rathbourne had waited a full hour for her to return from her errand before taking his leave.

Once she reached the privacy of her bedchamber, Deirdre removed a letter from her bodice and read it for the upteenth time. It had been given to her by the concierge of Armand's lodgings, and it made no more sense to her now than when she had first scanned its incoherent contents.

June 12, 1815

Deirdre,

Can you believe it? I—a turncoat! Please try to understand and forgive me. And don't worry. I'm grown-up now. I suppose Rathbourne has told you that Caro is about to become betrothed? I hope I shall see you when this is all over, and if not, God bless.

Affectionately,
Armand

She read it again and again, slowly, digesting every word, pulling apart his phrases and substituting her own interpretation. Some of it she made sense of almost immediately. The intelligence about Rathbourne's sister, Caro, gave her the clue to what the Earl had mentioned earlier that afternoon, something about a letter from home with disquieting news which concerned Armand. Lady Caro and Armand—yes, she could remember how they had looked at each other whenever she had seen them together in London. Strange that she had never once thought to ask Armand about Caro since they had arrived in Brussels. She wondered if they had been indiscreet enough to correspond with each other. She could well imagine how the news of Caro's betrothal could push Armand to some

299

desperate act. But what?

Reasoning that Armand's friends were the likeliest people to approach for a clue to his whereabouts, she left the hotel shortly after noon the following day and systematically began to search them out. They offered little in the way of information or reassurance, though they told her not to worry and that Armand was bound to show up within a day or two. Of the letter he had left for her, Deirdre said not a word, feeling that in some way she could not explain, it was vaguely incriminating.

She fell into a restless sleep, and wakened sometime during the night with all the pieces of the puzzle having fallen into place. She lit a candle and smoothed out the letter, reading it again but with new insight. Her face drained of color as each word hammered into her brain, confirming what her subconscious mind had grasped at. Armand had gone over to the enemy. The news of Caro's betrothal had pushed him over the edge. Had Rathbourne taken him to task, as only he could, for presuming to engage the affections of his sister? What a fickle lot those Cavanaughs were! Armand must have been consumed with despair at the news of Caro's desertion.

Oh Armand, Armand, she thought desperately. This could not be called a folly, or misdeed, or indiscretion, or by any other of the euphemisms she was in the habit of using to explain away her brother's foolhardiness. The penalty for this act of defiance was death. She remembered how Armand had told her that Rathbourne hated the French and had two young men hanged when they had gone over to the enemy. And Rathbourne had men out looking for Armand! He had told her so in the curricle. Pray God, they did not find him!

There was no one she could turn to in her distress, Rathbourne least of all, though she remembered how secure and safe she had felt in his arms in the aftermath of their lovemaking. But that, of course, was her imagination again. He had taken away her innocence, destroyed her honor, and made her a laughingstock, and she was fool enough to think that he had her best interests at heart. Idiot! she berated herself.

She put Armand's letter to the candle and watched as it blackened and curled, then shot into flames. She threw it in the empty grate. It was beyond her power to help Armand now. But she would protect him with the last breath in her body, and if that made her a traitor, then so be it.

Chapter Twenty

The day of the Duchess of Richmond's ball dawned auspiciously. The skies were clear and gave promise of a glorious summer's day. It was remarked with pleasure by mistress and maid throughout the city who were in a fever of excitement as they went about their business. Dazzling ball gowns were unwrapped and shaken out of their tissue paper; flat irons were heated on the black iron stoves and plied with careful vigor to erase each tiny and imaginary wrinkle from the voluminous folds of elegant satin and gauze creations; and large kettles of water were put on to boil for the scented baths of those ladies fortunate enough to have in their possession one of the gilt-edged cards of invitation to what promised to be the most glittering event of the Season.

Deirdre awakened with the beginnings of another blinding headache. Her first waking thought, as always, was of Armand, and she felt the familiar dread begin its slow seep into every nerve of her body, robbing her of the ability to think coherently. She lay back against the pillows and tried not to think, allowing the comforting noises of the hotel to soothe the incessant throb at her temples.

Solange entered on a softly spoken *"Bonjour,"* and went to the clothes press to unpack Deirdre's ball dress. She reached for the sea-foam gauze and Deirdre stopped her with a word.

"No!"

The maid hesitated, and waited for further instructions.

"The gold," said Deirdre firmly. She did not think that she could endure one more facetious remark about the effect the green dress had on her eyes, even supposing the color was all the crack and suited her to admiration. Besides, she had already worn it on three different occasions, and that was bound to be noted by the spiteful tabby cats whose sharp eyes never missed a thing. The simple pale gold satin and gauze would be passable, and truth to tell, Deirdre had lost interest in the trivia of what, in normal circumstances, would have occasioned many hours of pleasurable activity.

Solange beckoned to Deirdre, holding the dress up to the light for her inspection, and Deirdre obediently got out of bed and smoothed the gown over the front of her nightdress. As she observed herself in the looking glass, a pale shaft of sunlight bathed her in its soft halo, picking up the gold of the dress and reflecting its warmth in her creamy complexion and gold-streaked hair. It reminded her of a game she and Armand had played as children when they had gathered buttercups in the common and held them under each other's chin to determine whether the day would be fine or foul. It had never occurred to them, as children, that on a bright day, naturally, the yellow-tinted petals would cast a golden glow against the white of their skin. They had thought themselves, then, terribly clever at predicting the weather.

She handed the dress back to Solange with a murmured, "It will do," and wondered if there would ever again be another fine day in her life.

Later in the afternoon, she paid a visit to Mrs. Dawson. Her new scarlet spencer was ready and waiting for her, and Deirdre made an effort to pull herself together and made appropriate comments of appreciation for the excellent tailoring and fine stitchery of the accomplished seamstress. With nothing better to do with her time, she lingered and took charge of little William when his mother set herself to giving the two little girls a bath. It was difficult to remain in the dismals with three young children demanding attention, and Deirdre's problems gradually faded from the forefront of her mind.

As she took her leave toward the dinner hour, Mrs. Dawson remarked quietly in her ear, "You're not forgetting that you promised to look after the wee ones when the time comes?"

Deirdre signified that she had not forgotten.

"Then be ready for them tomorrow or the next day at the latest."

It was the first intimation Deirdre had received that the inevitable meeting between Wellington and Napoleon was imminent.

Lady Fenton did not place much credence on the intelligence that Deirdre had received from Mrs. Dawson.

"If that were so, my dear, you may be sure that the Duchess of Richmond would have canceled her ball, and Lord Uxbridge and his aides are here now, in the hotel, and quite possibly dressing for the ball this instant. Do you really suppose that Wellington would permit such a thing if Napoleon were on our doorstep?"

Deirdre had to admit that it did not seem likely, and she went off obediently to have her bath with its subsequent nap before the carriage was sent for to take them to the ball.

The rooms overhead were remarkably silent, and she wondered if Rathbourne would make it back in time for the ball. She tried to summon up all her defenses against him, but all she could think was that there was nothing she would like better than to lay her head against his chest and cry her heart out.

As it happened, the object of Deirdre's reflections was already in the hotel, although not in his own rooms for the moment. He was in conference with Lord Uxbridge, who had taken rooms for the night across the hall from his good friend and aide. Rathbourne's long booted legs were mired to the knee and his garments were covered in a thick coat of dust. He was slumped in a chair and gave every evidence of being bone weary to the point of exhaustion.

"Here, drink this," said Lord Uxbridge solicitously, and pressed a large glass of brandy into Rathbourne's long fingers. After a couple of long swallows, Rathbourne gave out a satisfied grunt.

"You've seen the Duke, then?" Uxbridge inquired.

"Yes, but I'm not sure if I've convinced him that Napoleon means to attack through Charleroi. The wily Corsican has been sighted from here to Ostend. Understandably, the Duke prefers to wait for more definite information before going off in every direction to tilt at windmills. He still expects the main attack to come on the road from Mons. Our commander hopes that I have the right of it, though. As you may remember, the area to the south of the Forest of Soignes is the terrain he prefers as the best defense for the city. But he mistrusts Napoleon, with good reason, I admit. He thinks the Charleroi diversion may be all a hum so that we will march off in one direction while the main attack comes from another."

"It's possible that the French may cut off our line of retreat through Halle, should, God forbid, we ever need one."

"Exactly what the Duke is afraid of. Hence, sixteen thousand of our troops are left to languish at a garrison that I am perfectly certain will not see action during this fight."

Uxbridge laughed at his friend's confidence. "Are you so sure of your sources?"

"Perfectly," replied Rathbourne easily. "I tell you the main body of Napoleon's army with his Imperial Guard will come at us through Charleroi."

"Engaging Marshall Blucher and his Prussians first?"

"It's possible."

"Divide and conquer?"

"That's what Napoleon hopes. The element of surprise is on his side, of course; that and the proliferation of conflicting intelligence reports which are reaching our commander by the minute. The enemy has quite possibly engaged the Prussians by this time. If he has, we shall soon hear of it."

"I still can't believe that we are under orders to attend this frivolous ball tonight when there is so much else we might be doing."

"Believe it! Wellington told me that he has no wish to start a panic in the city among the featherbrained British visitors. He wants the roads clear for the deployment of our forces, not choked with fleeing carriages and farmers' wagons. The presence of his senior officers at the ball is meant to allay suspicion and bolster morale. There's method in his madness."

"There always is, Rathbourne. Nevertheless, you should get some rest. As your commanding officer, I absolve you from the duty of attending Her Grace's ball this evening."

Rathbourne stood up and drained his glass in one gulp. "Thank you, but I would not dream of forgoing my last social engagement for some time to come. But I shall endeavor to catch forty winks, if you don't mind. Wake me when you are ready to dress and we'll go together."

As he reached the door, Uxbridge's soft-spoken question brought his head round. "Rathbourne, what do you think of our chances?"

"Oh, we shall win, if we give it all we've got."

"Now why do you say that?"

"It's a case of history repeating itself; battle tactics, Uxbridge, battle tactics." When he saw the Earl's bewildered expression, he went on to explain. "Napoleon deploys his troops in the manner of the ancient Macedonians; Wellington follows the Roman pattern. You hadn't noticed? Think about it and you'll see that I'm right."

"So? What if you are?"

"Only this. The Romans were invincible in pitched battles. Ask any Greek."

At No. 9, Rue de Centres, the residence of the Duke and Duchess of Richmond, the great ballroom blazed with the lights of a thousand candles. On the glittering floor beneath the orchestra gallery, young men in colorful regimentals whirled their partners to the steady tempo of the waltz. Deirdre was in the arms of Major Thornhill. She smiled often and said enough in reply to his courteous commonplaces to satisfy duty, but her eyes absently scanned the room for a set of arrogant shoulders with a head of thick mahogany curls.

She caught sight of Mrs. Dewinters in one of the shadowed alcoves that the candlelight did not quite reach. She was in conversation with some tall soldier in red and gold regimentals. Mrs. Dewinters's partner turned, giving Deirdre a clear view of his profile, and she expelled her breath on a small whisper of relief. It was Captain Roderick Ogilvie.

As the music drew to a close, there was a slight commotion at the door. Couples fell back as the Duke of Wellington, the only man who refused to wear the obligatory white dancing gloves, made his entrance. At his side was Lord Uxbridge and behind him, Rathbourne, with some other aides. They made an impressive picture with lashings of gold lacing on scarlet and blue tunics. Over one shoulder was carelessly draped a fur-edged pelisse. The assembled guests curtsied and bowed in the Duke's direction as if he had been the King of England. The expressions on the faces of Wellington and his staff were relaxed and smiling, giving the lie to the rumor which had circulated all evening that the army had been given its marching orders.

The dancers cleared the floor and a detachment of kilted Gordon Highlanders entered to the deafening skirl of the bagpipes. Each Highlander solemnly placed two crossed swords on the floor in front of him. The rhythm of the bagpipes quickened and the entertainment commenced. The furious battle dance seemed almost prophetic, and the eyes of all the spectators watched the nimble feet of the huge men as they strained not to touch the swords as the tempo of the dance grew wilder. Deirdre had heard of the superstition the Highlanders held to, that one touch on the sword meant death on the battlefield. Her eyes traveled from face to face, scrutinizing the uniformed men as they watched the movements of the Highlanders with breathless intensity. She knew then that the rumors were true. Napoleon had advanced upon Brussels and tomorrow the army would march out to meet him.

Her eyes flew to Rathbourne. He was watching her from across the room. As if he had read a signal in her eyes, he moved toward her, keeping her in his golden gaze. His hand circled her waist in a gesture of possession, and he swept her past the dancers, past the silent spectators, past the sentries stationed at the front entrance, and toward the rooms which were reserved for supper. Somewhere, a clock struck the hour.

"Midnight," said Deirdre breathlessly.

"Friday, June sixteen! Did you know that my birthday is on Sunday?"

"How old will you be?"

"One and thirty. Don't look like that, Dee. I assure you I intend to be around for many years to come, if only to plague the life out of you."

They were among the first to sit down for supper, but they hardly ate a bite. Before long, the room began to fill up. Deirdre noted that the Duke of Wellington was assiduous in his attentions to Lady Frances Webster, the lady who held first place in his heart and his bed, as rumor would have it, for the moment at least. Rathbourne read her mind.

"Deirdre, don't look so censorious. There are extenuating circumstances. You would know what I mean if you knew Wellington's Duchess."

Her cheeks reddened slightly and she looked away. "It's just so sordid and sad, really. Anyway, I've no right to judge the morals of anyone."

"True, but easier said than done."

He was mocking her, and to change the subject she said quickly, "When do you move out?"

"At dawn, but I'm not supposed to tell you."

Her lips parted, but the words would not come.

His hand covered hers briefly and he said in a conversational

309

tone, "If you look around, you will notice that many of the officers have left already to join their regiments."

Deirdre's eyes searched the diminishing throng of guests and saw that he spoke the truth. "Where are you off to?" she asked. "Or don't you know?"

"I will in a minute."

His eyes were on an aide who was conferring with the Duke and Lord Uxbridge. After a moment or two, they were joined by some of the other commanders, among them Picton, Somerset, and Ponsonby. All eyes were on Wellington and his staff as they moved apart to talk in whispers. Conversation at the tables languished; the clinking of champagne glasses gradually ceased; cutlery was laid aside; a foreboding silence filled the huge saloon.

Uxbridge bowed to the Duke and withdrew from the huddle. He came toward Rathbourne and said quietly in passing, "They've taken Charleroi. I'll see you at Quatre Bras at first light," and so saying he made for the exit.

He was the only commander to leave. The others resumed their places, and it was noted that the Duke seemed to be in high spirits. Conversation at the tables resumed; the hilarity became rowdier, and champagne was downed with increasing zest. Just when Deirdre felt that she could not endure another minute of the frenetic gaiety, Rathbourne pushed back his chair and reached for her.

"Time to go," he said against her ear.

She moved into the shelter of his arms and allowed him to lead her past the sentries and into the welcoming cool night air. He emitted a shrill whistle, and after a moment, a closed carriage with O'Toole in the box rolled to a halt in front of the torch-lit entrance.

"Get in, Deirdre," he told her softly, and dreamlike she moved to obey him.

"Where are you taking me?" she asked, not really caring what the answer might be. The present moment was all that seemed to matter.

"To your wedding," he replied, and she detected a note of steel behind the words.

For one unguarded moment, her heart gave a leap of joy, but other thoughts, less comforting, soon rushed in to caution her first instinctive response. Armand was a traitor, and by implication, so was she. If it should ever come to light, and she did not see how it could be prevented, the Earl would hate her with a virulence which she could not bear.

"Did you hear me?" he asked quietly from the depths of the coach's dark interior.

She turned her head in the direction of his voice. Her hand went out, and she traced the outline of his jaw. "This isn't necessary, you know." Her voice was breathless.

He turned her hand over and kissed it passionately on the open palm. "It's very necessary. Make up your mind to it, Dee."

It never occurred to her to ask how he could contrive to arrange their marriage when he had been out of Brussels for three days. He was Rathbourne. He could do anything when he put his mind to it. But this was one purpose she was determined to frustrate.

"Gareth," she began again, choosing her words with care, "I don't wish to be, can never be your wife, but I should be very, very happy to take you as my lover for as long as you wish it."

Her words lay between them for a long moment. He straightened.

Deirdre could feel his resentment fill the silence, and she cried out, "What have I said?"

"Your lover?" His tone lashed her with his anger. "By God, I was right. You don't think I am fit to be your husband or the father of your children. You look upon me as an object for your sexual gratification. Do you realize you have just offered me carte blanche?"

"Don't be absurd," she chided gently, trying to dispel his ugly humor. The last thing she wanted was to quarrel with him. "And if I did," she teased, "you may think of it as poetic

311

justice, retribution for all the ladies you have seduced in your time."

If she meant to placate him, she failed miserably.

"So we are back at that again, are we?" he asked wearily. "I am never to be given a chance to prove that I can aspire to anything more than a confirmed prodigal. I don't know why that should surprise me. I ought to be used to it by now."

"You're talking nonsense, Gareth. We've been through all this before. The reasons for my refusal to marry have nothing to do with you. They reside totally within myself. Why can't you accept it? If it's any consolation," she hesitated fractionally, then said very softly, "I love you." He was silent for so long that she wondered if she had offended him or if he believed her, and she rushed on with more feeling. "I never said that to anyone before."

"Then marry me!"

"I can't!"

"Nevertheless, you will!"

"I don't see how you can make me."

"Oh, that's simple—blackmail."

"Blackmail?"

"It's a newfangled word for a very old concept. I meant, of course, coercion." In an altered tone, he asked abruptly, "Deirdre, where is your brother?"

"Armand?" she asked cautiously, and felt every nerve in her body come alive as she sensed danger.

"Don't play for time. It won't do you a bit of good. Of course I mean Armand. What other brother do you have? Now tell me where he is."

When she could bring herself to answer, she sounded faintly amused. "My dear Rathbourne, how should I know? I am only his sister."

"Then I shall tell you. I have him under guard. You will see for yourself in a minute or two. Now Deirdre, what do you have to say to that?"

She tried to frame a suitable reply, but no words came. Her

312

mind went numb, and her body tensed as if waiting for a blow to fall.

"What do you think I should do with him?" he asked. "Hang him as a traitor?"

"Oh, no! Please, no!" The words broke from her on a sob.

"My dear, don't distress yourself. You must know I have no intention whatsoever of depriving myself of my one hold over you. I am not so stupid."

She should have felt anger, but his bitter words brought only a surge of relief. She leaned her head back on the squabs and closed her eyes.

"What?" he asked cynically. "No protestations of undying gratitude? I am disappointed in you, Deirdre. I see that you mean me to sink to the depths you believe I am capable of. Very well then. You may have your brother's life for a price, and you know what the price is. Does that satisfy you? You were right. I have no scruples where you are concerned. And you have no scruples where your brother is concerned. I think we make a pair. What do you think?"

She let the wave of his invective wash over her, hardly taking in a word that he said. "How did you find out?" she asked at length.

"Very easily. You confirmed my suspicions."

"I?" Her eyes opened wide, and she blinked rapidly, trying to glimpse his expression in the gloom.

"Yes, you. Armand's letter was read before you ever received it. You may remember that I told you he was on the verge of being arrested. When you started asking questions of his friends—and such questions, Dee, so obvious, really!—it was easy to put two and two together."

"What will happen to him?"

"What should happen to him? I shall make no report about him. He is my ward. He will soon be my brother-in-law. And when this is over, he will return with us to England. Does that satisfy you?"

"Yes."

313

"And are you prepared to make the supreme sacrifice for your brother?"

"If that will satisfy you."

"It does not satisfy me. But it will do."

They were married in the candlelit nave of a small stone church by a Walloon minister of the Reformed profession of faith. The wedding party was kept waiting until the arrival of Sir Thomas and Lady Fenton. It was not until later that Deirdre discovered that her aunt and uncle had been apprised of her wedding nuptials only after Rathbourne had spirited her away from the ball. He had contrived it, so her ladyship told Deirdre, her feathers thoroughly ruffled, so that Sir Thomas would be powerless to put a rub in the way of Rathbourne's plans, as if he would wish to deprive Deirdre of snatching the most eligible bachelor on both sides of the English Channel!

Deirdre soon perceived that even without Armand's unhappy intervention, her compliance had been a foregone conclusion. The sense of inevitability somehow made everything easier to bear.

Her heart leaped to her throat when she recognized Armand standing in the shadows. He gave her a brave, encouraging smile. Her eyes wandered to the man beside him, and she gave a start. Guy Landron, whom she had not seen since she left London, greeted her with a very grave, assessing look. She read concern in the directness of his expression, and returned a reassuring smile. It took her a full minute to register that the fair-haired gentleman on Armand's other side was Tony Cavanaugh, the Earl's cousin. She had not known that either man was in Brussels.

She made a move toward her brother but was stopped by Rathbourne's steady grip on her elbow. "The minister is waiting," he said curtly. "And time is of the essence."

It was over in a matter of minutes, and Rathbourne's ruby betrothal ring with a slim wedding band of gold lay snug around her finger. She managed only a short word with Armand before he left with the others, and even then, they said nothing of significance. But his smile was quite unrepentant as he wished his sister joy.

The ride back to the hotel was made in almost total silence. Deirdre found it very unnerving. It seemed to her that the Earl was already regretting that he had made her his wife. It was not until they had crossed the threshold of his rooms on the third floor of the d'Angleterre that she voiced the question that had revolved in her mind.

"Why was it so important for me to marry you?"

She could see that her question had angered him and she tried to pass over it lightly. "You see, I don't suffer from a surfeit of false modesty. I know my worth, and I cannot imagine why you should have settled for me when you could have done so much better for yourself. And I did not demand it of you."

She watched as he eased himself out of his scarlet tunic. Deirdre had not begun to undress and stood in the middle of the room feeling more awkward by the minute. She looked at him through the sweep of her dark lashes. For a man who had rushed her into marriage less than an hour before, he seemed to be uncommonly cold and unloverlike. She became conscious that her new husband had no intention of making things easy for her. She sat down on the edge of the bed and fumbled with the buttons at the back of her gown.

His expression was impenetrable. "I thought you might have guessed why I settled on you for my wife. At all events, there can never be any question of why you accepted me."

He was down to his pantaloons and glanced at her irritably. "I have to be gone in an hour, you know. It's imperative that this marriage be consummated. You see, I'm leaving no loophole—no chance later for an annulment, if you should ever take it into your head to seek one."

"You don't want me," she said in sudden enlightenment.

"You're wrong—which I shall very soon prove to you. Now

315

get undressed." There was a suggestion of impatience in his voice.

The last button gave way under her fingers, and she stepped out of her gown. "Then you want me against your will," she observed.

"And you married me against your will," he retaliated.

"Is that it? Is that the reason for this show of temper?"

"Yes, that's it! Now get your drawers off before I help you take them off. I don't think I could stand the caterwauling that *that* act would occasion."

She gave a little crow of triumph and his eyes narrowed on her. She twisted her body suggestively and wriggled demurely out of her white linen drawers and threw them with a feminine flounce on the nearest chair. He felt his blood, hot and thick, begin its familiar surge to every pulse point in his body, and was embarrassed to undress further and give her all the proof she needed of how much indeed he did want her.

"Douse the lights," he said harshly.

"Oh, I don't think so," she drawled. "I'm not the innocent I once was, you know. I don't frighten easily."

She left him no choice but to disrobe fully. His eyes were dark and turbulent as Deirdre's mischievous green eyes slowly assessed every naked inch of him.

"You'll do!" she said on a throaty laugh, and quickly crossed the distance between them.

She spread a hand across his bare chest and turned her head aside to evade his hungry kiss. "Gareth, listen to me," she said, and her eyes were shining and unguarded with a depth of affection he had often hoped for but had never dared expect to see in them. "Can't you tell why I was so reluctant to give my consent to our marriage this evening?"

"You've made your sentiments known before. I should have heeded them."

"Cawker!" she said with a sigh. She brushed his lips with the tips of her fingers, and kissed him lightly when he opened them to her. "I had already made up my mind to have you. It was this business with Armand which made me obstinate. How could I let you become involved with a couple of traitors? I thought you would hate me if you knew."

A look of something Deirdre could not quite name came and went in his eyes. He drew her firmly into the circle of his arms. "Does this mean you are finally admitting that you love me?" he asked against her ear between nips and nibbles of her earlobe.

"I thought I said as much in the carriage." Her hands slid over his shoulders. She pushed him slightly away, and spread them over his chest, testing the hardened muscles with the soft pads of her fingers. His breathing altered, became slower, deeper, less regular.

"I wasn't listening the first time you said it. Say it again," he managed raggedly, and his hands cupped her hips to fit her more snugly against the length of him.

"I love you."

"Is it so hard to say?"

"It must be," she murmured indistinctly as she nipped at his shoulders with her sharp teeth, "for I have yet to hear you say those words to me tonight."

He said them, and kissed her deeply. He repeated them and cupped her head with both hands, swinging her round and round as if leading her to the slow tempo of some music that only he could hear. When he pulled her down on the bed, he made to remove her chemise.

"Gently," she warned him as he slipped it over her head. "You never told me what excuse you gave your abigail for the torn stays and drawers."

"I told her a half-truth."

That got his attention. "What did you tell her?" His glance was wary and slightly disbelieving.

"That my horse fell on me when I tried to mount it."

He fell on top of her. "Lady Rathbourne, you think you have an answer for everything, don't you? Well, you'd better have an answer for this." He pulled her hand down to his groin and rubbed himself suggestively against it. "Well?" She gave him the answer he wanted.

"I don't want to go to Antwerp," she told him peevishly as he dressed an hour later. "I want to stay here, close to where you will be."

"Nevertheless, you'll do as I say. My cousin, Tony, will escort you. At least I can trust him to follow my wishes."

"Why is that?"

"For one reason, because I am the head of this family."

"And for another?"

"I hold the purse strings."

"Well, I hope you don't say as much to him. I find that attitude very arrogant and quite out of place. We're in the nineteenth century now, you know."

"That's as may be, but some things never change. Tony is not obtuse, like some I could name."

The time had come to part, and they spoke at random, reluctant to say the final words that would begin their separation.

He drew her into his arms and laid his cheek against her hair. "I hope you are pregnant."

"I thought you might." Her fingers absently smoothed the gold lace at his throat.

"Would it please you if you were?"

"Only if you can guarantee to give me babies with red hair." She was trying very hard not to cry, but the tears overflowed in spite of herself.

He kissed her swiftly and covered her hands with his, drawing them reluctantly away from him. "Deirdre, I want you to know that whatever I have done, I did because I love you. No, don't interrupt. Try to understand and . . . be generous and forgive me."

He tore himself away and left without a backward glance. Deirdre rushed to the bedroom windows and opened them wide. The Rue de là Madeleine was milling with people, and the noise of drum and bugle rose steadily as soldiers in uniform and heavily laden supply carts passed over the cobbled streets toward Grand' Place.

Rathbourne strode out of the hotel, and out of the blackness came a mounted O'Toole leading the Earl's gray. Another rider remained in the background. A lump caught in Deirdre's throat as Rathbourne swung himself into the saddle. He looked up and caught sight of her. After a heartbeat of a pause, he touched his fingers to his lips. A moment later, he dug his spurs into the gray's flanks and rode off with O'Toole into the night.

She looked at the clock on Rathbourne's dresser. It was four o'clock in the morning. She had been married for two hours.

Chapter Twenty-One

Deirdre awakened to what she at first supposed were the distant sounds of a severe thunderstorm, though sunlight was streaming into her bedchamber. She looked at her bedside clock and remarked that she had slept till well past noon. The thunderstorm persisted, but the rhythm was disturbingly regular, and for a long disoriented moment, she was at a loss to explain such a phenomenon. Then it came to her. Gunfire!

She leaped out of bed and dressed herself with trembling fingers and hastened downstairs. The corridors were choked with English patrons and their servants who had spent the night packing up their belongings and were frantic to remove themselves from the battle zone lest the city fall into French hands. The clamor of their panic-stricken orders and counterorders rose to an alarming pitch as Deirdre stumbled past an assortment of trunks and valises which were strewn around the halls.

She found her aunt, Mrs. Dewinters, and Tony Cavanaugh in the public dining room calmly consuming a late luncheon, and she was given to understand by Tony, who held a chair for her, that the sound of the big guns probably came from the vicinity of Quatre Bras, the crossroads which fell somewhere between the villages of Waterloo and Charleroi.

"Nothing to worry about," he said soothingly as he tucked

her chair under her knees. "It will be a long time before anything major happens. The two sides are just feeling each other out."

"But how can you be certain that it's Quatre Bras and not closer?" asked Lady Fenton, the treble in her voice clearly showing the strain of a long, sleepless night.

"Well, I'm not certain, of course, but all units are under orders to make for Quatre Bras, so it was a natural assumption to make."

Conjecture, however, could not be stifled by Tony's protestations to the contrary, and it was soon evident that nothing would placate Lady Fenton but a speedy removal to Antwerp. When Sir Thomas arrived, however, he soon scotched that notion. The roads throughout the city, he told them frankly, were choked with the carriages of fleeing visitors and native Belgians who knew what it was to endure the ferocity of a French occupation. To make matters worse, there were many units of soldiers still in the city and trying to rejoin their regiments in the south.

"Even a rider on horseback can't force a way through." He saw an expression of alarm cross Lady Fenton's face, and went on belatedly, "It's much safer to remain where we are for the present, my dear. We might easily get stranded in the middle of nowhere. Tomorrow is time enough to make the journey."

A glance out of the dining room windows, which gave out back and front, confirmed the truth of Sir Thomas's logic. Loaded carriages with angry coachmen, shouting passengers, and cursing ostlers, all at odds with each other, had blocked every exit to the hotel. If such scenes were repeated throughout Brussels, they would be lucky to make the outskirts of the city by nightfall. Tony said as much and continued, "Sir Thomas is right, and I, for one, have every confidence that Wellington will give Napoleon his just deserts." His words seemed to calm Lady Fenton, and Deirdre flicked him a grateful glance.

Mrs. Dewinters had said very little after her politely

tendered congratulations to Deirdre on her nuptials, and Deirdre felt a wave of sympathy for the actress. Whatever Mrs. Dewinters's past relationship had been with Rathbourne, Deirdre knew without a doubt that she, Deirdre, was in sole possession of her husband's heart. She tried not to let the pity she felt show in her eyes.

As it happened, the arrival of Mrs. Dawson with her children helped raise the spirits of all the ladies. It gave them something to do. Only Mrs. Dewinters showed a calm acceptance of the young woman's decision to leave her children in the care of strangers and follow her husband to the field of battle. Lady Fenton had, of course, heard rumors of such things happening in Spain, but it had always seemed to her to be a romantic fabrication put about by those disreputable periodicals which would stoop to anything to boost sales. She did everything in her power to dissuade the young wife and mother from a course of action which filled her with horror, but nothing she said made the least impression. In the face of so much determination and pluck, she felt vaguely ashamed. It helped her get a grip on the sense of panic which had been rising steadily since the Duchess of Richmond's ball.

Solange and Mrs. Dewinters took charge of the children, and for something to keep her hands and thoughts busy, Deirdre went out to the stables to give Lustre a good rubdown. As she brushed the powerful, glossy back and flanks of the whinnying filly with smooth easy strokes and made vaguely soothing noises, Deirdre traced the route to Bois de là Cambre and beyond that to the Forest of Soignes in her mind. It was on the way to the village of Waterloo, although Deirdre had never ridden so far. She remembered the night of the reception, just a week ago, at the beautiful Château de Soignes and wondered if Rathbourne was at that moment anywhere near it.

The rest of the day passed in a nightmare. The sound of the big guns could be heard intermittently well into evening, and there was constant turmoil outside the doors and windows of the hotel as rumor of first victory, then defeat, sent shock waves throughout the city. When the sound of the guns finally stopped as darkness descended, the citizens enjoyed their first respite of quiet in many long hours until a savage thunderstorm with torrential rain suddenly burst upon them, lasting well into the night.

The natural rhythm of their days was disrupted to such an extent that no one thought, throughout the hours of that long Friday, of having meals at regular intervals or going to bed at dusk. One ate when the mood struck and caught a nap at odd moments, fearful lest one miss any report of how things were faring with Wellington and his armies.

Thus it was that the Fenton party, along with other tardy guests of the hotel, were sitting down to a late supper shortly after midnight when they heard the ferocious clatter of horses' hooves on the cobblestones outside. There was a rush to the windows and they watched as the remnants of a Belgian and Dutch cavalry unit approached. The men were battle stained, their uniforms were torn and covered in mud; many of them were wounded and half falling off their mounts, and some of them were shouting the words "Quatre Bras," and warning the citizens to leave Brussels on the instant since Wellington had fallen and the road to the city was open.

It started a new wave of panic. The streets which had gradually quieted during the day were soon thronged with terrified Bruxellois and the remnants of the English making a desperate attempt to escape imminent disaster. Sir Thomas refused to be panicked, and he and Tony Cavanaugh left the hotel to try to discover if the report of Wellington's defeat was a fact or if the Belgians, as he suspected, had deserted the field of battle. They returned an hour later and calmed the fears of the few remaining hotel patrons by informing them that although some panic-stricken Belgian dragoons were fleeing to the north, many British units were still in the city with their officers and were under orders to make for Quatre Bras.

In face of the renewed activity of carts, carriages, and mounted horses outside the hotel, evidence that the news of

324

Wellington's defeat had spread like a forest fire, it was difficult to accept with equanimity Sir Thomas's calm assurances, but to venture out and become part of the mad mêlée on such a night was a fate that not even Lady Fenton would contemplate. They waited anxiously for further news.

Toward two o'clock in the morning, cartloads of wounded began pouring in. Most of the wounded were Dutch and Belgians, but there were a few British among them. Several such cartloads came to a halt outside the Hotel d'Angleterre and Deirdre's heart jumped when she recognized Dr. Shane McCallum.

Sir Thomas went to meet him, and within minutes, the wounded were being carried from the loaded wagons and the hotel had been taken over as a temporary hospital. Dr. McCallum gave them the first reliable intelligence they had received of how things stood with the allies.

"We still hold the crossroads, thank God. Things could be worse, but we're a long way from any decisive action."

There was little time for further talk, for many of the wounded were in urgent need of medical treatment, and Dr. McCallum let it be known that he expected the ladies to don their plainest frocks and assist him with the care of his patients. They worked through the night, tending wounds, sitting with the dying, soothing the nightmares of the shell-shocked victims, administering doses of laudanum, and generally making themselves useful. But the worst task of all was in assisting with amputations.

When Deirdre unhesitatingly obeyed Dr. McCallum's summons to assist him with a young British soldier who lay stretched out on a table, she had little idea what was expected of her until she looked with horror at the shattered arm and the implement in Dr. McCallum's hand. She swayed on her feet, and Mrs. Dewinters quickly stepped in and took over. The actress, dainty and dazzlingly beautiful, put on a performance somewhere between flirtation and cajolery which soon charmed the young patient into submission. His protest that he would be only half a man with the loss of his arm was laid to rest by a few softly spoken words in his ear. Mrs. Dewinters held a glass of brandy to his lips as the young man, a boy really, who hailed from Somerset, gulped it back. It was the only aid to blur the pain of surgery.

It was quickly over, and the patient was in spirits enough afterward to crack a joke about his good fortune. Deirdre, huddled in a chair, sick at heart and more frightened than she had ever been in her life, felt a wave of gratitude to a woman who could work such a transformation with a few smiles and words.

"What did you say to him?" she asked later, when most of the lights had been doused and they were making the rounds together.

Mrs. Dewinters gave her a long, hard look and took her time before replying. "I told him that I once had a lover who had lost an arm in battle and he was more man than I could hope to handle."

Before she could stop herself, Deirdre blurted out, "Truly?" then blushed scarlet at her lack of tact as much as the show of vulgar curiosity.

"Yes, truly!" said Mrs. Dewinters quietly. "He was my husband," and she swept up the stairs, leaving a contrite Deirdre to regret the sheen of tears that was clearly reflected in her eyes.

Deirdre rose at noon to a day of oppressive heat and gave herself a sponge bath before dressing. Lady Fenton and Solange had taken over the care of the Dawson children while Mrs. Dewinters and Deirdre, with some of the ladies of hardier sensibilities who had also been stranded in the hotel, became nurses and maids under the direction of Dr. McCallum. It was a division of labor which, if not agreeable to all, at the least was agreed upon by all.

Once the hotel had been turned into a hospital, there was no more talk of the Fenton party retreating to Antwerp. More wounded arrived by the hour, and it was perfectly obvious that the medical corps, such as it was, would be totally inadequate to deal with the main onslaught of wounded once the decisive battle was joined.

During the hours that Deirdre had slept, some British casualties had been conveyed to the makeshift hospital. The news which they brought was disquieting in the extreme, although Dr. McCallum summed it up lightly by saying, "The Prussians have taken a beating, it would seem. They're down, but not out by any means, and Wellington is still counting on them."

More was to follow. The Duke, by design, had evacuated his forces from Quatre Bras during the night and had fallen back closer to the city, to a ridge and valley just south of the Forest of Soignes which went by the name of Mont St. Jean. What was in the Duke's mind by such a maneuver was impossible to guess, but many of the men were disgruntled since they had held on to the crossroads at great personal cost.

The sound of the distant guns had become a constant, occasioning little remark. Shortly after Deirdre began her rounds, however, a new sound was heard which was at first unrecognizable.

"What is it?" Deirdre asked one of the older soldiers, who was lucky enough to have sustained nothing more severe than three cracked ribs and a broken leg when a loaded supply cart had run over him.

"Drums!"

The silence in the room lengthened, stretched taut, pulsed with throbbing emotion, and Deirdre felt the fine hairs on the nape of her neck rise.

The slow crescendo of marching boots and the irresistible tattoo of drums turned into the Rue de la Madeleine, and every man in the room reached for the nearest weapon. Those who could walk moved cautiously to the windows. Deirdre caught a glimpse of a sea of scarlet tunics with white lace and shakoes with bobbing white plumes. A cheer went up behind her and then a cry of "The Inniskillings! The Inniskillings! Go to it,

327

boys! Show those froggies what we're made of!"

Civilians were opening windows all along the street and calling out their encouragement. The phalanx of Inniskillings never wavered. Flowers were showered upon them, but not an eye flickered, no rank was broken.

"There will be no retreat now," said one battle-wise veteran into the silence of the room's interior. "These boys will stand to a man."

"Aye, they're too daft to know when retreat is expedient," derided the lone Highlander, the only dissenter in the censure on his commander-in-chief's decision to give up Quatre Bras.

His remark broke the tension. Laughter became general and confidence soared. Wellington's ill-advised retreat from Quatre Bras was spoken of no more.

Another furious storm broke overhead about three in the afternoon and continued well into the night, but nothing, it seemed, could dampen the good cheer that the sight of the Inniskillings had generated. If anything, hopes rose even higher. Soon, the word "Salamanca" was on everyone's lips.

"What's going on?" demanded Deirdre of Mrs. Dewinters, and she gestured to the rows of hardened soldiers whose stern features were relaxed into ludicrous, beatific smiles.

"Superstition! The veterans from Spain are remembering the eve of Salamanca when it rained cats and dogs."

"I don't understand," offered Deirdre.

"Rain before a battle is, to them, an omen, a good luck charm. Salamanca was, as you well know, a victory Wellington snatched from the French. They think history is repeating itself."

"You can't be serious!"

"Look at them, and you tell me." When Deirdre said nothing, the actress patted her comfortingly on the shoulder. "Quite right. My confidence resides in Wellington's ability also. And whatever the sentiments of the rank and file, I'm certain that the Duke is wishing the rain in Hades. Nevertheless, the superstition will make it a little easier for the men in the field to endure the soaking they are bound to have taken these last few days."

Hours later, when Deirdre stood at the long windows looking out at the pitch black of the night, she could see that there had been no letup in the storm. Behind her, most of the candles had been doused. Men were snoring and shifting restlessly in their sleep. The great clock in the hotel foyer chimed the hour. Midnight! Her mind was filled with impressions of the Duchess of Richmond's ball, and Rathbourne, in scarlet and gold, holding her in his warm golden gaze as he shepherded her into supper. Was it only two nights ago? Tomorrow was his birthday. Oh where was he and what was he doing?

She switched the curtains aside and stared blindly at the sheet water coursing down the misted windowpanes. Into her mind came the picture of Rathbourne soaked to the skin and sheltering from the elements under some scraggy hedgerow. Her reflections grew darker, and she shied away from them, purposely turning them into less frightening channels.

Her thoughts shifted to Armand and a fresh wave of uneasiness swamped her senses. When he failed to present himself at the hotel, as she had expected him to, it had occurred to her that Rathbourne had sent him to Antwerp, thinking that she would be there. She could not recall that Rathbourne had made any mention of how he would deal with the boy and the omission caused little shivers of trepidation to dance along her spine. Why had she not thought to ask him what he intended? But they had made a bargain. She fastened on that fact. Not for one moment did she believe that her husband had reneged on his promise. But there was something . . .

A small movement at her back was reflected in the dark mirror depths of the windowpane. It caught her eye and she dropped the curtain.

"You look all in." Tony Cavanaugh's voice was shaded with sympathy and she found it very hard not to dissolve into his arms. "Best get to bed while you have the chance. God knows

329

what tomorrow will bring."

Something stirred in her breast, some profound discontent which bewildering impressions of bloodied bandages and smashed bone and the stench of untended wounds had forged in her mind throughout two exhausting and horror-filled days.

"War is awful," she said, and she felt a rush of helpless pity, like the ripples from a pebble dropped into a pond, spread out from the row upon row of makeshift cots along the walls of the d'Angleterre's best public saloon to the combatants of both sides of the conflict on the slopes of Mont St. Jean and beyond, to the nameless, faceless wives and mothers in England and France who waited and prayed without ceasing for the safe return of their men. "When I see the effects of it, I can scarce take it in. How can civilized men face each other and inflict such horrible wounds? Death is one thing, but this—this suffering is beyond anything."

"What you need is a shot of brandy," said Tony, a frown clouding his eyes. She made a small, gesture of refusal, but he took her arm in a firm clasp.

"Rathbourne left you in my care. If he finds you the worse for wear when he returns, I shall be the one to pay for it. It's bad enough that I permitted you to stay in Brussels without adding to my list of crimes. Now come along and do as Cousin Tony bids you, there's a good girl."

She allowed him to lead her to a quiet corner of the hotel foyer. Within minutes, he had pressed a small glass into her hand and she was obediently sipping the fiery liquid.

He was watching her intently, and she managed a half smile.

"That's better," he said encouragingly, and rewarded her with another splash of cognac which he poured into her glass from an opened bottle in his hand.

Until this moment, Tony Cavanaugh had made very little impression on Deirdre. She obediently sipped the brandy under his watchful eye and tried to recall what she knew of him and decided that it was very little. He was a good friend to Armand, although older than he by a few years. His parents, as

330

she remembered, had both died when he was a child. He had no brothers or sisters, and had been raised with Rathbourne. On the death of Andrew, the Earl's brother, Tony Cavanaugh had become Rathbourne's heir. It occurred to her that Tony had probably lived most of his life in his cousin's shadow. In the few occasions when she had met him socially, he had always treated her with deference and respect, but then so had every gentleman of her acquaintance with the exception of her husband. She could see how it would be very easy for a man like Rathbourne to ride roughshod over his more retiring cousin.

"When did you arrive in Brussels?" she asked between sips of her brandy. She grimaced and tried to lay aside her glass, but he brought it back to her lips and admonished her to continue until she had drained the entire contents. She thought then that perhaps she had misjudged him. There was strength of purpose behind the mild-mannered exterior.

"Less than a week ago," he said in answer when he was satisfied that she meant to obey him.

"What brought you here?"

His eyes shifted from hers, and he replied evasively, "A family matter."

"Lady Caro?"

"Who told you? Armand? Rathbourne?"

"Oh both, in their different ways." Her words, as she had meant them to, gave the impression that she knew more than she did.

His guard relaxed and he said with a wry smile, "No real harm was done. A secret betrothal conducted by correspondence across the English Channel is, after all, nothing to get in a flap about. I wish Rathbourne could see it in that light, but I am afraid Armand has rubbed him the wrong way once too often."

She remarked very carefully, "I presume that there was a quarrel?"

"Oh, ferocious! You didn't know?"

331

She smiled confidingly. "They don't tell me everything, by any means, but I can imagine how it was between them."

"Yes, there's no love lost between them and they both have the deuce of a temper. I'm sure Rathbourne did not mean half of what he said. Empty threats, every one of them!"

Deirdre could not recall Rathbourne ever having made an empty threat in all the time she had known him, but she wasn't about to say so. Though she was dropping with fatigue, she was anxious to learn more.

"What kind of threats?"

"Oh, the usual, murder and mayhem! No really, I'm joking! There were words between them, nothing more."

It was evident that he was not about to reveal what had taken place between her husband and her brother. She dragged herself to her feet, and he rose with her.

"Try not to worry about them," he began, and then shook his head in derision. "What an inane thing to say! Of course you will worry about them. Just try to remember that Rathbourne is a veteran. He knows what he is doing, and he will look out for Armand."

Her expression froze. "Armand is with Rathbourne?"

He missed her soft inflection of shock. "I think he means to keep your brother with him, as a dispatch rider or some such thing. Armand wasn't too pleased about getting special treatment. Well, you can imagine how that would go against the grain. I still can't believe he turned traitor on me."

"Turned traitor?"

"He said that he had no intention of getting involved in this conflict. I believed him. Then he dons a uniform and rides off with Rathbourne. I've half a mind to follow him. But Rathbourne left you in my charge. He'd have me shot as a deserter if I were to leave you in the lurch."

Her mind refused to function properly. She allowed him to lead her to the staircase and went up to her room in a daze. Bits and pieces of Armand's letter came back to her. He had called himself a "turncoat." Had she been mistaken in thinking that he had gone over to the French? Was it, as Tony implied, that he had changed his mind and decided to enlist? That could not be right, for Rathbourne had said that he had found him and had him under guard. She was too weary to think straight. She peeled her gown from her aching limbs and lay down on the bed in her underthings. Who was the third rider with Rathbourne and O'Toole whom she had glimpsed in the darkness? Was it Armand? Oh God! Was this Rathbourne's way of punishing the boy—plucking him from one army and forcing him to fight on the other side? She might have known that he would not let Armand get off scot-free.

She moved restlessly, becoming aware of the cold night air against her skin, and she pulled the coverlet over her shoulders. The temperature was dropping, a welcome respite from the suffocating humidity of the last few days. She closed her eyes and tried not to think about the morrow.

Sunday dawned cool and, at long last, without a threat of the rain which had fallen relentlessly for almost thirty-six hours. Deirdre wakened to a barrage of cannon fire. She dressed quickly and went downstairs. The hotel was unnaturally quiet. She entered one of the makeshift wards and found men propped up in their cots looking to the windows, their faces subdued and grave. Smoke clouds could be seen wafting in over the city.

"Poor bastards," said one. "We're the lucky ones. I wouldn't want to be in their boots today."

There was no response, each man involved in his own private reflections.

Before long, the steady stream of medical wagons began their slow trek past the windows of the d'Angleterre with casualties from the previous day's fighting. The hotel was filled to capacity, and Deirdre went out to direct the drivers to other centers in Grand' Place. It was from the men in these wagons that the civilian population of Brussels received the only news of what was happening at the front.

Deirdre approached the first wagon. She would not have

recognized any of the battle-scarred occupants had she been their own mother. Mud, thick and glutinous, clung to them as if they had been dredged up from the bottom of a quagmire. Not a uniform, nor rank, nor age could be discerned among any of them. Gray, thought Deirdre, trying to contain her horror, gray, like the gray North sea; gray wraiths resurrected from a gray watery grave.

"Miss Deirdre, is that you?"

One of the gray ghosts had addressed her. She looked into a pair of intelligent blue eyes and the horror was dispelled a little.

"It's Seaton. I'm a friend of your brother. Don't you remember me?"

She looked carefully at the owner of the intelligent blue eyes, but she could not say, in all honesty, that she recognized him. The name, however, was familiar. William Seaton was one of the young bloods who had partnered her in the dance at the Château de Soignes and later, into the night, as an escort on their round of Brussels café life. There was nothing about him now, however, to give her any clue to placing him in Armand's circle of friends. A grotesque, bloodstained bandage covered his head, and every inch of his garments was saturated in slime.

"Of course I remember you, Seaton," she said diplomatically. "It's just that I am having trouble adjusting to thinking of you as a soldier. What happened to you and your comrades?"

The men began to stir as canteens of fresh water were brought out and distributed among them by the purposefully cheerful ladies who had volunteered as Dr. McCallum's aides.

"We were with Lord Uxbridge in the rear guard action on the Genappe road when our chaps pulled back to Mont St. Jean. Believe it or not, we're all of the Seventh Hussars, at your service ma'am, though you might not be able to tell by looking at us in these rags."

A few muted laughs from the wagon greeted this faint sally.

The driver of the first wagon came out of the hotel with Dr.

McCallum and some of the gentlemen who had been pressed into service. They were directed to a wagon farther down the column where the most seriously injured were to be found. It was seen at a glance that many of these pathetic cases had already undergone primitive surgery on the field. Deirdre forced herself to look away.

"What happened?" she asked for something to say to distract the attention of the somber-faced men from their unfortunate comrades. "Why did Wellington retreat? Are things so bad with us?"

"If you don't mind, Miss Deirdre, we prefer to call it a strategic pullback, not a retreat. The Duke doesn't tell the likes of us what is on his mind, but I have heard it from Armand, who heard it from Lord Rathbourne, that Wellington had the instincts of a wily old badger. At least, I think he said 'badger' or something close to it. At any rate, he's entrenched in his warren or words to that effect, and nothing will get him out."

Deirdre immediately fastened on the intelligence that was of most interest to her. "You talked to Armand? Where? When? How is he?"

"He's fine, don't worry. We huddled in the same leaky barn last night, which goes by the grand title of 'field hospital,' at a little place called Mont St. Jean. Rathbourne brought Armand in with a flesh wound to the arm. One of the French lancers had managed to nick him." He saw her look of alarm and went on hurriedly, "No really, I mean it. His wound isn't serious. Rathbourne said so. And even if it were, there are plenty of surgeons in the field to attend to him."

She wanted to ask him so much more, but the wagons had already begun to move off, the medical orderlies impatient to unload so that they might make the return trip to the front and take on a new batch of human cargo. Dr. McCallum called for her to assist him with some of the newer casualties, and for the next hour or so, Deirdre was too occupied to think of anything but what went on within the four walls of the d'Angleterre.

When Mrs. Dewinters came to relieve her, however, and she

had achieved the privacy of her own chamber, her thoughts chased themselves round in her head till she thought she would go mad. Try as she might, she could not make sense of all the flotsam and jetsam that floated about in her brain. Armand was a turncoat. Tony Cavanaugh had come from London to Brussels on a family matter. Lady Caro and Armand had contracted a secret betrothal. Rathbourne hated the French. Armand would never take up arms against his own countrymen. Rathbourne had taken Armand to the field hospital. Armand was wounded but Rathbourne said it was nothing serious. Her thoughts returned to that one fact again and again. Armand was wounded and in a field hospital on the edge of the Forest of Soignes, at the village of Mont St. Jean.

She moved restlessly around the room, absently picking up first one object then another and carefully returning them to their places. The Forest of Soignes wasn't so very far away. It was just beyond the Bois de là Cambre, and no farther, really, than Richmond was from London. She and Armand had often exercised their mounts there. If she were a man, she would think nothing of saddling her horse and making for it now.

The big guns started up again and Deirdre went to the window. A pall of smoke hung on the horizon and the smell of gunpowder and shot wafted in the air. She could smell it. What was happening out there? Where was Rathbourne? What was he doing?

Tony Cavanaugh had intimated that Rathbourne would look out for Armand, but that notion she rejected as a comforting fiction. Rathbourne did not like the boy, and had never tried to hide it from her. He had misled her—deliberately letting her think that he would send Armand to her when all the time he never had any intention of doing such a thing.

What game was Rathbourne playing? What did he intend to do with Armand? The solution which came to her mind was immediately rejected. She would not, could not believe it of him.

She turned back into the room and began a restless pacing.

The uncertainty was driving her to the brink of hysteria. The shrieks of infants at play reached her from the courtyard, and she recalled that the Dawson children were enjoying their first outdoor game in two days of almost monsoon rains. Deirdre halted in her tracks. Mrs. Dawson would not be so easily deterred from pursuing her purpose. At this very moment, there were women at the front watching and waiting for word of their loved ones. Mrs. Dawson was one of them.

She went to the washstand and poured some cold water into a basin from a china pitcher. She stripped naked and as she massaged the rough washcloth over her clammy skin, her thoughts became less frantic, more coherent, focused. By the time she had friction-dried her body with an unbleached linen towel, her skin was glowing and she felt refreshed and ready for almost anything. From the clothes press against the wall she selected her new scarlet pelisse with its gold frogging. She would need its warmth, for after a three-day heat wave, the temperature had dipped drastically. In the drawer of a mahogany dresser, she found a pair of embroidery scissors. She carefully unbound her long tresses and twisted them into a rope. In the mirror, she observed closely as she pulled the rope of hair taut and held it above the crown of her head while her right hand came up and the scissors ruthlessly sheared through the long swathe. Satisfied with the boyish aspect of the reflection which stared solemnly back at her, she negligently swept scissors and the discarded rope of hair into a drawer. Her mind was already racing ahead. Lustre, at all events, she reflected, would welcome the exercise and could be depended upon to find her way to the Forest of Soignes even with blinkers on.

Chapter Twenty-Two

The road out of Brussels toward the Forest of Soignes and the battle zone was thick with traffic moving with all dispatch in a northerly direction. The slight youth in muddied regimentals and mounted on a fresh horse was compelled to turn aside from time to time to permit the passage of heavily laden peasant carts, baggage horses, and wagon loads of army wives and camp followers which threatened to sweep all before them. An hour or so later, well to the rear of the wagon carts, came ragged bands of battle-stained soldiers in the tatters of uniforms of every description. Some looked to be dazed and ready to faint from weariness. Others bent sideways glances on the young dispatch rider, their knowing eyes narrowing on the fresh horse beneath him which would quickly carry them away from the hell they had left behind.

Deirdre reined in and looked over the weary exodus of motley men which passed before her. She was anxious to set a faster pace but was loath to bring attention to herself lest a closer inspection reveal that beneath the military disguise was a frightened slip of a girl whose nerves were honed to rapier point. Her hand moved to the brace of pistols at her belt which she had "borrowed" along with the other accoutrements of a soldier from a locker at the Hotel d'Angleterre, and confidence returned.

A foot soldier with a glazed expression left his companions and stumbled toward her. Instinct warned her a second before he leaped for the horse's head. Simultaneously, she dug her spurs into Lustre's flanks and whipped out her pistol, grasping it by the barrel. As horse and rider leaped forward, she brought the butt of the pistol down on her attacker's head. He fell to his knees, but another took his place, and some behind fanned out to prevent her advance. She twisted the gun in her hand as Lustre shot forward and rode straight for the thin line of men. She leveled her pistol and pulled the trigger. One man went reeling backward, but the explosion terrified the horse beneath her. Lustre reared, almost unseating Deirdre from the saddle. For a paralyzing moment, she thought she had lost control. She dug in her spurs and flattened herself over her mount's neck. Lustre bolted, running down the line of menacing men before they had time to regroup and exact vengeance for their fallen comrades.

Horse and rider pushed forward and did not slow their pace until the ranks of the departing refugees had considerably thinned. The experience left Deirdre shaken, nor was the horse beneath her eager to pursue the direction her mistress had chosen, for as they entered that part of the road which took them through the Forest of Soignes, the sound and fury of the battle grew louder, stronger, more intimidating.

Deirdre stroked her mount's neck and crooned soothingly, though she herself was trembling with alarm. Through the tall stands of beech trees which flanked either side of the road, she caught glimpses of soldiers making their way to the north. It was only later that she discovered they were a small part of the thousands of deserters who had melted like snow into the surrounding countryside when it looked as if Wellington had lost the battle.

The roar of cannon intensified and Deirdre slowed her mount to a walk. All about her, acrid and tear-blinding, the smoke from the guns cast a gloomy pall, filtering out the purple rays of the setting sun. The road ahead took on a threatening aspect.

She was almost upon them before she saw them. Line upon line of men in French colors. Her heart leaped to her mouth, and she turned off the road to take refuge among the trees, watching anxiously as they drew level. It seemed to her in those few desperate moments that the road to Brussels was open and the French were advancing. It took some time for her numbed brain to register that the scarlet-coated infantrymen who marched beside the dejected lines of silent French soldiers were escorting a detachment of prisoners of war.

As the last of them went by, she swung out of the trees and dug in her heels. The road before her lay open, and the villages of Waterloo and Mont St. Jean lay just ahead.

Waterloo gave every appearance of being deserted except for a few of the local inhabitants, and Deirdre did not linger. A mile or so farther along she came out of the trees and saw a cluster of cottages which made up the hamlet of Mont St. Jean. For an agonizing moment, she thought that she had stumbled onto the battlefield. The smoke of cannon at this point was so dense that it took several minutes for her to grasp that the scores of shadowy figures, some mounted, most on foot, were garbed predominantly in British colors. She urged her mount forward and passed unmolested through ragged lines of soldiers who were slumped dejectedly before the thatched hovels. Most of them had sustained injuries and had been brought by comrades to the makeshift field hospital for treatment. She scanned their weary faces. It did seem to her that things were going well for Wellington.

Beyond the cottages, there was a fork in the road, and on the left a farm with outhouses. She made straight for the stone building, half expecting at any moment to be challenged, but no one tried to stop her. She dismounted and tied the reins of her horse to the hitching post. To the left of the farmhouse, the door of the barn stood open. Four men with a blanket suspended like a litter which cradled a fallen comrade were maneuvering themselves across the threshold. Deirdre put her head down and followed in their wake.

Inside the huge barn, men were laid out on row upon row of straw pallets. The stench of unwashed bodies was overpowering. Deirdre forced down a sudden, compulsive nausea and tried to shut her ears to the cries and moans that filled the room. As her eyes grew accusomed to the gloom, she saw grim-faced surgeons working at long tables, and women holding lanterns above them. Others were moving from pallet to pallet checking on patients. Men were begging to have their wounds attended to or to be put out of their misery. Some were wandering in a daze between the rows of injured and had to be forcibly restrained. Only the most pressing cases were given immediate medical attention. She recalled the orderly wards of the Hotel d'Angleterre which she had fled only hours before and thought that she had now entered Bedlam.

One of the doctors observed her as she stood irresolute. "You can go back to your unit now, lad," he said, "unless you've been sent here to help us."

A few minutes passed and the surgeon looked up from his gruesome task. He was bleeding one of the patients. Deirdre had not moved an inch. She had never before witnessed the operation, not even at the d'Angleterre, since Dr. McCallum was one of the few physicians who did not hold with a practice which he regarded as a useless convention, but which his contemporaries assiduously employed in spite of, so he said, any scientific evidence to show that it was beneficial—quite the reverse.

"What is it, lad?" the doctor asked in a gentler tone. "Are you looking for someone?"

"Sir, I was told my brother was here."

He gestured into the room. "Take a look around. We don't have time to ask for identities."

It took all her courage to move among the pallets of grotesquely wounded men. Some were already dead. She tried to get a hold of herself, and whispered Armand's name urgently as she moved like a shadow from pallet to pallet. No one answered her, and she was filled with a sense of despair.

A shaft of light fell across her path as the door was opened, and a scarlet-coated dragoon stood silhouetted in the doorway. Deirdre looked up and became instantly alert. There was something familiar in the man's stance. She pulled herself slowly upright and watched with a guarded expression as he took a step or two into the room. She came face to face with O'Toole. His eyes narrowed, then moved indifferently over her, and he strode to a pallet Deirdre had already investigated.

"What happened to the boy who was here this morning?" she heard him ask one of the women in his soft Irish brogue.

"St. Jean? Oh, he went back to his unit."

Deirdre heard a muttered imprecation, and O'Toole turned on his heel and strode out. She sank back on her heels and covered her face with her hands. Her desperate, terror-filled ride had been for nothing. Armand had slipped through her fingers. Where was Armand? Where was Rathbourne?

She stumbled to her feet and ran after O'Toole. He was mounted on a huge gray and making for the battlefield. She shouted his name, but little could be heard above the deafening barrage of gunfire. She raced back to the farmhouse to collect her mount, and wheeled to follow him. The guns suddenly ceased and a terrible silence descended. Deirdre reined in. Everywhere, men raised their heads to listen. On her right, she saw the sun low in the sky. Soon it would be too dark to continue the fighting, and she wondered if hostilities had ceased for the day. She moved cautiously forward, although she had lost sight of O'Toole in the thick haze. She looked behind her, and caught a glimpse of men mounting up. Without warning, she came out onto the crest of a broad ridge. And then she heard it.

Far off to her right, men were cheering. It was taken up and spread all along the ridge, like the blaze of a sudden, windswept forest fire soaring high out of control. Men were cheering, and the jubilant cries of hoarse English voices rose to a tremendous

343

pitch. The battle had turned, and the victors roared their triumph. And then, as suddenly as it had begun, the cheering stopped.

Deirdre saw that there was no sense in going further. O'Toole had been swallowed up in the dense smoke, and everywhere men and horses were on the move. She pulled on the reins to direct her mount to retrace their steps, her reasons for being there suddenly appearing wild and irrational, the act of a deranged woman. Before she could complete the movement, however, there was a thundering at her back and a dozen cheering Horse Guards with outstretched sabers came dashing out of the smoke.

"Up and at them," she heard the leader shout, and Lustre, faltering before the furious onslaught, sprang forward, and horse and rider were swept into the charge.

They took a low hedge, and the smoke suddenly cleared. Below them lay a valley bathed in the rays of a fine summer sunset, and for one blinding moment, Deirdre felt her spirits soar as the gagging fog was left behind. And then the horror of what lay before her swamped every sense.

On the fields of trampled rye, beneath the pounding hooves of their charging mounts, were littered the twisted bodies of the dead and dying. On the slopes of the valley was chaos—a mass of surging British infantry with bayonets brutally cutting and thrusting a way through the lines of Napoleon's retreating Imperial Guard. As their line of escape was cut off by the solid wall of their fleeing comrades, men wheeled and fought with the ferocity of cornered tigers. The ground shook with the hoofbeats of thousands of screaming horses as the French lancers and cuirassiers poured up the muddy incline, their brass helmets gleaming brightly, and engaged their British counterparts in a rearguard action to the mingled roars of *"Vive L'Empereur!"* "England and St. George!" and "Scotland Forever!" their battle cries rising above the hoarse shouts of the fallen.

Down the slippery slope of the bloodied field they rode hell for leather, and Deirdre clung helplessly to the saddle, inexorably swept along by the frenzied onrush of horse and rider on either side, and curved sabers flashed cruelly high above men's heads. From nowhere, fifty feet in front of them, appeared a detachment of French dragoons wheeling to meet them head-on, and men singled each other out, digging in their spurs as they flew at each other's throats.

Horses and riders came together on the bone-on-bone grind of straining bodies, and steel beat furiously against steel with no quarter asked or given. Deirdre looked into the maddened eyes of a charging dragoon as he forced his way through to her, his sword sullied with blood, and raised to cut her down. She fumbled in her belt, leveled her pistol, and fired. His eyes widened in shocked surprise, but he pushed forward as if the dark stain which spread across the front of his green tunic was of no consequence.

Flight was impossible, nor did she think of it. Every sense was heightened, every instinct vibrant and alive to her danger. Without thinking, she dug in her heels and leaped forward to meet her attacker. No plan formed in her mind. Her actions were purely reflex as she swung her feet free of the stirrups, and one leg slid smoothly over Lustre's neck. Her eyes locked on the dragoon's raised sword arm and every muscle coiled like a spring. As the saber began its descent, she threw herself bodily from the saddle to meet it.

The impact of her sudden movement threw the charger back on its haunches and both riders went tumbling to the ground in a tangle of limbs. She clung tenaciously to the arm that went rigid beneath her, tensing for the thrust of steel that would end her struggles, but the body beneath her gradually relaxed. Deirdre lifted her head and looked down into the staring eyes of a dead man. A sob rose in her throat.

She dragged herself to her feet and swung into the saddle, her eyes frantically searching for an escape from the bloody carnage. It was then that she saw him—Armand, mounted, and only a dozen yards to her left, swinging his blade as two French lancers came charging toward him. She opened her mouth to scream, but no sound came. As if in a nightmare, when limbs become leaden and refuse to obey the urgent commands of the brain, she remained frozen, her eyes staring in horror, refusing to accept what she could plainly see. A fresh burst of French artillery fire kicked up the ground at her feet, and the shock galvanized her into action.

Screaming her brother's name as if it were a bloodcurdling battle cry, she leaped forward, her face contorted in fury. She saw the lancer at Armand's back poise his lance to thrust, and she flung herself at him, her arms twisting around his neck like a vise, and she used every ounce of strength to drag him back. His charger reared and twisted beneath the struggling bodies. Deirdre saw Armand go down and a cry of anguish tore from her throat. Her grip slackened momentarily, and the lancer took full advantage. His elbow connected ferociously with her ribs and sent her flying. She hit the ground with a sickening thud and the breath was knocked out of her. Stars exploded in her head. She raised herself on one shaky elbow, then fell back, sinking into oblivion.

When she came to herself, the sun had set, and the noise of battle had receded. She lay unmoving for a long time, trying to make sense of the faint sounds around her, her mind grappling with the unrecognizable cries of creatures of the night which seemed to have crawled out of their burrows to wander over the field. A rush of memory flooded her brain, and she struggled to a sitting position. And then she recognized the animal cries for what they were—the pitiful moans of the wounded and dying crying weakly for water and the relief of a quick death.

Her head sank to her knees, and she filled her lungs with several long steadying breaths. Every muscle in her body ached as if she had taken a beating and she tasted blood on her lips although her mouth was parched. She lifted her head and looked about her. Small fires burned here and there on the battlefield, and the moon cast its ghostly rays upon the scene of death and destruction.

She pulled herself to her feet and tried to get her bearings. Armand had fallen only yards from where she had taken a tumble. She moved in circles calling his name, feeling her way blindly, shutting her mind to the horror about her. And then she found him.

He was warm and breathing, but he made no response to her urgent pleas that he waken. She worked quickly, her hands and fingers testing bones and flesh through the sodden tunic. She found the injury on his left shoulder. She tore his clothing open and pressed her fingers into the ragged wound. His shirt and tunic were drenched with blood and her relief gave way to panic. She was too weak to move him. Nor would she find him again among so many slain even if she did go for help, and that was impossible, for Lustre had vanished, was perhaps at that very moment one of the carcasses that littered the field. She fell back on prayer and a measure of calm returned.

She quickly unbuttoned her spencer and wrenched off her fine linen shirt. She wadded it into a thick pad and looked around for something to bind it tightly against the hole in Armand's shoulder. There was nothing.

It took every ounce of willpower to ignore the cries of the injured as she stumbled among the broken bodies, frantically searching for a corpse to strip of some article of clothing to make into bindings. She deliberately numbed her brain as she went about her ghastly business, steeling herself to touch the faces of the men about her till she found one that was cold and rigid in death. Within minutes she was back at Armand's side, and deftly bound his wound with the tattered remnants of a young French ensign's shirt. She rebuttoned her brother's tunic and sat back on her haunches.

She knew that there would be no relief, no medical help coming until first light. She had never before considered the inhumanity of such neglect but the cruelty of the practice, unintentional though it might be, struck her suddenly with full force. Men who might easily live with immediate medical attention were being left to die in their hundreds while their comrades made themselves comfortable for the night. She thought of Mrs. Dawson and the other women who followed their men on the march and knew without a doubt that they at least would be wandering the field looking for loved ones who had not yet returned.

Her eyes picked out dark shapes flitting among the fallen. She was about to cry out for help, but the sound froze in her throat as she saw corpses stripped naked and relieved of everything of value. Looters had begun their ghoulish work. They spread out across the field, carrying off their booty like jackals scavenging on leftovers after the lion has gorged himself on his kill.

The gutteral sounds of German reached Deirdre's ears as two Prussian soldiers turned over one of the wounded. A young French voice pleaded for mercy. There was the flash of steel, and the voice was suddenly cut off. Rage, white hot and passionate, tore through Deirdre. In a day of unmitigated horror, that one cold-blooded, wanton act surpassed everything.

She scrambled on her knees among the corpses, searching with frenzied fingers, and found a pair of pistols primed and ready to fire. Satisfied that the powder was bone dry, she braced herself on her knees before Armand like a shield and sat back on her heels to wait. When the Prussians were only yards from her, she cocked the pistols.

"Was wollen sie?" she asked on a low snarl.

The men straightened and one of them laughed.

"Ein Englischer?" he ventured in an amused tone, and moved cautiously forward.

"Come one step closer and I'll blow your brains out," she said in faultless German.

Their eyes narrowed on the dark shape hugging the ground. It did not seem possible that such a slight form could pose any threat that two burly men could not handle with ease.

"Wir sind freunde," said one placatingly, "friends," he

added in English to make sure his meaning was not mistaken.

Allies they might be, but Deirdre knew that there was no love lost between the British and Prussians. No questions would be asked on the morrow about the night's work. And dead men tell no tales.

She sensed their intent as the bolder of the two edged closer. Two shots were all that she had, one for each of them, and if she failed . . . She waited with eyes and ears straining as she took aim.

The Prussian had advanced to within a foot of her. Without warning his hand shot out, and as she felt the quick stab of fire along her arm, she simultaneously discharged the pistol in her right hand. He went spinning backward and fell in a deformed heap.

His companion hesitated. Deirdre transferred the pistol in her left hand to her right, scarcely aware of the warm blood dripping from her fingers. Her heart was pounding furiously against her bruised ribs, but fear was far from her thoughts. That would come later.

"*Warum warten sie?* What are you waiting for?" she challenged softly. "Try and take me and I'll give you what I gave your friend." The shape cursed softly and moved silently away, slinking like a whipped cur into the shadows, and Deirdre lowered the heavy pistol to the ground. Her breath, which she had controlled perfectly until that moment, tore through her lungs in ragged gasps and she began to retch.

"Gareth, oh Gareth," she heard herself sob, and fought back the attack of hysteria that threatened to overwhelm her. The night was far from over, and it did no good to speculate on what had become of her husband. Nor could he help her now. She had to rely on her own resources. She tucked her left forearm under her right armpit to stanch the flow of blood and brought up the pistol, resting it against her knees. She huddled closer to Armand, sharing her body heat.

He stirred. "Caro?" he whispered on a rustle of sound.

"Hush, darling. You'll be with her soon."

349

The answer seemed to satisfy him, for he drifted off to sleep, or unconsciousness, and Deirdre was left to her thoughts during her long, lonely vigil.

The rest of the night was uneventful, for most looters were cowards and moved away from the ferocious hellion brandishing the wicked-looking pistol to avail themselves of easier pickings. At first light, the medical wagons came for them and they were conveyed to the village of Mont St. Jean. Since Deirdre's wound was not considered critical, she was left to wait till noon outside the thatched cottages until a surgeon was available to clean and suture the gash on her arm. It was from the surgeon that she learned that Lord Uxbridge had been hit in the knee by almost the last shot of the battle and had been taken to Waterloo.

"That doesn't sound too serious," she said hopefully.

"Not a bit of it," was the cheerful rejoinder. "He's lost the leg, of course, but that's of little consequence. Considering that he had eight horses shot from under him during the day, he should think himself lucky."

Deirdre, still posing as a young dispatch rider, fought back the unmanly tears. "What of Rathbourne? How did he fare, or don't you know?"

"Like the Duke, not a scratch on him as usual. He left with the army at dawn to chase the French to the gates of Paris."

She would have asked more, but by the time she had swallowed the hard lump which had formed in her throat, the surgeon had moved on. Deirdre put down her head and wept openly, careless of the softened expressions on the faces of hardened soldiers who wished they were brave enough to follow the young lad's example.

By evening, the road to Brussels was lined with the elegant carriages of its wealthier citizens who had sent their well-sprung vehicles to transport the wounded to a heroes' welcome in the city they had saved from the designs of a little Corsican megalomaniac. Brother and sister slept through most of the comfortable journey, Deirdre through sheer fatigue, and

350

Armand under the sedation of a large draft of laudanum. When they arrived at the Hotel d'Angleterre just before nightfall, Deirdre took charge and had Armand put straight to bed, refusing to answer a single question about her extraordinary appearance or her whereabouts until she had bathed and dined. Her own questions to Armand she resolved to leave till morning when it was to be hoped a good night's rest would work a salutary change in him.

When she finally met with her anxious relatives before retiring to bed, she told them the bare facts, omitting anything that implied she had been in any kind of danger.

"Just like a picnic to Twickenham," intoned Tony Cavanaugh with a quizzical elevation of one elegant eyebrow.

In other circumstances, Deirdre would have received a severe tongue-lashing, but Lord Uxbridge had arrived from the front with his ever faithful aide, Seymour, and the hotel was in an uproar as special beds and chairs were examined and removed to his lordship's rooms for his exclusive use. With so much going on, and since their niece seemed to have suffered no ill effects with the exception of a gash on the arm which she made light of, Sir Thomas and Lady Fenton decided to let sleeping dogs lie. Indeed, it was Deirdre's shorn locks which provoked her aunt to anything resembling real anger.

"How could you, Deirdre?" she asked plaintively. "Fashion, you eschew, the bloom of youth is fading, and apart from a trim figure and fine complexion, you have little else to boast of. It was your one claim to distinction. God knows what Rathbourne will say."

Tony flashed a commiserating grin, and Deirdre bit back a laugh, only too thankful to have been let off so lightly.

On the following morning, when she opened the door to Armand's chamber, she found him sitting up in bed and looking a little hollow-eyed, but quite obviously on the mend. Deirdre crossed the room and sank on her knees beside the bed.

One hand reached out to touch his face. "Pale but interesting," she managed lightly, then her arms went round

351

his waist and she put down her head and wept. His hands idly fingered her soft, feathery tresses. When she finally looked up, she saw that his eyelashes were beaded with moisture.

"That was you, standing guard over me through the night, wasn't it?" he asked softly.

She nodded dumbly, and fumbled in her pocket for a handkerchief. When she had told him the whole story of how she had come to be swept up in the final charge, he burst out savagely, "Dee! It's a miracle you are alive! Don't think I'm not grateful. You probably saved my life. But you carry things too far. When are you going to let me live my own life? To come after me like that when I told you I was enlisting passes the bounds of anything!"

"But you didn't tell me you were enlisting!" she defended. "You told me that you were a turncoat, and I surmised the worst."

"What does that mean?"

"That you had gone over to the enemy."

He looked dumbfounded. "You thought I was a traitor?"

"Don't look so shocked." She got to her feet and said with a break in her voice, "What should I think when you said all those wild things and Rathbourne thrashed you for it? You never mentioned a word in your letter about enlising. How should I know what was on your mind?"

"You actually thought that I could betray my family, my friends, my country, my name? And I thought you knew me!"

Her eyes dropped before the look in his, but she said levelly, "None of your friends knew where you were. Why didn't you tell someone?"

"It all happened so suddenly. Tony told me about Caro. There seemed nothing to hold me back. Besides, Rathbourne knew. Why didn't you apply to him? He is your husband, for God's sake."

"Rathbourne knew?"

Armand missed the flicker of shock in her eyes. "Certainly he knew. How he found out, I don't know, but that bear of a fellow, his watchdog, what's his name . . . ?"

"O'Toole."

"He hauled me off to answer to my guardian. Damn impertinence! He's only a servant, after all."

"And Rathbourne didn't try to stop you?"

"Devil the bit of it! He said that, all things considered, he thought it was the best solution."

"What did he mean by that?"

"I never gave it much thought at the time. I was too relieved to be let go. Who knows? Perhaps he hoped I would become one of the casualties. That would certainly solve some of his problems," he concluded bitterly.

"Does he really hate you so much?" she asked in a voice striving to remain calm. She came and sat on the edge of the bed and took his hand.

His eyes were troubled, though he said easily enough, "No, I don't really believe that. Rathbourne may dislike me intensely, but he's not a fiend. We have had our differences, it's true. Even if he does despise me, he would never go that far."

"What differences?" she coaxed, giving him a perfect opportunity to unburden himself about Lady Caro. But on that subject her brother remained discouragingly silent.

A communication from her husband arrived soon thereafter having made a circuitous route by way of Antwerp to find her. The contents were brief and to the point. Under his cousin's escort, she was to make for Belmont, Rathbourne's seat in Warickshire, where his mother and sister had taken up residence for the summer. Guy Landron had been sent ahead to smooth the way for her arrival. The Earl would join her as soon as his stint with Wellington was over and the world was once and forever rid of Napoleon Bonaparte. Rathbourne made no mention of her brother; no explanation was tendered for Armand's disappearance from Brussels just before the battle; no regrets offered for the part he had played in keeping her in ignorance of an event that was bound to affect her profoundly. There were no endearments, no tender expressions to soften directions he might just as easily have sent to a servant. He had signed it simply "Rathbourne," in Deirdre's eyes, the final insult.

She read the missive several times, then tore it into shreds. She did not think that she could ever forgive Rathbourne for the deception he had perpetrated. How could he do it to her? In suspecting Armand of being a traitor, a conviction which Rathbourne had ruthlessly exploited, she had been made to suffer agonies. Nor did the list of his iniquities end there. The torment of being in ignorance of Armand's fate for three days had propelled her into a course of action which she would remember for the rest of her days. It had been in Rathbourne's power to protect Armand, but he had sent him off to battle like so much cannon fodder—an untried, untutored, raw recruit. For what purpose?

Who could fathom the mind of such a man or explain his conduct? It seemed to her that Armand had earned the Earl's dislike from the very beginning, over the affair with Mrs. Dewinters. And once Rathbourne was roused, there was no placating him, not that Armand had made the slightest push to reconcile their differences. Far from it, as she was first to admit, but his youthful defiance did not merit such implacable enmity. The affair with Caro coming when it did must have been the last straw. Had Armand's carelessly uttered words been close to the truth? Did Rathbourne really want the boy dead so that he would be out of Caro's reach once and for all?

Fragments of conversations came back to her. Armand warning her off the Earl because he was no gentleman; his nom de guerre was "le Sauvage"; he hated the French with a passion. That he hated Armand was self-evident. Could she be in love with such a man, a man who could stop at nothing to gain his ends?

Her thoughts strayed to Vauxhall, then moved on to the night he had cheated her at cards at Lord Winslow's gaming establishment. Finally, she thought of the coach ride after the Duchess of Richmond's ball, and his threats about Armand.

The man was utterly without conscience as he had repeatedly proved in his conduct with respect to herself.

His glib tongue had almost beguiled her into thinking that he loved her. She should have known better! Always, *always* in the past, she had had her defenses in place ready to deflect the first serious attempt to engage her heart. How had he managed to slip under her guard? Of all people, she more than anyone had ample evidence of the unscrupulous lengths the male animal would stoop to in the game of conquest, and how little declarations of love counted when passion was spent. He wanted her, was obsessed with her, lusted after her. Hadn't his lovemaking proved that the man was a sensualist? That wasn't love! If he truly loved her, he would never have put her through this hell.

He expected her to retire to Belmont and await his pleasure. As his wife, she was bound to comply with his wishes, and Armand, as his ward, was in no better case. The authority of a husband or guardian under the law was almost inviolable, and short of murdering his dependents, he was given a free hand to abuse them in any way he saw fit. Fool that she was to have put herself so completely into his power! And more fool still for wishing that he were with her, and she could be folded into his arms and unburden her heart to him.

Chapter Twenty-Three

In the week that followed the battle, a steady stream of
dignitaries passed through the portals of the Hotel d'Angleterre with no other object than to pay homage to Lord
Uxbridge, the man who, time and time again, had thrown back
the legendary French lancers and cuirassiers. That he proved
to be the most popular guest of any note that the hotel had
ever boasted of was not to be wondered at, for a smile was
never far from his lips, and he was in such high spirits, despite
bouts of pain, that it was impossible to feel sorry for him, at
least in his presence.

As it turned out, there was no question of Deirdre's
immediate removal to Belmont. Armand developed a fever, and
Dr. McCallum advised that he be given time to convalesce
before attempting a journey which was bound to fatigue him.
Deirdre was only too happy to delay an event which filled her
with dread, and they remained where they were with Deirdre
dividing her time as companion-nurse equally between her
brother and Lord Uxbridge who found himself in much the
same pass as Armand. Of the two patients, there was never any
doubt that Uxbridge had the better temper.

The first lists of casualties were published a few days after
the battle. The names seemed to go on forever, and were
expected to double when many of the worst injured succumbed

357

to their wounds. General Picton was gone, as was Ponsonby of the Scots' Greys, their heroic deaths instilling as much pride as regret in what was left of their regiments. Deirdre scanned the lists with a heavy heart, recognizing the names of many of the officers who had squired her at various dos in Brussels. The omissions, however, occasioned much heartfelt relief to their friends. When Tony Cavanaugh exclaimed that Roderick Ogilvie's name was not among the casualties, Mrs. Dewinters got up without saying a word and left the room, leaving Deirdre and Tony to look after her in wonder.

That night over dinner, Mrs. Dewinters made it known that she would be returning to London the following morning since there was no longer anything to keep her in Brussels. An uncomfortable silence descended over their party, and Deirdre could almost feel the pitying looks which were cast in her direction. It seemed that everyone was aware of the woman's past relationship to Rathbourne, and speculated on whether their affair was over and done with or merely suspended until such time as it was decently possible for Rathbourne to renew the liaison in light of his nuptials. Deirdre tried to appear natural but inwardly she was seething. The embarrassment of her predicament was one more bone of contention that one day soon she hoped to settle with her husband. She sawed into the piece of rare sirloin on her plate, stabbed it with her fork, and purposefully chewed the tender morsel into gratifying oblivion. When she raised her eyes to Cavanaugh's, she saw the gentle raillery in his barely suppressed grin, and she tried to reciprocate, though she feared that she had failed miserably.

He found her later in Armand's chamber, where she was attempting with indifferent success to teach her brother some of the finer points of the game of picquet. Cavanaugh pulled up a chair and watched silently as they played out a hand, with Deirdre giving a running commentary, and Armand watching her every move intently.

"Pity I hadn't known that little play when I accepted Rathbourne's challenge that night at Watiers," he said ruefully as Deirdre gathered up the cards and began to shuffle them expertly.

"I doubt if that would have made a jot of difference," mused Tony. "Picquet is Rathbourne's game. I hear he made a study of it after some chit bested him at some houseparty or other years ago."

"Now you tell me," groaned Armand.

Tony flashed an apologetic half smile. "I never did find out—did you manage to come up with blunt to recover your vowels?"

"I took care of it," said Deirdre, and looked curiously at her husband's cousin.

Armand threw out a card. "Tony offered me a thousand to help me out. But it was only a drop in the bucket. I shan't forget it in a hurry, though, Tony. You're the best of fellows."

"Oh, don't mention it. I felt responsible. How was I to know what Rathbourne was about when I took you to see him? He only told me that he wished to speak to you."

Deirdre's eyes lifted from the perusal of the cards in her hand. "So it *was* a deliberate attempt to put Armand into dun territory!" she exclaimed, and immediately regretted saying as much to a stranger.

Cavanaugh looked startled. "Oh, I say, surely not. Rathbourne is not that vicious. I think it was merely his way of warning Armand away from . . ." He faltered, and ended miserably, "I beg your pardon."

"Mrs. Dewinters," Deirdre added gratuitously. "Oh, don't look so crestfallen, Tony. You haven't shocked me, I assure you. Gareth has taken me into his confidence." It was far from the truth, but it galled her to think that everyone believed her the complete dupe.

"It's Maria I came to talk to you about," he began diffidently. "I thought I might give her my escort to London, if you don't mind, since you are in no position to leave at present. I should be back within the week, and then we can return to town together, if you like." His hand moved to his cravat and he adjusted it with compulsive fingers, quite ruining the effect of its intricate folds.

Deirdre wondered at his embarrassment. He could hardly look her in the eye. And then, it came to her.

"Has Rathbourne asked you to look after Mrs. Dewinters as well?" He shifted uncomfortably, and she said gently, "You needn't answer that. Of course you must escort her. But don't trouble about us. There's no saying how long we may continue in Brussels. You mustn't allow Rathbourne to take control of your life, you know. He will if you don't stand up to him, oh yes he will! I give you my word that we shall make for Belmont, just as soon as Armand is better. Now go to London with an easy conscience, and take up the threads of your own life."

He protested, but Deirdre soon overcame every objection he raised, and the matter was finally settled between them. Her composure outwardly remained unruffled, but inwardly she staggered from the disclosure that Rathbourne was in some sort still tied to his former mistress.

One episode ended very happily for Deirdre, however, and that was the business of Lustre. Deirdre could not bring herself to mention the loss of the prize bit of blood to Lord Uxbridge. Happily, Lustre was returned without a scratch. Lord Uxbridge assumed that the horse had been requisitioned or stolen, which amounted to the same thing, and Deirdre chose not to confess her own culpability in the matter.

She spent part of each afternoon reading to the Earl in his private parlor. He managed to get about on crutches tolerably well, and never complained in her hearing, though she knew that he often suffered dreadfully. Deirdre's admiration for the man grew apace, and she was sensible of the fact that in the months she had come to know him, her opinion of his character had undergone such a change that she would never have recognized the Earl as the object of the scathing diatribe she had once made to her friend Serena.

On one occasion, she was reading to him from *Waverley*, a novel which Uxbridge particularly favored, by an unknown author, though rumor had it that it was written by Walter Scott, when the door was pushed open and a lady in traveling clothes with a young infant hanging on her skirts took a few steps into the room and halted. Deirdre put down the book in her hand, and looked inquiringly from Uxbridge to the woman whose eyes were brimming with tears.

The Earl raised himself on one elbow, extended his hand, and said, "Oh Char, oh my dear," in a voice that Deirdre would not have recognized as his own.

Lady Uxbridge, for so Deirdre supposed the lady to be, then flung herself upon her husband, who gathered her and his young son in his arms. Deirdre slipped from the room unobserved.

A short time later, she was sent for to be formally introduced. What Deirdre had expected in Uxbridge's Countess was a far cry from the lady who smiled so warmly at her. Char Wellesley was said to have stolen the sought-after Lord Henry Paget, as Uxbridge then was, from his wife, one of the reigning beauties of the ton. On first impression, Deirdre would never have given the Countess a second glance, and she wondered how Uxbridge could prefer the quiet mouse of a woman to the dazzling Caroline Villiers, now the Duchess of Argyll.

Second impressions were more favorable, however. It was very evident that Uxbridge and his wife were devoted to each other, and Lady Uxbridge was friendliness itself, showing every courtesy to the slip of a girl who, so she avowed, had shown such kindness to her husband. That Deirdre had also married Rathbourne, an obvious favorite with Lady Char, was very much to Deirdre's credit.

"I was so relieved when my dear Paget told me that yours was a love match," said Lady Uxbridge confidingly, as the two women shared a pot of tea in Uxbridge's private parlor. Dr. McCallum had called only moments before and was with the Earl in the next room. "I know Rathbourne has told you all about our wretched sufferings and the guilt I don't suppose we shall ever be free of."

Deirdre did not know what she should say and busied herself with her cup and saucer. Her reticence went unremarked by the older woman.

"But those days are best forgotten. Now tell me all about you and Gareth."

The expurgated version of the courtship which Deirdre hesitatingly embarked upon was close enough to the facts, so she consoled herself, that no one could call her an unmitigated liar. It seemed to her, however, that since she had fallen in with Rathbourne, she was habitually spouting a twisted version of the truth. It troubled her greatly, for it had always been in her nature to be transparently honest.

It came to her that that was not entirely the case, for when she was an infant, her stepfather had very gently broken her of a mendacity that was fast becoming a habit by encouraging her to forgo a treat whenever she found herself telling a half-truth. He had put her on her honor, and she had doggedly owned up to every falsehood. His pride in her success had filled her with pleasure. The memory was a happy one, and she was overcome with nostalgia. She could not remember when she had last thought of her stepfather with anything but hostility. She allowed the memory to revolve slowly in her mind, and in some odd way, she felt soothed, as if a throbbing wound had lost some of its power to hurt her.

Lady Uxbridge's soft accents recalled her to the present, and she dutifully accepted a marzipan from the proffered dish of sweets. "Delicious," she murmured politely.

When Dr. McCallum called Lady Char to the sickroom, Deirdre offered to amuse the small boy, whose nurse had suffered dreadfully from *mal de mer* on the crossing to Ostend, and who had taken to her bed as soon as the swaying coach had pulled in at the hotel. Young Clarence, four years old and just beginning to test parental authority to its limits, had other ideas and nothing could persuade him to remove from the vicinity of a father whom he had not seen for three months.

362

Lord Uxbridge, happily for the little urchin who seemed to be able to twist his doting papa round his thumb, vociferously aided and abetted the boy. Lady Char and Deirdre exchanged a smile and Deirdre withdrew to leave the little family to their reunion.

When Deirdre descended the stairs alone Solange could not hide her disappointment. The Dawson children had been removed from her care days before when Mrs. Dawson had collected her offspring and returned to her lodgings to await a summon from her husband to join him in Paris when British forces should take the city—a foregone conclusion, since the allies were meeting little opposition as they streamed southward into France.

Deirdre looked in on Armand and found him sleeping, and went in search of her aunt. The hotel was almost empty of patients, since most had already been removed to England, and time hung heavily on her hands.

"How is Lord Uxbridge?" asked Lady Fenton, looking up from a letter she was writing to one of her many offspring.

"Oh, I think his recovery is assured with Lady Char now in attendance."

Lady Fenton sniffed. "It's just as well Armand is ready to be moved. No one will think it odd in you to leave for home at this juncture."

Deirdre looked questioningly at her aunt as her fingers idly turned the pages of the morning paper. She noted that a small frown of concentration furrowed her aunt's brow.

"We must, of course, be polite to Lady Uxbridge as long as we are confined under the same roof, but it won't do to become too friendly with her. Not that I have anything against her personally, you understand. I don't know the woman. But to court her friendship would taint you in the eyes of the ton."

"I cannot believe I am hearing this."

Lady Fenton faltered under Deirdre's cool appraisal. "She's not accepted anywhere," she went on to explain. "If you were known to be taking her up, no one of any significance would ever darken your doors. I'm not saying that's how it should be, Deirdre. I am only telling you how it is in our circles."

The paper was laid aside and Deirdre said mildly, "But Lord Uxbridge is accepted everywhere, is he not?"

"Oh well, he is a man. No one expects gentlemen to behave any better than they should. I can tell by your face that you think I'm being hypocritical. Perhaps you are right. But just remember, I didn't make the rules. None of the Pagets will have anything to do with her, and I doubt if Uxbridge's sister, Lady Capet, will show herself here now that the Countess is in residence."

"People can be so cruel and unforgiving!" Deirdre said feelingly.

"So they can. But just remember your own sentiments when St. Jean eloped with that woman and left your mother to fend for herself. The cases are not dissimilar, and I don't recall you ever having a good word to say about your stepfather."

A vivid recollection came to Deirdre of the last time she had seen her stepfather before his death. She had watched from an upstairs window as he had ascended the front steps of their dismal lodgings. He wanted to visit with his children, so her mother had informed them gently that morning over breakfast. To Armand, it had meant little. To Deirdre, it brought emotions so confused and painful that she had become wretchedly sick. She hated him for his rejection, and tried to smother the longing to be held comfortingly in his arms. In her child's logic, she had long since divined that if only she had been his real daughter, as Armand was his real son, he never would have deserted her mother, and they would still be living happily together.

She had hidden herself in the attic, refusing to come from her hiding place even when she heard his dear voice calling her name. When she finally descended the stairs after he had gone, her mother said little, but looked at her with sad, reproachful eyes and had given her a small velvet box, a gift from her papa. Inside was the St. Jean emerald, the only thing of value he had left. She had never seen him again.

She shook her head as if to deny that the child of her memory could possibly be related to herself.

"Think about it, Deirdre," she heard her aunt's voice say as if from a distance, "and you will see that I am right."

"Oh no," said Deirdre. "Oh no. I think I am just beginning to see how wrong I have been about everything."

In the days that followed, Lady Char and Deirdre were often in each other's company, and in spite of her aunt's misgivings, Deirdre could not help responding to the Countess's shy overtures of friendship. In the course of conversation, they spoke of Uxbridge House in Burlington Gardens and naturally Deirdre mentioned her friend Serena, the Uxbridges' next door neighbor. After that, any reservation on Deirdre's part vanished, for Lady Char said without rancor or any hint of self-pity that Serena Kinnaird was the only hostess in London whose home was open to her. Within an hour of making Lady Char's acquaintance, Deirdre had known that she liked the woman; after a week, she regarded her as one of her closest friends.

She attempted to pen a letter to Serena, explaining all that had happened in the fortnight since she had last written. To justify how she had come to marry a man she had vehemently declared she detested, however, as well as to account for her becoming on the best of terms with a couple whose conduct she had at one time severely condemned, was beyond her capabilities, and she gave up the attempt. She simply wrote that she would be home by the beginning of July and that there was much that she had to tell her friend. To her husband, she wrote not one word, nor did she receive any communication from him.

As it happened, Deirdre and Armand came home to London with great, though unexpected, ceremony. The Prince Regent, having placed the royal yacht at the disposal of Lady Uxbridge, and having declared that "he loved Uxbridge, that he was his best officer and his best subject," thereupon elevated him to the title of Marquess of Anglesey. It was in the royal yacht, as friends of the newly created Marquess and Marchioness, that brother and sister made the return journey from Ostend.

"Although," said Lady Char with a hint of amusement in her voice, "they could make me the Angel Gabriel's assistant, and it still wouldn't make a jot of difference. Some portals are harder to enter than the pearly gates."

They spent a night on board the royal yacht in the harbor at Deal and set off early the following morning for London in the crested carriage of Anglesey, as Uxbridge was now called. Lord Clarence and his nurse, with Lady Anglesey's abigail, were in the carriage which followed. As they crossed Westminster Bridge, a number of people recognized the Marquess or the crest on his carriage. Soon there was a boisterous throng of well-wishers which made passage impossible. Before the occupants of the coach knew what was happening, the horses were removed from their traces and men harnessed themselves to the carriage and dragged it through the cheering crowds. They entered the park by Storey's Gate, which was normally reserved for royalty. Numerous horsemen turned aside to accompany the carriage on its triumphal journey up St. James Street. Finally, they turned into Burlington Gardens.

On the steps of Uxbridge House, Lord Anglesey addressed a few words to the jubilant crowds before ascending the steps on his crutches. It could not be doubted that the tumultuous welcome had made a deep impression on him, as indeed it had on everyone present.

Deirdre and Armand took an immediate farewell of the Angleseys with promises on both sides of a future reunion either in town or at their respective country residences. Since Rathbourne House on Picadilly had been shut up for the Season, and Deirdre was loath to open her husband's house for only one night and be compelled to give directions to a set of servants who were completely unfamiliar to her, she had made up her mind that they should spend a night or two in a hotel.

366

She said as much to her friend Serena, to whose home they had repaired as a matter of course since she lived practically on the doorstep of Uxbridge House.

Serena would have none of it and prevailed upon her reluctant friend to accept her hospitality for a few days. "For I think that there is much that needs to be discussed between friends who have been, or were at one time, closer than sisters," she said in a tone which Deirdre found more disconcerting than she was willing to allow.

After dinner, leaving the men to their port in the dining room, the ladies retired to Serena's dressing room, where Serena collapsed upon a stuffed chintz chair, folded her arms across her chest without a word, and elevated her delicate black brows. A smile lurked in the depths of her eyes, however, robbing her threatening posture of any genuine displeasure.

"You must find my actions a trifle inconsistent," Deirdre ventured when she saw that Serena was determined to put her on the defensive.

"Totally incomprehensible," intoned Serena with unrelenting severity, and then spoiled the effect by smiling fondly at Deirdre. "Ninnyhammer! Don't you think I know you've been fighting your attraction to Gareth Cavanaugh since we made our bows together as schoolroom misses?"

"How could you know such a thing? I never said anything to you."

"That's how I knew, dunce! It was so out of character. Every other one of our beaux was fair game for examining under a microscope. The laughs we used to have at their expense! It really wasn't kind in us to hold them up to ridicule, even if it was merely girlish mischief and we did it only in private. But Gareth Cavanaugh was off limits from the very beginning, as I recall."

"You exaggerate," said Deirdre distantly. "It was only that Gareth's foibles didn't lend themselves to being made light of."

367

"You mean his reputation, of course? That doesn't signify. Reggie explained it to me. He says that Rathbourne's sin in the eyes of the ton was in thumbing his nose at them. He didn't give a fig for public opinion, and could not be forgiven for it. But I've told you that before. So! You've finally come to your senses! Do you know, I was beginning to think that you were too dense to see that you were meant for each other? How did he manage to persuade you?"

Deirdre blushed to the roots of her hair, and began to stammer out an incoherent explanation. Serena took pity on her friend and broke in with a twinkle, "I'm sure, I'm sorry I asked. No, don't roast me, Dee. My morals are not in question. And to think my grandmother always held you up as a pattern card of morality. Shame on you, Deirdre! Which brings me to something else. How came you to be on such familiar terms with the Uxbridges—I mean of course, the Angleseys? What a turnabout after what you last said to me about their affair."

Deirdre shook her head and grinned ruefully. She did not know what answer to make, and delayed by taking a turn around the room before sitting herself on the stool at Serena's dressing table. "I can't explain what I don't understand myself," she said frankly. "I used to think I knew the difference between right and wrong. Now I'm not so sure. How can I be the judge of something I know nothing about? I can only say that the Angleseys are amongst the kindest people I have ever known, and I think that the shabby way Lady Char has been treated is the worst kind of hypocrisy. I've given up thinking I have all the answers, I suppose. It's made me think I may have been wrong about lots of things."

There was something in Deirdre's voice that gave Serena occasion for pause. She studied her friend closely, then said in a gentle tone, "Your stepfather, for instance?"

"Perhaps. Children see everything in black and white. I never tried to understand his position. And now it's too late. I know that he wasn't happy, either with us or without us. But oh, how I loved him! No, I am not ready to forgive him yet. Not yet. Now," said Deirdre on a brighter note, "tell me about you and yours."

It was Armand who pushed for their removal to Belmont. Deirdre would have been happy to delay their departure indefinitely. Once the decision was taken, however, she resigned herself to her unhappy fate, but she saw no reason why Armand should share it. To every persuasion of his sister that he go home to Marcliff, however, Armand was adamantly opposed. He said that he was done with acting the fool, that he had given his guardian his word to follow his wishes to the letter, and that was the end of it. As they set out for Warwickshire in one of Serena's well-sprung carriages with borrowed coachmen, Deirdre wondered if Armand's newly acquired docility had anything to do with Lady Caro's being in residence at Belmont. She hoped that it had not, but feared the worst.

It was pitch black when the coach pulled up a little ways from the dimly lit entrance to Belmont, and it was evident that they were not expected. Few lights shone from the forbidding dark walls, and the massive carved doors stood bolted against them. Deirdre and Armand descended from the carriage and, telling the coachmen to wait, crossed over a narrow cobbled bridge.

"You did send word that we were arriving today?" asked Armand as he looked doubtfully at the huge scarred doors which barred their entrance.

"Naturally," responded Deirdre. "Serena sent off one of her grooms with my letter the day before yesterday. This welcome must be deliberate. There's no love lost, as I hear, between Rathbourne and his mother. No doubt, she lumps me with him."

Armand patted Deirdre on the cheek with brotherly

369

affection. "Too bad that old battle-ax doesn't know that she is dealing with a veteran of Waterloo. I can almost feel sorry for her."

"Break the door down, Armand," said Deirdre dryly, and she calmly stripped the kid gloves from her fingers.

Armand obligingly banged the knocker on the door, and after an interval, it swung open. Deirdre sailed past a sleepy night porter and entered a dark tunnel which gave onto an immense grassy courtyard.

"Good God!" said Armand at Deirdre's elbow. "I think it's a castle, or some such thing. That little bridge we crossed must have been over a moat. Poor Dee! You didn't know, did you?"

"Of course I didn't," she snapped irritably, "and if Rathbourne thinks I am going to make my home in a fortress, he'd best think again."

They pressed the reluctant night porter into service and, after some delay, were ushered across the courtyard to another set of doors which led into the great stone-flagged hall of the Castle of Belmont.

"*Ad altiora tendo*—I aim for higher things, the Rathbourne motto," said Armand by way of explanation as he examined the Rathbourne shield and crest above the ornately carved oak fireplace which could, thought Deirdre, quite easily have roasted a couple of oxen at one go.

"Can you imagine this place in winter?" she asked with unfeigned horror as she took in the vast interior with several suits of armor displayed in various corners.

"Is that a horse?" she said in awe, and moved to a huge window alcove where a stuffed destrier with full battle regalia, including silver breastplate and headpiece with black plumes, stood poised as if ready to charge.

"This place must be the armory." Armand spoke with mingled admiration and amusement as he took in the blackened armor and antiquated weapons which adorned the stone walls. "What a collection!"

"This isn't a home, it's a museum," said Deirdre, and sniffed her displeasure.

"Now mind your manners, Dee, or you'll find yourself confined to the dungeons. I say, I wonder where they are? What fun we shall have here."

Before they could speculate further, however, Guy Landron came down the stairs, his face a picture of consternation.

"Lady Rathbourne! Welcome to Belmont," he said, and using his cane, deftly crossed the space between them. He took both Deirdre's hands in his. Armand's presence he acknowledged with a curt nod of the head but an affably uttered, "St. Jean, good to see you again."

As they mounted the great staircase to the upstairs library, Landron gave lackeys terse instructions to find and lead the coach into the courtyard, and dispose of the baggage in appropritae bedrooms which had been made ready weeks before. The housekeeper, a slight nonentity of a woman who looked as if she might be frightened of her own shadow, went off muttering under her breath to procure a pot of tea and a cold collation for the weary travelers.

As Landron ushered brother and sister into the library he asked, "Why didn't you send word that you were arriving today?"

They entered a charmingly appointed saloon.

"I thought I did," said Deirdre mildly.

Her feet sank into the plush pile of a luxurious Axminster carpet, and she noted with approval that the stone walls were generously hung with various tapestries. Of books there was nary a sign.

"What a charming and unusual library," she intoned politely.

A small movement drew her eyes to two ladies who reclined in Jacobean armchairs flanking the cavernous grate. The younger laid aside her embroidery and rose to her feet. Her golden gaze alighted on Deirdre briefly, then locked on the

371

darkly handsome young man at her back. It was Deirdre who broke the charged silence.

She ignored Lady Caro and addressed herself to her mother-in-law. "Mother Rathbourne, how good of you to wait up for me!" She swept into the room and kissed the Dowager Countess on both cheeks. A pair of astute amber eyes gave her a level look, neither overt hostility nor friendliness revealed in their tawny depths.

"So you're the girl Rathbourne finally settled on," said the Dowager, her quick eyes taking in Deirdre from the tip of her disheveled bonnet which had lost its feather to the scuffed half boots which covered Deirdre's travel dusty feet. "You're not in his usual style, are you? Oh, don't look daggers at me! I assure you, I've paid you a compliment. I don't know what I expected, but I'm more relieved than I can say to find that you're a lady. You wouldn't believe the trollops he's tried to palm off on me . . ."

Landron coughed and made as if to interrupt her ladyship's diatribe. She rounded on him.

"Oh, don't get your bowels in an uproar, Guy. I shan't eat the girl. And as for you two children," she went on caustically, riveting Armand and Caro in turn with a piercing look, "you can stop making sheep's eyes at each other behind my back. If you want my opinion, Rathbourne wants his head examined having you both under the same roof. I warned him at the outset that all the Cavanaughs were sensualists, but when did he ever listen to a word I had to say?"

Armand's shoulders shook, and Lady Caro said, "Mama," in a strangled undertone.

For the next half hour or so, the Dowager Countess rattled on in the same vein as the late arrivals availed themselves of the leftovers of what had evidently been an atrocious dinner. It did not surprise Deirdre that the dishes were generously heaped. The food was inedible.

Mr. Landron tried without much success to break into Lady

Rathbourne's long litany of complaints, but Deirdre waved him to silence and heard them out with as much interest as patience. When she had finally satisfied the pangs of hunger and dabbed her lips delicately with the linen napkin, she said commiseratingly, "I don't doubt that Rathbourne has much to answer for. He never listens to me either. As for the servants, now that there are two Lady Rathbournes to direct them, I'm perfectly sure that we can make them toe the line, and if not, then we shall simply get rid of them."

"Get rid of them? Don't think I wouldn't like to make a clean sweep of the lot of them. I only put up with them at Rathbourne's express command. I have no authority, as you'll soon find out."

"Nonsense," said Deirdre briskly. "We act first, and ask Rathbourne's permission afterward."

A slight coughing at the door brought all heads round. An old man with bald pate and bent shoulders stood on the threshold. In his frail hands, which shook alarmingly, he held a tarnished silver tray with one solitary letter upon it. It took a minute for it to register on Deirdre's mind that the threadbare rags on his back were the livery of the House of Rathbourne.

"Yes, Beecham, what is it?" asked Lady Rathbourne at the top of her lungs, and waved him in with a frantic gesture.

Beecham entered and tendered the tray to his mistress.

Deirdre recognized the writing on the note and said, "Don't trouble to read it. I know the contents. It's the letter I sent by special courier informing you that Armand and I should arrive this evening. I wonder why it was delayed?" She looked questioningly at the butler.

"No good asking Beecham. He's as deaf as a doornail. You see how it is."

"Then we shall have to get by with lip reading," said Deirdre with awful finality, "or Beecham will have to go." She looked the old retainer straight in the eyes and said very softly, "Thank you, Beecham. That will be all."

He stood hesitating for a long, uncertain moment, then bowed and shuffled out of the room. Armand dissolved into fits of laughter.

Deirdre bent a quelling look on her brother and rose to her feet in one graceful movement. "Lady Rathbourne, would you be so kind as to give me your arm and show me to my rooms? Guy, I leave you in charge of the children. Give them five minutes alone then conduct them to their respective chambers. I think we owe them that much," she said quickly before Rathbourne's mother could voice a protest. "And Guy, I trust that their quarters are in different wings of the house? If not, perhaps you could have one of the servants see to it? It's no good looking at me like that, children. I quite agree with my goodmother. Rathbourne's wits must have gone abegging when he permitted you two to live under the same roof."

The Dowager Countess looked with new respect at Deirdre. "Do you know, gooddaughter, I have the happy presentiment that you are the best thing that has happened to the House of Cavanaugh since Charles the Second elevated the fifth baron to the earldom."

"Thank you," said Deirdre. "I hope you are of the same mind in a month or so when I have turned Belmont inside out. Oh, by the way, Guy, I should like to meet with all the servants in the Great Hall tomorrow morning, particularly cook and Beecham. Would you see to it for me? Shall we say eight o'clock? And of course, Mother Rathbourne, I shall want you by my side. We shall begin as we mean to go on."

Guy Landron looked appreciatively at the new mistress of Belmont. The running of Rathbourne's house had always been the domain of the Earl's mother, and so the old housekeeper had told him, she had done well enough until the estrangement with her son. After that, the servants had taken advantage like naughty children playing one parent off against the other. Rathbourne's five-year stint with the army had only aggravated matters, and Lady Rathbourne had all but resigned herself to the shoddy service which had become the mark of her servants. Landron thought that it looked to be an interesting week or two before his employer returned home.

He shut the door to the library very softly, and began a slow tour of the gallery which overlooked the Great Hall. He too wondered at Rathbourne's logic in having St. Jean at Belmont when anyone could see how his presence affected Lady Caro. Young they might be, but there was nothing childish about the looks they gave each other. He hoped Deirdre could handle her brother, for he didn't much like the thought of playing nursemaid to two naughty children until their guardian should take charge.

On the other side of the library door, Lady Caro had just turned on a brilliant smile with which she hoped to dazzle Armand. "You're cross with me," she said pettishly when she saw that he was not susceptible to her lures.

Armand negligently crossed one booted foot over the other and brought his fingertips to drum absently against each other. "You're damned right I'm cross with you. D'you realize how nearly your brother came to murdering me? What the devil possessed you to perpetrate that lie? There was no secret betrothal between us, and you know it."

"Well, what do you call it when a gentleman kisses a girl passionately, yes, and other things as well which I shan't mention, and tells her that he loves her to distraction?"

"I call it damned stupid!" He jumped to his feet and came to tower over her. He was struck, as he had been the first time he had ever set eyes on her, by the glorious tawny coloring. She looked like a young leopardess who had just caught a whiff of danger. Her eyes slanted up at him, watchful and wary. His voice gentled. "How could you possibly have thought that I had made you pregnant? Caro, I hardly touched you."

"It's all very well saying that now," she answered crossly, "but how was I to know? No one ever told me that *that* was how a man got a woman with child. To be frank, I don't think I want babies, no, not even yours."

"I could make you change your mind very easily," he

375

drawled with a suggestive smile, then suddenly recalling himself, "but that's not the point. Your brother was convinced that I'd ruined you! He could have killed me! How on earth could you have been so careless as to let your mother get hold of that letter?"

"I had nothing to do with it. I gave it to Tony, and he left it lying around. Mama recognized the writing, and the rest you can imagine. She sent *him* off to Brussels, and I was incarcerated here at Belmont to await my brother's pleasure. Oh, don't look so stricken. Gareth never could gainsay me anything I wanted. He'll come round in time."

He shook his head as if he could not believe that anyone could be so obtuse. "How can I make you understand? I told you then as I tell you now, Rathbourne will never consent to our marriage."

"Did you ask him?"

"Of course I didn't ask him! I'm not stupid. What have I got to offer a girl in your position? I must have been mad to reply to your letters. Tony should never have agreed to act as our go-between. How did you get him to do it?"

Caro made no response to his question but put out one hand and caught him by the sleeve. "Armand, it's no good taking on so." She pulled herself to her feet and stood gazing up at him, her eyes tear-bright and darkening to sable. Her hands moved to his shoulders. "My dear, I mean to have you, and that's all there is to it," she said simply.

"And what about your betrothal?" He was weakening and damn if that languorous smile on her lips didn't prove that she knew it.

"What betrothal?" she asked huskily.

"Tony said that you were on the point of accepting one of your many offers."

"No, dear, Mama was on the point of accepting one of my many offers. That's why I made up the story about our prior engagement. Were you jealous?" She flicked back a dark lock of hair that had fallen across his forehead.

His arms encircled her waist. "They'll never allow it," he said softly, and he kissed her very swiftly on the lips, then pulled back to gauge her reaction.

"We'll persuade them somehow," was the throaty rejoinder. Her fingers coiled in his dark curls, and she pulled his head down.

"Oh no, love, oh no," he groaned weakly, but he crushed her to him just the same, and kissed her so shamelessly that there was never any doubt of who carried off the honors in that encounter.

Upstairs in the west wing of the private apartments, Martha, a young maid of an age with Deirdre, was occupied in unpacking her ladyship's boxes.

She curtsied at her young mistress's entrance. Deirdre acknowledged the gesture with a smile and glanced around the candlelit chamber. She had an impression of shabbiness, a grandeur that had gone to seed, but she was too weary to take much in. She longed for the comfort of a hot bath, but such luxuries, so she had discovered, were beyond the imagination of the residents at Belmont, and she thought of Marcliff with regret and of the servants, few though they were in number, whom she had trained to run the household with the precision of a corps of artillery gunners.

As the abigail unpacked Deirdre's boxes and put away her things, Deirdre suffered the discomfort of a cold sponge bath and made monosyllabic replies to the spate of chatter which emanated from the maid. Something caught her interest, however, and she asked at length, "What Servants' and Tenants' Ball?"

"The last one, ma'am, afore his lordship went off to Spain. That were the first time I ever wore a grown-up gown, like this." She held up one of Deirdre's pale muslins and went on hopefully. "Me ma says that now that Belmont has a new mistress and his lordship is finally settled, mayhap we'll go back to the old ways and have a ball again every year."

"Would that please you?"

"Oh m'um!" Martha's eyes were shining. "It's the grandest thing I ever was at in my life."

"Tell me about it," said Deirdre, her interest piqued.

Martha's pinched face softened, taking on a faraway expression, and her faltering accents gradually warmed as she began, diffidently at first, then with more confidence, to describe an event that had made a deep impression on her young mind. She told of the months of preparation throughout the castle and of the night itself, just after harvest was in, when the Great Hall was lavishly garlanded with fresh flowers and sheaves of wheat, and an orchestra with violins, imported from London, played beguilingly from the gallery. As protocol demanded, the ball was opened when his lordship led the housekeeper into the first dance, and the lady of the house was partnered by the august butler. So vividly did Martha tell her tale that Deirdre could almost hear the sweet strains of the orchestra and smell the oxen roasting on spits in the great fireplace as two hundred guests sat down at long trestle tables which had been pushed back against the walls, and devoured the special dishes which cook and her helpers had painstakingly prepared weeks in advance, and she could almost taste Martha's excitement as servants and tenants opened the small gifts which had been set at the place of every man, woman, and child.

Deirdre slipped between the cold linen sheets smelling of lavender and smiled with faint regret. "A Servants' and Tenants' Ball sounds marvelous, Martha, but scarcely practicable. I would die of shame before I'd let my neighbors see the squalor inside this old heap of stones. I can't see how such a thing is to be accomplished, can you?"

Martha became involved in emptying out the china wash basin and tidying away the towels which Deirdre had discarded. "No, m'um," she agreed politely, then cautiously, as an afterthought, "but my old ma always says that there's nothing like a good party to get the house spanking clean from attics to cellars."

"Does she now?" asked Deirdre, and paused as if she was giving the matter some serious thought. "It occurs to me that your old ma knows a thing or two. Perhaps we shall have a ball," she mused aloud, "yes perhaps we shall, if I can be persuaded, that is, that I won't live to regret it."

"Oh no, m'um! You never would," said Martha seriously, and Deirdre smiled to herself.

Chapter Twenty-Four

Deirdre stretched languidly like some replete jungle feline, and she buried herself deeper into the warm depression the weight of her body had formed in the cushion of fragrant hay. A sound which was very close to a purr caught in her throat, and a slow smile of pleasure touched her lips. She felt happier and more relaxed than she had done in a long, long time. Her thoughts drifted, resisting the pull to consciousness, and she turned on her side as if to turn her back on the reality of scores of servants who were turning Belmont Castle upside down and inside out in preparation for the ball which was only a month away.

A small pang of guilt intruded on her pleasant reveries, but she smothered it. They could do without her direction for an hour or two, and she would not reveal her secret retreat above the hayloft in the stables and be at the beck and call of every scullery maid in Belmont for every minute of the day. She filled her lungs, breathing deeply of the comforting aromas of fresh hay, sweating horseflesh, and the mellow tang of old polished leather. Something stroked against her back, and she moved slightly to accommodate it, supposing in her drowsiness that one of the stable cats was seeking her warmth.

Under her palm, she felt her breasts swell, and the bud of a nipple tightened against her stays. Her bodice loosened as if in obedience to her half-formed thought. Her eyelids fluttered, and a small frown furrowed her brow. A hand buried itself in her short-cropped tresses and Deirdre came fully awake. She sat up with a start, and her bodice dropped to her waist, baring her breasts. She looked down in bewilderment, gazing at her nakedness, and at the long masculine fingers which caressed her flesh, indolently kneading the soft mounds to a voluptuous sensitivity.

"You!" she breathed, turning fully to be bathed in the brightness of his langorous, golden gaze. Rathbourne raised himself, and she twisted slightly away from him as if to protect her nudity from his devouring eyes.

"Deirdre," he murmured against her neck, and he slipped out of his pristine white shirt to reveal the tanned, muscular physique which rippled with each sure movement. "Deirdre," he said again, and cupped her shoulders, sinking his parted lips into the soft warmth of her nape. She felt the heat of his naked torso as it brushed sensuously against her back, heating her skin to a feverish glow.

She moaned, her scattering thoughts losing focus, and the knot of resentment she had patiently nursed in the weeks since she had last seen him splintered into a thousand fragments.

"Unjust," she whispered on a breath of a sound, and twisted slightly to block the marauding hands which moved purposefully to cup her breasts. His hands followed her, and his thumbs lazily stroked the swelling nipples, coaxing her body to a sweet oblivion of everything but him.

"Unjust," she breathed again, shrugging his hands off, her mind groping to hang on to the feeling of ill-usage which was fast slipping from her. "We must talk," she said slowly and deliberately, but could not recall exactly what it was she wished to say to him.

"Yes," he agreed, and forced her gently but relentlessly into the hay, "but only love talk. Everything else can wait for this."

He came down on her, deliberately brushing and teasing the tender rise of her breasts with the soft mat of dark hair on his chest. She groaned, and her lips parted slightly. He swiftly captured them, cupping her chin in both hands, forcing her lips wider as he buried his mouth in her honeyed warmth. The kiss gentled to a slow exploration as if he wished to refresh his senses with the taste of her on his tongue and lips, and awaken her to the pleasure of his body. But passion outstripped reason, and his hands and mouth burned and bruised with his raging haste to possess her. She splayed her fingers against his chest, restraining him, and he released her at once.

She pushed herself to a sitting position, her arms hugging her knees. He was manipulating her into surrender and she fought against it.

He raised on one elbow and ran the fingers of one hand down the length of her bare arm. "Deirdre?" he said coaxingly, his need for her hoarsening his voice to a whisper of liquid sound, "I've waited almost two months for this. Even if I wanted to, I don't think I could let you turn me away now. You can give in gracefully, or . . ."

His hand grasped her ankle and began a slow and tantalizing exploration beneath the folds of her skirts, and his warm, erratic breath fanned her shoulder. He parted her knees, easily overcoming her slight resistance, and his fingers moved higher and deftly untied the strings of her drawers. His palm burrowed inside to the warmth of her abdomen, languidly massaging the taut muscles till he felt them relax against the flat of his hand.

"Deirdre, love, we don't want all these clothes between us, do we?" he asked, and soothed her with words of love as he stripped her to her chemise.

"You're my wife, and I love you," he reassured, and he quickly divested himself of his pantaloons and hessians. "I want to be as close to you as I can. Words can't possibly express what I am feeling for you at this moment. I want to show you with my body, and . . ."

She turned into him on a soft cry, and words became superfluous. He pressed her back and drowned her senses with lavishly bestowed caresses and slow, seductive kisses. He stroked her ceaselessly, as if he would rediscover the imprint of each curve and hollow against his hand, and when she opened herself to him, holding nothing in reserve, he fought to control the hot surge of passion that swept through him like the incoming tide.

"What is it you want from me?" he teased with mock innocence, and his fingers worked their irresistible magic, his touch as light as snow melting on the moist warmth of her skin. Her knees snapped together and she bared her teeth at him. "Gareth Cavanaugh," she ground out, then she sucked in her breath as he pressed her knees apart and entered her deeply. "Gareth Cavanaugh," she repeated, but on a breath of a sound as his mouth smothered her lips, swallowing her soft cries as she rose to meet him, the rising tempo of their rhythm heating their feverish skin till it was dewed with moisture.

He tried to prolong their pleasure, but she resisted when he made to still her movements. "No!" she protested when his hands clamped on her hips to hold her passive. "No!" and she moved sinuously, arching herself into him.

He drew his breath on a ragged gasp and his control shattered. He reared over her. "Deirdre, oh Deirdre," he groaned, his voice a whisper of apology and he drove into her. But she was beyond him, the ripples of sensual pleasure already convulsing her body. She dissolved against him, her nails compulsively raking his back, and he heard his name on her lips as his own cry of release tore from his throat.

She became aware that his idly caressing hands had, by degrees, become purposeful, deliberately brushing against the pleasure pulses of her body. "No," she said negligently, still savoring the gift of repleteness which his lovemaking always brought to her.

"Yes," he corrected uncompromisingly, and he swept his hands possessively over her nakedness. She caught them with her own and said on a laugh, "Gareth, it's too soon."

His answer was to capture her lips, forcing them open, and

384

the strength of his rising passion stirred her. She made a weak attempt to shake him off, but he held her fast, impervious to her halfhearted protests.

When she determined the earnestness of his purpose, she thought to make him a gift of herself, to let him use her as he would for his own gratification, but the generous gesture was not to his liking. He wanted her breathless with desire, as he was, and he devoted himself to feeding her passion with unlimited patience and skill. When he heard her deep-drawn gasps as her lungs gulped in air, he rewarded her by giving her what her body now demanded.

"Again?" he asked on a low laugh of masculine triumph.

"Gareth," she warned, and sighed with relief as he brought himself fully into her. "Again," she pleaded, and locked her arms behind his neck, drawing his head down.

But he had himself well in hand, and seemed to take a perverse pleasure in evading her shy attempts to bring him to climax. It forced her to a boldness which delighted him. Her hands caressed and teased and her softly murmured words of entreaty drove his passion to boiling point. When he finally allowed her lips to connect with his, he tasted the blaze of uninhibited desire on her moistly open mouth and his bridled ardor exploded through him.

The aftermath almost became another prelude, but Deirdre was now sensitive to his mood swings, and she thwarted his intent by scrambling to her knees and warding him off with both hands. He had half moved to catch her and draw her back, but when he saw the determined light in her eyes, he sank back on his haunches, gave a regretful sigh, and resigned himself to what he knew must follow.

She dressed quickly, keeping a wary eye on him as he reluctantly donned his own hastily discarded garments.

"What happened to your hair?" he asked, mentioning her shorn locks for the first time, and his eyes darkened.

She touched one hand guiltily to the wispy gold strands on her nape and shrugged off his black look. "I had it cut. But

385

that's not what I wish to speak to you about, so don't try to turn the subject."

It occurred to her then that she could scarcely ring a peal over him when she had just allowed him to make passionate love to her. She bit her lip, wondering if he had contrived the whole thing for that very purpose. A quick look at the barely suppressed mockery lurking in the depths of his eyes confirmed her suspicion. He would, oh yes, he would!

She surprised herself as much as him by her opening remark. "You didn't even give me a chance to say 'welcome home.'"

The eybrows shot up. "I have no complaint about my welcome home," and a smile creased his face when he saw the blush come and go under her skin. He picked up a straw and ran his teeth over it, his eyes never leaving hers for an instant.

"Oh, it's no good taking you to task," she said petulantly. "You have a plausible explanation for everything. But what you did to me was wrong. You used my fears for Armand to force me to your will."

He stretched out in a leisurely manner, and clasped his hands behind his head. "That was a mistake," he said calmly, "an impulse that I regretted almost as soon as I indulged it. I've been in Intelligence work too long, I suppose, and find it hard not to carry the methods I use there into my private life. I beg your pardon."

Her expression was arrested. "You were in Intelligence work? You never said a word to me."

"That, my dear, is the nature of the game; cloak and dagger stuff. It was safer for you not to know, given the fact that my interest in you was common knowledge."

"What a whisker! It was your liaison with Mrs. Dewinters that was common knowledge, and don't try to deny it!"

He looked at her with amused indulgence. "Did I gammon you too? I confess that my bruised pride was soothed by your jealousy." He saw the dangerous glitter in her eyes and his smile deepened. "Nevertheless, my fictionary affair with

Maria was to throw sand in the eyes of the watching world and to protect you. I told you many times that there was nothing between us. You wouldn't listen. Am I to be blamed for your lack of faith in me?"

The man had an answer for everything. But Deirdre was determined to keep him in the wrong.

"Was that fair to her?"

He shrugged negligently. "Maria was one of our best agents. She understood the risks she was running. We've worked together before."

She sat looking at him in silence for some moments. He could almost hear her mind working as she absorbed this piece of information and reviewed his past iniquities one by one. He was not overly troubled. He had spent two months perfecting the responses he would make to every possible accusation she could come up with.

"Why are you telling me this now?" she said finally.

"Because now it is safe to tell you. Bonaparte is now far away on the island of St. Helena. In Brussels, with Napoleon and his cohorts practically on our doorstep, you were in danger. It was better for you to be in ignorance of my activities. Even now, you must treat what I have told you with the utmost confidence. Some people have long memories and carry a grudge. But I thought I owed you an explanation."

"Thank you, that is very generous of you," she said scathingly, and he suppressed a smile.

He watched in fascination as she chewed on her lower lip. He had taken the wind out of her sails and he could see that she was not best pleased by it.

"Are you satisfied now, love?"

"No! Everything is just too pat." Her face brightened a little and instinct warned him to be cautious. "To get back to Armand," she said in dulcet accents. "If you regretted the impulse to use him to blackmail me, as you say, why did you not tell me at once? Why did you let me go on thinking the worst?"

387

"Because explanations would have taken time and led us into all kinds of difficulties. We had less than two hours together. I had better things to do with my time than quarrel with you about your brother. It was, for God's sake, our wedding night."

"But to let me think that he would be safe, when all the time he was with you and—"

"I know. I took the coward's way out. But I couldn't stop the boy, and I honestly did my best. I set O'Toole to guard him with his life. When Armand took a scratch, I put him in the infirmary. I thought I had done my duty. O'Toole was with him. He left him for an hour or so, and when he went back to check on him, Armand was gone. I didn't know what to think. We heard after the battle that he had fallen on the field with a friend who went to help him. O'Toole and I looked for him all that night, but there were so many corpses, so many wounded. It was hopeless. Can you imagine what I went through thinking that I might have to face you with your brother's death?"

His eyes were very frank and his expression somber. That part of his story she had verified for herself. She shuddered, remembering the events of that day and the long night of terror.

"And Armand's affair with your sister had nothing to do with your decision to let him enlist?"

His face darkened, but he said easily enough, "So that's what you thought! It never ceases to amaze me how swift you are to think the worst. No. And the decision to enlist was his, not mine. You may defile me as you will for my attempt to blackmail you. That I deserve. But acquit me at least of wishing your brother ill."

She looked slightly shamefaced, and he continued more gently, "Good God, Deirdre, I think I have some excuse for doing everything in my power to give you the protection of my name. You, I know, will say I was only doing what suited me. Think again. No man wishes to be tied to a woman who hates him, or worse, is indifferent to him. I was thinking of your happiness as much as my own. Perhaps I was high-handed. Very well, I admit I was, if you say so. But only because the obstacles to overcoming your objections to me were as ridiculous as they were immovable. I knew that you loved me five years ago before I went to Spain. You look surprised. I assure you Deirdre, I knew. No woman ever responded to my kisses with such unpracticed though unwilling ardor. It inflamed me; captivated me; enslaved me. I thought I could easily overcome your resistance. But I didn't understand the nature of the barriers between us." He stretched and rose to his feet with feline grace, then went to stand at the open dormer window with his back to her. Deirdre remained on her knees, drinking in his lean muscled form and the glints of gold in his hair where the sun touched it.

"Love is awful, isn't it? When I first found you, I thought I was the luckiest man alive. But you, even loving me, thought I was like the dirt beneath your feet. So—I was a womanizer and a gambler, and all the other things you called me. What of it? It had nothing to do with us. Do you suppose I was happy with that sort of life? I was as miserable as hell! And lonely too, for all my boon companions." He turned to look at her, and her eyes dropped under the blaze of his. "Your love could have made all the difference in the world to me, but you withheld it, for no damn good reason! And I, God help me, let you. When I found you again, things were exactly the same between us. I knew then that I would be a fool to let you go a second time. Your aunt explained something of your background to me. And I quizzed your friend, Serena. I knew that you would not be persuaded by logic or by your own heart. So, I stooped to other means—cheating, abduction, blackmail. Not very gentlemanly, I grant you, but I make no apology for what I did."

She heard the soft tread of his boots as he crossed the floor to her. He knelt down beside her and his long fingers clasped her chin and brought her head up. She raised her eyes to his and saw the bright laughter mocking her.

"No, I make no apologies," he repeated softly. "For you, my love, are very, very pregnant, and I am the happiest man in the world."

She tried to snatch his hand away, but he held her securely. A faint blush colored her complexion. "I am not very, very pregnant," she protested. "Only two months. And I don't see how you can tell. And furthermore, I don't want to know how you can tell either," she concluded hurriedly when she saw the devilish glint in his eyes.

"Are you happy, love?"

Something in his voice gave her pause. There was no change in either his expression or his posture, but there was a tension there that betrayed he was hanging on her words.

"More than I deserve," she said, and was rewarded for her honesty by being tumbled into his arms and pressed backward into the soft bed of hay.

"Is that all you can think about?" she asked weakly when he began to disrobe her.

He made no answer, but as very soon afterward it was all that Deirdre could think about as well, she decided wisely that the question had become irrelevant and did not press him for an answer.

Dinner was not the unqualified success that Deirdre had hoped it would be. The undercurrents that eddied back and forth between various family members put a definite dampener on what ought to have been a joyful homecoming. Lady Caro and Armand had obviously had a falling-out and pointedly ignored each other. Armand and her husband exchanged wary glances like two dogs circling each other before a fight, and the Dowager and Rathbourne were at loggerheads within minutes of the first course being served. The burden of conversation fell on Deirdre and Guy Landron.

The meal itself, as well as the service, was excellent, however, and Rathbourne commented on it.

"Did you finally get rid of Mrs. Petrie?" he asked Deirdre as he savored a mouthful of baked turbot smothered in a smooth lobster sauce.

"No. We are merely the beneficiaries of her attempts to persuade me that there is no need to hire a chef from London for our Tenants' and Servants' Ball."

Beecham entered with two footmen, and Rathbourne watched with veiled interest as they served the next course with a precision which was as welcome to him as it was unfamiliar.

When the servants withdrew, Rathbourne looked down the length of the table at Deirdre and drawled, "I think I've divined your strategy. A Tenants' and Servants' Ball, you say? Doesn't that come close to corrupting the innocent? And who, may I ask, is going to pay the shot for this Bacchinalian revelry? Dee, I'm shocked at your deviousness."

Mistaking the nature of this gentle cajolery, the Dowager interrupted her flow of small talk with Mr. Landron and, turning on her son, said in withering accents, "Hold your tongue, sir, if you cannot find anything good to say of the girl. You've been so much in petticoat company that your address begins to smack of the gutter. In the month that she has been here, Deirdre has done wonders at Belmont, and everyone knows it. If you had been home, as you ought to have been, instead of galavanting all over Europe with those disreputable friends of yours, things might never have come to this sorry pass. Why, my gooddaughter has done more to see to my comfort and peace of mind than my own flesh and blood."

Visibly smarting under his mother's staggering tirade, Rathbourne bristled, but his voice, when he spoke, betrayed no emotion. "Thank you. And now that you have vented your spleen on my character and comrades, perhaps you would be so kind as to tell me why a mere slip of a girl should accomplish in one month what you could not do in five years?"

Deirdre and Armand exchanged a quick glance. His face showed only mild amusement, but his sister was deeply embarrassed. She felt like an eavesdropper and wished only to escape from a quarrel that would have been better conducted in private. She stole a quick glance at Landron and Caro. Both were pretending an inordinate interest in the food on the plate in front of them. She opened her mouth to make a comment, any comment about the dinner, the room, the weather, but the Dowager was before her.

She sniffed and said in a voice that was tremulous with emotion. "The servants never paid me any mind. Why should they, when my own son made it very plain that I was only in his house on sufferance? I had no authority, and everyone knew it, from the girl who cleans out the grates to old Beecham, who never liked me even when your father was alive. Your instructions to me were that none of the older retainers were to be let go unless you authorized it. How could you authorize it when you were not here? Perhaps I was not as clever as Deirdre. I admit it. But I was here as seldom as possible. After I lost Andrew, I could not bear all the memories of the happier times we shared in Belmont."

As the Dowager spoke, a pall descended on the table, each person uncomfortably aware that he was intruding upon a private grief. It was Deirdre who broke the protracted silence.

"Well, I hope you will recall those happier times, goodmother," she said prosaically, "and share them with your grandchildren. It's very likely that another Andrew will be running around this fortress in a year of two." Then she added very gently, "You will be depriving him of his birthright if you deny him your memories, especially those of his namesake. Memories can be very comforting if you cherish the happy ones. And now," she continued with forced brightness as her eyes traveled the arrested faces of the guests at her board, "shall we repair to the tapestry room to have coffee and brandy? I refuse to relinquish my husband to the obligatory port on his first night home."

"Do you mean the library?" asked Rathbourne as he offered Deirdre his arm.

"No, I mean the tapestry room. You'll soon get the hang of it, Rathbourne. The servants did, and it's made life so much easier. The library is the room with books in it; the tapestry room has tapestries hanging on the walls; the dining room—"

"Don't tell me. It's the room where we dine."

"You've got it. Simple, isn't it? It was so confusing to ask the servants to serve coffee in the library and have them deliver trays to the new library which used to be the old dining room, and if you said that you would see someone in the drawing room, Beecham might or might not show them into the tapestry room when you meant the blue saloon, and—"

"Yes," he interrupted with a laugh, "I get your drift. We Cavanaughs, from one generation to another, have changed rooms around to suit our own convenience. Somehow the old names stuck. I see how the servants might have taken advantage."

"Oh, not 'might,' Gareth. *Did*, unashamedly and invariably," she responded with a twinkle.

He smiled at her with a tenderness which made her heart constrict. "Do you know, I love your proprietary air? I am beginning to feel that I really belong to you at last. Now tell me what you think of Belmont."

As they slowly mounted the Great Hall staircase in retinue, Deirdre surreptitiously ran her fingers over the ballustrade and was glad to note that not a trace of dust adhered to her fingers. Rathbourne's keen eyes missed nothing. He grinned.

"Well?" he demanded.

"I found Belmont a bit daunting at first, like its master," she confided archly. "But I intend to lick them both into shape."

"I hope you mean that literally," he said in an undertone. "At least with respect to the master." Deirdre colored and turned on him wrathfully. "I know," he interposed. "Male crudity again. Better get used to it, Dee. I shall be as crude as I please." He flicked her mischievously on her upturned nose. "You make the temptation irresistible, you know."

The remainder of the evening began only marginally more

comfortably. Deirdre, now alert to the barbs which flew between mother and son, contrived to deflect each thrust before any irreparable damage could be done. She felt like a governess presiding over the nursery, and longed to knock their heads together. It was not in her power, however, and she was forced to resort to diplomacy, never one of her strong suits.

She recognized the similarity of temperament and that unbending will which was common to both and which inevitably led to confrontation. Their history of bad feelings and cruel words, she knew, could not be easily overcome or forgiven. Roderick Ogilvie had told her that the estrangement had begun when Andrew, the younger son, had lost his life in the climbing accident in Scotland, but she could not believe that Rathbourne and his mother had ever been on terms of intimacy. It seemed to her, as she observed the thrust and parry of their verbal exchanges, that what was needed were some happy memories that they could both look back on with pleasure. She hoped she could find a way to provide some.

Her eyes shifted to Lady Caro, and her heart sank. The chit was unashamedly flirting with Guy Landron. Nor was that provoking gentleman averse to playing her game. Armand's dark eyes smoldered and his lips were set in a thin line.

Deirdre went into action. She opened the card table and retrieved a pack of cards from a drawer. No sooner had she begun to shuffle them than she was joined, as she knew she would be, by her husband and her brother.

"Sit down, Rathbourne," she commanded. "These are cards I brought with me from Brussels. I'd like to see what you can do when everything is above board. Armand can look out for my interests and keep tally."

He chuckled and slid into the seat next to hers. "I could beat you blindfolded," he challenged outrageously. Something caught his eye and his hand closed over the back of her wrist. He turned her arm over and his eyes traveled the ugly red scar which ran from elbow to armpit.

"How did this come about?" he asked, and his eyes became alert when Deirdre and Armand exchanged wary glances.

"It's only a scratch," she answered, and tried to pull her arm away.

"Who did the embroidery?" His tone was casual—too casual by half for Deirdre's comfort.

To evade a straight answer was one thing, but Deirdre had no wish to begin her married life on lies and subterfuge. He would be angry, but she could weather that. "One of the army doctors at Waterloo. I forget his name. It's a long story. I'll tell you later when we are alone," she said quietly.

He let her go and picked up the cards she had dealt him. "What stakes do we play for?"

Deirdre breathed more easily. "No stakes. The loser pays a forfeit. It's more fun that way."

"What kind of forfeit?"

"Heavens, I don't know. Armand, what kind of forfeits did we pay when we were children?"

"Horrid ones," he said, and a grin tugged at the corners of his mouth. "You once made me kiss Farmer Sykes's prize sow. For that peccadillo I got a beating from Papa."

"Nonsense!" said Deirdre unsympathetically. "You got the beating for rolling about in the pigsty in your Sunday best."

"Well, she wouldn't hold still!"

The game commenced and before very long the hilarity at the card table attracted the other members of the party. Soon everyone had joined in. The forfeits for the losers were chosen with a view to making them appear as ridiculous as possible. Deirdre and Mr. Landron, who were both known to be indifferent musicians, were made to sing one verse of "Greensleeves" in harmony, a labor which set everyone to groaning and covering their ears with their hands. Armand and Lady Caro, at Deirdre's instigation, and with much prompting, were compelled to recite "The Lovesick Frog," a ditty which lent itself to the substitution of the names of persons present, a circumstance which the young couple used to good effect, roasting everyone in turn. And the Dowager, who foolishly owned to lapsing into a childish lisp when she became excited, was made to twist her tongue around some piece of nonsense having to do with silly servants shining silver shoes in Simon's sunny solarium. It brought the house down. Only Rathbourne, as the unbeaten champion, stood aloof from the absurd antics of his companions. It was Armand who remarked upon it with a look which Rathbourne immediately distrusted.

"When we were children," Armand reminded Deirdre, flicking a malevolent glance at his brother-in-law, "the winner was made to stand on the roof of the outside privy and shout, 'I'm the king of the castle,' and the losers had to bow down and chant 'Amen! Amen! Amen!'"

"Not a chance," Rathbourne interjected, and he shifted uneasily under the hard stares of five pairs of interested eyes.

"It's Deirdre's game, Gareth," said his mother on her dignity. "She should decide what's to become of you."

Everyone looked to Deirdre for direction. She walked slowly in a circle round the Earl as if deep in thought.

"He can choose his own forfeit," she said finally, and silenced the derisive hoots with a slight movement of her hand. "After all, when we were children, who didn't want to stand on top of the privy and be king of the castle? Show us then, my Lord Rathbourne, what you are made of. Take your seats, ladies and gentlemen. And Gareth," she added softly, "this had better be good."

They took their places, and all eyes turned expectantly upon the Earl. "Caro, ring for Beecham if you would be so kind," he drawled, and negligently adjusted the lace at his sleeve. "Ah, Beecham, a glass of Drambuie, if you please."

Within minutes, a small crystal goblet filled to the brim with the amber liquid was tendered to the Earl on a spotless silver tray. He removed a linen handkerchief from his coat pocket and wrapped it round the stem of the glass. Beecham then lit a taper from one of the candles and brought it to his master. Rathbourne put the taper to the goblet, and the heated

Drambuie burst into flame. He put the fiery liquid to his lips and drank it back in one gulp, emptying the glass. He replaced the empty goblet on the tray and said affably, "Thank you, Beecham. That will be all."

He turned his saturnine countenance full face toward his open-mouthed audience. "It's nothing, really," he said with a deprecatory shrug of his broad shoulders. "I learned the trick at Oxford when I joined the Holy Grail Society, now defunct of course."

No one moved and he felt impelled to add, "It's one of the initiation rites."

As the door closed on the departing butler, Landron got to his feet and raised his glass in a toast. "For he's the king of the castle," he intoned solemnly, and five awestruck voices chanted, "Amen! Amen! Amen!"

Deirdre had little hope that her husband would forget about the scar on her arm, nor did he. They were undressing for bed when he asked her again to explain the cause of the injury she had suffered. Deirdre, though determined to make a clean breast of everything, began to describe the horror of the battle and its aftermath with an understatement which made the whole sorry episode sound ludicrous even to her own ears. It did not fool him for an instant. He asked a few terse questions which she answered evasively. When he pressed her, however, she concealed nothing. He was at first thunderstruck, and then he exploded with a white hot anger.

"It was you who was seen going to Armand's aid when he was attacked by lancers, wasn't it?" he demanded furiously.

She tried to placate him, but her calm assurances seemed only to invite him to a greater wrath.

"Do you think I will permit my wife to endanger her life in that wanton fashion? You flaunted my express wishes! How dared you expose yourself to such peril? Of course, Armand! That explains everything!" He grabbed her by the arms and shook her roughly. "When are you going to allow that brother of yours to stand on his own two feet?" He threw her from him, and she fell against the bed. She made no move to rise, but remained on her knees, meekly accepting the chastisement she felt in some sort she had deserved.

He turned on her. His eyes were flashing and his mouth was tight-lipped. "What you did, for whatever reason, was an intolerable breach of my trust. Must I remind you that you are my wife? By God, you had better remember it in future or it will be very much the worse for you. I *will* have your obedience, or you shall feel the weight of my hand. Do I make myself clear?" and he raised his hand as if to strike her.

Deirdre had prepared herself to accept the rough edge of his tongue. She knew that he would be sorely provoked by her conduct. But this vicious form of address shocked her to the core. In a moment, her anger blazed to as great a heat as his own.

"How dare you threaten me! Doesn't it mean anything to you that I saved Armand's life? The doctor said—"

"I'm not interested in excuses. Nor am I interested in St. Jean. A husband takes precedence over a brother. Remember that in future, or by God, I'll take steps to see that you do."

"Then I wish I had never married you," she lashed out, and turned her back on him.

In a castle with more bedchambers than Deirdre could number, she had expected Rathbourne to have his own suite of rooms. His baggage, however, was strewn around the floor, making it very obvious that where she was, he intended to be also. She wished she could slam out of the door and find a quiet hole where she could be miserable in comfort, but no other rooms were ready to receive guests and it seemed ill advised to test a temper that was already at boiling point. She climbed into the high tester bed with as much dignity as she could muster and curled herself into a ball on the far edge of the mattress.

She was to discover that though quarreling might make her averse to the intimacies of married life, it had no such effect on her husband. She tried to remain cold and impassive in his arms, but he seduced her to passion with mortifying ease.

398

Though he was gentle with her, she was never in any doubt that he meant to show her who was master and exact his own peculiar retribution for the last angry words she had flung at him. It was a long time before he finally gave in to her distracted pleas for release from a torment that was driving her to delirium.

When it was over, she burst into tears. He cradled her in his arms, cherishing her with unending caresses, soothing her with extravagant endearments.

"Deirdre, don't cry. There's no need. You know I would cut off my arm sooner than hurt you. But what you did was wrong. My God, if I had lost you . . ."

His ragged voice and trembling limbs betrayed the strength of his emotion. It was a long time before Deirdre could find the means to comfort him. Words proved inadequate. Their protracted lovemaking was as inevitable as it was necessary, but it could not heal the one serious difference that still divided them.

Sleep, when it came to Deirdre, was fitful and filled with terrifying presentiments. She was mounted on Lustre, riding madly into battle to ward off one of the French lancers who threatened Armand's back. Armand went down, and Deirdre screamed. The lancer turned to face her and drew back his lance to finish her off. And she saw that it was Rathbourne. He smiled grotesquely and he aimed the bloodied point of his spear at her breast. She leveled her pistol, but her fingers refused to pull the trigger.

Chapter Twenty-Five

Over the next week or so it became customary for the residents of the castle and its environs to catch glimpses of the master of Belmont and his lady as they rode out on an early morning ramble. There was nothing desultory about these excursions, however, for Rathbourne had it in his mind to familiarize Deirdre with every corner and every facet of his domain. He was so eager, so touchingly desirous of her good opinion, that Deirdre determined to be suitably admiring. If Rathbourne hoped to impress her, he succeeded beyond his dreams.

Until the Earl's return from Paris, Deirdre had never ventured far from the castle walls unless it was to the stables which lay just beyond the footbridge over the dry moat. Rathbourne now gave Deirdre her first intimation of the extent of his vast holdings and an inkling of the sort of moneyed aristocracy into which she had married.

It soon became evident that the Earl, as much as anything, wanted to show her off, and she was introduced to a veritable army of personages who devoted their energies to enriching the land for their lord and, as Rathbourne would have it, enriching themselves into the bargain—gamekeepers and under-gamekeepers, gardeners and under-gardeners, woodsmen, parkmen, gatehouse keepers, bricklayers, plasterers, painters, sawyers, and gravel diggers, as well as the tenants and laborers who farmed the land for him. His holdings took in several villages, and the disposition of a dozen church livings was in his hands. There was even a clerk of works on his payroll. It had never occurred to Deirdre that Rathbourne, whom she had once accused of being a lightweight, had that kind of background. It was hard to justify her pride in her own dear Marcliff, which, in comparison, seemed like a pauper's hovel.

After one such foray, as they returned to Belmont, they stopped to rest their horses at a ford across the River Avon. Deirdre threw herself down on the grassy bank and leaned back on her elbows.

"Why didn't you tell me before we were married that you owned half of England?" she demanded.

"Hardly!" he reproved, and came to tower over her, his face in shadow so that Deirdre could not read his expression. "Besides, a sixth sense warned me that all this"—he gestured vaguely with a slight movement of his hand—"might well work against me. Was I wrong?"

"Probably not. Still, you ought to have given me some sort of warning."

"Why?"

She brushed angrily at the skirt of her riding habit. "Because . . . because . . ." she blustered, "because your wife must needs be a public figure. That sort of life doesn't appeal to me. From now on, everything I do will be sifted by a fine-tooth comb. I'm a private sort of person. Nobody ever noticed me before. Now I shall be under constant scrutiny."

He threw himself down beside her and said quite impenitently, "True! The worst of it is, of course, that half of the gossip will be mere fabrication, or at the very least, exaggeration. I've lived with it most of my life." His fingertips, a butterfly caress, brushed her cheek. "I know it's not pleasant, but you'll learn in time to ignore it."

"Is that what happened to you? Serena said something . . ."

"No. I won't claim an innocence I am not entitled to, not even to gain your good opinion. I was everything you said I was. But *that* was the folly of youth. You could have converted me to a pattern card of rectitude very easily if you had chosen to."

"No I couldn't." She hugged her knees and rested her chin on the cross of her arms. "We had different devils driving us. But I was just as driven as you were. We met at the wrong time, that is all."

"Not for me. And it was more than lust, as you once threw at me! You gave my thoughts a new direction. I thought of you constantly as you are now, by my side, as my consort, helping me to build a future for our children and our children's children. My God, I could still throttle you, Dee, when I think that you have cheated me of five years."

"I would have made you miserable then. The Fates have been kind to us. Let's not quibble about something we can't change. I've done a lot of growing up since I first met you. And suddenly the future looks much brighter." She turned a brilliant smile on him and found herself swiftly pinioned beneath him. She felt the weight of her skirts as he dragged them up.

She struggled wildly. "Let me go, you devil!" She laughed up at him. "All it needs is one yokel to catch a glimpse of us and it will be all over the county that the master of Belmont has been tumbling some precocious wench in the hay."

"But you're my wife," he protested.

"Who would believe it? You have a castle with scores of bedchambers. No man with such resources at his disposal would make love to his wife in the open, as if they were field animals."

He let her go reluctantly. "You win this time, but don't expect such consideration in future." He kissed her lingeringly, then abruptly hauled her to her feet. "Once my people see that the master of Belmont is desperately in love with his wife," he said reasonably, "they'll be disappointed if I don't

403

shock them."

"Incorrigible," she flashed at him, but her eyes were smiling.

They returned to Belmont in perfect amity. At the stables, Deirdre came face to face with O'Toole, and remembering Brussels and how much the man was in her husband's confidence, she dropped her eyes and her cheeks took on a healthy glow. She became tongue-tied as she welcomed him home, and even more incoherent as she attempted to thank him for his care of her brother at Waterloo.

Rathbourne chuckled, and winked broadly at his groom. "What Lady Rathbourne means to say, O'Toole, is that she hopes her hoydenish behavior in the past hasn't given you a lasting disgust of her. For some unfathomable reason, she values your good opinion more than she does mine."

Deirdre's blush deepened, but O'Toole's matter-of-fact disclaimer to knowing anything of a nature which could possibly detract from the high regard in which he had always held her ladyship did much to smooth her ruffled sensibilities.

"How long has O'Toole been in your employ?" she asked Rathbourne as they made their way across the castle bailey.

"Forever. I inherited him. O'Toole was my father's under-groom as a lad, as I remember, but a nurse to me from the time I was in leading strings."

"You seem to be on terms of intimacy with him."

He gave the matter some thought. "Very true. It comes, I suppose, from our long association, that and my brother and I being left very much to our own devices when we were children. Our parents never seemed to have time for us. When one's father was so frequently absent or unavailable, it was natural to find a father figure to replace him. O'Toole was always there, though the poor man could have seen us far enough on occasion."

He pushed open the solid, carved door which gave on to the Great Hall, and he stood aside to permit Deirdre to enter. "My father was never there for me either," she said, and suddenly turned into him with a little sob catching in her throat.

His arms went round her, and he held her in a loose, comforting clasp till the bout of weeping subsided. "Deirdre," he murmured. "Oh Dee, I'll try to make it up to you." He was shaking with emotion. He turned her face up and gently brushed the tears from her eyes. He could not have felt closer to her if he had entered her and was filling her with his own hungry body. "Deirdre," he said again, and when her mouth opened to gulp in air, he ran the tip of his tongue over the soft swell of her parted lips. Her mouth opened wider to permit his entry, and on a sudden surge of passion, he plunged his tongue into the moistly hot recess in an intimacy that had her melt into him on a mewling whimper.

Inevitably, his body took fire. He crushed her closer, beyond caring for the curious stares of the odd footman and housemaid who passed through the Great Hall. At length, he pulled himself together, caught her wrist in an unrelenting grip, and half dragged her behind him up the long staircase to their bedchamber.

When the door was shut with a resounding slam, there was many a jest and knowing wink between maid and manservant, and Deirdre's devoted lackeys went about their business with a lighter step and a smile on their faces. Love was in the air, and so Martha's old ma said to Beecham as he presided over the servants' hall at luncheon, it warmed the cockles of the servants' hearts to see that the young master had lost the blighting look which he had habitually worn since the accident to his brother.

That cynic, however, merely remarked that as far as he was concerned, the top-lofty Earl had finally met his comeuppance and no bad thing either.

It was a slightly shamefaced Deirdre who descended the stairs an hour or so later. Rathbourne had taken himself off to attend to estate business with Guy Landron, and she had belatedly realized that her regular interview with Beecham to discuss the day's disposal of servants' duties had come and

405

gone. Since everyone seemed to be managing without her direction, she happily thought to steal a few minutes' solitary reflection in her secret retreat above the hayloft.

As she was crossing the courtyard, or bailey, as the servants referred to it, she caught a glimpse of Caro making her way through the gatehouse to the bridge over the dry moat. Deirdre quickened her step to catch her up, but when some minutes later she came out of the dark entrance, there was no sign of her sister-in-law. On her right were the stables; on her left, hidden by a thick screen of trees, was the Little Chapel and graveyard where all the Cavanaughs were finally laid to rest. Since the chapel had burned down the previous year during a ferocious late summer thunderstorm, and it was only an empty shell of a building, it did not seem likely that Lady Caro would have any business there. Deirdre made for the stables.

Her search of the stables and its environs proved fruitless and twenty minutes later saw Deirdre retracing her steps to follow the well-worn path that led to the Little Chapel. There was nothing of a particular nature she wished to impart to Caro, nothing that could not wait for another place and hour, but a feeling of disquietude which she could not shake had roused an inexplicable anxiety in her heart.

As she rounded the east wall of the building, she heard masculine voices raised in anger. From the corner of her eye she saw Guy Landron with the reins of two restive horses in his hand. His free arm was clamped securely around a weeping, struggling Lady Caro. But it was on the two men who were shouting at each other that Deirdre's eyes became riveted.

"By God, St. Jean, this passes all bounds," she heard Rathbourne say in a rigidly controlled tone.

Armand's head went back, and he said furiously, "Think what you like. I have nothing to say to you. But if you lay a hand on Caro, I swear I'll kill you."

Deirdre watched in horror as the riding crop in Rathbourne's hand rose and descended with full force against Armand's shoulder. She was sure Armand would make some

406

move to defend himself, but he stood like a statue, grim-faced and white-lipped, his knees slightly buckling. Rathbourne raised the crop again, and without thinking, Deirdre flew at him. She grabbed for his hand and in the next instant she was sent reeling backward as Rathbourne shook her off with a savage, involuntary movement, and the crop caught her a stinging blow across the cheek. She stumbled, and Armand caught her in his arms.

"Deirdre," she heard Rathbourne say in a stricken voice, and his hand went out to her. She flinched from him, and he drew back as if stung.

A slow flush suffused his face. He felt betrayed, like some blissfully ignorant husband who suddenly discovers that his wife has cuckolded him. He would not allow that the provocation was great. She had rushed to Armand's defense, as she always did, without making the least push to discover the facts of the case. She was his wife, he worshipped her, but the galling truth was that he would never be first in her loyalties or affections. That place was reserved for St. Jean.

A wave of bitter anger rose in his gorge as he eyed the pair who stood so defiantly before him. Deirdre was half turned into Armand's arms, as if she was seeking protection from the wrath of a violent husband. After the intimacy they had shared, and so recently, that little gesture cut him more than anything.

He fixed her with a look of quiet menace. "Get away from him," he said curtly, "or by God you'll take the thrashing he deserves."

"For God's sake, Gareth!" exclaimed Guy Landron, and the girl in his arms renewed her attempts to free herself.

"It's all my fault," Lady Caro sobbed. "I followed Armand here. He warned me to keep my distance. Armand, for pity's sake tell him."

Armand waved her to silence. "Do as you wish with me," he gritted out, "but leave Deirdre out of this. I would have thought that even a man of your violent nature would give some thought to his wife's condition."

"Armand, no," Deirdre interrupted, "he didn't mean anything by it. It was just temper—"

"For God's sake will you get away from him?" roared Rathbourne, and made as if to snatch his wife out of the other man's arms.

Armand thrust Deirdre behind him and stood glaring into the stormy eyes of the Earl. "Thrash me and have done with it," he said cuttingly, "but leave my sister alone."

"Armand, tell him I'm to blame," cried Lady Caro brokenly. "Oh why didn't I listen to you?"

"Don't say another word, Caro. We shall be married once you have come of age, as I promised, and there is nothing he can do to prevent it."

"Over my dead body," said Rathbourne venomously. "D'you think I'd let my sister marry a penniless ne'er-do-well? You'll never get your thriftless paws on a penny of her fortune as long as I live!"

Deirdre had no intention of allowing the two people she loved best in the world to come to cuffs with each other. She stepped swiftly between them and laid a restraining hand on the Earl's chest. "No," she pleaded. Neither man paid her the least attention.

Armand's lip curled. "Keep Caro's fortune with my goodwill. If rumor is anything to go by, you'll need it to keep all your bits of muslin in handkerchiefs. La Divine Dewinters's sojourn in Paris this last month cost you a pretty penny or two, or so I've been told."

Deirdre's eyes opened wide and she looked a question at Rathbourne. "Mrs. Dewinters was in Paris?" she asked softly. There was an appeal in her eyes, but Rathbourne ruthlessly crushed the impulse to respond to it.

Armand looked stricken. "Dee, oh Dee! I am sorry. I never meant for you to know."

Her expression hardened, and her glittering eyes swept the Earl's stiff figure in slightly contemptuous dismissal. "No! Nor did Rathbourne, I shouldn't wonder," she drawled.

The silence stretched taut, and Rathbourne and Deirdre held each other in a coldly calculating gaze. The Earl's eyes shifted to Armand and narrowed.

"You seem remarkably well informed of my movements, St. Jean," he said with a calm that deceived no one. He ignored his wife but was aware of her slight movement as she turned away from him and into Armand's arms. "I'd like to know who it was who gave you that piece of misinformation."

Armand ignored the query, but addressed himself to Caro. "I'll get word to you somehow. Remember, he can't force you to marry anyone. Wait for me. Everything will work out."

"And how to you propose to support a wife?" Rathbourne jeered.

"He can have Marcliff," interposed Deirdre quickly, voicing a thought which had taken hold in her mind for some weeks past. "It's a good living, Armand," she added when she saw her brother shake his head.

"It's not that, Dee. It's simply that—"

"It's simply that Marcliff belongs to me," finished Rathbourne silkily.

Deirdre looked at him as if he had just crawled out from under a stone. "It belongs to me," she stated unequivocally.

"That was before our marriage. When you married me, everything you owned became mine, even the clothes on your back. You weren't very wise, Dee. You should have insisted on settlements and so on before our marriage. You have nothing. You are in fact a pauper, a suppliant dependent on my good graces." He added very softly, "It were wiser for you if you remembered that fact, and learned to be more conciliatory."

Guy Landron, who had witnessed the scene with growing impatience, suddenly burst out, "Gareth! Why are you doing this? You know that's not—"

"Quiet!" thundered the Earl. "When I want your opinion, Landron, I shall ask for it. I don't need anyone telling me how to manage my wife."

"Let us go, Rathbourne," said Deirdre in a voice that was devoid of feeling, no mean achievement considering that she was reeling from a rush of emotions she had yet to examine and identify. "Marcliff means nothing to you. You don't need it."

He moved to take the reins of his mount from Landron's hand. "Get her under lock and key," he said curtly, indicating Caro with a slight movement of his head. He turned back to brother and sister.

"Oh no!" he said, addressing Deirdre in a voice as soft as velvet. "You are carrying a burden which is significant for the House of Cavanaugh, or had you forgotten? Once you are relieved of it, then we shall see. You stay. As for St. Jean, he will be out of here just as soon as I decide what to do with him. Meanwhile, O'Toole can take him in hand. He can move his things into the stable quarters and eat with the grooms. But let me catch him once more with my sister, and I'll thrash him to within an inch of his life."

He swung into the saddle and wheeled his horse to face her. "Don't think to coddle him or protect him from my authority. And Dee, if you're not inside the walls of Belmont in five minutes, you won't like the consequences."

As he disappeared from view behind the trees, the starch seemed to go out of Deirdre and she collapsed against Armand. She was past tears and recriminations. She rested her head against his shoulder and felt unexpectedly comforted. Never once in her memory had Armand been the one to offer solace. Her head lifted, and she looked at him curiously. His eyes were shadowed with concern.

"He found you with Caro," she stated.

"And thought the worst," he added, unable to keep the bitterness from his voice.

"Was he wrong?"

"He was wrong," Armand answered forcefully. "But he never believes any good of me."

"You sound disappointed."

Armand lifted his shoulder and gazed off into space. "I

410

suppose I had come round. He's not the man I was led to believe. In many ways I admire him. I thought he was warming to me. If only Caro were not so hot at hand, things might have been different."

"She's a headstrong girl."

"I'll tame her."

He was so young, yet so sure of himself. But Rathbourne would never permit it. In the past, she had always contrived, by one means or another, to put things right for Armand. Suddenly, she felt helpless, without the resources to take care of her own life let alone manage the affairs of another. She moved restlessly away from him, and went to sit on the dry stone wall which enclosed the graveyard. He followed at a leisurely pace.

"What's to be done?" she asked, in a small, forlorn voice. With Marcliff gone, there was no place they could call home. She went on a little desperately, "I must have time to think."

"No, Dee. I've already decided what's to be done. There are one or two avenues open to me when I reach my majority next month. I can always take up Uncle Thomas on his offer to find me a post in the diplomatic corps. And Uxbridge once said something about a military career. I rather enjoyed being a Hussar."

"That takes money. You heard Rathbourne. We're paupers."

"I could earn enough in one night at faro to buy my commission. Don't look like that, Dee. Really, I have no interest in gaming now."

She looked at him for a long moment, as if she was seeing him with new eyes, and her spirits lifted a little. "Aunt Rosemary always said it would take something catastrophic to bring you to your senses. She was right."

He laughed. "I suppose that's one way of describing Caro. She's certainly turned my life upside down. I can't say as I am sorry though. Quite the reverse."

A thought came to Deirdre. "Mrs. Dewinters," she blurted

411

out, "how did you come to hear that she was in Paris?"

"Tony wrote to me. I'm truly sorry, Dee. I'd call Rathbourne out, but he would never accept my challenge." He kicked a loose pebble viciously with the toe of his boot.

"Don't even think of it!"

"No, seriously, I wouldn't like to put paid to the life of Caro's brother, whatever the provocation. But I could, oh yes I could. I'll send for you once I'm settled."

"No. It's too late for that. He'd never let me go. You heard him."

"But Dee . . ."

"No!" she said flatly. "You have your own life to lead. You've told me that often enough. I can't help you now. So make something of yourself and make me proud of you."

"I intend to. Keep an eye on Caro for me. This will be hard on her."

She looked at him consideringly. "Armand, is this going to last? I mean, you've been in love so many times before."

"Oh no. I've never been in love before," he said simply. "I only thought I was. Trust me, Dee. This will last." His tone was quietly confident.

She almost smiled, but the effort wrinkled the raw cut of Rathbourne's crop across her cheek and she put up her hand gingerly. The violence to her own person was easily forgotten. He had never meant to hurt her, of that she was certain. But his vicious attack on her brother was another matter. If she had not put a stop to it, there was no saying how far his vindictiveness might not have taken him. And he had not disputed Armand's allegations that Mrs. Dewinters had been with him in Paris. And then there was Marcliff. Her mind could not take everything in. How was it possible for the intimacy they had shared only hours before to suddenly be shattered, like some fragile glass ball that a willful child had carelessly tossed from the castle ramparts? A sound caught her ear and she turned.

Her eyes were drawn to a poste chaise and four which came

412

bowling along the drive. It slowed to take the incline toward the castle walls but it was soon lost to sight in the trees.

"Visitors," observed Armand. "What timing! We'd better not dally. Rathbourne's temper is on a short leash. For myself, I don't give a rap. But if he cuts up at you again, I'll do something no doubt I shall regret."

When they entered the Great Hall, they heard Rathbourne's sardonic laughter. He caught sight of Deirdre and strolled toward her. His eyes held hers with a tawny intensity that belied his easy assurance.

"We have guests, my dear," he drawled smoothly, and put a proprietary hand on her elbow, ignoring her slight resistance as he brought her forward. Deirdre recognized the tall figure of Tony Cavanaugh in conversation with a woman. The cloying scent of carnations tickled Deirdre's nose. She stiffened.

"Look whom Tony has brought for a visit," said Rathbourne somewhere between spite and mockery.

Deirdre's chin lifted a fraction and she held out her hand. "Mrs. Dewinters, hot foot from Paris! We *are* honored. Welcome to my husband's home." She managed a creditable smile.

Mrs. Dewinters's eyes swept up and met Deirdre's. They traveled to Rathbourne. "Paris?" she asked innocently.

"Deirdre knows," said Rathbourne with a malicious smile, and turned aside to give directions to two footmen who had been called to dispose of the baggage which the porter had deposited in the hall.

Conversation became general though a trifle awkward, and Deirdre soon took her leave with the excuse that one of the stable cats had inadvertently scratched her and she must attend to the wound before blood poisoning had a chance to set in. She took Armand's arm and swept from the hall as if she hadn't a care in the world. Tony soon wandered off and Rathbourne turned on Mrs. Dewinters.

"To what do I owe the honor?" he asked coldly.

She stripped the gloves from her fingers, patted him

commiseratingly on the cheek, and said mildly, "There, there, Rathbourne. I've ruffled your feathers. But it really was imperative that I speak to you. Shall we repair to your study, or somewhere private? I bring you a message from our lord and master."

"Grant sent you?"

"The same."

Without a word, he led the way out of the Great Hall and along the west wing till they came to an open door. Mrs. Dewinters entered ahead of him and looked around the large room with interested eyes. The green painted paneling on the walls with its intricately carved molding picked out in gilt was a perfect background for the matching coffered ceiling. On the floor was a crimson Aubusson with a border in green and gold, and crimson damask curtains and chairs upholstered in the same design were placed against the walls.

"Impressive," she said softly, and plumped herself down on a newly upholstered chair. "This room belongs more properly in a palace."

Rathbourne settled himself behind a massive, leather-topped desk. "You wouldn't have thought so a month or so ago, before Deirdre took charge. What that girl has done is beyond belief."

"Oh, I believe it. You forget, I was with her at the Hotel d'Angleterre when it was turned into a hospital. It was she who organized the whole thing and arranged the watches so that someone would be on duty to look out for our patients all through the night. Do I detect a note of pride in your voice?"

"And if you do?"

"I could have sworn that you were at daggers drawn only a moment ago. D'you know, I had the strangest feeling it had something to with my being in Paris when I was supposed to be in London. Was I wrong?"

"What message do you bring from Grant?" he asked, pointedly ignoring the question. He poured himself a shot of brandy from a decanter on his desk.

She took the hint and said without preamble, and in a matter-of-fact tone, "I'm here to warn you. Grant came across some documents in Paris after you left. It seems that the person who betrayed your identity to the French when you were in Brussels passed the information along through a French network in London."

"Interesting. Go on," he said, and absently sipped his drink as if her words were of little import.

It was impossible to tell from his shuttered expression what he was thinking. Grant had warned her that Rathbourne would minimize any threat to his person, though she had known that already. She sighed inaudibly and tried again. "Gareth, you must take this seriously. The informant was English, and a considerable sum of money changed hands. You must know what that suggests."

"Certainly. I was not betrayed for a cause but for profit by someone who was either in my confidence or close enough to divine the truth about me. I still don't see why you had to create difficulties for both of us by coming out here to tell me in person."

She flushed a little at that, but said evenly, "It wasn't my idea. It was Grant's. He thought my word might carry some weight with you. I told him not to rely too much upon it, but as you see, he wouldn't listen."

At the faint reprimand in her words, the color under his skin heightened. "Yes, well, Grant doesn't know as much as he thinks he does about my private life."

"You mean, he didn't know that you used me in Brussels to make Deirdre jealous? Oh you needn't scowl at me like that, Rathbourne. I knew what you were up to, whatever you might pretend to the contrary. It suited me to acquire an aura of respectability, otherwise I would have sent you to the roustabouts."

Under Rathbourne's watchful gaze, she painstakingly pleated and unpleated a fold of her peacock blue silk skirt. Her eyes lifted and looked frankly into his. "Gareth, I want the rumors of our pretended liaison scotched before they have a chance to circulate in London."

"It's a bit late for that now," he answered impatiently. "And your coming here like this will only aggravate matters."

"Perhaps I'm putting this badly. Let me explain. I have taken steps to exonerate your good name and mine. You may expect to see an article in *The Times* in the very near future applauding our work as agents in His Majesty's Service. Our liaison will be seen for what it was—a cover for our activities."

"The devil I will!"

"The devil has nothing to do with it. Grant himself is breaking the story to the press."

"With what object?"

"I thought I told you. I want to be respectable."

He gave her a shrewd look from under slanted dark brows. "Would this craving for respectability on your part have anything to do with Roderick Ogilvie?"

She was aware of a slight easing of tension across his shoulders. That one involuntary gesture spoke volumes. It told her he was relieved that she had transferred her interest to another. She stifled a last pang of regret and forced a smile.

"It has everything to do with Roddy. I hope we may be married by the end of the month."

"Hope?" One questioning brow shot up.

"He hasn't asked me yet. But I think he will."

"May I wish you happy? Deirdre will be pleased," and, he thought privately, his wife's pleasure could not exceed his own by half at this welcome intelligence.

"Will she?"

"What does that mean?"

"Oh nothing much. Just that some women hate to lose an old beau. Roddy paid Deirdre an excessive amount of attention at one time."

"So I noticed," responded the Earl dryly, and took a long swallow of the drink in his hand.

She thought it wise to ignore this faint jibe. "To get back to the reason I came here in the first place," she said with decision.

"Yes? Is there more to tell?"

"Grant's nose! It's been troubling him of late."

"I'm listening."

"He thinks that someone still wants you dead—that there was more to your betrayal than the thirty pieces of silver that exchanged hands. Can you think of anyone who wants you dead, Gareth?"

"A score of people. I have never been one to cultivate a vulgar popularity."

"But no one in particular?"

He seemed to consider. "Several I could name right off the bat. What are you suggesting?"

"Nothing at all. Grant merely wants to put you on your guard. If I've done that much, I've done my duty. Oh yes, there was one other thing. Have you had any brushes with death in the last year or so when you were on English soil?"

"As a matter of fact, I have. But those were accidents."

"Were they? Are you sure?"

"Even if they weren't, there were plenty of spies in England who could have put a period to my existence, and very easily too."

"Possibly, but Grant says that the French only discovered your identity when you were in Brussels. You were safe from their agents before then. Think about it, Gareth. Who hates you enough to want you dead?"

Rathbourne did think about it. Grant's intuition, he knew from experience, was not to be lightly sloughed off. It had saved his bacon and that of his agents in the field on numerous occasions. A new and sinister significance was suddenly revealed in incidents which he had, in his innocence, formerly regarded as merely annoying misadventures. And if there was a perpetrator behind these acts, he deduced that it must be someone whose enmity he had incurred within the last year. Only one name came readily to mind.

Dinner that evening was an awkward affair, though Rathbourne gave every evidence of having recovered his spirits. Only one eye he studiously avoided, and that was Guy Landron's. Rathbourne was still smarting from the altercation which had taken place before dinner in his study. Damn if he would put up with the impertinence of others telling him how to manage his affairs! And how in Hades did Deirdre contrive to win the loyalty of others so effortlessly—his mother, his sister, his steward, his servants. It was uncanny! Only O'Toole remained loyal to his master. What he wouldn't give, though, to be first in her loyalties! He watched covertly as she played his hostess with consummate skill, and his eye softened.

His one inept attempt to reestablish himself in her good graces, however, was met with reproachful eyes and a cold shoulder. Thereafter it was Mrs. Dewinters, a little surprised, but a good deal gratified nevertheless, who came under the full force of his considerable charm. His attitude, thought Deirdre darkly, was like that of a felon who has decided he might as well be hanged for a sheep as a lamb. In her mind's eye, she began to construct the scaffold from which she would gladly see him dangle.

The Dowager, characteristically of late taking her cue from her daughter-in-law, retreated behind a wall of glacial politeness, and spoke to her son only when directly addressed. She wondered at Caro's and Armand's absence from the table, but could not bring herself to voice the question, so incensed was she to see a son of hers blatantly neglect a sweet innocent like Deirdre for a woman of dubious reputation. It was only from a wish to please Deirdre, who hated ill-bred displays of the family's dirty linen, especially in public, that the Dowager resolutely put her tongue between her teeth and bit down on it.

As if sensing the unasked question on everyone's mind, Rathbourne easily explained away the absence of the two youngest members of the household. If anyone doubted his glib explanation, no one ventured to contradict him to his face.

"Is Armand in the suds again?" Cavanaugh asked Deirdre in

418

an amused undertone. They had removed to the tapestry room to linger over tea and a tray of Mrs. Petrie's mouth-watering sweets. Rathbourne was fully occupied in reminiscing with Mrs. Dewinters about mutual acquaintances in Paris. Their low laughter was exclusive and exuded a familiarity of long standing. Deirdre's jaundiced eye took in the actress's long-sleeved creation in scarlet silk which suited her dark, dramatic beauty to perfection.

She became aware of Tony's interested gaze. "Need you ask?" she replied, and she refilled his empty cup from the gleaming silver teapot on the low polished rosewood table at her elbow.

"Don't look so serious. It's nothing new, after all."

Deirdre flicked a wrathful glance at her husband. "This is different, Tony. There can never be a reconciliation after today."

His expression grew grave. "Is Armand confined to his room?" he asked softly.

"No. To the stables. He'll be gone in a day or two. Tony, why is Mrs. Dewinters here?"

"I didn't invite her," he answered quickly. "And nothing would have induced me to bring her if I had thought for one moment that her affair with Rathbourne wasn't over."

"He denies that there is anything between them."

"Then believe him."

"You don't, so why should I?"

There was no chance for further conversation, for Rathbourne was on his feet and peremptorily demanding that all the gentlemen repair to the billiards room for a game of billiards before retiring. The Dowager rose also, stifled a yawn, and made her excuses, saying that she had been ready for bed for an age.

The door closed, leaving Mrs. Dewinters and Deirdre the only occupants of the room.

"How was your stay in Paris?" Deirdre intoned politely, wondering how she could ever have thought to make a friend of the beautiful creature who sat so at ease and so totally unconcerned for the havoc she had wrecked in her life.

Mrs. Dewinters's expression softened. "Paris," she said, "is the city for lovers. I was fortunate to have as my guide a man who had spent some time there and knew the city intimately."

Deirdre recalled Rathbourne's malicious jibe that he had learned the art of lovemaking in the brothels of Paris, and her smile became fixed. "Your decision to remove to Paris was very sudden, was it not?" she asked with a creditable attempt at civility.

"Not really. I was hoping he would send for me, and he did."

"And did he induce you to come to Belmont also?"

Mrs. Dewinters looked at Deirdre oddly. "No, he tried to prevent it. But I felt impelled to disregard his wishes in this matter." She set her cup and saucer aside and said with a puzzled frown, "Gareth has told you about us, has he not?"

This was too much for Deirdre. Her smile faded and she said scathingly, "My dear, it seems that the whole world knew before I did."

"But this is ridiculous. You can't be jealous. I know that he paid you some attention when you first arrived in Brussels, but you must have seen how it was between us."

This last brought Deirdre to her feet. "Certainly I saw how it was. You are welcome to him. I think you deserve each other. Do help yourself to more tea, and it goes without saying, to anything else which has taken your fancy. What a stupid thing to say—you already have." She sailed with regal dignity past the open-mouthed actress, and made for the door. On the threshold, she turned back and said over her shoulder, "If you should chance to see my husband before I do, which I make no doubt you will, you may tell him I've gone out for a breath of fresh air. The stench of carnations in this room is practically suffocating! And furthermore," she added pettishly, her eyes sweeping the diminutive actress from head to toe, "long sleeves may be all the crack on the continent, but in England, that fashion fell flat on its face. So, you see, Serena doesn't know everything." And Deirdre swept out of the room in a rustle of skirts.

Mrs. Dewinters looked after her hostess for a long bewildered moment, then comprehension gradually dawned. "Rathbourne," she warned the empty room in withering accents. "Damn you, Rathbourne! You've done it again!"

Chapter Twenty-Six

Though the night was balmy, and there was not a cloud in the sky to shade the glitter of the full moon as it frosted the castle walls with its silvery reflection, Deirdre did not linger in her solidary walk around the perimeter of the bailey. Rathbourne, who was used to accompanying her every evening before they turned in, did not put in an appearance, and Deirdre told herself firmly that it was no less than she expected, and she almost convinced herself that she wasn't disappointed in the least at his desertion. In other circumstances, her fertile imagination would have peopled the courtyard with knights on their magnificent destriers preparing to ride off to the Crusades, with fair ladies on the ramparts throwing down their favors to their chosen champions. But her thoughts on this night were far from pleasant and soon turned from Rathbourne and his immutable dislike of Armand to the scene in the tapestry room with Mrs. Dewinters. That her husband had transferred his affections to the actress never once entered Deirdre's head, but it made her blood boil to think how easily he had reverted to form in Paris when she was not present to act as a restraint on his baser nature.

When she finally retired to her bedchamber, there was no comfort to be found there either. She sent Martha away and, without bothering to undress, lay down on the bed, trying to bring her fragmented thoughts into some semblance of order. But she was in no mood to be rational. She was buffeted by a whirlwind of emotions which left her feeling like a rag doll that had had the stuffing knocked out of it. "If this is love," she thought miserably, "I wish it had never been invented," and she began to imagine a world that had never been infected by that bane of humanity, deciding that it must be a very happy place indeed.

She must have dozed, because she came to herself with a start. For a long moment she thought that she was back in her room at the Hotel d'Angleterre and that she had been awakened by the sound of the guns in the distance. Something wasn't right. She got swiftly to her feet and opened the bedroom door. Sounds of muffled voices reached her ears. She quickened her pace along the corridor till she came to the gallery which overlooked the Great Hall. Her hand rested lightly on the balustrade, and she looked down. Servants were hurrying about, but her eyes were drawn to a settee before the huge stone fireplace. O'Toole was bending over a half-swooning Rathbourne, whose face was as white as a sheet. She watched as Rathbourne's dark jacket was eased over his shoulders. One arm of his white linen shirt was soaked crimson with blood.

Deirdre gave a little cry, then went racing down the stairs at breakneck speed and flung herself across the hall till she was on her knees before her husband. O'Toole moved back a pace, and Deirdre's nimble fingers began to undo the small pearl buttons of Rathbourne's shirt.

"What happened?" she asked O'Toole as she worked to remove the bloodied garment.

Rathbourne struggled to a sitting position. "It's a scratch, nothing more," he said weakly, and pushed her hand away. "Why weren't you in the bailey? I waited for you to join me for our walk. You didn't appear."

Deirdre heard the petulance in his voice, and a wave of relief washed over her. She managed a weak smile. An injured man who could take his wife to task over some paltry transgression could not, in her opinion, be at death's door. She splayed both hands over his chest and pushed him back into the cushions. "O'Toole, get brandy," she said in a no-nonsense voice. "Oh, Beecham, thank you." She took a bowl of hot water and clean towels from the butler's hands and set them on the floor at her knees. As she worked on Rathbourne's arm, she gave a spate of orders to waiting servants and they moved quickly to do her bidding. Rathbourne watched her through half-lidded eyes.

"This wound was caused by a gunshot," said Deirdre at last, and her fingers stilled. "The ball went clean through your arm. You're very fortunate. What happened?"

The doors to the Great Hall were flung open and Tony Cavanaugh, with Guy Landron close behind, came in at a run.

"What the devil is going on?" asked Guy Landron tersely. "I heard a shot. My God, Gareth, who did this to you?"

Deirdre took the glass of brandy which O'Toole had procured and pressed it to Rathbourne's lips. Her stern manner persuaded him that it would be futile to argue. He drank it back in a few swallows. O'Toole took the empty glass, and Deirdre immediately began to dress her husband's wound.

Tony was impatient for answers. "I was on the ramparts, having a quiet smoke before turning in, when I heard the shot. What the devil happened?"

"You didn't by any chance see who did it, did you?" asked Rathbourne, his eyes never wavering from his wife's tense face.

"No! All I saw as I ran down the stairs was Armand running toward the gatehouse. I say, do you think he might be after the blighter who did this to you?"

"Oh no, I don't think so for a minute." Rathbourne's eyes locked on Deirdre's and her hand bandaging his arm shook.

"Tony," she interposed quietly, "are you sure it was Armand you saw? Did you get a clear view of him?"

He looked curiously at Deirdre's intent expression. "Well,

no! It was so dark. I might easily have been mistaken," he said a little too quickly, and Rathbourne's soft expletive silenced him.

Deirdre shook her head, but Rathbourne went on with devastating calm, "You heard him threaten me earlier."

"I heard you both threaten each other!" she cried defensively. It was as if they were the only two people in the room. "Gareth, no," she said, her eyes pleading for understanding. "Armand is incapable of such an act."

He didn't argue the point, but struggled to his feet and eased into the fresh shirt O'Toole had brought for him. Deirdre sat back on her heels and watched miserably as he donned his dark coat.

"You should see a doctor," she said, but her words made no impression on him.

"Fetch St. Jean," he said to O'Toole curtly, and the groom, with an uneasy glance in the general direction of Deirdre, turned on his heel and swiftly left the hall.

It was a full half hour before he returned, and the intelligence he brought to his master appeared to damn Armand even more. The boy was nowhere to be found, and the pistol which O'Toole kept in the tackroom was gone also. Only Rathbourne could meet Deirdre's eyes.

"Are you satisfied now?" he asked with an edge of impatience in his voice.

"No! But I see that it satisfies you." She rose to her feet and stood to her full height, a suggestion of defiance in her posture, giving him back look for look. "What do you intend to do?"

Rathbourne did not trouble to answer her. He turned to O'Toole. "Rouse the stable hands and the gardeners. I want every available man ready in five minutes. We'll flush him out if we do this systematically. He won't get far."

Tony laid a restraining hand on his cousin's arm. "Perhaps I should stay with Deirdre," he suggested, his eyes clouding with worry. "She shouldn't be left alone at a time like this."

Deirdre flashed him a grateful glance.

426

"She won't be," Rathbourne turned to Beecham. "Get the Dowager. Tell her to stay with her ladyship." His gaze traveled to Landron and Lord Tony. "If you wouldn't mind, gentlemen, I'd like a word in private with my wife. I'll be with you directly."

He watched them go and turned back to Deirdre, his expression somber. "I want you to stay out of this, whatever happens." His voice was harsh, forceful but not angry.

Deirdre looked at him, her eyes wide with misery. "Nothing will ever convince me that my brother would attack you in this way. This was the act of a coward. Whatever else Armand is, he is not that."

Her words, she could see, were wasted on him in his ugly mood.

"If he is innocent, he has nothing to fear. That I do promise."

"And if he is guilty? Will you show compassion?"

The words lay between them like some sort of test. Again, he said nothing and Deirdre sank down on the sofa. Her demeanor was one of abject resignation, as if she had bowed to the inevitable.

Rathbourne was not sure if he trusted this new docility in his wife. But events were moving quickly and time was of the essence. He said impatiently, "Just trust me, for God's sake. Surely that's not too much to ask? Stay here, in the Hall, till I return. And that's an order!"

When she heard the Great Hall doors crash to at his back, her head came up, and her body tensed for action. She remained poised, ready for flight for a moment longer, then she was off like a shot up the great stairs to her room.

The pistol was kept for safekeeping in the bottom of a trunk in the dressing room she shared with Rathbourne. It was a keepsake of Waterloo—a grim reminder of that long night's vigil when she had stood guard over her brother. She had never thought she might ever have need of it again. Against the flat of her hand, its weight was very reassuring. She checked to see if

427

it was loaded. For a long reflective moment she stared at the weapon in her hand, then she moved with decision, her steps taking her to the stairs and the great doors that led to the courtyard.

The castle walls were ablaze with the light from scores of pitch torches which servants were hastening to secure in their brackets. Their flickering light, abetted by the full moon and clear sky, made some impression on what in normal circumstances would have been a forbidding darkness. From the entrance steps of the Great Hall, Deirdre could see men gathering at the gatehouse, and Rathbourne's commanding voice rang out as he issued orders to his subordinates. Fearful that she might be seen, and having no wish to retreat to the Great Hall where it was very possible that Beecham had returned with the Dowager, she moved stealthily, keeping to the castle walls and finally reaching her destination—a flight of steep stone steps which would take her up to the ramparts of the North Tower. When she came out on the castle walls, she paused, shoulders hunched over, laboring to regain her breath after the hard climb. After a moment or two, she leaned out over the stone parapet and looked down. The North Tower was to the right of the gatehouse and barbican and an excellent lookout in times past when Belmont had been under siege. The throng of men in the bailey was thinning as they moved purposefully out through the castle gate. Deirdre moved quickly to the other side of the ramparts. She watched them as they disappeared into the trees, some with lanterns in their hands, others like link boys brandishing pitch torches high above their heads. More lights were coming from the stables and she waited till the two parties of men converged.

Wearily, she sagged against the hard wall of the parapet and sank slowly to her haunches. From her high perch, she had an unobstructed view of the countryside for miles around. By following the path of the torches, it was her design to keep track of what was going on. If Armand was caught, she was sure he would be brought to either the castle or the stables and she

428

had no intention of allowing her husband or anyone else for that matter to exclude her from what she knew would be a stormy interview. Her mind refused to take her beyond that point.

She had meant every word she had said to Rathbourne. His assailant could not possibly have been Armand. The boy was a hot-tempered hellion; she had never denied it. But this attack on Rathbourne was the act of a coward, or perhaps, she thought hopefully, it had been an accident and the perpetrator was too ashamed to admit to it. Rathbourne was known to have a foul temper and a rough tongue, and the servants' respect for their master, so she had observed, was based more on fear than on affection. The more she thought about it, the more reasonable her explanation appeared to her.

She remembered, then, that Armand had been seen in the bailey at the time of the attack, and her confidence faltered. If the boy had seen something, why hadn't he come forward?

She leaned her head back on the parapet and closed her eyes, and her thoughts went spinning off in every direction trying to find some plausible explanation to exonerate Armand's odd behavior. Some memory teased her mind. She concentrated on it, and by degrees, it sharpened and came slowly into focus. It was the day after Waterloo, when she had confessed to Armand that she had suspected him of turning traitor. She remembered that he had humbled her by his outraged profession of innocence. His words came back to her.

"You actually thought that I could betray my family, my friends, my country, my name? And I thought you knew me!"

She breathed more easily, and something deep within her let go, as if a hand squeezing her heart had suddenly relaxed its hold. He was innocent! If she had ever doubted it, she knew it now. He was incapable of such a craven murder attempt, just as she had told Rathbourne! But how to convince her husband of that fact!

Her eyes opened slowly, and the hot tears were released to course down her cheeks. The stars overhead, the same stars which had watched over the destiny of succeeding generations of Cavanaughs for centuries, seemed remote and uncaring of her fate. She moved her head slightly, as if to avoid their cold, dispassionate stare, and her glance passed idly over the bulwark of the North Tower then came back with a start. A light was shining from one of the lookout embrasures. She was almost certain it had not been there a few moments before. Deirdre scrambled to her feet and quickly covered the few steps along the rampart walk that took her to the door of the disused guard room of the tower. She wrenched the door open and almost screamed her fright. Instinctively, she brought up the pistol in her hand. "Tony!" she exclaimed, and her voice throbbed with relief. Tony Cavanaugh looked to be almost as startled as she.

"Deirdre! What the devil . . . ?" He looked at the object in her hand and his eyes narrowed.

She followed his gaze and the pistol was quickly lowered.

"What are you doing with that?" he asked with a suggestion of suspicion in his voice. Behind him, on the floor, she could see a lantern and the flickering light in the darkness of the tower reassured her.

"I don't feel dressed without it," she responded with a flippancy she was far from feeling, and made as if to push past him.

His arms came and caught her shoulders. "Wait!" And then on a less urgent note, "Deirdre, Armand is here. He's all right, but I think he's foxed or some such thing. Don't be alarmed."

He stood aside and Deirdre saw the form huddled on the flagstones of the floor. Armand was half propped against the wall and his eyes were closed. At his elbow was an empty brandy bottle, and the stench of strong spirits assaulted Deirdre's nostrils.

Wordlessly, she moved to kneel beside him and she felt for his pulse. It was beating erratically, but it was strong.

"How did you find him?" she asked over her shoulder, and she smoothed Armand's tousled locks back from his forehead.

"I knew all along that he was here, but I had no wish to give Rathbourne wind of it—not when he was in a mood to do murder."

She looked a little surprised at this but merely responded, "You knew? But you said that you saw Armand making for the gatehouse."

"That was no lie. But he turned aside before reaching it. It's my guess that Armand saw who shot at Rathbourne, but knowing he himself would come under suspicion, ran for cover. I have merely put Rathbourne off the scent. The boy is within the walls of the fortress. Rathbourne is searching on the outside. Perhaps I should not have mentioned his name at all, but it never occurred to me that Rathbourne would jump to conclusions."

There was something in his logic that was not quite right, but Deirdre was too anxious about her brother's position to spend precious moments sifting through long explanations.

"But why would he come here and drink himself into a stupor? It doesn't make sense."

Cavanaugh shrugged. "Who knows? It's my surmise that he was in his cups before he came through the barbican tonight. We'll just have to contain our curiosity until the boy comes round. But what's to be done? Shall I call off the search and tell Rathbourne that Armand has been found?"

"No!" Deirdre's quick denial silenced him. She needed time to think, but her brain was sluggish, unable or unwilling to grapple with the onslaught of problems which pressed upon her. "No," she repeated more quietly. "Perhaps I am being overcautious, but I would feel happier if Armand were away from Belmont altogether."

He looked at her for a long considering moment, then nodded. "I was afraid it would come to this. Their quarrel must have been ferocious."

"It was," she acknowledged, but did not elaborate.

"Deirdre," he said reasonably, "try not to put too much credence on all the gossip you have heard about Gareth. It's

431

grossly exaggerated, you know."

"What is?"

"Oh, you know, the stories that he somehow engineered Andrew's death in that climbing accident; his implacable hatred of the French, or anyone who opposes him for that matter; his cruelty . . ."

"You've been listening to Armand," she interrupted with sudden insight, and wished that Tony had not chosen that moment to regale her with a litany of Rathbourne's iniquities.

"Oh no." He sounded surprised. "These stories about Rathbourne have been circulating for years now. I know he is a hard man, but I can't believe that he is . . . well, without conscience."

Deirdre did not believe it either, not in her heart of hearts. If it were only herself she had to consider, she could face him without a tremor. But she did not have the right to take a chance on her brother's safety.

"Can you saddle and fetch mounts for us without being seen?" She spoke with a new resolve. "I'd like to take Armand to our home in Henley."

"I can try. It shouldn't be too difficult."

"Good. Hide the horses well, then come up here and give me a hand with Armand. I'll never manage to get him down those steps on my own. D'you mind if I keep the lantern? I don't care to be left in total darkness."

"No, I don't mind at all."

He watched with interest as Deirdre brought up the barrel of the pistol and cradled it in the crook of one arm.

"D'you know how to use that thing?" he asked doubtfully.

She gave him a long level look. "Oh, yes, Tony," she answered. The frown left her brows and her voice firmed. "Never doubt it for a moment."

"You know, you're a remarkable girl," and his voice held bemusement as well as admiration. "If I'd found you before Rathbourne . . . who knows?" and he laughed deprecatingly, but his eyes were watchful.

"No, if Rathbourne hadn't found me, I would still be . . ." Her voice drifted away as if she had become suddenly distanced in time and space. "No," she said more forcefully, but she smiled to take the sting out of that one annihilating word.

"If you say so," he said gravely, and moved to the head of the stairs. "I'll be back as soon as I can."

She listened to the stealthy sounds of his footfalls as he descended the circular flight of inside stairs of the tower. The door creaked as he closed it behind him. Then there was silence.

She turned back to Armand and grasped him by the shoulders. "Wake up, you besotted fool!" she said impatiently. He groaned and tried to push her hands away. "Armand, wake up. You must pull yourself out of this drunken stupor."

She had to strain to catch his slurred words. "Caro? Must . . . see . . . Caro."

"Why must you?"

He struggled to answer her question, but his head lolled on her shoulder.

Nothing she did could rouse him again, and she wondered abstractly how they would manage to get him, in his intoxicated condition, out of the tower and into the saddle. If only Rathbourne had given her some clue about the fate that might await Armand if he believed him guilty, she would be tempted to remain where they were till her husband's anger had time to cool and Armand could come to his senses and explain the damning evidence against him. But his silence had been almost a threat, and she would be a fool not to take Rathbourne seriously. She settled down beside the inert form of her brother to await Tony's return.

The door at the bottom of the stairs opened, and Deirdre's head came up. She had not expected Tony to return for some time. Something must have gone wrong. She got cautiously to her feet and peered down the well of the staircase, but could see nothing in the dense gloom.

"Tony?" she queried softly.

There was no answer. The footsteps halted, then after a pause, began to climb again, but more rapidly. She steadied herself with one hand behind her against the wall, and raised the pistol. He rounded the corner and the light from the lantern clearly illumined the austere set of his features.

"Rathbourne," she said on a whisper, and stumbled back till the hem of her skirts brushed the prone figure of her brother.

Rathbourne took in everything at a glance. He observed Armand's huddled form at her feet, and his eyes, like molten gold, moved from the empty bottle then sliced to the weapon in Deirdre's hand.

"So, it's come to this!" and a travesty of a smile twisted his mouth. "What now, Deirdre?" Then on a softer, more intimidating note, "Do you intend to shoot me dead?"

He took a step toward her, and Deirdre leveled the pistol. Her chin lifted and her eyes met his unflinchingly.

"What do you intend to do with Armand?" she parried, and was surprised that her voice betrayed nothing of her inner trepidation.

"I don't have to answer to you for my actions in this instance. Perhaps you've forgotten that St. Jean shot at me earlier this evening? I shall tell you once, and only once, not to interfere in what is between your brother and me. Do I make myself clear? Now step aside." There was no softening, no offer of compromise in his stern tone.

Her arm straightened and she pointed the pistol at his heart. "Come one step closer, Rathbourne, and it'll be the last thing you do. Ever," she added for emphasis.

His eyes smoldered. "I believe you would pull the trigger."

"Believe it!"

He averted his head, and one hand came up to ravage his dark locks in a weary, bemused gesture. "Deirdre, oh Deirdre!" and in the next instant his foot lashed out and caught her a crushing blow on the wrist. She cried out and the pistol went spinning from her grasp. It came to rest against the door leading to the battlements.

Rathbourne strolled to the door and picked up the pistol. He weighed it in the palm of his hand. "So now we know where we stand," he said quietly, and laughed in a way that made Deirdre press back away from him.

"You don't mind if I dispose of this—what is it?—a momento of Waterloo? The weapon you used on the Prussian?" Her silence confirmed his words. "I thought as much," and he thrust open the door to the battlements. She watched as he threw the pistol from the threshold to arc over the rampart walls. Then he turned back, and at the little half smile on his lips, something inside Deirdre shriveled.

"What do you mean to do?" she asked tremulously, and stepped in front of Armand as if by shielding him from the Earl's murderous eyes, she could make him invisible. The gesture was not lost on Rathbourne. His eyes blazed.

"Why, what should I do, but what I should have done long since—sever every connection with you and your family. Oh don't look so worried, madam wife. I won't harm your precious brother. You wanted compassion? You have it! You wanted Marcliff? It's yours! I give it back to you, gladly. I hope you and St. Jean will be very happy there. It's what you always wanted, isn't it? He's the only man in your life that counts for anything, the only one who, right or wrong, you trust implicitly. Oh, don't shake your head at me in that innocent fashion. You proved once and for all, when you pointed that pistol at my heart, where your loyalty lies—not with me, that's for certain. What a fool I was to think that once, just once, you would put yourself completely into my hands. But it was not to be, and I, thank God, have come to my senses." He turned away as if the sight of her disgusted him, and threw one last barb over his shoulder. "It's time to cut my losses. See that you are packed and ready to leave for Marcliff first thing tomorrow. You can stay there till my child is born. After that . . . we'll see."

As shock and weariness began to take their toll on her, Deirdre's teeth began to chatter and she clamped her jaws tightly together. Her misery was too deep for tears. She had failed him, and she did not know how to put things right.

She tried to think of something to say in her defense, but the words would not come. The set of his shoulders, his air of remoteness, one fist clenching and unclenching as he leaned the press of his weight against the wall—everything warned her that he was in no frame of mind to listen.

She said miserably, "Gareth, I'm so sorry."

He remained unmoving, and she had to strain to hear his words. "So am I, Deirdre. So am I."

They neither of them heard the soft footfalls on the stairs until Tony Cavanaugh emerged from the stairwell. "Touching, very touching, and so disappointing!" he said conversationally.

A shaft of light was caught and reflected back from the object Cavanaugh held in his right hand, and Deirdre saw that it was a pistol.

"You can put that away," she said wearily. "Rathbourne never had any intention of harming Armand."

Cavanaugh smiled unpleasantly. "Oh, I never thought for a minute that he did." And he brought up the pistol in a threatening gesture.

Deirdre felt a shaft of purest apprehension, and the fine hairs on the nape of her neck stood on end. Her eyes darted to Rathbourne's, and she read the warning that flared in their depths.

Rathbourne pushed from the wall but his posture remained relaxed. "So, it was you. I thought as much."

"Did you?" asked Cavanaugh in a negligent tone, though the white of his knuckles around the butt of the pistol in his hand betrayed a control that was rigidly imposed. "I take leave to doubt that. If you had, you would have murdered me in some quiet spot before now without the least compunction."

"Not murder, Tony, execute. There is a difference, you know, though I suppose it wouldn't have mattered to you since the result would have been exactly the same. You were, and

436

still are, a traitor. I suggest that what I had in mind would have been preferable to a long, drawn-out trial and a public hanging." He willed his voice to tell the lie convincingly. "Even should you silence Deirdre and me, you won't get away with it. They know who you are." His voice sank and he said quietly, "The game is over. Give it up, Tony, and I'll be generous, I promise you."

Cavanaugh's well-bred mask of indifference slipped. He stared wild-eyed for a moment, then visibly struggled to get a grip on himself. "I don't think so." He shook his head as if to clear it. "No. If you had put two and two together, I would have been a dead man."

"And so you are. I spared you only because there was some doubt that St. Jean was your accomplice. I had to know the truth about him."

"And what have you discovered?"

"I knew he was innocent as soon as I saw that pistol in your hand. I'd recognize it anywhere. O'Toole keeps it in the tackroom."

A laugh was startled out of Tony. "Clever, oh very clever, Gareth. But just for argument's sake. Supposing St. Jean had been my accomplice, what fate would you have had in store for him then?"

"You know the answer to that question as well as I do."

"A convenient accident?"

The words hung on the air, and Deirdre's eyes fastened on the impassive form of her husband. Their eyes met. He made no answer, and after a moment turned away from her.

Tony's laugh had an ugly ring to it. "Since it makes no difference now, I don't mind admitting that the boy is a pawn, nothing more. D'you know, Rathbourne, you and I are both diabolical? I don't think there is much to choose between us. Deirdre, do you still prefer him?"

Deirdre felt as if her brain were frozen. With paralyzing slowness, she managed to stammer, "I don't understand this."

Rathbourne saw her distress, and made a move to lessen the

distance that separated them.

"Don't!" and the pistol in Cavanaugh's hand was nervously jerked up.

"Gareth, what's going on?" she pleaded.

"As you see, my dear, my cousin is finally showing his colors." He turned slightly to address Tony. "I didn't think you had it in you. Up till now, you have stayed very much in the background and let others do your dirty work. Oh wait, now I get it." One hand went to his head in a gesture of impatience. "When you lured me up here to find Armand, was Deirdre supposed to blow my brains out when I came up those stairs? She would have, you know, oh yes she would have if I hadn't disarmed her. Your scheme almost came off, if it's any consolation."

"What scheme?" asked Deirdre, her voice rising with the panic which was racing to every nerve end in her body. In the circular chamber, in the dim light from the lone lantern which had been set on the massive flagstones, the features of the two protagonists assumed a sinister and inhuman aspect. The scene was like a nightmare which she longed to waken from.

"Well, Tony, shall you tell her or shall I?" she heard her husband's voice drawl with its usual sangfroid.

"Oh you, by all means, Gareth. I'd be obliged if you would keep it brief. Though I think it will be a long time before your lackeys return."

The smile that twisted Cavanaugh's lips was chilling and a shiver of alarm pierced Deirdre's heart. It was as if she had been touched by the ghastly breath of some ancient shade which stalked the castle walls. Tony Cavanaugh was a stranger to her! There was a satanic mesmerizing light in his eyes. It came to her that he was in no hurry to bring things to a head, but was savoring every moment of the novelty of having Rathbourne compelled to do his will.

"Where shall we begin?" asked Rathbourne, and his eyes, heavy-lidded, looked steadily into the fever-bright eyes of his cousin. "Did it begin when we were children, Tony?"

"Indubitably," was the amused rejoinder.

"You hid it well."

"What other course was open to me? I lived on your family's charity. But I hated you even then. You thought yourself cock of the walk—and so you were. I was just the poor relation. It was Andrew's death that made me see how fragile your claim to the title and estates was."

"But you didn't act then. You should have, you know. I was more trusting when I was younger."

"True. But I myself was more of an idealist. When you went off to Spain, I thought the French would do the deed for me."

"How galling for you when I returned after five years without a scratch. Then, of course, you took a hand in things."

"Much good it did me. Really, Gareth, you're like the proverbial cat with nine lives. Footpads, French assassins, even fire left you untouched. Armand was my last hope."

"In some things I'm remarkably lucky, but by no means in all," replied the Earl in a deprecating tone.

"Your luck has just run out."

"Don't count on it."

Deirdre stirred and said, as if coming back from a distance, "Where does Armand come into all this? I don't understand. How does he come to be here in the tower?"

"Oh, that was easily accomplished," said Cavanaugh. "I lured him here with a note, forged of course, from cousin Caro. The poor boy is really smitten with her. Just a suggestion from me that Rathbourne had unleashed the full force of his anger against the girl, and Armand was beside himself."

"And the brandy?" asked Rathbourne quietly.

"Oh that was to while away the time. Drugged, of course. It will be hours before the poor boy comes to himself."

Relief flooded Deirdre. "Then Armand was never your accomplice," she cried.

"Not knowingly, of course. He was only a dupe. But oh Deirdre," Cavanaugh went on with a slight shake of his head, "you were a complication I never counted on. D'you know, my dear, every time I set the stage for something to happen between your brother and Rathbourne, there you were, pouring oil on troubled waters. It really was too bad in you. Forgive me, my dear, I had hoped that there might be a different ending to our story. But with Rathbourne gone, you wouldn't have turned to me. You confirmed that not half an hour ago."

Rathbourne made a slight movement, and the pistol was jerked up to cover him. "Easy," said Tony softly. "D'you know, I am rather enjoying this, old boy? For once in our long and unhappy association, I am the one who is calling the shots. How does it feel? Don't bother to answer. I can see from your face that you relish it as little as I did all those years."

Sudden comprehension blinded Deirdre. "You want Gareth dead and you intend Armand to take the blame for it! It was you who set them against each other!"

"Oh, I don't take all the credit. They both cooperated admirably. You were the only fly in the ointment, as I've already explained. Really, it would have been so much simpler if there had been a duel. Armand would have blown your brains out, Gareth. Do you know that? His marksmanship is faultless. Ah well, it was not to be. Luckily, I walked in on a scenario today that I would never have been able to contrive in a hundred years. D'you know, when I searched Armand out tonight, I could scarcely take in what he told me? Honestly, I couldn't have managed it better myself. You must see that I could not let this opportunity go to waste. It was sheer bad luck on my part that you eluded me in the courtyard. That bullet was meant for your heart. Still, things have worked out rather well. Armand is already the prime suspect."

Deirdre would have given anything to feel the weight of her loaded pistol in her hand. Worse than anything was the calm complacency of the man who was intent on snuffing out their lives as if they had been a couple of cockroaches. In that instant, fear was superseded by a wave of anger and she knew she could not allow it.

440

Her mind feverishly did a quick assessment of their situation. There was only one charge in the pistol. He would use it on Rathbourne, she was sure, and with him out of the way, she would be no match for Tony's superior strength. He would kill Rathbourne. Armand would be accused of the murder and very probably hang for it. Her own life was forfeit, as well as that of her unborn babe. Four lives would be sacrificed to the insane ambitions and greed of one madman. Perhaps two of those lives might be saved if she could draw his fire to herself. Her eyes traveled the chamber searching for some means of evening the odds. Her gaze came to rest on Rathbourne. As if he could read her mind, his eyes blazed. Deirdre felt as if he had reached out to scald her.

Tony's voice, soft as down, interrupted her thoughts. "Shall we take a walk on the ramparts? It's rather close in here. And Gareth, don't try anything, or Deirdre gets it first. Ah, I see you left the door open. Thank you. That is very convenient. Did you expect O'Toole to come dashing through it? I thought as much. Well, he won't. I took care of him when you entered the tower. When he comes round, he'll make an excellent witness against Armand. I like to leave everything tidy, as you see. After you, Gareth."

Rathbourne hesitated for only a moment. "I don't suppose that there is any point in asking you to let Deirdre go? It will be your word against hers, and everyone will think she is merely trying to shield St. Jean. Think about it, for God's sake, man. She can't hurt you."

"Good try, cousin, but it won't serve. It's possible that the child Deirdre is carrying is your heir. Then I would be in no better case than I am at present. Good God, when I heard from Armand that she was pregnant, you can imagine how I felt. And you know," he said to Deirdre in a tone that held a suggestion of disappointment, "I did give you a chance earlier, but you turned me down. I'm very fond of you—no, really."

Rathbourne looked as if he might argue the point, but when the gun was raised to Deirdre's head, he took a swift step that

441

took him onto the battlements.

Tony propelled Deirdre toward the open door. When she crossed the threshold, she stumbled and fell to one knee. She was ruthlessly yanked to her feet and in that moment she swung round and thrust desperately upward at the hand which held the pistol. A shot rang out, and Deirdre screamed. Before the smoke had cleared, Rathbourne had lunged for his cousin. The two men fell heavily against the pediment, and the spent pistol went rattling harmlessly along the rampart walk into the Stygian darkness.

Deirdre watched in heart-stopping terror as the indistinguishable forms swayed perilously close to the edge of the battlements and the long drop down to the bailey, each frantically searching for a weakness to exploit. Rathbourne's long fingers closed around his adversary's throat. Cavanaugh gagged, but before the Earl could tighten his murderous grip, his cousin's fist came up and lashed with unerring accuracy at the wound on Rathbourne's arm. Deirdre heard her husband's sharp intake of breath. His grip slackened and Tony pressed his advantage. He surged against Rathbourne in a desperate attempt to fling him backward through a gap in the ramparts. Rathbourne's fingers curled and clung tenaciously to the stone pediment, but it was evident to Deirdre that in his weakened condition, he could not hold on for long.

"Deirdre, save yourself! Get away from here—now!" he choked out between labored gasps of breath. The fingers of one hand were ruthlessly prised open and he slipped farther over the edge of the wall.

Deirdre picked up her skirts and went racing through the tower door. In a moment, she was back, and in her hand she held the lantern. Blinding fear for Rathbourne's safety made her heedless of all danger. She threw herself on the back of the man she had so unwisely trusted, and brought the lantern down with every ounce of her strength. The glass shattered and a stream of hot oil drenched both Deirdre and Cavanaugh.

In that instant, he twisted sharply and swung at her with a

vicious blow of his fist, sending her hurtling along the opposite wall of the ramparts. She tried to raise herself, then sank to her knees in a haze of pain.

Cavanaugh recognized his jeopardy, but it was too late. There was a flash and a wall of flame engulfed him from head to toe, even as his frenzied fingers worked to wrench off his oil-soaked garments. In a matter of seconds, he blazed like one of the pitch torches which lit up the bailey far below. Deirdre saw Rathbourne drag himself to safety, and her shoulders heaved with the wracking sobs of mingled pain and relief.

A bloodcurdling scream rent the air, and the writhing man, in a maddened panic, flung himself along the battlements to the far flight of stairs which led to the courtyard. Voices below raised an alarm, and men pointed at the horrendous spectacle silhouetted against the dark skyline. The flaming figure became more frenzied and paused irresolutely at the head of the stone stairs, then began a reckless descent, but in his haste, he stumbled. Deirdre watched, horrified as he poised for a split second in midair, then went hurtling into space, his demented scream of protest suddenly cut off far below as he hit the ground. She turned her head into the parapet and wept.

Chapter Twenty-Seven

The door to Rathbourne's study was thrown open with an ear-splitting clatter, and the Earl raised his besotted head from his desk and groaned his displeasure. One eye opened wearily as he heard the muffled treads on the rug as they crossed the room to the window, and in the next instant the heavy damask curtains were thrown wide to allow a blinding glare to penetrate to his bleary gaze.

"Beecham! What the devil do you think you're about? Close those curtains at once, d'you hear?" Then on a more plaintive note, "Can't a man be allowed to drown his sorrows in peace?"

The firm tread of the butler approached his lordship's desk. "I beg your pardon, my lord," intoned Beecham with exaggerated gravity. "Had I known you were here, I should not have intruded." He sniffed and bent to retrieve the two empty brandy bottles that were rolling at Rathbourne's feet.

The Earl decided that that was one lie it was wiser to let pass. "Since you're here, you may send John to me with another bottle," he said, striving to keep the slur from his speech.

"John, your lordship?" queried the butler.

Rathbourne frowned. Was the man drunk or something? "You heard me, Beecham—John, the first footman."

Beecham raised his eyes to the ceiling, a gesture which was

lost on the Earl since his head was again cradled in his arms. "The first footman's name is Jeremiah," said Beecham reasonably.

The Earl's head lifted and his bloodshot eyes regarded the stoic butler in mild perplexity. "What d'you mean the first footman's name is Jeremiah? The first footman's name in Belmont has always been John, just as the second footman's name has always been James, and the third footman's name, Charles. It's been like that for generations."

"Nevertheless, my lord, the first footman's name is Jeremiah, the second footman's name is Obadiah, and the third footman's name is Bartholomew."

The Earl's shoulders straightened and he bent a sinister look from under black, slanting brows at his impassive butler. "Oh?" he said with deceptive mildness, "and whose idea was it, may I ask, to permit the footmen to revert to their given names?" He could smell insurrection here, and he meant to put a stop to it before the infection spread.

"It was her ladyship's doing, your lordship. She thought that the custom at Belmont of naming the footmen and maids for convenience was . . . barbaric."

"To which ladyship are we referring, Beecham?"

"To Miss Deirdre, sir."

The Earl's brows elevated at this familiarity. "Miss Deirdre?" he queried in arctic accents.

"Yes sir. She asked me to address her as such to distinguish her from the other Lady Rathbourne, your mother."

Rathbourne's lips thinned. "And do you tell me, Beecham, that 'Miss Deirdre,'" he emphasized, "addresses the respective footmen as Jeremiah, Obadiah, and Bartholomew? Good God, what a mouthful!"

The butler's lips were as thin as the Earl's. "Oh, no, my lord. She calls Jeremiah, Jerry, Obadiah is Obi, and—"

"Don't tell me," interrupted the Earl with a devilish smile, "Bartholomew is Bart."

"Quite so, sir."

"And what handle, pray, does Miss Deirdre give to you?"

"Me, sir?"

"Yes, sir. You, sir."

The corners of Beecham's lips turned up. "She calls me 'Cecy,' sir."

"Cecy?"

"Yes, sir."

"And your name is . . . ?"

"Cecil."

"I see." The Earl studied the erect figure of his butler for a long moment. "Beecham," he said softly, and very deliberately, "send John to me with a bottle as soon as may be, and let us hear no more of this nonsense. Do you take my meaning?"

"Certainly, sir," said Beecham with well-bred stoicism, and silently left the room.

The Earl leaned back in his chair and closed his eyes. Damn if the battle lines weren't being drawn up already—his mother, his sister, and now his servants! This was Deirdre's doing! How dare she calmly pack up her bits and pieces and take her leave of him when he was the injured party! How dare she look at him from the carriage window with those reproachful eyes of hers as if he were the one who should beg pardon! And to leave him alone, to fend off the barbs of three incensed women—well, that was the worst infamy of all! She knew, oh yes, she knew that he hadn't wanted her to go! She was doing this to punish him. Well, she would catch cold at that, if that was her little game! He laughed, but even to his own ears, the sound had a hollow ring to it.

"Gareth!" said Mr. Guy Landron from the threshold. "So this is where you've been hiding yourself! God, you look awful! Did you sleep in those clothes?"

"No. I had my valet put them through the mangle 'cause I rather like the casual look!"

447

"Don't cut up at me, old chap," said Mr. Landron with perfect affability. "I'm not the one who deserted the sinking ship."

The Earl leaned one disconsolate elbow on his desk, chin in hand. "Guy," he said musingly, "d'you know that I call my valet 'Edward'?"

"I believe so. Why?"

"All my valets have been called 'Edward.' Even my batmen in Spain were called 'Edward.'"

"What a coincidence."

"No, not really. The thing is, I always call them 'Edward' irregardless of the names they were christened with."

"You do? Whatever for?"

"Because," said Rathbourne reasonably, "it's so much easier to remember their names that way."

"Oh, I'm sure."

"It's been a family tradition for generations."

"How odd!"

"D'you think it's wrong?"

Mr. Landron suppressed a smile. "Let me put it this way. How many valets have you had?"

"Oodles! They never stay for more than a sixmonth or so."

"I wonder why?"

The Earl caught the gleam of laughter in his friend's eye and he said pettishly, "Oh I might have known that you would take her part. Everybody does."

Mr. Landron said nothing, but he turned away to hide a broad smile. A lackey entered and approached the Earl with a fresh bottle of brandy on a silver tray.

Rathbourne noted that the tray was spotty and a frown gathered across his brow. "Well, put it down, man! I suppose I shall have to resign myself to . . . oh, never mind, just put it down."

The first footman did as he was bid and waited patiently for his dismissal. Rathbourne eyed him speculatively. "Thank you ... Jeremiah?" The lackey nodded, and smiled his pleasure. "Thank you, Jeremiah, that will be all."

Mr. Landron looked to be surprised. When the footman had made his exit, he observed, "I thought his name was John."

"Oh, never mind, it's a long story. What day is it?"

"This is Thursday, a week to the day since Deirdre left."

"I'm perfectly well aware of how long it has been since my wife deserted me," said Rathbourne frigidly.

"Six days since the departure of Mrs. Dewinters," went on Landron as though the Earl had not spoken, "and two days since the departure of your dear mama to visit her sister in Bath. I wonder who next will desert you?"

"Are you thinking of leaving my employ, Guy?" asked Rathbourne, his suspicions roused.

"Certainly not," disclaimed Mr. Landron, "though I must admit, since Deirdre's departure, it's no pleasure being in Belmont—back to cold baths, inedible dinners, candles that drip and smoke atrociously. If one didn't know better, one would think that the servants had it in for you, Gareth. I suggest that you stop playing the fool and go fetch her back."

"Fetch her back? After all that she has done to me? You must be mad!"

"What has she done to you?"

Rathbourne rose and swayed slightly on his feet. "What has she done to me? She damn near killed me, that's what!"

"I don't believe it!"

"No, because you weren't there. I tell you she pulled a pistol on me, and threatened to blow a hole in me."

"She never would! If you don't know that, you don't know her at all."

"Oh, that's easy enough for you to say! You didn't come under that cool, detached scrutiny, as though she were measuring me for a shroud. There wasn't a tremor in her hand as she pointed that pistol at my heart."

"Gareth, this is ridiculous. The girl saved your life! You

449

forget that I came onto the ramparts just as she broke that lantern over Tony Cavanaugh's back. It's a miracle she didn't set herself on fire as well."

"Did I ask her to save my life? I did not! I told her to leave, but of course, she wouldn't listen!"

"Gareth, that's not fair! Deirdre wasn't to know that I was keeping watch over you. When I heard that shot, I tell you, I thought I was too late. And this gammy leg of mine, well, I nearly was too late, wasn't I?"

"No! It was Deirdre who forced Cavanaugh's hand. I had no choice but to go for him then. Why can't she do as she is told?"

Landron's brows knit together. "Honestly, Gareth, I'm disgusted with you. You sound just like Deirdre's brother! The two of you don't know how fortunate you are to have won the love of such a woman. I wouldn't mind being in your shoes."

A sneer distorted the Earl's handsome features. "Oh, it's St. Jean she really loves. I come a poor second best." It came to him then, that the two bottles of brandy he had consumed during a long night of dissipation had loosened his tongue.

Landron made a gesture of impatience. "I warned you from the very beginning how it was with Deirdre and her brother. She is used to being a mother to him. He doesn't like it any better than you do. What she needs is a houseful of her own brats to mother. Well," continued Landron, flashing the Earl a speculative look, "she'll have at least one babe to look after."

"She'll have a damn sight more than that!" snapped Rathbourne.

A smile lit up Landron's thin face. "Now you're making sense."

The Earl stared at his companion's smiling face for a long, thoughtful moment, then he silently shook his head. He took a few unsteady paces toward the open door, stopped suddenly, and retraced his steps until he was eye to eye with Landron.

"I can forgive her everything," he said on an aggrieved note, "except the episode with the pistol. And it's no good saying

450

that she wouldn't have pulled the trigger. We'll never know that for sure, will we? I shall never forgive her for that— never!"

He weaved toward the door. His hand closed around the lintel to steady himself and he turned back and said with exaggerated dignity, "Not unless she particularly asks me to."

His eyes traveled to the windows and the bright sunlight that was streaming through. He noted dourly that Beecham had forgotten to close the curtains. He compressed his lips tightly together and said stiffly, and rather inconsequentially to Mr. Landron's ears, "Jeremiah, Obadiah, and Bartholomew be damned!"

The blaze of sunlight in the courtyard blinded his eyes and he put his head down to avoid its penetrating glare. What he needed to clear his befuddled senses, he suddenly decided, was a brisk ride across hill and dale. There was no Deirdre to accompany him, but he would be very happy, so he assured himself, to make do with O'Toole. His spirits lifted a little. His groom was one worthy on whose loyalty he could always count.

As he made his way toward the gatehouse, his eyes lifted involuntarily to the North Tower and the ramparts where he had very nearly lost his Deirdre. He stilled as the memory of that night came rushing back. His mouth went dry and his heart began to race against his ribs.

That night, and its aftermath, had been worse than any in his five years as a soldier. To risk his own life was one thing, but for Deirdre to put herself in such jeopardy was something he would not tolerate. He would throttle her first before he would let her put him through an experience like that again!

He had managed to keep her name out of the inquest, nor had she or Armand been placed anywhere near the scene of the "accident" since he and Landron had spirited them away before anyone had thought to take a look on the battlements. The shot that had come from O'Toole's pistol was easily accounted for. Rathbourne had explained to the coroner that he had fired it to call off the searchers when he found his young brother-in-law safe but decidedly the worse for drink in the castle keep. Young bucks, he had intimated confidentially, weren't always wise enough to inform their elders of their movements and the ladies were always apt to panic when their fledglings left the roost. His own trifling wound he had dismissed as a prank that had gone wrong, or at the very worst, a minor misdemeanor—and he had no intention of bringing the unfortunate perpetrator to book for something that was very obviously an accident.

The coroner had brought in a verdict of accidental death, a foregone conclusion in light of the evidence that Tony Cavanaugh was used to enjoying a quiet smoke on the ramparts before turning in whenever he stayed at Belmont. It was surmised that he was trying to light his cigar from the lantern when it shattered and sprayed him with burning oil. And so the good name of Tony and all the Cavanaughs had been preserved.

It was after the inquest that Deirdre had quietly packed her bags and had taken off for Marcliff with Armand. He was willing to own that he had expected some kind of set-down for his coldness of manner in the few days since his cousin's death, but that was because she had damn near murdered him—the husband who adored her—with that ugly brute of a pistol she had picked up at Waterloo.

He was on the point of moving off when his eye was caught by the sun's reflection on some object that lay at the edge of the tower. It was Deirdre's pistol. No one had given it a thought since the night of Cavanaugh's death. He picked it up and remembered how calmly Deirdre had aimed it at his heart. God how that memory would haunt him to the end of his days. He clenched his teeth.

Would she or would she not have pulled the trigger if he had laid a hand on her brother? It was a question that tore at his insides, burned his mind, kept him sleepless at nights until he drowned his pain with the insensate solace that was to be found only from a bottle.

He extended his arm and aimed for the branch of a plane tree some twenty paces away. Would she, or wouldn't she? His finger curled around the trigger. He cocked the pistol. Would she, or . . . ? He pulled the trigger.

"Deirdre! Have you read the paper this morning?"

Deirdre turned from the upstairs drawing room window which gave a clear view of the driveway with its fine avenue of elms to the entrance of Marcliff, and she looked absently at her brother. "What paper?"

"*The Times*, of course," replied Armand with a touch of asperity. He noted the dull eyes and the pallor of his sister's cheeks and his voice gentled. "You'll find this of interest. Listen, Deirdre:

"'A private ceremony is to take place at St. James on September seventh, at which time The Right Honourable, Major the Earl of Rathbourne, is to be presented with a commemorative sword to mark his outstanding services to King and Country. Rathbourne, who has served with the 7th Hussars for the last five years in Europe, and was seconded to special duties in the war against Napoleon, is credited with running the counterespionage ring which effectively destroyed the reliability of French Intelligence in the months preceding Waterloo.

"'Mrs. Maria Dewinters, well-known London actress, who worked closely with the Earl in Spain and latterly in Belgium, is to be thanked personally by the Prince Regent for services rendered to His Majesty.

"'The Earl of Rathbourne, readers may remember, was married on June sixteenth, just two days before the glorious Battle of Waterloo, to the former Miss Deirdre Fenton. Mrs. Dewinters is to be married in Paris at the end of this month to Captain Roderick Ogilvie of the Horse Guards. An announcement of the engagement is to be found elsewhere in this edition of *The Times*.

"'May the editors of this periodical be the first to congratulate . . .'"

"Let me see that," exclaimed Deirdre, and she wrested the paper from Armand's grasp. She read it through twice, then turned the pages impatiently till she found the page with the announcements of forthcoming marriages.

"God, I feel awful," said Armand when Deirdre's eyes finally looked up to meet his. "When I think of what I accused him of with Maria Dewinters in Paris!" He groaned and his head went down to his hands. "Tony Cavanaugh! How could I have let him dupe me like that . . . from the very beginning! Oh, I hope to God he's roasting in hell!"

"Well, Gareth should have said something! How were we to know?"

"He wouldn't though. A man like Rathbourne wouldn't stoop to defend himself from a scurrilous attack on his character. I should have believed better of him! How could I have been so dense! Even in Brussels, I learned how highly the men of the 7th regard him!"

"What about his hatred of the French?"

"I got that from Tony Cavanaugh, as well as the story about the two young men he had hanged for desertion! Deserters are shot, not hanged. But Tony had a plausible explanation for everything."

"Oh," said Deirdre softly, and plumped herself down into a chair.

"I wonder," said Armand musingly, "if Cavanaugh poisoned Rathbourne's mind against me in the same way? That would explain some of his antipathy."

"I think I'm to blame for the rest."

"You?"

"He didn't like the way I protected you."

"No? Well neither do I, in retrospect. An occasional thrashing when I was a lad might have been the making of me."

"Armand!" she protested.

"It's true. If I'd had a man like Rathbourne for my guardian

454

in the last, oh, five years or so, I wouldn't have pursued my own pleasures quite so hotly nor dragged you into dun territory with me."

"Because you'd be terrified to face Rathbourne's ire?"

He looked surprised. "Oh no. Because I'd be determined to win his good opinion."

It was now Deirdre's turn to be surprised. "Armand! Do you know what you are saying? It's true that we've misjudged Rathbourne on many points, but I cannot forget, if you can, that if you *had* been a traitor, he would have arranged an accident for you—or so Tony Cavanaugh said, and Rathbourne did not deny it."

"Oh that!" Armand said dismissively, as if the intelligence were of little consequence. "What else should he do with a traitor?"

Deirdre was appalled. "But you're my *brother!*"

"All the more reason that I meet with an accident. D'you think Rathbourne would take the trouble to protect my good name if I weren't your brother? I'm obliged to him for his consideration."

"This is awful! I cannot believe that you really mean what you are saying."

"There, there! I didn't mean to upset you, but yes, I meant every word. And it's too bad in you, Dee, if that's what is keeping you apart from your husband. Try to remember his background. His work was in Intelligence. He's spent more than five years fighting in a cause he believes in. What do you expect of him?"

Deirdre had no answer, but she reflected on Armand's words for the rest of the morning. Armand donned his oldest clothes and went to help the stud groom in the stables, and Deirdre pored over her ledgers. She wondered how things were working out at Belmont and hoped that there had been no backsliding among the servants.

They were sitting down to a late luncheon when they heard the carriage wheels outside. Armand strode to the window and after a moment said tersely, "It's Caro."

Deirdre was only a minute or so behind Armand as he hastened from the room and descended the narrow paneled staircase. She followed him at leisure to the front vestibule, and was met by the sight of Caro in Armand's arms, sobbing wildly, and a sheepish O'Toole, hat in hand, standing irresolute in the doorway. At the sight of Deirdre, a look of patent relief crossed his face.

"Oh Armand, don't send me back to that horrid, horrid place," sobbed Caro uncontrollably. "Please, oh please let me stay here with Deirdre. I'll be good, I promise, and I'll never *ever* disobey you again, word of honor!"

"There, there, darling," said Armand soothingly, and then trenchantly, "If Rathbourne has been threatening you in any way, he'll have me to answer to."

So much, thought Deirdre with a touch of cynicism, for the short-lived desire to win his admired brother-in-law's approval. "Armand, take Caro upstairs and offer her some refreshment," she said a little dryly but with commendable composure, though she trembled to think what might happen if Rathbourne was hot on the heels of his runaway sister. "I'll be there in a minute or so."

As soon as they had turned the half landing, Deirdre turned on O'Toole. "What's this about, O'Toole?"

He looked down at the toes of his black boots and said rather shamefaced, "It's the master, Miss Deirdre. And sure if he hasna been in one of his black moods since you left us! There's no reasoning with him. Most of the time he's in his cups, and in a devil of a temper. He's not eating; he doesn't trouble to change his clothes or look to his appearance. He's threatening to put the young miss in a convent. You'll not be surprised to hear, will you, that I couldna turn away the lass when she begged me to bring her to you?"

"But her mother . . ."

". . . has gone to Bath to get away from Belmont. There's no one there for Lady Caro to confide in but the servants."

456

"Oh dear. What's to be done?"

"You couldna see your way to sending the young lady to her mother in Bath, could you, miss?"

"Will you take her, O'Toole?"

A look of regret crossed O'Toole's face. "I'm sorry, Miss Deirdre. That I couldna do. The master would never forgive it. Perhaps it were better if someone else could do the honors? I took the precaution of bringing Lady Caro's maid. She's in the carriage. The coachmen are impatient to be off. You see," he added by way of explanation, "they're good lads but they know the Earl's temper, and he'll not be more than a couple of hours behind us."

"But O'Toole, if he's only an hour or two behind you, he'll soon catch them up. D'you think it's wise . . ."

O'Toole's smile verged on the apologetic. "I was hoping, Miss Deirdre, that you could throw the master off the scent."

"Throw him off the scent?" she echoed foolishly.

"Give him the wrong directions."

"You mean, lie to my husband?" she asked on a note of alarm.

"Or, if you prefer, find some way to delay him. I think it would be very easy for you to do."

Deirdre looked into the shrewd eyes of her husband's groom. "Oh," she said, and her eyes dropped. After an infinitestimal pause, her eyes lifted, and O'Toole observed with no little relief that their expression was speculative rather than hostile.

"I daresay I can think of some way to make him linger," she said with a casualness that deceived no one. "He's very fond of a game of cards."

"A game of cards might just do the trick, Miss Deirdre," intoned O'Toole musingly, "if, that is, the stakes were such as to interest his lordship. With a bit o' luck, he might even be persuaded to stay the night."

Deirdre colored slightly but said with a candor which completely disarmed the groom, "Much as I would wish it, that

457

doesn't seem likely. His skill is formidable. I could never hope to beat him."

"Never beat the master? Never say so! I know a thing or two that will even up the odds. I'd be more than happy to show you, miss."

The corners of Deirdre's mouth lifted imperceptibly and she linked her arm with O'Toole's. "What's your Christian name?" she asked shyly, and she directed their steps to the kitchen door at the end of the hall.

"Patrick, miss. Why d'you want to know?"

"Pat! It has a nice ring to it. Naturally, I would never use it public. That would be an impertinence. But when there's no one around to hear us, I don't see why we can't be the best of friends, do you?"

O'Toole's eyes softened. This girl definitely had a way with her. No wonder his lordship was besotted. "It would make me very happy to hear my name on your lips," he said with unaccustomed gallantry, "except," he amended with a swift return of caution, "in the master's hearing."

"Oh! That goes without saying," and with a confident swish of her skirts, Deirdre led the admiring groom to the best dinner he had consumed in a fortnight.

In the upstairs parlor, Armand wrested Lady Caro's viselike grip from his neck and said irritably, "Caro! Behave yourself! Your conduct resembles more that of a lightskirt than the gently bred lady of quality that you are. Now sit down and compose yourself."

He straightened his cravat and watched warily as the lady spun away from him and plumped herself down on a rose damask chair. She removed her high poke bonnet and a cascade of fire spilled in soft waves over her shoulders. He forced his breathing to a slower pace.

"Well, you should know," she pouted.

"I beg your pardon?"

"About lightskirts."

The wary expression in his eyes intensified. "I don't think

458

I follow."

"Don't you?" There was a martial glint in her eye. "You needn't stand there like Innocence personified—or perhaps I should say, petrified. I've had it all explained to me. I think men are disgusting." She averted her head, and Armand felt a shaft of pure fear penetrate his heart.

"Caro," he cried, and in two swift strides, he was before her chair. He kneeled in front of her and possessed himself of her hands. "Caro, darling! That part of my life is over and done with. You cannot think that, loving you, other women would hold any interest for me."

She sniffed, and made a halfhearted attempt to drag her hands from his fierce clasp.

"Caro!" he cried again, and gripped her chin in one hand, forcing her to look at him. "If I don't have you, I have nothing. Why else am I doing all this?"

"All what?" she asked pettishly, though the passion in his voice had considerably mollified her.

"Why, reforming my life—making something of myself, taking a position at the Admiralty under Uncle John's second cousin; forswearing gaming and duels and—"

"Lightskirts?" she supplied unhelpfully.

"I was about to say my boon companions," he responded through stiff lips.

"Then lightskirts are still on the agenda?"

"Caro! You know that's not what I meant." There was a note of genuine anguish in his voice, and the lady relented somewhat on hearing it.

"But Armand, you needn't go to all these extremes for me. Mama explained it all. When I come of age, I come into a considerable fortune, and Gareth has no control over it once I marry."

"I wouldn't touch a penny of it," he exclaimed hotly. "Your mother explained it to you?" he asked when the full import of her words had penetrated his consciousness. "You can't mean that she approves of our liaison?"

"Of course she does." Caro looked at him in some surprise. "Why shouldn't she?"

"Because," he said morosely, "I have nothing to offer a girl like you."

"That's preposterous!"

"Oh?" He looked to be unconvinced.

She put out a tentative hand and touched his lips. "Mama explained that to me too," she said softly. "You'd never know it, but she's dreadfully romantic. Love! Mama believes in it. She says that we Cavanaughs are fated to love only once. We have a history, so it seems, of single-minded devotion to only one person. We're like swans. When a Cavanaugh finds that his love is unrequited, the consequences are often tragic. I never knew before that my father pursued my mother for five years. She hated him. He finally abducted her and she was forced to marry him. It was only later that she came to love him."

He took her hand and kissed it passionately. "The St. Jeans' history is quite different. But I mean to change that."

She said nothing, but there was a question in her eyes.

"I learned only recently that my father, poor wretch, deserted my mother when I was still in short coats. I don't know why I wasn't told sooner! It seems that he became infatuated with some mercenary vixen who bled him of every penny he had. When she left him, he was too ashamed to come back to us."

"How did you find out?"

"Your brother told me just before we left Belmont."

"Isn't that just like Gareth! He had no right to—"

"He had every right," Armand broke in impatiently. He ran a distracted hand through his hair. "I don't think I shall ever understand the logic of women! Men are not little boys to be cosseted and protected at every turn. I expected better of Deirdre. If only I had known, I might have been a help to her. Instead of which . . ." He faltered to a halt, his eyes staring off into space.

"Have you spoken to her about it?"

Armand shook his head. "Not yet. I'm too angry, and she is too . . . well, low in spirits. The time is not right. One day though, we shall have to have this out."

She laid a restraining hand on his sleeve. "Don't be too hard on her. Who was there to advise her? Now that she has Gareth, things will be different."

"I daresay, if ever they get together again, which doesn't seem very likely at this point in time."

"Nonsense. That's why I'm here."

"What?"

"To get them together again. It's Mama's dearest wish. She and O'Toole concocted this scheme before she removed to Bath. Gareth is bound to come after me. But I won't be here. Mama said that you are to escort me to Bath so that Gareth can have a clear field with Deirdre."

"I'll do no such thing," he stated emphatically. "I refuse to put your reputation at risk."

Lady Caro's eyes flashed with anger. "If you are afraid that I shall attack you in the closed carriage, let me assure you, sir, that my abigail will be there to protect you. Of course," she grated through clenched teeth, "if I had been one of your lightskirts, I expect you would have got rid of my abigail to make mad, passionate love to me."

"But Caro," Armand soothed without much success, "you must see how, loving you as I do, I cannot possibly take advantage of you."

Lady Caro's brows drew together. She tossed her head. "I don't think," she said in withering accents, "that I shall ever understand the logic of men."

Armand looked at her for a long, thoughtful moment. He sighed. He shook his head. Finally, he said in a resigned tone, "Have it your own way." His arms went round her waist and he drew her forward till their bodies were locked together. "I disclaim any responsibility for what follows," he warned her.

She tipped up her head till their lips were only inches apart.

461

"I absolve you," she murmured on an uneven breath.

Armand's head descended, and the lady in his arms was very soon aware that a long engagement would not suit her at all. She wondered how soon the combined influence of three determined women could wear down the resolve of a brother who was known to be soft-hearted to a degree, in spite of appearances to the contrary.

Chapter Twenty-Eight

It was closer to three hours rather than the expected two before Deirdre heard the clatter of her husband's curricle at the front entrance. She opened the sitting room door a crack and cautiously peeped out. Annie, Deirdre's abigail and general maid of all work, had gone to answer the peremptory summons of the knocker. Deirdre glided noiselessly to the head of the stairs, hoping to divine her husband's temper by the tone of his opening remarks to her servants. It was the merest bad luck that, after Annie had taken his lordship's hat and coat, he should happen to run into O'Toole as the groom came out of the kitchen.

The silence was arctic, but no less chilling was Rathbourne's voice as he coldly intoned, *"Et tu Brute?"* and before Annie could show him the way, he was taking the stairs two at a time. Deirdre whisked herself into the room and had just taken up her place at the card table, where she was engaged in playing a solitary game of picquet, when his lordship entered.

Deirdre blinked. O'Toole had led her to expect a hollow-eyed wraith with two days' growth of beard on his face. Rathbourne looked to be insultingly healthy and well groomed. His tanned features were set off admirably by his mahogany, windblown locks, giving him an even more rakish appearance than usual, and his snug-fitting blue superfine emphasized the breadth of

463

his shoulders. She was conscious of the tight-fitting beige pantaloons over muscled thighs but dared not drop her gaze to appraise him further since his eyes had narrowed on her face. He was an absolutely magnificent creature, a young lion, and that she had held off such a specimen for one hour, never mind five years, seemed totally incomprehensible. She noted the hard set of his features and did not think that she would very easily worm her way back into his good graces.

"So this is Marcliff," he said carelessly, and shut the door behind him with a snap. "It's very nice," he elaborated, and his eyes moved slowly about the room before coming to rest on Deirdre.

Deirdre was conscious of his hard scrutiny, and as he crossed the distance that separated them in a few leisurely strides, she composed herself to sit unmoving until he was done looking her over.

He selected a comfortable soft upholstered chair next to the sofa she occupied and sat himself down, crossing one booted foot over the other with negligent grace.

"You look awful!" he said baldly, his bright gaze lingering on the dark smudges under her eyes and the pale cheeks. "It's obvious that you're not looking after yourself. If you'd remained at Belmont, where you ought to be . . ."

"If memory serves," she said with icy dignity, "I was told to leave. Nor was the order rescinded."

"Oh that!" He waved his hand in a dismissive gesture and answered her playfully. "When have you ever done as I have asked? I told you to remain in Henley and you bolted for Dover; I instructed you to make for Antwerp, and you entrenched yourself in Brussels; I warned you not to leave the Great Hall, and you immediatley made for the ramparts. How could I know that in this instance you meant to act like a conformable wife? I am not a mind reader. Besides, I don't believe for a minute that you left on my say-so. Oh no, Dee, you cannot lay the blame for this ridiculous separation at my door."

Deirdre shot him a quelling look from under slashed brows, then she remembered that she had a task to perform. She blinked as if to dispel the frown in her eyes and she gave him a perfect view of her small even white teeth through the parted curve of her lips.

"May I offer you tea, or something?" she asked in her best hostess manner.

"The 'something' will do nicely, thank you. Sherry perhaps?" He watched her movements covertly as she rose and with her usual grace went to pull the rope that would ring a bell in the pantry. Hope flared in his heart. She hadn't annihilated him with that rapier tongue of hers, as only she could, nor had he been ordered off the property at gunpoint. In fact, she was behaving in a suspiciously amenable manner. What was she up to? The temptation to tumble her into his arms and kiss her senseless was ruthlessly crushed.

A decanter of sherry and two glasses were duly procured and Rathbourne noted with no little approval but scant surprise that the appointments and service at Marcliff were impeccable. Belmont, no less than he, was missing the touch of its mistress. He almost said so, but caught himself in time. After all she had made him suffer, he should be paddling her backside! What the devil had possessed him to accept her hospitality as if he were a guest and she the grande dame? It had put him at a definite disadvantage.

"Where are they?" he asked without preamble, and his mouth set in a cruel line. If she was shielding St. Jean again . . .

Deirdre watched him warily over the rim of her glass. She had observed the play of emotions that had crossed his face and had deduced that his lordship was in one of his volatile moods. Instinct warned her to be cautious. Very cautious.

"Who, dear?" she prevaricated, and set the sherry aside untouched. With a practiced flick of her wrist, she flipped over the two hands of cards, face up, which lay on the table in front of her.

Rathbourne's glittering eyes followed the deft movements of

her fingers. He watched mesmerized as she selected a card from one set and discarded it on the table. She then repeated the process with the other hand.

"What, may I ask, are you doing?" he asked with restrained impatience.

Her eyes lifted and her long, curly lashes batted up at him. "I'm playing out a hand of picquet," she managed with wide-eyed innocence.

"Picquet? And whom do you play against?"

"Myself."

Her eyes lowered and her attention became fixed on the cards on the table.

Rathbourne shook off the suspicion that he was being toyed with. He had an explosive temper. His wife knew it. The poor girl was probably shaking in her shoes, expecting momentarily to come under the full lash of his tongue. His expression softened. He would, he decided, be generous in victory.

His voice gentled. "Tell me where they are, Deirdre. You must know that I cannot permit my sister to make a runaway marriage. If, in a year or two, they still feel as strongly, and St. Jean has proved to me that his way of life is more settled, then I may be persuaded to change my mind." His offer, he thought, was magnanimous.

He looked into a pair of stormy green eyes and his confidence faltered.

"My brother," said Deirdre through clenched teeth, "would never do anything to compromise Lady Caro. Unlike some I could name, Armand *is* a gentleman."

"What does that mean?" he asked angrily.

"It means that your sister's virtue is safe with my brother, which is more than could be said of mine when you decided you wanted me."

His color heightened, but he managed to say with tolerable calm, "Our cases are entirely different. I never wanted to . . . It was your obstinacy . . . If you had . . . Oh what's the use? You'll never understand."

466

He bolted the sherry in his hand and got to his feet in one lithe movement. "Where are they?" he demanded, and his voice held a suggestion of menace.

"How badly do you want to know?" asked Deirdre, and ignoring the threatening figure who loomed over her, she flexed her fingers and dealt another pair of cards.

His long fingers closed over her wrist. "Deirdre," he warned at the end of his patience.

"What can you do if I don't tell you?" she asked coolly. "Beat me? I think not—oh, not that you wouldn't like to, but in my delicate condition, you wouldn't take that chance. How will you find them if I don't give you their direction? They could be on the way to Gretna Green, or Brussels, or perhaps to my friend in Aberdeen." She flashed him a commiserating smile. "Poor Gareth! You know to your cost how easily I can lay a false trail."

"Deirdre," he protested in mingled exasperation and anger. That she should believe him capable of hurting her in any way was a shaft that had slipped under his guard. "How could you even think that I would beat you, whatever the provocation?"

"Oh, don't tell me! I know! You'll beat me for that remark."

He saw that she was laughing at him, and he was slightly mollified. "It's only a figure of speech, after all."

"So I've learned," she intoned politely. "But to get back to business. I have the information you want, and there's only one way you'll get it out of me."

"How?" he asked, and something kindled in his eyes.

"We're both gamblers, as events have proved. Let the cards decide. The loser pays a forfeit."

His eyes brightened to amber. "Picquet?" he asked with new interest, and pulled his chair closer to the card table and sat down.

"Naturally!"

"You're on! Foolish girl, you know you cannot win." He gathered the cards into his hands with a flourish, and grinned wickedly as he shuffled them and dealt them each a hand.

467

He saw a fleeting smile that bordered on the self-congratulatory curve her mouth and he said with belated caution, "In the very faint chance that I should lose, what forfeit do you have in mind for me?"

"Only an hour of your time," Deirdre responded smoothly, and her eyes lifted to look guilelessly into his.

"An hour of my time? For what purpose?"

"That would be telling," she said cryptically, and her lashes lowered to conceal her expression.

Rathbourne's brows snapped together, but a moment's reflection convinced him that he had nothing to fear. At picquet, he was invincible. He relaxed and said with unfeigned good humor, "Shall we commence play?"

Thirty minutes later the Earl pushed back his chair and said accusingly, "You've been practicing!"

"What a poor loser you are to be sure," said Deirdre pleasantly, and quickly slipped the cards into the drawer at the side of the card table. "Are you trying to weasel out of paying your forfeit?"

His expression was guarded. "Certainly not! One hour of my time, Deirdre, and not a minute more. Now, how may I serve you?"

Wordlessly, Deirdre rose to her feet and walked to the door. The Earl watched through narrowed eyes as she turned the key in the lock. She then stalked to the open window and threw the key out onto the driveway below. He heard the faint rattle as steel struck cobblestones.

She turned back to him. "You are now my prisoner, as I was once yours."

Green eyes, wide and unblinking, stared into golden. Rathbourne leaned into the soft upholstery at his back and said softly, "And if I am?"

Deirdre took a deep breath. "And I learned from you that in some circumstances, only desperate measures will suffice."

Her fingers moved to the small row of buttons at the bodice of her spencer, and with slow, deliberate movements, she eased

468

them, one by one, out of their buttonholes. She dragged the spencer from her shoulders and threw it with studied carelessness on the back of a chair. Her breasts rose and fell as if she was laboring under some profound emotion. Rathbourne saw it and a pulse sprang to life at his temple.

"Deirdre," he growled deep in his throat, and his hands moved involuntarily to wrench the immaculate neckcloth from his throat. "This had better mean what I think it means. I won't let you turn back now." His coat and shirt quickly followed his cravat to the floor, but his fingers at the waistband of his pantaloons stilled when he heard his wife's icy accents.

"I," she said deliberately and with great dignity, as she struggled in vain to undo the button at the back of her gown, "I am supposed to be seducing you. What the devil do you mean by cooperating?"

A great gust of laughter convulsed the Earl. "Seducing me?" he asked incredulously. "Deirdre, don't you know that seduction can only take place when one of the partners is reluctant?"

"Well, of course I know that," she said crossly, and gave up the attempt to undo the buttons at her back. "I'll just have to make love to you with my clothes on," she said prosaically. She lifted her skirts and gave the Earl a perfect view of her shapely legs as she carefully unrolled each silk stocking in turn.

He beat back a dizzying wave of desire. "Deirdre," he said hoarsely, "there's no need to seduce me."

"There is every need," she retorted, and Rathbourne groaned as she began to wriggle suggestively out of her drawers.

"But why?" he asked, his eyes lazy as he watched her movements.

Deirdre's head came up and she looked at him as if he had been the village idiot. "Well, isn't it obvious? I have to persuade you to my will. If it can work for a man, I don't see why it shouldn't work for a woman also!"

Rathbourne savaged his locks with a distracted hand and

469

moved automatically to Deirdre's best damask-covered sofa. "But I didn't persuade you when I seduced you. You ran away from me . . . to Brussels."

"Damn, so I did!" said Deirdre with a hint of irritation. She stepped out of her drawers and, with commendable aplomb, threw them on the growing pile of her discarded clothes. "It'll have to be the other method then. What did you call it? Oh yes, now I remember, blackmail."

"Blackmail?"

She moved gracefully and came to stand over him. "I am a bit muddled about the process, but I think a little blackmail with a healthy doze of seduction thrown in for good measure should persuade you to my will."

His hand reached out and caught her wrist, not hard, but with enough force to ensure that the adorable creature standing before him in such tempting deshabille would find her escape cut off if she were foolish enough to make the attempt to flee him.

"But what is your will, Dee?" he asked softly.

Her free hand came to rest on his naked shoulder and she leaned down till her face was only inches from his. He turned his head up, and the tip of her tongue, warm and sensuous, traced the swell of his bottom lip. He held himself in rigid control and groaned. "Tell me."

"My will," she said earnestly, "as you well know, is to breed a houseful of babies with soft red tresses."

He administered a rough shake and she fell into his arms. "And?" he prompted.

Her eyes were bright with laughter. "And to be by your side, as your consort, helping to build a future for our children and our children's children."

He made to crush her to him, but she spread her fingers against his chest to ward him off.

"And," she continued with quiet persistence, "to make our home a place of welcome to all the members of our families, yes, and in-laws too, even if we would like to see them at

470

Jericho on occasion."

His eyes bathed her in a golden haze. "Aren't you going to insist on settlements and so on?"

"Oh that! I never doubted for a minute that you had made some provision for me."

"Thank you for that. And Maria Dewinters?"

She hung her head. "I read the papers this morning. I owe her an apology, and you also."

"Dee, how *could* you think, for one minute, that I would ever want another woman after what we have been to each other?"

"Do you love me so much?" she asked archly, and smiled into his eyes.

"No, you conceited wench. I can scarcely handle one woman. What makes you think I'd be fool enough to take on two?"

"Gareth Cavanaugh, you'd better kiss me now before we start quarreling," said Deirdre through her teeth.

Much later, Deirdre looked at the clock on the mantlepiece and said languidly, "Your hour is up, Rathbourne. I have to let you go now."

"Mmm!" said his lordship noncommitally, having no desire to be ousted from a position which was eminently satisfying to him. "I'm a generous loser. I'll give you another hour."

"But don't you wish to know where Caro and Armand have gone?"

"Not particularly," and he shifted her in his arms to bring her lips back to his searching kiss.

"But . . . but . . . isn't that what you came to Marcliff for in the first place?" she asked in slight bemusement.

"That was only one of the reasons. You've convinced me that Armand is a pattern card of rectitude. Where are they? On the way to my mother in Bath by now, I shouldn't wonder. Oh well," went on his lordship philosophically, "that should keep them out of our hair for a week or so at least."

471

His lips moved to the pulse at Deirdre's throat and she made a slight movement to evade the heat of his lips.

"Gareth?"

"Mmm?"

"I have a confession to make."

"Tell me later," he murmured as his lips dropped lower.

"Promise you won't be angry?"

His head came up, and he looked searchingly into her luminous green eyes. "What is it?"

"I'm not only a gambler and a blackmailer but I'm also . . . please forgive me, my dear, a cheat."

"A cheat?"

She nodded dumbly and said in a small voice, "I didn't beat you at cards just now. I cheated." She saw his blank look and explained, "The cards were marked. I knew every card that was in your hand before play started, Gareth," she went on a little desperately when she saw that he still did not understand how far she was sunk in iniquity, "you didn't stand a chance from the moment you entered this room."

He saw her serious expression and a smile of deepest tenderness gentled his features. "Ninnyhammer," he purred against her ear, "I've known *that* since the moment I first set eyes on you. Don't give it another thought. If I had won, the forfeit I intended to exact from you was identical."

"You didn't want to know where Caro was?"

"Oh that," he responded dismissively. "I know you too well to think that you would have loaned your support to anything havey-cavey. And I'd no real wish to dash all over England to look for that headstrong sister of mine. Armand wanted responsibility? He has his wish! Let him try and tame her. I can't even manage the one slip of a girl who happens to be my own wife."

Deirdre could feel the steady beat of his heart at her breast. She looked up through the veil of her lashes, and a wave of tenderness caused a sudden tightness in her chest. One hand went up to smooth the rough edge of the scar on his cheek, and she was submerged in a rush of memory. She scarcely recognized the girl who, even loving him then, at Vauxhall, had struck out in blind fury, passionately denying the strength of the attachment between them. That his love had endured time and distance and every imaginable obstacle she had thrown in his path seemed like a miracle to her. Nor could she be sorry for that almost frightening ruthlessness of purpose in him which had compelled her to accept his claims upon her. A well of gratitude opened up deep within her. It bubbled up like fresh spring water drenching the parched earth with its life-giving properties. She was filled with a sense of well-being, of coming home, and she knew then that the man whom she had been so reluctant to love, whom she had mistrusted without foundation, was the one person in the world with whom her happiness was most secure.

She drew a deep breath and said unsteadily, "Gareth, that night on the castle walls, when I threatened you with that pistol."

"Yes . . . the pistol. I think that hurt more than anything. I would have put you to the test, you know, but I expected O'Toole to be right behind Tony. I couldn't take the chance that, if you had pulled the trigger, he might not want to take a paltry revenge. I had to disarm you, and quickly."

"You would have put me to the test? You were so sure I wouldn't pull the trigger?"

"No, my love. In that moment of truth I would have given anything to know if you would have chosen your brother over me."

Her eyes, tear bright, she said shakily, "You might have been very, very dead."

"Then I would have had my answer." His face was grave but in his eyes she discerned a glint of laughter.

"About the pistol," she began, but his fingers sealed her lips.

"I know. I found it, oh, days later. It wasn't loaded."

"No."

"But why?"

"Because . . . because, I found I could only go so far. If the gun were armed, I don't think I could have pointed it at you. An empty pistol was a better defense than nothing. When you forced me to choose between the two people I love most in the world, it was the best compromise I could come up with."

"I was insanely jealous. Can you forgive me? I wanted, from the very beginning, to share the burden of your brother with you. But you would have none of it. And if ever I did try to instill some sense of responsibility in him, you—"

"I know. I was there to ruin whatever good you might have done." He pulled back his head to study her more closely and Deirdre continued, "Armand himself said as much, and more. He said that if he'd had you or someone like you for his guardian for the past five years, he might not have become such a scapegrace. I think he rather hero-worships you."

"Oh, that's going too far."

An impish light danced in Deirdre's eyes. "That's what I told him."

She received a rough shake for that piece of impertinence and she nestled closer in his arms. His lordship was not insensible of the advantages of his position and he administered another rough shake with most agreeable results.

"Gareth?"

"Mmm?"

"You said that Caro was only one reason you came to Marcliff. What was the other?"

Rathbourne's mouth reluctantly halted its slow exploration of Deirdre's shoulder and collarbone. "To take you back to your proper domain, of course."

"Did you miss me a little?" she asked coyly.

"More than a little," he responded with gratifying ardor.

"Yes? Go on."

"My dear, how could I not? Every day of your absence became more of a torment to me."

"How so?" she prodded, and her silky lashes fluttered down in artless confusion.

"It was the candles that finally broke down my resistance."

"The candles?" she asked, and the artless pose was gone in an instant.

His lordship's lips remained grave. "The candles were the last straw in a week of utter frustration. Wellington, at Waterloo, could not have felt more desperate. You're my last hope. With you by my side, I expect we shall manage to turn the tide of the battle."

"Waterloo? Battle? What the devil are you talking about?"

"Can't you guess? Then I shall explain, though it pains me to tell you. Deirdre, there's insurrection in the ranks at Belmont. Either that, or some evil spirit has put a hex on my once tranquil existence. The signs are unmistakable. Do you wish me to enumerate?" Taking his wife's wide-eyed silence for acquiescence, his lordship warmed to his subject. "There isn't a candle in the castle that doesn't smoke and drip over—oh, everything. There's a constant fog in the house of an evening when they're lit that is positively intolerable. The silver seems to have been attacked by an incurable disease, I think it's called tarnish; the fires won't light in the grates anymore; water, in defiance of natural law, can't be brought to the boil, so I've had to make do with a cold bath every night; the servants have been struck with a peculiar form of amnesia—they're so confused they can't remember the dining room from the tapestry room; no one answers to his name any longer, it doesn't matter whether you call him John or Jeremiah; cook can't recall how to boil eggs, let alone dress the high cuisine we were fortunate enough to sample when you were in residence; there's no mail, nothing ever gets delivered—no, not even if it bears the Royal Seal; but most heinous of all, and something which I refuse to tolerate an instant longer—my best brandy has turned into vinegar. You can see how it is with me. I've been brought to my knees. You're my last hope, Deirdre—the reinforcements I'm counting on. If you can't see your way to doing your duty, I'm done for."

"And the reason you wish me to return to Belmont . . ." she began in outraged accents.

". . . is to make my life more comfortable," concluded the Earl suavely.

The silence which ensued was ominous. Then a furious spate of invective broke from her ladyship's lips. The Earl winced to hear it. After a moment, his arms tightened around Deirdre's warm, struggling body, and he proceeded, quite ruthlessly, to kiss her into silence.

When her movements had stilled under the onslaught of his fervent embrace, he lifted his head and looked down with satisfaction into her smoky eyes. "And that, madam wife, is the third reason I came to fetch you back to Belmont. Now what do you have to say to that?"

But coherent speech was beyond Deirdre. A strangled sound halfway between a moan and a whimper fell from her lips. She tried to speak, but intelligible words were beyond her, and his lordship, who evidently understood perfectly his beloved's inarticulate form of address, gave himself up to persuading his lady that words between lovers were totally superfluous.

Have You Missed Any of
These Thrilling Novels
of Romantic Suspense
by Elsie Lee?

SATAN'S COAST   (2172-0, $2.95)

THE SEASON OF EVIL   (1970-X, $2.95

SILENCE IS GOLDEN   (2045-7, $2.95)

THE DIPLOMATIC LOVER   (2234, $2.95)

THE SPY AT THE VILLA
    MIRANDA   (2096-1, $2.95)